Portrait of Adam Mickiewicz by Alexander Pushkin, c. 1830
(pen and ink on paper)

PAN TADEUSZ

OR

THE LAST FORAY IN LITHUANIA

A TALE OF THE POLISH NOBILITY

IN THE YEARS 1811 and 1812

IN *TWELVE BOOKS*

BY

ADAM MICKIEWICZ

TRANSLATED BY

CHRISTOPHER ADAM ZAKRZEWSKI

ZMOK
BOOKS

BOOK INSTITUTE

©POLAND

This publication has been supported by the ©POLAND Translation Program

PAN TADEUSZ – OR THE LAST FORAY IN LITHUANIA A TALE OF THE POLISH NOBILITY IN THE YEARS 1811 AND 1812 IN TWELVE BOOKS

By Adam Mickiewicz, translated by Christopher Adam Zakrzewski
Cover design by Vincent Rospond with an illustration by Michał Andriolli
This edition published in 2019

Winged Hussar Publishing, is an imprint of

Pike and Powder Publishing Group LLC
1525 Hulse Rd, Unit 1   1 Craven Lane, Box 66066
Point Pleasant, NJ 08742   Lawrence, NJ 08648-66066

Copyright © Christopher Adam Zakrzewski
ISBN 978-1-94530-75-6
LCN 2019931548

Bibliographical References and Index
1. Fiction. 2. Poland. 3. Historical Romantic

Pike and Powder Publishing Group LLC All rights reserved
For more information on Pike and Powder Publishing Group, LLC,
visit us at www.PikeandPowder.com & www.wingedhussarpublishing.com

twitter: @pike_powder
facebook: @PikeandPowder

TABLE OF CONTENTS

Cast of Main Characters   2

Book One: The Manor   4

Book Two: The Castle   26

Book Three: Romantic Pursuits   45

Book Four: Diplomacy & The Hunt   64

Book Five: The Quarrel   87

Book Six: The Noble Village   109

Book Seven: The Council   124

Book Eight: The Foray   138

Book Nine: The Battle   156

Book Ten: Emigration. Jacek   175

Book Eleven: The Year 1812   196

Book Twelve: Let Us Love One Another!   212

Note on the Spelling of Names   233

Notes   234

CAST OF MAIN CHARACTERS

PAN TADEUSZ (the eponymous hero; nephew of Judge Soplica)

JUDGE SOPLICA (uncle of Tadeusz and younger brother of Jacek)

JACEK SOPLICA (the Judge's disgraced brother; father of Tadeusz)

ROBAK (Franciscan friar, priest, and alms quester)

SOPHIA (Sophie; ward of Telimena)

TELIMENA (Sophie's guardian; distant relation of the Judge; a notorious flirt)

THE STEWARD (Tadeusz Hreczecha; kinsman of the Judge; skilled in the ancient art of knife-throwing)

THE PANTLER (Horeszko; former holder of the disputed castle)

THE WARDEN (Gervase of the noble village of Rembaïlo; last retainer of the Horeszko family; variously styled *The Old Boy, Half Goat* and *Scarpate*; wielder of *Jackknife*)

THE COURT USHER (Protase Balthazar Brzechalski; habitué of the hemp patch)

THE COUNT (a distant relative of the Horeszko family; an anglophile with Quixotic leanings)

THE CHAMBERLAIN (president of the district boundary court)

THE NOTARY (Bolesta; styled *The Preacher*; owner of the greyhound Scut)

THE ASSESSOR (the acid-tongued owner of the greyhound Peregrine)

RYKOV (Captain Nikita Nikitich; an honest Russian soldier)

MAJOR PLUT (Rykov's superior officer; a renegade Pole)

YANKEL (a Jewish innkeeper and Polish patriot; a maestro of first repute)

MATTHIAS (Dobrzynski; patriarch of the noble village of Dobrzyn; variously styled *Cock o' the Steeple, Hipsmiter, Matthias of Matthiases,* and *Little King*; lover of rabbits and wielder of *The Switch*)

BUCHMAN (an estate manager from Kleck; weaver of sound political arguments and disciple of Jean Jacques Rousseau)

THE BAPTIST (wielder of *Sprinkling Broom*), *WATERING CAN, SACK, THE RAZOR, THE PRUSSIAN* (all members of the Dobrzynski clan)

GENERALS DOMBROWSKI, KNIAZIEWICZ (historical personages)

BOOK ONE: THE MANOR

Argument: The young master's return. A first encounter in a little room, a second at table. The Judge's weighty lesson on the polite arts. The Chamberlain's political reflections on fashion. Beginning of the dispute over Scut and Peregrine. The Steward's lamentation. The last court usher. A glance at the political state of affairs in Lithuania and Europe of the time.

Lithuania – my homeland. You are like health; to lose you is to cease taking you for granted. Now that I grieve your loss, I see your beauty and show it forth in all its splendor.

O Holy Virgin, who guard the bright hill of Czestochowa; who shed your morning beams from Vilna's Ostra Gate! You that mount sentinel over Novogrodek's castle and pious townsfolk! In my childhood, once, you healed me by a wondrous sign. Placed under your protection by my sobbing mother, I raised my life-less eyelids and soon felt strong enough to walk unaided to the threshold of your shrine, where I offered thanks to God for re-storing my life. Even so, by a sign, shall you restore us to the bo-som of our land. Until that day dawns, bear my yearning heart to those richly wooded hills, those verdant meadows stretched along blue Niemen's banks. Bear it hence to those painted corn-fields, gilded with wheat and silvered with rye, where the rape-seed glows amber yellow, the buckwheat shimmers white as the snow, the clover mantles with a maidenly blush; and all this belted round by a green boundary strip, where, here and yon, a pear serenely stands.

Years ago, amid those fields, in a grove of birches overlook-ing a small brook, there stood an all-timber manor house with foundations of solid stone. From a distance, the whitewashed walls shone the clearer against the line of dark-green lombardies that broke the autumn winds. While none too large, the house was spruce and trim. There was a mighty barn, thatched and bursting with corn. Three heaping straw ricks stood beside it – clearly, the region grew grain in superabundance. Everything about the domain, from the galaxy of shining shocks, which ran the length and breadth of the fields, to the host of seasonable plows working the vast black loamy tracts left in fallow (all neat-ly tilled like garden plots) – all this was proof that order and plenty made their dwelling here. The gate stood fastened back, a clear sign to passers-by that all were welcome, all received with open arms.

In through this very gate, a young master drove his two-horse britzka. He circled the courtyard, backed up to the porch, and jumped out. Left unattended, the horses fell to grazing on the grass and drew slowly away in the direction of the gate. The house seemed deserted. The porch door was shut fast – hasp fitted over the staple with a peg slipped through. Loath to seek help in the servants' quarters, the traveler undid the door himself and ran inside. Great was his impatience to salute the house. He hadn't seen the place for years, not since leaving for the distant city to finish his schooling there. The longed-for day had come at last.

Fondly and keenly he scanned those ancient old walls so dear to him. He saw the same furnishings, the same rich tapestries that had amused him for as long as he could remember. True, they were smaller now, not quite as lovely as they had seemed. The same oils adorned the walls. Here stood Kosciuszko in his Cracow coat, sword raised in both hands, eyes upcast. Such was the attitude he struck on the altar steps when he swore to drive the three powers from Polish soil – or fall upon the sword himself. There, dagger poised over his breast, the robed Rejtan sat lamenting his nation's lost liberty. Before him lay *Phaedo* and *Cato's Life*. Next: the comely sad-faced youth, Jasinski, with his fast bosom friend Korsak beside him. Knee-deep in slain Muscovites, they hew the foe on Praga's ramparts, while the city burns all round. Even the old grandfather clock in the alcove stood remembered. With childish delight, the traveler pulled the cord to hear the old Dombrowski mazurka chime.

On through the house he ran, seeking out the room he had occupied of old as a boy of ten. He entered, swept the walls with round, astonished eyes, and drew back. A woman's room! But whose? His uncle was an old bachelor, and his aunt had been living in Saint Petersburg for years. The housekeeper's? Surely not! A pianoforte? With books and scores tossed in a careless heap on top? Sweet disarray! No wizened old hands had wrought it. Here, spread over the arm of a nearby chair, was a white frock, fresh off the peg. On the windowsills yonder stood pots of scented flowers – aster, violet, geranium, and stock gillyflower.

The traveler drew up at one of the windows. Another marvel! Where stinging nettle had once run riot at the orchard's edge, there now lay a small garden traversed by a network of paths. Clumps of mint and ribbon grass grew there in profusion. Enclosing the plot was a delicate cross rail fence bordered with tremulous white daisies. Plainly, the beds had just been sprinkled – yonder stood the can with water in it – yet not a glimpse of the gardener anywhere. Evidently, she was here a moment ago, for the gate, recently nudged open, still rocked on its hinges. The dint of a dainty foot bereft of stocking and shoe lay impressed in the scattering of powdery sand nearby. Distinctly outlined, the hollow in the snow-white sand was not deep; clearly, the foot that made it was light and nimble – one that, in running, scarcely grazed the ground.

Long stood the traveler by the open window, musing, admiring the prospect, snuffing up the scent of the flowers. Turning to where the violets grew yonder, he swept the pathways with curious eyes. Once again, his gaze hovered over the tiny footprints. He was puzzling over these traces, wondering whose they might be, when, chancing to look up, he noticed a girl in a white undergarment perched on the fence within hail of the house. The garment covered her svelte figure from the bosom down, leaving her swan-like neck and shoulders bare. Never, save in the early morning hours – certainly never in the presence of men – did Lithuanian girls go about in this state of undress. Even now, in the absence of spectators, she made good the wanting veil by holding her hands crossed over her bosom. Her hair, the ringlets yet to be brushed out, was a mass of little knots folded into tiny white pods. A curious head adornment, for it flamed in the sun like the crown of glory depicted on a sacred image.

Her face eluded the traveler's eye. She was standing with her back toward him, seeking someone out in the fields far below. Suddenly, descrying the party, she clapped her hands and gave out a peal of laughter. Like a white bird she alighted from the fence and flew across the sward. Even before the young traveler was aware of it, she'd threaded the rails, cleared the flowerbeds, darted up a plank that stood propped against the window ledge, and burst – fleet, noiseless, radiant as a moonbeam – into the room. Trilling softly to herself, she seized her frock, ran to the mirror, and only then laid eyes on the lad. The frock slipped from her fingers. She paled with shock and fright. The young man's face crimsoned as when a cloud meets the rising sun. Half closing his eyes, veiling them with his hand, he fumbled for a word of apology, bowed and drew back. The girl gave out a faint, painful cry like a child startled in its sleep. The lad looked up in alarm, but she had fled the room. Bewildered, heart pounding, he made himself scarce, wondering if this strange encounter should cause him shame, amusement, or sheer delight.

Meanwhile, the arrival of the new guest at the porch had not escaped notice in the servants' quarters. Already, his horses stood in the stable, crunching on the ample portion of oats and hay that every decent country house provides. The Judge wouldn't dream of dispatching his guests' horses to the Jewish inn, as was the fashion now. True, his servants hadn't come out to greet the caller, but it would be wrong to suppose they were remiss in their duties. They had been waiting for the Chief Steward to change his clothes after overseeing the banquet preparations at the rear of the house. The Steward stood in for the lord of the manor. He was a distant kinsman of the Judge and a friend of the house; to him belonged the task of greeting and minding the guests. On catching sight of the new arrival, he had stolen back to the servants' quarters – he could hardly receive a caller in his homespun dustcoat! – and there scrambled into the Sunday suit he'd laid out in the morning – for, he'd known since then that he would be seated at dinner with a large party of invited guests.

The Steward recognized the traveler from a distance. Uttering a cry, he flung out his arms, fell on his neck, and saluted him. Followed that confused stream of discourse in which the interlocutors try to squeeze years of events into the compass of a few brief words: scraps of narrative interrupted by queries, cries, sighs, then a fresh round of hugs. At last, after satisfying his curiosity on many points, the Steward informed the lad of the day's events.

"Well done, Tadeusz," he said; they'd christened the boy after Kosciuszko, to honor the year of war in which he was born. "Yes, Tadeusz, you could scarcely have timed it better. Just when we have so many marriageable young ladies present. Your uncle has a mind to see you wedded soon, and we've girls aplenty! For days, folks have been coming up in droves to hear the court settle our long-standing boundary dispute with the Count. He'll be paying us a visit tomorrow. The Chamberlain, his wife, and daughters have already arrived. Our youth went for a leisurely shoot in the forest, while the elders and womenfolk took a notion to inspect the harvest in the adjacent field – they'll be waiting for the youngsters by now. Shall we walk down? In no time, we'll meet your uncle, the Chamberlain, his wife, daughters, and the rest of the ladyships."

The Steward and Tadeusz took the road to the forest. They talked the whole way down, never slaking their thirst for more news. Meanwhile, the sun was gaining the utmost ends of the sky. Less brilliant now, though shedding a broader beam, it glowed with the hale ruddiness of a plowman retiring home to his rest. The radiant disk settled over the forest. A dim mist arose, thickening limb and crown, merging the trees into a solid mass. The forest bulked black like a vast building with its roof set ablaze. At last, sinking below, the sun flashed among the tree-trunks like candlelight through a slatted shutter, and went out. All sound of reaping and hay-raking ceased thereupon. Precisely as the Judge decreed: on his domain, all fieldwork closed at sunset. The Lord of the Universe knew best when to call it a day. When his toiler, the sun, retired from the sky, the farmer took his cue and vacated the fields – so ran his maxim. And to the honest Bailiff, the Judge's will was sacred, so that even the wagons they'd just begun to load with rye were forced to return to the barn unfilled, while the beasts of burden delighted in the ease of their yoke.

The entire company was even now repairing home from the forest. Despite their buoyant spirits, they walked in orderly array. The children and their tutor led the train. After them came the Judge with the Chamberlain's wife. The Chamberlain and his family followed to the side. Then came the elders, followed closely by the young people – damsels outpacing the lads by half a step, as decorum demanded. No one compelled this observance of order, no one played marshal here. Men and women instinctively knew their place. The Judge clung to ancient custom. Years, birth, rank, and wit had all to receive their due regard, he was wont to say. All great races and nations observed order; without it, families and nations died out. And so, the rule of order came naturally to all the inmates of the manor. Relations, strangers, or guests biding even briefly there, soon fell in with the prescribed usages of the house.

Solemn and brief was the Judge's greeting. Offering his hand to his nephew's lips, he kissed his brow and gave him welcome. Though he said little in the presence of the guests, it was plain to all by the tears he swept away with the sleeve of his robe that he loved Tadeusz dearly.

Forsaking field, forest, meadow, and pasturage, man and beast were wending their way homeward in the master's footsteps. Here, squeezing into the lane, raising clouds of dust, ran a flock of bleating sheep. A herd of Tyrolean heifers came ambling behind, brass bells swaying. Horses flew whinnying down from the freshly mown field yonder. All made eagerly for the well, where the creaking sweep decanted its drafts into the wooden troughs.

Though weary and beset by his company, the Judge was not one to shirk the weighty duties of the farm. Taking leave of his guests, he guided his steps down to the well. "No time like the evening for the master to inspect his stock," he was fond of saying. He insisted on discharging the office himself, for 'nothing so fattened the colt as the lord's solicitous eye.'

The Steward and the Court Usher stood candle in hand at the manor door. They were at odds, having words. In the Steward's absence, Protase had ordered the banquet table removed and installed in the castle ruins, which stood in clear view at the edge of the forest. Why the relocation? The Steward made a wry face and muttered his regrets. The Judge was stunned. But it was too late, the deed done, past undoing. Better to extend their regrets to the guests and escort them to the castle.

The Court Usher took full advantage of their walk down to explain why he'd crossed his master's plans. There was no room in the house to seat so large a host of honored guests. The castle hall was spacious, in good repair, its vault intact – true, there was a crack in one of the walls, no panes in the sashes; but this was summertime. The cellars? Sir! Spitting distance away. On he rambled, tipping winks to the Judge. By his look and mien, it was clear that more compelling reasons lurked in the back of his mind.

The castle stood some two thousand paces back from the house. This splendid pile of imposing bulk was the ancient seat of the Horeszkos, whose last heir had perished during the time of troubles. State seizures, careless trustees, and awards of court had reduced the domain to rack and ruin. The bulk of the estate went into liquidation to pay off the numerous creditors. The residue fell to distant relations in the female line. No one cared to take the castle. The cost of its upkeep was more than the local gentry could afford. But then the neighboring Count, a wealthy squire distantly related to the Horeszkos, came of age, and, returning from his travels abroad, took a fancy to the pile. He made much of its Gothic architecture – this despite the Judge producing papers to prove the builder was no Goth but a master architect from Vilna. The Count's show of interest in the castle was all it took to set the Judge thinking along similar lines. No one knew why. Both laid claims at the district court. The case went before the Senate. From there, it worked its way back to the court, then went before the Governor's Council. Finally, after great expense and a dozen edicts, the case was remanded again to the boundary court.

The Court Usher was quite right. The castle hall could comfortably seat all the members of the bar as well as the invited guests. Ample as a refectory, the chamber had a high vaulted ceiling, supporting pillars, a stone-flagged floor, and clean, spartanly appointed walls. Frontlets of stag and roebuck stood mounted all round with the date and place of their acquisition inscribed thereon and the hunter's name and arms carved into the wall below. The Horeszko Half Goat emblazoned the vault.

Entering in orderly fashion, the guests drew up in a circle around the table. To the Chamberlain – it being the privilege of his office and senior years – belonged the post of honor. Bowing to the ladies, elders, and youth, he approached the table. The Franciscan took his station beside him, and the Judge, his – next to the Franciscan. The Friar recited a brief benison in the Latin tongue; the men took vodka, whereupon they all sat down and tucked quietly into the beet-leaf soup – chilled Lithuanian-style.

Youngster though he was, Tadeusz shared the head of the table with the lady guests and the Chamberlain. Between him and his uncle stood an empty seat crying for an occupant. The Judge kept glancing at it and the door with an air of expectation. Tadeusz followed his uncle's gaze with his eye. Now it flew to the door, now it alighted on the vacant seat. Remarkable thing! All around him sat ladies at whom no prince would have looked down his nose. All were of gentle birth, young and pretty, yet here was Tadeusz staring at a vacant seat. The place was a riddle. But young people delight in reading riddles. Thus distracted, Tadeusz spoke scarcely a word to the Chamberlain's comely daughter seated beside him. Not once did he change her plate or fill her goblet or seek to entertain the ladies with the courteous talk prescribed by table etiquette. The unclaimed seat held him spellbound; indeed, it stood empty no longer – his thoughts had filled it. A thousand guesses thronged around it. So, after a cloudburst, the marsh frogs come swarming over a solitary meadow. A lone figure holds sway among them, as when, on a calm day, the lily of the lake rears her pale brow above the waters.

The servants brought in the third course. Decanting a finger of wine into Mistress Rose's goblet, then nudging a salver of salted cucumbers toward his youngest lass, the Chamberlain suddenly remarked:

"Alas, it is I, your old and fumble-fisted father, who must wait on you, my dears."

Instantly several lads sprang up to serve them.

The Judge eyed Tadeusz askance. Arranging the sleeves of his robe, he poured himself a bumper of Hungarian wine and spoke forth:

"It is the custom, nowadays, to send our youth to the capital to study. I do not deny that our sons and grandsons surpass their elders in book learning. Yet I am constantly given to observe how much they suffer from their lack of schooling in the domain of the polite arts. Time was when young nobles went for periods of training in the courts of great lords. I myself spent ten years as an attendant of the Royal Governor, the Chamberlain's father." Here the Judge gave the Chamberlain's knee a squeeze. "It was he who groomed me to serve the public. Not until he had made a man of me did he release me from his charge. My house shall always hold his memory dear. Each day, I pray *Eternal Rest* for his soul. If I left his court to take up the tillage of our fields and have profited less than others that stood worthier of the Governor's grace (and later rose to our country's highest offices!), at least no one here shall lay a lapse of courtesy or good manners to my charge. I say this without hesitation: courtesy is no easy art, nor is it of small account. Not easy, for there's more involved than showing a graceful leg or greeting every mother's son with a smile. Such fashionable manners may belong to the merchant class, but they are not the ways of Old Poland – or the nobility.

"Everyone deserves respect. Aye, but not without distinctions. Kindness towards children, a husband's public regard for his wife, a master's for his servant – all these are expressions of courtesy, but each in its own way. Considerable study is needed to appraise a man correctly and render him his due respect. Not even our elders exempted themselves from such learning. Our great lords cultivated polite discourse as the living history of our land. The conversations of our landed gentry filled the pages of the county chronicle. Thus came our brother nobles to feel that they were men of consequence, esteemed none too lightly. And so, our nobility safeguarded their manners. Today we no longer ask, 'Who is he?' 'What is his family?' 'Whom has he lived with?' 'What has he accomplished?' So long as he is not a beggar or a government spy, he enters wherever he pleases. As Emperor Vespasian cared little for the smell of his money or the hand or land it came from, so no one troubles now to take stock of a man's birth and manners. Legal tender and the stamp of currency are all that matter these days; and so, we value our friends as our Jew values his minted coin."

The Judge regarded his guests one by one. Though he spoke with power and eloquence, he knew that today's youth lacked patience, finding long speeches – even the most eloquent ones – tedious. But they were all attention. With a glance of his eye, he addressed the Chamberlain. The latter, forbearing to interrupt him, had been signifying assent with frequent nods of his head. The Judge remained silent. At last, upon securing another nod, he charged the Chamberlain's cup and his own, and resumed his theme:

"Now, courtesy's no trifling matter. By learning to value, as we ought, the years, noble birth, manners, and qualities of another, we learn to value ourselves. A nobleman gauges his weight by setting himself against his brother on the opposing scale. But what is even more deserving of your attention, gentlemen, is the courtesy a young man owes the fairer sex, the more especially, when substance and a noble house enhance the lady's natural grace and merits. This is the path to the heart's affections. It paves the way to splendid alliances. So thought our elders, and yet—"

The Judge broke off; and turning thereupon to his nephew, he shook his head and fired him a stern glance. Clearly, he had said his piece.

The Chamberlain tapped his gilded snuffbox. "Come now, Judge," said he. "In former times, things were worse. These days, I wonder if even we elders haven't changed with the times. Today's youth may not be as bad as we think; anyhow, I see less scandal now. Oh, I recall when the mania for all things French first greeted our land, when fashionable young men fell upon us from abroad in hordes worse than the Nogai Tatars. Here, in our own land, they reviled our Creator, the beliefs of our forebears, our laws, our customs, even our time-honored garments. What a sorry sight they were! Sallow-faced puppies drawling through their noses, if they had one at all, brandishing pamphlets and newspapers of every sort, espousing new-fangled religions, laws, and modes of dress. That rabble held our minds in thrall, for when God wishes to punish a people, he first robs them of their reason. The wiser heads among us lacked the nerve to cross those fops. The whole nation feared them like the pest. Everyone felt the contagion's lurking germ. We inveighed against those dandies, yet we aped them withal. We changed our faith, our manner of speech, our laws and dress. A masquerade! A carnival of license, swift on the heels of which came the season of Lent – bondage!

"Though I was but a young boy then, I remember the Cupbearer's son fetching up in front of my father's house in Oszmiana district. He was the first in Lithuania to parade himself in the Gallic style. People swarmed about him like swallows around a buzzard. Sorely envied the house before which his two-wheeled conveyance stood parked. They called the thing a *cabriolet* in French. In place of footmen, two small dogs sat perched on the trunk. On the coachman's seat towered a bizarre specimen of a German valet, lean as a lath, with long meager shanks like hop poles. He sported silk hose, low shoes with silver buckles, and he wore his queue encased in a bag.

"The equipage sent the elders into hoots of laughter. Our rustics blessed themselves, swearing a Venetian devil was abroad in a German coach. As for the Cupbearer's son, his appearance baffled description. Enough that he put us in mind of an ape or parrot in an outlandish peruke, which he likened to the Golden Fleece and we, to a plain case of the elflock. If any among us thought our Polish apparel better than aping foreign fashions, then we kept our own counsel, lest we incensed the youth; for, they would have decried us as culture's foes, impedi-

ments to progress, and traitors to our land. Such were the prej-
udices holding sway in those times.

"The Cupbearer's son declared his aim to refine our ways,
reform our system of rule and bring in a constitution. Eloquent
Frenchmen, he claimed, had made a discovery: all men are created equal. Now, hasn't Holy Writ always taught this? Doesn't
every parish priest prate of it from the pulpit? The doctrine's
old. Its application, aye, there's the rub! But so befogged were
we then that we set no store by the older things of the world
unless a French gazette took note of them. For all his talk of
equality, the Cupbearer's son became a marquis. Titles, as you
know, originate in Paris, and marquisates were all in vogue. But
fashion changed, and our marquis promptly became a democrat.
When, under Bonaparte, the winds of fashion changed yet again,
our democrat returned from Paris a baron. Had he lived another
year, the dear baron would doubtless have re-espoused the democratic cause. Paris prides herself upon her frequent about-faces
of fashion. Whatever France contrives is bound to appeal to the
Polish race.

"Thank God it is not the lure of fashionable duds, of poking around printers' booths for new laws, or of refining the art of
speech in the coffeehouses of Paris that draws our youth abroad
today. Napoleon's a quick, impetuous man with little time for
fashions and idle talk. Today we hear the roar of ordnance! Our
old hearts swell with pride that our countrymen should again be
the talk of the world. Glory is ours, and so our Commonwealth
shall rise again. The tree of liberty always springs from the laurels. Yet, alas for us, the years drag on so. We stand idle, and
our boys have yet far to come. The waiting's long, even news is
scarce. Father Robak!" he said to the Friar, lowering his voice. "I
hear you bring news from across the Niemen. Perhaps you have
intelligence of our troops?"

"None. None at all," said Robak with a careless air. Plainly, the talk unsettled him. "Politics bores me. The letter from
Warsaw touches on our congregation's business. Franciscan
matter! Why discuss it at the table? It's none of the laity's concern."

Saying this, he glanced sidelong down the table at their
Muscovite guest. It was Captain Rykov, a seasoned old soldier
who stood quartered in the neighboring village. The Judge had
invited him out of courtesy. Until now, he had been eating heart-

ily and taken little part in the talk; but at the mention of Warsaw, he looked up.

"Ah, Chamberlain!" said he. "Always curious about Bonaparte. Mind always set on Warsaw. The Fatherland, eh? Rykov's
no spy, though he speaks your Polish tongue. The Fatherland!
I know those sentiments, understand them well. You Poles, we
Russkies, eh? Right now, we're not at war – an armistice! We
eat and sup together. Our boys at the advance posts knock back
vodkas and chum with the French. But when the huzzah breaks
forth, prepare for a cannonade! We Muscovites have a saying,
'Love the one you love to thump.' 'Clasp your crony close, then
dust him good and proper like an overcoat.'

"I say there will be war," he went on. "Just the other day,
the staff adjutant called on Major Plut. 'Prepare to march,' says
he. On Turkey? France? It's all the same. But then Bonaparte's
a rare bird all right. With our Suvorov gone, he may trounce us
yet. When our troops marched on the French, word went out
Bonaparte had magic. But Suvorov knew the black arts too, so it
was spell against spell! On the battlefield once, we looked about
us – no sign of Bonaparte. He'd turned himself into a fox. So,
Suvorov becomes a hound. Bonaparte takes another shape. Now
he's a cat. Starts slashing with his claws, then presto! Suvorov's
a pony. Now see what becomes of Bonaparte."

Here Rykov broke off and resumed eating.

A footman announced the fourth course. Even as he did
so, the side door swung open, and in swept a young and comely
new guest. Her abrupt entrance, her lofty stature, her beauty
and attire drew the eyes of the guests. They rose as a body to
greet her; clearly, all save Tadeusz had made the woman's ac-
quaintance. Svelte, full-figured, and charmingly endowed, she
had on a low-cut frock of rose-colored satin with short sleeves
and a thread-lace collar. She fiddled with her gilded fan – a play-
thing, as it wasn't hot. When she whirred it, the bauble scattered a rich shower of sparks. Bareheaded, she wore her hair up
in a cluster of ringlets interlaced with pink ribbons, with a peep
of diamond – like a star in the comet's tress – within. In a word:
gala dress! All just too-too, muttered some, for a weekday in the
country. Though her frock was short, her foot eluded the eye.
She moved swiftly, or better, she glided along like the Twelfth
Night puppets which little boys, concealed in the booth, slide
across the stage.

Greeting the guests with a slight bow, she made for the
seat reserved for her. Alas! Easier thought than done. The Man-
or was short of chairs. The company sat on four benches at right
angles to each other. Either a whole row would have to move,
or she overleap the bench. But she managed deftly to squeeze
in between two benches. Like a billiard ball she glided around
the table, clearing the corridor that the guests made for her. As
she swept past Tadeusz, she caught her flounce on a protruding knee, stumbled, and inadvertently steadied herself on the
youth's shoulder. Begging his pardon, she took her seat between
him and the Judge. But, evidently, she had no appetite. She
whirred her fan, then twirled it by the stem. Now she straightened her collar of Flemish lace, now she smoothed her hair and
bright-hued ribbons.

After a lapse of four minutes, talk picked up again, this
time at the far end of the table – in an undertone at first, then
loud enough to be heard. The men's talk ran upon the day's hunt.
A spirited exchange arose between the Notary and the Assessor
over the former's bobbed greyhound. Passionately fond of his
dog, the Notary insisted Scut had brought the hare to book. To
spite him, the Assessor claimed the crown for his dog, Peregrine.
Each sought the backing of the guests. Soon all were taking
sides, some championing Scut, others, Peregrine, some claiming
to be experts, others, eyewitnesses.

"My apologies, dear," muttered the Judge to his new partner at table. "But we couldn't delay any longer. The guests were
hungry after their ramble in the fields. I took it you wouldn't be
dining with us tonight."

At this, he poured the Chamberlain and himself a bumper;
then, he struck up a quiet conversation on a political theme.

With both ends of the table thus engaged, Tadeusz took
leisure to study the stranger. Yes, he'd suspected whose seat it
was the instant he laid eyes on it! He felt the blood mount in
his cheeks. His heart beat with a strange vigor. So, the mystery puzzling him stood solved! So, fate ordained that the one
sitting next to him should be the very beauty he'd glimpsed in
the twilight. True, she seemed taller now that she was dressed.
Clothes had a way of making a person look bigger or smaller.
Her hair, it now appeared, was long and raven-black, not short
and blonde, as he'd imagined seeing in the garden. No doubt the
setting sun's rays and the reddish tint they imparted explained

the fact. He hadn't caught the gardener's face; she'd fled his gaze too swiftly. But the mind will divine fair looks. The lad imagined her with dark eyes, a cherry-red mouth, and a light-skin complexion. This woman's eyes, mouth, and face matched his image perfectly. Where the two seemed to differ most was in age. The one in the garden had seemed a young girl, while here was a woman of mature years. But youth does not probe into beauty's birth certificate. To the eyes of a youth, every demoiselle is young, every beauty his peer. To an innocent lad, every heart's pride is a tender maiden.

Although Tadeusz was just shy of twenty and grew up in the great city of Vilna, he had been confided to the care of a watchful priest who raised him in the stern rules of old-fashioned virtue. In consequence, Tadeusz brought back to his native hearth not only a pure soul, a lively mind and upright heart, but also a strong yen to break loose. Even before leaving the city, he had vowed to taste the long-denied freedoms of country life. He was conscious of his good looks, his youth, his vigor. He came by his robust health honestly. After all, he was a Soplica, and everyone knew the Soplicas were a strong and sturdy breed, apt at soldiering, less so at book learning.

Tadeusz brought no disgrace upon his fathers. He rode ably and walked with a stout stride. He was by no means dull-witted, though he'd made little progress in his studies, on which his uncle spared no expense. Anyhow, shooting a gun and handling a sword were more in his line. He knew he was going for a soldier. Such was his father's instruction in his last will and testament. All through school, the lad had longed for the soldier's drum; but then his uncle suddenly took a new mind. He recalled him home with plans for marriage and handing down the estate, first a small hamlet then the rest of the domain.

None of these gifts and qualities escaped the discerning eye of Tadeusz's companion at table. She appraised his tall, handsome build, his burly shoulders and ample chest. She studied his face, which blushed furiously each time his eyes met hers. Soon, he, too, was master of his eyes and was staring at her ardently. She returned the gaze. Their four eyes burned, face to face, like *rorate* candles.

She struck up a conversation – in French at first. Seeing as the lad had been at school in the city, she sought out his views on new books and authors. His replies brought on fresh queries.

But then she launched into painting, music, dance, even sculpture. Letters, brush, score, she was equally at home with them all! The show of knowledge rendered Tadeusz speechless. Terrified of being made an object of ridicule, he stammered out his answers like a schoolboy before his master. Happily, the master was pretty and lenient. Guessing the cause of his dismay, she turned to less taxing, less erudite matters – rural living, its tedium and bothers. She spoke of its diversions, of apportioning one's time, so as to sweeten life in the country and make it more pleasurable.

Tadeusz's replies became increasingly bolder. Within half an hour, the pair were fast friends, partaking even in squabbles and jokes. Rolling three bread pills between her thumb and finger, she set them on the table before him: he must choose between three parties. He picked the nearest, whereupon the Chamberlain's two daughters sitting close by signaled their displeasure with a frown. Tadeusz's partner laughed, but she refrained from attaching a name to the lucky pill.

Meanwhile, the far end of the table was engaged in other games. Peregrine's champions had suddenly grown in strength and were mounting a furious assault on the Scuts. The contest ran high, and the last courses stood untasted. Both factions were up on their feet, yelling and draining their cups. By far the most impassioned among them was Notary Bolesta. Given the floor, he went on like a millrace, gracing his speech with expressive gestures. He had served on the bar, where his habit of extravagant gesticulation earned him the nickname of *Preacher*. Just now, he was concluding his account, arms pulled in, elbows thrust back, two long-nailed index fingers representing the greyhounds' leads pointed forward:

"See-ho! Together we, the Assessor and I, slip our leashes like the hammers of a double released at the touch of the trigger. See-ho! They're off! The hare makes a sprint for the field, the hounds right on his bob." The Notary ran his hands over the table, uncannily mimicking the dogs' movements with his fingers. "Right on his bob! In a trice, they head him from the forest. Then, whoosh! Peregrine puts on speed. Aye, he's a fleet one, though hot-headed. He leads Scut by so much, by a whisker. But I knew he'd muff it. Rare old puss our game! He makes as if straight for the field, hounds fast on his traces. Crafty puss!

No sooner does he sense the pack bunching up behind him than
zip! He jinks to the right and turns a somersault. The fool dogs
swerve to the right after him. But then, after just two bounds,
lickety-split! He jinks to the left and the dogs veer left after him.
Now he's making his point to the forest – and that's when my
Scut goes WHAP!"

Here, bending over, the Notary ran his fingers to the other side of the table and roared "WHAP!" right above Tadeusz's
ear.

The outburst caught Tadeusz and his partner in the
midst of their *tête à tête*. Instinctively, the two heads withdrew
from each other like the crowns of close-set trees sundered by a
gust of wind. A pair of hands lying close together under the table
flew apart, and two faces broke out into a single blush. Tadeusz
strove to hide his distraction.

"No doubt you are right, Mr. Notary," said he. "Your
bobbed one's a handsome beast, no disputing. If he should be as
good at seizing his—"

"Good at seizing!?" bridled Bolesta. "My prize hound not
good at seizing?"

Again, Tadeusz expressed delight that such a handsome
animal should be accounted faultless in every respect. Only he
regretted he'd seen the beast but once, homeward bound from
the forest, and hadn't had time to form an estimate of the greyhound's qualities.

Here the Assessor took bitter umbrage. Dropping his
cup from his hand, he pierced the youth with a basilisk glance.
Though smaller than Bolesta, of slighter build, and less given to
vociferating and gesturing, he was the awe of every masquerade
party, ballroom, or regional diet. They said he had a sting in his
tongue and could turn out witticisms worthy of the farmer's almanac – all of them barbed and cutting. Formerly a man of substance, he had squandered his own and his brother's inheritance
by moving in high society. Now, he'd entered the government
service to make a name for himself in the county. He was inordinately fond of hunting – and not just for the sport of it. The peal
of the horn and the sight of a ring of beaters recalled the days
of his youth when he had employed scores of hunters and kept
a kennel of first-rate hounds. Of the former hounds, only two
remained; and now a shadow of doubt hung over one of them.

Stroking his side whiskers, the Assessor leaned over toward Tadeusz.

"A bobbed greyhound is like a nobleman sans berth," said he with a laugh, a laugh that dripped with venom. "A tail gives the hound a clear edge on speed. And you, sir, take its absence for a virtue? But why not put the case to your auntie? Though Mistress Telimena lives in the capital and only recently bides in our parts, yet I daresay she knows more about the course than the callow sportsman, for knowledge, surely, comes with years."

Scarcely expecting such a thunderbolt, Tadeusz rose in dismay. For a moment, he stood speechless, glaring at his rival with an eye that grew increasingly grimmer and more ominous. Fortunately, the Chamberlain chose this very moment to sneeze twice.

"*Vivat!*" they cried in a chorus.

His Excellency bowed to his guests then beat a slow tattoo on his snuffbox. Wrought of gold, with a diamond inlay, the snuffbox boasted a miniature of King Stanislas on the inside of the lid. It had been the proud gift of His Majesty to the Chamberlain's father, and now the Chamberlain carried it proudly after his father. A rap on the lid signaled his wish to address the party. The guests fell silent, all attention.

"Esteemed gentlemen! Fellow nobles!" said he. "The field, the forest, these are the hunter's forum. Such matters I do not decide indoors, and so I shall defer our session until tomorrow. No further rejoinders today. Mr. Usher! Declare the case adjourned to the fields, where the Count and his entire shooting party have agreed to join us. You, dear Judge and neighbor, shall be so kind as to accompany us, as will, I trust, Mistress Telimena and our gracious ladyships. In a word, we shall organize a splendid day of sport, as befits the occasion. Nor shall our Steward refuse us his company!"

And with that, he passed his snuffbox down to the Steward who sat with the hunters at the foot of the table.

All this time, the Steward had been listening in silence, squinting his eyes, resisting the efforts of the youth to draw him into the conversation – he being the most experienced hunter in the district. Long he held his peace, musing over the pinch of snuff in his fingers. At last, drawing the grains into his nostrils and sneezing with such violence as to send echoes reverberating through the hall, he shook his head and smiled a rueful smile.

"Ah!" said he. "How this saddens and astonishes an old gaffer like me. What would our hunters have said on seeing so large an assembly of lords and nobles having to adjudicate on a greyhound's stern? What would old Reytan say, were he raised to life? Why, he'd slink right back to his grave in Lachowicze! And what of old Niesiolowski? Aye, the governor – owner of the world's finest bloodhounds. Two hundred shooters and a hundred cartloads of nets he kept in the grand lordly fashion at his castle in Woroncza! All these years he remains shut up like a hermit in his hall, and no one has enticed him out for a hunt. Why, he even refused Bialopiotrowicz himself! But what quarry would he be hunting on your shoots, gentlemen? Some glory for a man of his stature to go haring after a rabbit, as they do nowadays. In the sportsman's lingo of my day, it was the wild boar, the bear, the wolf, and the elk that passed for noble game. A beast innocent of tusk, horn, or claw fell to the paid servant or manorial flunkey. No self-respecting nobleman took into his hand a gun bearing the indignity of firing small shot. True, they kept their hounds on hand, for now and anon, riding home, they would start some hapless hare. Then, for a lark, they'd slip the leashes and watch the youngsters urge their hobbies after it; though, in truth, even then they scarcely bothered to watch, much less argue over a hound. So, Your Excellency, pray revoke your bidding. Forgive me, but I cannot hunt this way. Never will I take part in it. My name is Hreczecha, and no Hreczecha since the days of King Lech ever went chasing after a jackrabbit . . ."

The young people's laughter drowned out the rest of his discourse. Meanwhile, the party rose from the table. The Chamberlain – it being the privilege of his post and senior years – was the first to leave. Out he swept, bowing to the ladies, elders and youth. The Judge and the Franciscan followed. Upon reaching the door, the Judge offered his arm to the Chamberlain's wife. Tadeusz went next, linking arms with Telimena, then the Assessor with the Carver's daughter and, last, Notary Bolesta with the Steward's lass.

Tadeusz walked to the barn with several of the guests. Bewildered, angry and dejected, he was at pains to sort out the day's events – the encounter at the house and dinner with his companion at table. Especially galling to him was the word 'auntie,' which buzzed around his ear like an irritating fly. He wanted to learn more about Telimena from the Court Usher, but he

was unable to find him, or the Steward either; for, the two servi-
tors had left with the guests directly after the meal, to prepare
their beds. The women and the elders were sleeping in the man-
or. The youth would bed down in the barn. Upon Tadeusz, the
Judge enjoined the task of escorting them there.

Within half an hour, save for the watchman's calls, there
reigned over Soplica Manor a hushed stillness as profound as
that over a cloister upon the bell for prayer. The guests were
sound asleep. The Judge alone forwent his repose. As lord of the
manor, he was busy laying plans for the morrow's course and the
breakfast to follow. Instructions went out to the overseers, fore-
men, helpers, clerks, bailiff-mistress, huntsmen, and grooms. At
last, after running his eye over the day's accounts, the Judge
gave the Usher leave to undress him.

Protase unfastened his waist-sash. It was a true nobleman's belt, crafted in Slutsk, woven from strands of gold and
hung with gleaming tassels as thick as a panache. Gold brocade
with a pattern of purple flowers lined one side, and black satin
with silver checkers the other. The article could be worn on either side, gold on gala days, black in seasons of mourning. None
but the Usher knew how to undo and fold the belt. He was per-
forming this very office as he closed his argument:

"So, yes," said he, "I removed the tables to the castle.
Show me the harm done. No one suffered as a result, and you
may even profit by it. The whole case revolves around the castle.
Now legal title is vested in us; and despite the strong conten-
tions of the other side, I aim to prove it. Who bids his guests
dine with him at the castle proves he holds possession there – or
takes it! We shall even serve writs on the opposition to appear as
witnesses. I recall similar cases in my day."

But the Judge was already fast asleep. The Usher tip-
toed into the hallway. Taking a seat beside a candle, he reached
into his pocket and drew out a notebook. The article – it was a
court calendar – served him like the daily missal. At home or
away, he was never without it. Listed in it were all the actions
he had called before the bench and many others he'd learned of
later. To the layman, the calendar consisted of stark columns of
names. To the Court Usher, it conjured up images sublime. And
so, leafing through the pages, he fell to reminiscing: Oginski ver-
sus Wizgird; The Black Friars v. Rymsza; Rymsza v. Wysogird;

Radziwill v. Mme. Wereszczaka; Giedroyces v. Rdultowski; Obuchowicz v. the Jewish Kahal; Juracha v. Piotrowski; Maleski v. Mickiewicz; and, last, the Count v. Soplica. And, as he scanned the names, he recalled the famous cases and the circumstances attending them. Before his eyes appeared the court, the disputants and witnesses. He saw himself attired in his white tunic and navy-blue robe, one hand upon his saber, the other beckoning to the parties to approach the bench. "Come to order!" he called. And so, he mused on. At length, after saying his night prayers, the last of Lithuania's court ushers, nodded off to sleep.

Such were the sport and contests in Lithuania's rustic purlieus when the rest of the world foundered in a welter of blood and tears; when, compassed by a cloud of regiments, armed with field-pieces innumerable, that Indomitable One, that martial god yoked both gold and silver eagles to his war chariot and winged his way from the Libyan sands to the lofty Alps, raining bolt after bolt upon the Pyramids, Tabor, Marengo, Ulm, and Austerlitz. Victory was his van, conquest his rear. Glory, swelling with deeds of valor, great with heroes' names, thundered northward from the Nile, until, at Niemen's banks, she dashed herself like a wave on the rock of the Russian line, a wall of steel barring Lithuania from news that Moscow dreaded like the plague.

And yet, ever and anon, like a stone dropped from heaven, news came even to Lithuania. An old beggar lacking a leg or an arm would appear at the door for a crust of bread. On receiving his alms, he would cast wary glances around the courtyard. Only when assured that the place was clear of Russian soldiers, Hebrew skullcaps, and scarlet collars would he make himself known: an old legionary dragging his bones back to the native soil he could no longer defend. How the entire household, servants and all, choked back their tears and fell about his neck! Led to the board, he spun tales as fabulous as any fable. Of Dombrowski enlisting Poles in the Lombard plains. Of his attempts to reach Poland from Italy. Of the victorious Kniaziewicz issuing orders from the Capitol. Of the hundred bloody flags he'd seized from Caesar's descendants and cast at the feet of the French. Of Jablonowski faring forth with his Danube Legion to exotic climes where the pepper was reared, cane sugar refined; and where, among fragrant groves in the flourish of eternal spring, he rained destruction on the black folk and pined for home.

The old campaigner's tales spread quietly throughout the countryside. A young lad who heard them would suddenly vanish from his home. With Muscovites in pursuit, he would beat a stealthy path through wood and slough, then, plunging into the Niemen, swim submerged to the other side, to the old Crown's banks, where a friendly, 'Welcome, mate!' was sure to greet his ears. Only after scaling a rock, and calling out, "Till we meet again!" to the Muscovite on the other side, would he walk away. Gorecki made it across. So did Patz, Obuchowicz, Piotrowski, Obolewski, Kupsc, Rozycki, Janowicz, Brochocki, Giedymin, the brothers Bernatowicz, the Miezejewskis, and many others. They forsook their kin, their beloved land, and all their worldly goods, which the Tsarist treasury promptly seized and consigned to her coffers.

From time to time, an alms quester would arrive from a distant friary. Upon acquainting himself with the manor holders, he would show them the gazette he'd stuffed inside the lining of his scapulary. Recorded in the newssheet were the muster and nominal rolls of every legion together with an account of the heroic feats or tragic death of each of the officers. Thus, after many a year, a family had first news of the life, glorious deeds, and death of their son – and the whole house would go into mourning. Whom they mourned, they shied from saying. The neighborhood could only guess. Silent sorrow or quiet expressions of joy were the gentry's only means of spreading the news.

Now it appeared that Robak was one such secret quester. Not seldom was he observed holding private converse with the Judge. After each such meeting, a fresh piece of news would go the round of the district. Judging by his exterior, he had not always gone about in a hooded habit or spent his years within cloistered walls. From a point between his right ear and temple, a scar traveled a handbreadth across the dome of his skull. His chin bore the mark of a grazing shaft or ball; clearly, he hadn't won these from reading the sacramentary. But it was not just the stern gaze and the scars. The very way he carried himself and his manner of address had a military air about them. At the mass, when with upraised arms he turned from the altar to the people to say, *"Pax vobiscum!"* he would do so smartly, in a single sweep, as if executing a right about face at the captain's command. He barked out the cadences of the liturgy in the tone of an officer addressing a squadron – so remarked the boys who served him at the mass. Indeed, Robak seemed far better versed in political affairs than in the lives of the saints. While questing for alms, he often tarried in the district town where he had a string of errands to run. Sometimes, he received letters, which he never opened with strangers present. Other times, he dispatched messengers, but where he sent them, and why, he did not say. Often, he'd steal away at night and visit the manor holders. He conferred endlessly with the gentry, made frequent calls on the neighboring hamlets, and stopped by the taverns to chat with the rustics; invariably he spoke of events abroad.

So now the Judge, who had been asleep for an hour, was the object of such a visit; clearly, the Friar had news to impart.

BOOK TWO: THE CASTLE

Argument: Coursing with greyhounds. A sightseer at the castle.
The last of the Horeszko retainers recounts the story of his late mas-
ter. A glance at the garden. A girl among the cucumbers. Breakfast.
Telimena's anecdote of Saint Petersburg. A fresh outbreak of hostilities
over Scut and Peregrine. Father Robak's intervention. The Steward's
discourse. A wager. Let's go mushrooming!

Who among us can forget the days when, as growing lads, we'd
shoulder a gun and strike out whistling into the fields? Neither
ridge nor fence stood in our way. When we cleared a baulk, the
idea of trespassing never crossed our minds. In Lithuania, the
hunter is like a ship sweeping the seas. He takes whichever path
he fancies, roams the wastes at will. And when he sweeps the
heavens with his eye, he is like a prophet reading the omens. No
cloud but a host of visible signs! Or again, he is like a sorcerer
holding colloquy with mother earth, who, while mute to the town
dweller, prompts the hunter's ear with a vast compass of sounds.

There rasps the corncrake. Idle to spy him out: he weaves
through the meadow grass like a pike in the Niemen. Overhead, plunged equally deep in the heavens, the skylark peals
his springtime matins. Yonder shrills the broad eagle's wing,
startling the sparrows even as the comet dismays the tsars; and
the hawk, poised in the clear blue vault, beats his wing like a
butterfly impaled on a pin; then, spying a bird or leveret in the
field below, he drops like a shooting star.

When will the Lord vouchsafe an end to our wanderings?
When shall we be settled again in our ancestral fields? Oh, to
serve with a cavalry that rides against the hare! A foot soldiery
that marches on the birds! To bear no arms but the hook and the
scythe. To scan no columns other than those of our household
accounts.

Morning had broken over Soplica Manor. Even now, the
sun shone down upon the barn, filtering in through cracks in the
dark thatch. Ribbons of golden light came flickering through,
flooding the dark-green, fresh-mown hay on which the youth had
made their beds. As a young lass wakes her sweetheart with a
grain-spike, so, with his morning rays, the sun teased the lips

of the sleeping guests. Sparrows frisked and chirped among the rafters. Thrice gaggled the ganders. Turkeys and ducks took up the refrain like an echo. The bawls of the driven cattle filled the air.

The youth were up and about. Only Tadeusz, the last to fall asleep, snored on. So much had last night's banquet upset him that the crowing cock found him still tossing and turning, unable to sleep. At last, the heaped-up hay engulfed him like a wave and bore him off. Now dead to the world he lay. A cool stream of air fanned his eyes, as, with a loud crash, the creaking barn door burst open and in came the Friar, Father Robak, swishing his knotted rope girdle.

"*Surge, puer!*" he roared and lay into Tadeusz's back with the knots of his belt.

The courtyard rang out with the cries of the gathering hunt. Men were walking their nags or still arriving in their dog-carts. Scarcely could the yard contain such a throng! The bugles shrilled, the kennel gates flew open, and out tore the hounds, babbling with joy. Driven frantic by the sight of the horses and huntsmen's leads, the dogs raced around the yard; but they soon ran up and yielded their necks to the leash. All this promised a splendid run; and at last, the Chamberlain gave the order to ride.

Slowly, in single file, the hunt moved out. Once past the gate, they quickened their pace and fanned out in loose array. The Notary and the Assessor rode headmost. Despite occasional glances of mutual loathing, they kept a civil tongue, as dueling principals do when riding out to the field of honor. No one sensed the rancor seething in their hearts. Bolesta led Scut; the Assessor, Peregrine. The womenfolk, drawn in open carriages, followed behind, while the young men cantered alongside, engaging the damsels in light raillery.

Father Robak paced the courtyard with leisurely strides, finishing his morning devotions. Now and again, frowning one minute, smiling the next, he glanced at Tadeusz. At last, he crooked a finger for the lad. Tadeusz drew up, but Robak only tapped the side of his nose in an ominous manner. No amount of urging and pleading would induce him to make himself clear. Refusing to answer, or even favor the lad with a glance, the Friar drew up his hood and finished his prayers. With that, Tadeusz galloped off to rejoin the hunt.

The huntsmen had just checked their hounds. The entire
field stood dead in their tracks, waving silence, eyes intent upon
a rock near which the Judge had halted. He had spotted the game
and was making signs with his hands. They understood him and
remained perfectly still; meanwhile, the Notary and the Assessor approached at a slow trot. Tadeusz, being closer, reached the
Judge first. Drawing up beside his uncle, he probed the prospect
with his eye. It was a good while since he had been in the field.
Not easy to catch sight of a hare in that gray expanse, the more
so, as the terrain lay strewn with stones. The Judge pointed it
out. There, pressed against a rock, sat the hapless beast, ears
bolt upright, red eye riveted on the hunters. Alive to its plight,
yet frozen by their gaze, the hare cowered in terror by the rock,
inert as that rock itself. Meanwhile, the cloud of dust in the field
drew steadily closer. Scut strained furiously at the leash, behind
him sped Peregrine the Fleet. Then, with one voice, the Notary
and the Assessor hallooed and vanished in a smother of dust on
the heels of their hounds.

Just as the hunt raced off in pursuit of the hare, the
Count emerged from the woods by the castle. The whole district
knew his lordship was incapable of showing up at the appointed
hour. Once again, he had overslept and vented his spleen on
the servants. As soon as he spotted the hunters in the field, he
set off after them at a gallop, the skirts of his long white coat
of English cut flapping wildly in the wind. Behind him rode his
serving-men. Each sported a shiny black mushroom-shaped cap,
a short jacket, white pantaloons, and stripe-lined top boots. At
home, the Count insisted his servants so costumed should be
called *jockeys*.

Just as the mounted party gained the bottom of the
meadow, the Count spied the castle and drew rein. Never before had he set eyes on the ruins at dawn. It was hard to believe these were the same walls, so much did the early morning
light enhance and refresh their lines. The new prospect filled
him with wonder. Thrusting up from the dew-mist, the turret
seemed twice its real height. The tin-sheeted roof shone gold
in the sunlight. In the window frames below, the broken panes
bent the morning beams into bows of prismatic light. The lower
floors stood veiled in mist. Hidden from view were the fissures
and flaws. Now and again, the distant halloos of the hunt came
floating by on the wind and rebounded off the walls. One would

swear that they hailed from within the castle; that under the mantle of mist, the walls stood rebuilt and teemed once more with human life.

Now the Count was fond of rare and novel sights. He called them romantic, as he owned to a romantic cast of mind – though in truth he was an incurable crank. When riding to hounds or coursing hares, he had a habit of halting sharply and gazing upward with the mournful watchfulness of a cat eyeing a sparrow high in a pine. Not seldom would he roam the groves without gun or hound like a runaway recruit, or sit motionless on the marges of a brook, his head bent over the stream like the heron's when he stares at the fish with a ravenous eye. Such were the Count's peculiar ways. People thought him a little daft, though they held him in high esteem, for he was well-born and rich, favorably disposed to the rustics and friendly to neighbor and Hebrew alike.

Swinging off the path, the Count put his horse across the field and drew up at the castle gate. Alone at last, he heaved a sigh and gazed at the walls. He was reaching for his drawing materials and setting down to sketch the lines, when, glancing aside, he observed a man standing some twenty yards distant. Evidently, the fellow was a devotee of scenic prospects like himself, for he was standing with his hands in his pockets, gazing up at the castle walls, as if reckoning the stones. The Count knew him at once but was fain to call several times before Gervase took notice.

Gervase was of noble stock – a servant of the former castle holder and the last remaining retainer of the Horeszko family. He was a tall, grizzled old master with a hale, rugged face furrowed with wrinkles and a mien both morose and stern. Once famous among the nobility for his good cheer, he had soured since the battle in which the last castle heir perished. No longer did he attend weddings and the annual fairs. Gone were the days when he amused others with his witty jests. No longer did his face spread with smiles.

He dressed in the old Horeszko livery, a yellow dress coat with a faded galloon trim that must have been gold in its day. The coat was embroidered all over in silk with the Horeszko bearing; hence the sobriquet *Half Goat* by which he was generally known. Sometimes, also, he went by the name of *Old Boy* from the familiar address he constantly used. Other times, he went by

Scarpate after the numerous scars seaming his bald skull. His real name, however, was Rembaïlo – his blazon was unknown – and he called himself *Warden* because years ago he had held that office at the castle. A hefty truss of keys still hung from his belt by a silver-tasseled cord. True, for years there had been nothing to lock, for the ruined castle gaped wide open. But he eventually found two doors, repaired and hung them at his own expense; and so he amused himself twice daily with turning the locks. He had even taken up lodgings in one of the empty chambers. Though he might easily have lived on the Count's charity, he chose not to, for he was always pining for the past and never felt well unless he could breathe the castle air.

As soon as he saw the Count, he snatched off his hat and, bowing to the kinsman of his lords, revealed to view his great shining skull, which numerous saber cuts had scored like the ball of a mace. Stroking it with his hand, he approached the Count, bowed profoundly again, then addressed him in doleful tones:

"Greetings, old boy . . . young master. Forgive the address, my lord Count. It is my way, you know, no disrespect. All the Horeszkos used to say, 'old boy.' My master, the late Pantler, said it all the time. Is it true, sir, you would stint a penny for the litigation and yield the castle to Soplica? I shouldn't have believed it, but now everyone's noising it about the countryside."

And gazing at the castle, he heaved one sigh after another.

"It is no wonder," said the Count. "The expense is great, and the tedium still greater. I dearly wish the matter were closed, but the tiresome old squire has dug in his heels. He knew he would wear me out in the courts. I cannot hold out any longer. Today, I shall lay down my arms and accept such terms as the court awards."

"Terms!?" cried Gervase. "Make terms with Soplica? The Soplicas, old boy?" He made a face, as if the very word confounded him. "Terms with the Soplicas? Come, my boy, you must be joking, eh? The castle, the ancestral seat of the Horeszkos, pass into Soplica hands? Only get you down from your horse, sir. Let us go into the castle. Come see for yourself. You do not know what you are saying. Come! No shying from me! Dismount, I say."

And he held the stirrup for his lordship to dismount.

They entered the castle. Gervase drew up at the threshold of the great hall.

"Here," said he, "would the former holders and their entourage lounge in their chairs after dinner. Here would my master settle disputes among the villagers. When in a good flow of spirits, he amused his guests with beguiling tales or delighted in another's yarn or jest. Meanwhile, in the courtyard, the youth exercised with wooden swords or broke my master's Turkish ponies to saddle."

They entered the hall. Gervase spoke on:

"If you counted all the stones in this vast paved chamber, you would still fall short of the number of wine casks we broached here in the old days. Name the occasion, a call to Parliament or the regional diet, my master's saint's day, a hunting meet – just name it, and the nobility would be lowering their belts into the cellars for a hogshead. On banquet nights, a small orchestra stood in yonder gallery, playing airs on the organ and sundry instruments. When we raised a pledge, the horns pealed forth from the choir as on Judgment Day. Toasts followed in orderly succession. The first brimmer we raised to His Majesty the King, the second to the Primate, the next three to the Queen, the nobility, and the Commonwealth respectively. Then came the sixth and final toast, 'Let us love one another! *Vivat!* A long life!' That was the rouse that never ended. Raised at sundown, it rang forth clear until sunrise, at which time carriages and dogcarts would be lining up to bear each guest to his lodging."

They passed through several chambers. Gervase remained silent, fixing his gaze now on the walls, anon on the vault. A sad recollection struck him here, a pleasant one there. At times, the words "Forever fled!" seemed poised on his lips. At times, he would nod his head sadly or wave his arm in the air; clearly, memory itself was a torment to him and he strove to drive it away. At last, they fetched up in the old hall of mirrors upstairs. The mirrors had long since gone. The frames hung empty. Paneless windows gave onto a gallery that commanded a clear view of the castle gate. Entering thereon, Gervase buried his head in his hands. When at last he looked up, his face bore a look of intense sadness and despair.

Unable to divine what all this meant, the Count felt strangely moved. He stared into the old man's face and squeezed his hand. For a while, they stood silent together; then, shaking his raised fist, Gervase broke the silence.

"No terms, old boy! There can be no peace between Soplica and Horeszko blood. Know that Horeszko blood runs in
your veins. You are kin to the Pantler by your mother, the Royal Huntsman's wife. Her mother was the cadet daughter of the
Chatelain, who in turn, as everyone knows, was my lord's mater-
nal uncle. Now listen to this tale of your kith and kin, for it all
happened here in this castle, in this very hall.

"My late lamented lord, the Pantler, was the first gentleman of the district, a man of family and substance. He had
an only child, a daughter, the very picture of an angel. Young
noblemen and notables alike wooed her by the score. Among
the nobility there was a hotheaded ruffian by the name of Jacek Soplica. People jokingly styled him *The Governor*; and, in
truth, he had clout in the province, for he held the whole Soplica
clan under his thumb, commanding their three hundred votes
as he pleased. Yet all he owned in the world was a landholding
of paltry size, a saber, and a pair of whiskers that spanned his
face from ear to ear. Now the Pantler often invited this fellow
to dine with him at the castle, especially during the regional
diets, for my lord's kinsmen and supporters found him favorable
to their causes. Alas, their affecting of his company went to his
head. Before long he was entertaining thoughts of wedding the
Pantler's daughter. More and more he imposed himself on the
castle. Soon, he had settled in like one of the family. He was all
set to ask for her hand when they got wind of it and served him
a bowl of black soup at the table. Seems the lass had been sweet
on him all along but hadn't breathed a word of it to her parents.

"Those were the Kosciuszko days. My master declared
for the Constitution of May Third. He was mustering the nobility to go to the aid of the Confederates, when, without warning
one night, the Muscovites encircled the castle. We scarce had
time to bolt the lower doors and sound the alarm with a mortar
shot. The castle's only inmates then were my lord Pantler and
his lady, myself, the cook and his two turnspits (besotted the
three of them), the priest, the footman and four stout-hearted
Haiduks. So, we seize our long guns and take to the windows.
With a 'huzzah!', the Muscovites come bursting across the terrace from the gate. We greet them with a fusillade, ten muskets
strong, 'Back, you sons . . .!' You couldn't see a thing outside. The
servants poured a steady fire from the lower floors. My lord and

I sniped away from the gallery above.

"All was blowing great guns, though we stood in mortal peril. Twenty muskets lay here upon these very boards. We fired one, they passed us another. In this service, our priest gave a good account of himself, as did the Pantler's wife, his daughter, and her servant-companions. We were but three sharpshooters, yet we fired without pausing for breath. The Muscovite infantry rained a hail of bullets on us from below. Our firepower was weaker, but we had height in our favor, and our aim was true. Three times the *muzhiks* pressed up to the doors, and each time three fell to the dust. So they leg it to the lumber house. Meanwhile, it was growing light. Gun in hand, the Pantler steps blithely out into the gallery. The instant a Muscovite shows his pate from behind the lumber house, my master lets him have it. And each time, for his aim was spot-on, another black shako goes tumbling over the grass. Soon, they were loath to venture out.

"Seeing the foe in disarray, the Pantler decided to mount a sally. Seizing his saber, he barked orders to his men below and, turning to me, yelled, 'Come, Gervase, follow—' At that instant, a shot rang out from beyond the gate. The Pantler's cry died on his lips. His face turned red then ghastly white. He tried to speak and coughed up blood. Then I notice the wound. The ball had struck him square in the chest. He staggered back, pointing toward the gate. I recognized the knave – Soplica! Aye, I could tell him by his build and whiskers. It was his shot that felled my lord. I saw it! The villain still had his musket up. Smoke was rising from the barrel. I drew a bead on him. The rogue stood motionless as a statue. Two shots I fired, and twice I missed. Rage – or was it grief? – hampered my aim. The women screamed. I turned and looked. My lord lay dead!"

Here Gervase broke into sobs. Moments later he closed his tale.

"By now the Muscovites were hacking down the doors. With my lord Pantler dead, I stood there, helpless, insensible to what was passing around me. Luckily, Parafianowicz arrived in the nick of time – he and two hundred Mickiewicz folk from Horbatowicz, a large noble family, stout-hearted to a man and long-time sworn foes of Soplica.

"Thus perished a mighty, pious, upstanding man whose house boasted seats in the Senate, ribboned orders, and hetman's maces. Though he was a father to the peasants and a brother to the nobility, yet he had no son after him to swear vengeance at his grave. Yet loyal servants he had! I smeared his blood over my blade, my rapier called *Jackknife*. You must have heard of my rapier. Used to be the talk of every parliament, regional diet, and annual fair! I vowed to notch it on every Soplica neck in the district. No session of parliament, no bazaar, no armed foray would I let pass without hunting them out. Two, I hacked down in a brawl, another two, in a duel, and still another, I burned alive in a wooden shack during the raid on Korelicze with Rymsza. We broiled him there like a loach. Those whose ears I lopped off do not enter into the reckoning! One Soplica has yet to receive a token from me. I refer to the born brother of that whiskered knave. He lives still and takes pride in his wealth. His land encroaches on the castle grounds. He enjoys the respect of the district, holds an office. Aye, the Judge! And to him you'd hand the castle? Allow his impious feet to wipe the Pantler's blood from these boards? Not whilst I live! So long as Gervase hath an ounce of courage in his veins and strength to match, so long as with one little finger he is able to wield his Jackknife, which hangs even now on the wall, Soplica shall never take possession of the castle."

"Ah!" exclaimed the Count, raising his hands. "What a good premonition, my falling in love with these ruins. I hadn't realized all the treasures they contained. What dramatic scenes! What a tale! Gervase, when I am restored to the castle of my fathers, I shall appoint you burgrave of these walls. Your tale stirs me deeply. What a shame you did not bring me here at the midnight hour. Amid these ruins I should have sat draped in my cloak, whilst you held me rapt with these tales of murderous deeds. Pity you lack the gift of narration. Oft have I heard and read of such happenings. No Scottish or English lord's castle, no German count's hall is without its tale of blood and slaughter; no ancient house without report of some perfidy or sanguinary deed whence vengeance devolves on the heirs; and now for the first time I hear of such a case in Poland. Aye, I feel stout-hearted Horeszko blood stir in my veins. I know my debt to glory and my kin. So be it! No more parley with Soplica, though it come to pistols or blade. Honor demands it!"

So saying, he strode solemnly off, while Gervase followed behind in profound silence. Still muttering to himself, the Count halted at the gate; then, casting a last backward glance at the castle, he leapt on his horse and closed his rambling monologue:

"What a pity old Soplica has no spouse or comely daughter with qualities arousing my deepest devotion. Loving her yet prevented from seeking her hand. Aye, that would thicken the plot! True love here, sworn duty there. Here vengeance, there affection . . ."

With that, he dug in his rowels and sped off toward the Manor. Just then, the hunt emerged from the far side of the forest. Now the Count was an avid sportsman. No sooner did he catch sight of the hunters than all preceding thoughts went by the board. Off he sped to join the chase. On past the gate, garden, and fence he rode; then, glancing aside upon rounding a bend, he drew up by the fence. Here stood an orchard.

Fruit-trees, planted in rows, shaded an ample field. Beneath the trees lay the cottage garden. Here, bowing his venerable head, the cabbage sits brooding on the fate of the plant kingdom. Yonder, entwining his pods around the carrot's green locks, the slim bean trains a thousand eyes upon his beloved. There nods the maize her golden tassels. Here and yon swells the stout gourd's paunch; a fair piece from his parent vine he'd rolled – a guest among the crimson beets. Each bed lies parted by a ridge; and ranged like sentries along each earthwork stand the cypresses of the cottage garden – hemp shrubs, silent, straight, and green. Hemp's odor and leafage afford the plot a means of defense. Snakes daren't pass through the leaves. The scent is lethal to grub and insect alike. Farther back, the painted poppy rears his whitish stalks. You fancy a swarm of butterflies – wings trembling, iridescent, shimmering like precious stones – balance on those stalks. Even so the poppy's variety of hues beguiles the eye; and in the midst of these blooms, like the full moon among the stars, the sunflower turns his fiery face from east to west.

All along the fence line stretched a row of rounded hillocks where neither tree, nor shrub, nor yet flower grew. Here, grown to splendor, lay the cucumber patch. A rippling broadloom of leaves overspread the beds. In their midst walked a young girl all draped in white. Knee-deep through the luxuriant growth she waded. Descending into the furrows, she seemed to breast the waves of leafage, bath in their verdure. A straw hat shaded her head. Two pink ribbons and a stray twine of flaxen hair flickered under the brim. Slung over her elbow was a wicker basket. Her gaze was lowered, her right hand raised; and even as a bathing damsel stoops to drive away the minnows nibbling at her feet, so she, basket in arm, bent to pluck up a fruit that grazed her foot or caught her eye.

The Count stood perfectly still, enchanted by the scene. Hearing his companions ride up from behind, he made signs for them to halt. They drew rein, and he, craning his neck, resumed his watch. So does the long-billed crane wait in ambush at a distance from his flock. Upon one stilt, alert-eyed, he stands, a stone gripped in his upraised claw to combat sleep.

A swish across the head and shoulders woke the Count from his reverie. There stood Friar Robak with the knotted ropes of his girdle in his upraised hand.

"So," cried he, "it's cucumbers you want, eh? I'll give you cucumbers! Oh, beware, your lordship, this bed holds no fruitage for you. Nothing shall come of it."

And waving a threatening finger, he arranged his hood and stalked off.

The Count, laughing inwardly and at the same time cursing the unexpected intrusion, lingered on. He turned his gaze back to the garden, but the girl was no longer there. He caught a glimpse of a white dress and pink ribbon vanishing into the manor window. The path she'd cut through the beds was plain to see, for the leaves, spurned by her nimble foot, still tossed. For an instant longer they trembled, then grew still again. So with a body of water when grazed by the swallow's wing. Only the little basket remained. There it lay where the girl had dropped it – overturned, bobbing on a sea of green leaves, its cargo of fruit gone to the bottom.

Moments later, all was quiet and solitude. The Count, all ears, fixed his gaze on the house. He mused on, his riders still stirless behind him. At length, like an empty hive upon the return of the swarm, the hushed, deserted house awoke with sounds: murmurs at first, then audible talk, then boisterous shouts. The hunt was back, and the servants were bestirring themselves with breakfast.

Great was the stir and commotion in the house. Food, silverware, and bottles were brought out. The hunters, still in their green shooting jackets, sauntered from room to room, plate in hand, eating, drinking, or leaning against the window jambs and talking of guns, hounds, and hares. The Judge sat at the table with the Chamberlain and the Chamberlain's wife. The young women chatted quietly in the corner. There was no standing on ceremony here, as at luncheon or dinner – clearly, a new custom in an old-fashioned Polish household. By no means pleased with this want of order, the Judge put up with it at breakfast time.

An array of dishes suited to men's and women's palates lay spread on the table. Trays provided with a complete coffee service came whisking out – enormous trays, handsomely painted with floral motifs. Upon each tray stood a fragrantly steaming coffeepot fashioned from beaten tin, a set of gilded cups of Saxon porcelain, and a dainty cream-jug.

No nation serves a better cup of coffee than does Poland. Ancient custom requires every decent Polish household to employ a maid charged expressly with the task of preparing the coffee. For this, she needs to procure beans of the finest quality from the city or the trading wherries. She stands entrusted with the secret of its brewing, for the nectar must be black as coal, clear as amber, fragrant as mocha, and thick as honey. As to the importance of good cream in coffee, it is common knowledge and easy to come by in the country. First thing in the morning, the maid sets the pots upon the stove to steep, then repairs to the dairy. After skimming off the topmost layer of cream, she apportions it into the little jugs, one per setting so as to vest each cup in its own coat of skin.

The older women, having risen earlier and taken their coffee, prepared a special drink for themselves: a bowl of mulled ale, whitened with cream and swirling with cheese curds, finely chopped. An assortment of cold meats lay prepared for the men – succulent goose-breast, sliced ham and ox-tongue, all of exquisite quality, home-cured and smoked in juniper. Last of all, they brought in the main course, beef stew and gravy. Such was the hearty refection served at the Judge's house.

Two separate companies stood gathered in adjoining rooms. The elders sat around a small table discussing the latest farming methods and the Tsar's increasingly stern edicts. The Chamberlain appraised the current rumors of war, drawing his conclusions. Meanwhile, the Steward's daughter, donning a pair of blue spectacles, entertained the Chamberlain's wife with a deck of tarot cards.

The youth congregated in the adjacent room. Here, talk ran upon the morning's hunt, though without the customary strife and rowdiness. The Notary and the Assessor, mighty orators both, foremost connoisseurs in the hunting-craft and first-rate marksmen, sat sullenly opposite each other. Apparently, each had slipped his leash correctly. Each was certain his hound would bring the quarry to book, when, on a level stretch, the hunt happened upon a peasant's parcel of uncut grain. The hare nipped right in. Just as Scut and Peregrine were about to seize it, the Judge checked the riders at the boundary mark. Enraged as they were, they were forced to call off the chase. The hounds emerged quarryless. No one knew for certain if the hare had been given best or been chopped by Scut's, or Peregrine's, or both sets of jaws. Opinions diverged, and so the contest raged on.

Meanwhile, gazing absentmindedly from side to side, the old Steward strolled through the adjoining rooms. He took no interest in the general talk, for he was employed upon other matters. Leather flapper in hand, he halted here and there, ruminated for an instant, then plastered a fly to the wall.

Tadeusz and Telimena stood alone in the connecting doorway. They spoke softly, as the two groups of guests were not far apart. Only now did Tadeusz learn that his Auntie Telimena was a woman of substance; that by the canons of the church they were not too closely related – indeed, it was doubtful that she and her nephew had any blood in common, though the Judge was in the habit of calling her sister; mutual kin of theirs had styled them so, despite their disparity in years. Finally he learned that Auntie Telimena had lived a good while in Saint Petersburg and there rendered the Judge a number of invaluable services. For this reason, the Judge held her in high repute and was pleased in public, out of vanity perhaps, to style himself her brother; to which, for friendship's sake, Telimena raised no objection. All these revelations came as a relief to Tadeusz. A great many other confidential things passed between them; and all this took place in one short while.

Meantime, in the room to the right, the Notary was baiting the Assessor.

"I told you the hunt would draw a blank," said he off-handedly. "Too early yet with grain still in the ear and so many peasants' plots standing unharvested, which explains the Count's absence today, despite the invitation. The Count knows

all about hunting, the time, the place. You've only to get him
started on the subject. Having spent the better part of his life
abroad, he takes a dim view of our barbarous hunting habits.
We flout the laws and government regulations, show scant respect for landmarks and boundaries, and ride roughshod over
private land without the owner's knowledge. Spring or summer
we course the fields and forests. Sometimes, we punish the fox in
molting season and allow our hounds to run down, or torment, a
laden doe in the winter grain, thereby wreaking great harm on
our game. Hence the Count's painful admission that Muscovy
enjoys more civilization than we, for there at least you have the
Tsar's hunting edicts, police surveillance, and penalties to fit the
crime."

      Telimena was facing the room to the left, fanning her
shoulders with a cotton batiste handkerchief. "So help me," said
she, "the Count is right. I know Russia well. You doubt me when
I insist her stern vigilance is laudable in its way. But I have
been to Saint Petersburg, and more than once. Sweet memories!
Charming, bygone times! What a city! Have any of you been to
Pieter? I will show you a plan if you like. I always keep one in my
escritoire.

      "Every summer, Petersburg society deserts the city for
the *dacha*, a summer mansion – *dacha* is their word for country
house. I lived in such a house. It stood on a man-made knoll
overlooking the Neva at an ideal distance from town. Ah, what
a place! I still have a plan in my escritoire. Anyhow, to my great
misfortune, a little *chinovnik*, a minor police functionary, leased
the house next door. He kept a number of wolfhounds. You've no
idea what a torment it is having a petty clerk and his dogs live
next door. I'd no sooner step out into the garden with my book
to enjoy the moon and evening air, than one of these ferocious
gazehounds would fly up, ears pricking, tail swishing. I often
took fright at the sight of them. In my heart, I knew grief would
come from these dogs. And that's exactly what happened.

      "I'd just stepped out one morning when, at my very feet,
one of these hounds choked the life out of my dear darling *bolonka*. Ah, what a sweet little doggie she was! – the gift of Prince
Sukin himself. Clever little thing. Quick as a squirrel. I'd show
you a picture, only it would mean a trip to my escritoire. The
shock of seeing her lifeless before me brought on fainting spells,
muscular spasms, and heart palpitations.

"My health might have taken still worse a turn if the Master of the Imperial Hunt, Kirilo Gavrilich Kozodushin, hadn't popped in for a visit. On learning the cause of my dudgeon, he had the clerk dragged in by the ear. There he stood, the hapless wretch, pale and trembling, out of all possession. 'You dare' – thundered Kirilo Gavrilich – 'to stalk a laden hind in the spring, and under the Tsar's very nose!' In vain did the stupefied clerk swear he hadn't been out stalking, and that, if it pleased His Excellency, the quarry was a dog, not a doe. 'Blackguard!' roared Kirilo Gavrilich. 'You presume to know more about venery and wild game than I, Kozodushin, the Tsar's *Jaegermeister*? Let the Chief of Police judge between us.' They summoned the police chief and launched an official inquiry. 'I' – stated Kozodushin – 'swear he was stalking a doe. The dolt here says it was a lapdog. Now you judge between us. Who's better in the know?' The police chief knew his duty. Aghast at the clerk's sauciness, he took him aside and urged him, in brotherly fashion, to make a clean breast of it. Thus appeased, Kirilo Gavrilich agreed to put in a word and have the wretch's sentence lightened. And that was that. The hounds were strung up. The clerk spent a month in the clink. This little incident kept us in stitches the entire evening. By the next day, it was the talk of the town. The *Jaegermeister* had interposed on behalf of my lapdog. And I know for a fact, the incident drew a hearty guffaw from the Emperor himself."

Laughter rang out in both rooms.

All this time, the Judge had been engaged in a round of matrimony with Father Robak. When Telimena began her anecdote, he had been on the point of making an important play, spades being trumps, and the Priest was barely breathing from excitement. Listening intently, chin upraised, his hand poised for the casting, the Judge heard out the tale while the Franciscan sat waiting in the direst suspense. Finally, the story told, the Judge cast his queen of spades, laughed, and spoke forth:

"If people wish to praise the Germans for their culture and Muscovites for their law and order, let them! If Greater Poland wants to learn from the Swabians how to litigate over a fox or have a hound arrested for trespassing on somebody's spinney, by all means, say I. But, thank heaven, we in Lithuania stand on our old ways. We have plenty of game to go around. Never shall you see us launching police inquiries over such trifles. Here we've no shortage of grain. No one starves if a hound goes coursing through the spring wheat or rye. All the same, I draw the line at the peasant's baulk."

"Small wonder, sir," piped up the Bailiff from the other room. "You pay through the nose for such game. Our rustics rub their hands at the sight of your hounds tearing through their standing crop. A dozen shaken ears of rye and you compensate them with a haycock. Even then it's not quits. Often, they receive a bonus of a thaler. Depend on it, sir, our peasantry's getting cheeky. If only . . ."

The Judge never heard the rest of the Bailiff's remarks. Their discourse had sparked a dozen more exchanges, anecdotes, tales, and, finally, quarrels.

Entirely forgotten in the fray, Tadeusz and Telimena had eyes only for each other. Telimena was delighted to see Tadeusz so amused by her anecdote. The youth, in turn, plied her with compliments. Telimena's speech grew slower and softer. With all the noise around them, Tadeusz feigned not to hear and replied in whispers. By now he'd drawn so close to Telimena that he could feel the pleasant warmth of her brow on his face. He held his breath, caught her sighs with his lips. His eye seized on every sparkle of her glance – when, suddenly, there flashed by between them a fly, followed directly by the swish of the Steward's swatter.

Lithuania swarms with flies. Among them thrives a species of housefly known as the noble. Except for his broader thorax and larger abdomen, he resembles every other fly in color and shape. When flying, he drones and bombinates intolerably. And he is strong enough to perforate a spider's web! Caught in the toils, he will buzz for three days on end, nor will he flinch at grappling with the spider. All this, the Steward had had occasion to observe. More than this: he claimed it was from these very flies that the lesser folk sprang. The noble was to the common fly what the queen bee was to the swarm. His extinction meant the end of the entire strain. Needless to say, holding to other views on the genesis of the fly, neither the housekeeper nor the village priest gave the Steward's hypothesis the time of day. But the Steward held fast to tradition. No sooner would he spot such a fly than off he'd go after him.

Precisely one of these nobles had droned past his ear. Twice, he flailed and – heavens! – missed. He swung a third time and all but took out the window. Addled by this commotion, the fly spotted two figures blocking his retreat through the doorway. In desperation, he hurled himself right between their noses. Even there the Steward's arm went after him. So lusty was the stroke that the two heads started back like the two halves of a thunder-cloven tree. Both heads struck a bruising blow against the doorpost.

Fortunately, no one observed the incident, for what had passed for polite, if loud and lively, conversation in the far room was building up to an explosive crescendo. When fox hunters deployed in an extended line enter the forest, you hear the occasional cracking of tree limbs, random gunshots and the babble of the hounds. But when one of the hunters chances to rouse a wild boar, he sets in motion a general hue and cry so tumultuous that all the trees of the forest give tongue. So it is with conversation: talk moves along at a leisurely pace until it alights upon an engaging topic like a wild boar. The boar on this occasion was the Notary and Assessor's fierce contest over their prize hounds. The dispute was of short duration. Much was accomplished in an instant's compass. Such a volley of words and invectives they fired off in a single breath that the first three stages of a quarrel – insult, anger, and challenge – had long since passed, and the pair were addressing for battle.

The guests in the adjacent room leapt up and surged through the doorway, sweeping aside the couple presiding there like bi-fronted Janus of the threshold.

Even before Tadeusz or Telimena had time to smooth their ruffled hair, the menacing noises had died down. Murmurs and laughter rippled through the crowd. A truce brokered by the Friar stood declared. Despite his age, Robak was a burly fellow of broad-shouldered build. No sooner had the Assessor closed with the Notary and the two were squaring for battle than he seized both men by the back of the collar, cracked their heads together like a pair of Easter eggs, and, spreading his arms like a fingerpost, flung them to opposite corners of the room. For a while he stood there, arms spread wide, repeating, *"Pax, pax, pax vobiscum!* Peace be with you!"*

The two sides stood thunderstruck, some laughed out loud. Their deference to a man of the cloth checked any impulse to rebuke him; and, after such a display of strength, no one was disposed to lift an arm against him. But now that the Friar had restored peace to the gathering, it was clear he had no interest in proving his prowess. Without further threat to the brawlers, without so much as a snort of anger, he arranged his hood, and, thrusting his hands under his belt, quietly took his leave.

Meanwhile, the Judge and the Chamberlain interposed themselves between the two sides. The Steward, roused as from a deep meditation, stepped forward and eyed the throng fiercely. Wherever a murmur arose, he silenced it with a priest-like flourish of his leather aspergillum. At last, raising the fly swatter solemnly like a marshal's mace, he called them to order.

"Becalm yourselves!" he repeated. "And give thought, you foremost hunters of our district, to the scandalous effects of your contention. Have you any idea? Behold our youth, the hope of our country, the ones supposed to bring fame to our forests and groves. Alas, as it is, our youth neglect the hunt. And now they may have fresh cause to despise it. See? The very ones that ought to be setting them an example bring home nothing but tumult and brawls! You might also show regard for my silver hair, for I knew greater sportsmen than you. Often was I called to judge between them.

"Who in Lithuania's forests measured up to Tadeusz Reytan? And who, when it came to deploying beaters or closing with wild game, stood equal to our Bialopiotrowicz? Show me a marksman today of the caliber of noble Zegota, who could pick off a sprinting jackrabbit with a pistol! I knew Terajewicz; a stout pike was all he used to hunt wild boar. And Budrewicz: why, he'd wrestle Bruin down with his bare hands! Such were the men our forests once knew. And when it came to quarrels, how did they settle the matter? They called on an arbiter and laid their stakes. Oginski forfeited two thousand hectares of woodland over a wolf. A badger once cost Niesiolowski several villages! So, gentlemen, take after your elders and settle your score, only place more modest stakes, for words are an idle wind, and there is no end to verbal disputes. Why waste breath over a hare? Choose your arbiters and yield in good faith to their verdict. For my part, I shall entreat the Judge to impose no limits on the master of the hounds, even if it means leading the course through a cornfield. I trust he will grant us this boon."

And saying this, the Steward squeezed the Judge's knee.

"My horse!" cried the Notary. "I shall stake my horse and harness. More than that, I shall swear an affidavit before the district court and pledge this ring to our referee as payment."

"And I," said the Assessor, "shall wager my shagreen dog collars with their inlaid rings of gold and my exquisitely wrought velvet leash with its glittering precious stone of matching craft. I had planned to leave these articles to my future children in the event that I should marry. They were Prince Dominic's gift to me when he, Marshal Sanguszko, General Mejen, and I went on a hunt together and I set my hounds against theirs. There, unprecedented in the annals of hunting, I bagged a half dozen hare with one bitch. We'd been hunting on the Kupisko Common. The prince, unable to restrain himself, leapt from his horse, clasped my famous Kite by the neck, and, after kissing her three times on the head and patting her thrice on the snout, declared, 'Now shall you be called Queen of Kupisko!' Even so does Napoleon make of his generals princes of the locality on which they have won their signal victory."

But Telimena was growing weary of all this strife. She longed for a breath of air outside but needed a companion.

"Gentlemen," said she, taking a basket off the peg. "I see you mean to stay cooped up inside. But I have a mind for mushrooming. Who cares to may follow me."

With that, she draped her head in a red cashmere shawl, seized the Chamberlain's youngest daughter by the hand, and, gathering up her skirts above the ankles, took her leave. Without a word, Tadeusz hastened after her.

The proposal of an outing delighted the Judge. Here was a way of clearing the air!

"Gentlemen," he announced. "To the woods, for mushrooms! Who graces our table with the finest *milkcap* shall sit by the loveliest young lady. I shall appoint her myself. And should a lady so grace the board, the pick of our boys shall be hers."

BOOK THREE: ROMANTIC PURSUITS

Argument: The Count's sally into the garden. A mysterious nymph tends the geese. The mushroom hunters. A comparison with the wandering shades of Elysium. Varieties of wild mushroom. Telimena at her Temple of Musings. Consultations touching Tadeusz's future. The Count as landscape painter. Tadeusz's pictorial views on trees and clouds. The Count's thoughts on art. The bell. A note. A bear, my lordship!

The Count was even now making for home; yet he kept drawing rein and turning his head back toward the garden. Once again, he imagined he caught a glimpse of the mysterious white dress in the manor window. Again, some weightless object floated to the ground, crossed the garden in the twinkling of an eye, and shone clear among the green cucumbers. So does a fugitive sunbeam break through a cloud and fall on a slab of flint in the field or a sheet of water in the green meadow.

Alighting from his horse, the Count dismissed his men and ran stealthily back to the garden. In no time, he gained the fence, found an opening, and slipped through like a wolf entering the sheepfold. Alas, he walked right into a row of dry gooseberry bushes. The little gardener looked round, startled by the rustling, but she saw nothing to alarm her. All the same, she ran to the far end of the garden; meanwhile, slipping sideways through the great leaves of wild rhubarb and yellow dock, the Count dropped down on all fours and, hopping frog-fashion through the grass, crept noiselessly up to within a few yards of the girl. He raised his head. A marvelous prospect burst upon his eyes.

Here, in this corner of the garden, grew cherry-trees, sparsely planted. The whole area stood deliberately sown with a wide assortment of crops: wheat, maize, broad bean, English pea, bearded barley, millet, even the odd flower and shrub. Conceived for the protection of the domestic fowl, this brainchild of the housekeeper – a famous mistress by the surname of Banty née Cockalorum – signaled an epoch in the annals of poultry farming. Today, it is common knowledge, but then, it was a novelty known only to the few initiates. In time, it made its way into the pages of the almanac under the title, *Remedies for Hawks and Kites: A New Method of Raising Barnyard Fowl*. Here was the garden.

Chanticleer, strutting his watch, had only to halt, poise his beak, cock his comb sideways (the better to sweep the clouds with his eye), spy a hovering hawk, and sound the alarm. At once, the hens would seek refuge in the grain patch. Even the geese and the peafowl, and even the startled doves, when baulked of the safety of the gables, sought shelter there. For the moment, no enemy hovered in sight. The fierce summer sun blazed alone in the sky. The birds sought out the shade of the covert. Some basked in the grass, others wallowed in the sand.

Rearing above the heads of the birds stood a knot of tiny human heads. All were hatless, bare-necked and had short tow-white hair. In their midst, standing a head taller, and with longer hair, was a maiden; and directly behind the tots sat a peacock with its hoop of nacreous tail feathers fully expanded. Set against the deep blue backdrop of the tail feathers, the little white heads stood out in bold relief – the bolder for the eyespots that set off each head with a starry wreath. There in the grain they shone, clearly visible through the screen of golden maize-stalks, silver-veined ribbon grass, blushful love-lies-bleeding, and green-leaved mallow. Tone and shape blended together to suggest a trelliswork of silver and gold that swayed in the breeze like a diaphanous veil.

Hanging like an airy canopy over this polychrome of flowers and grains was a radiant mist of mayflies – or *dames*, as they are commonly called. Almost viewless, they danced on four gauze-like wings as clear as glass; and though they emitted a faint humming sound, they seemed scarcely to stir. The girl swept the air with some gray tassel-like object resembling a tuft of ostrich feathers. Evidently, she was driving the golden rain of insects from the little tots' heads. A horn-like object gleamed in her other hand, some feeding vessel, for she was lowering it by turns to each of the urchins' mouths. The Count took this object for Amalthea's golden horn.

Even while so engaged, the girl kept glancing back at the gooseberry patch; clearly, she was still mindful of the disturbance there. Little did she know that her prowler had crept up from the opposite side and was even now worming his way across the garden beds. Suddenly, he leapt out from the burdocks. Glancing up, she saw him bowing low before her, just four beds away. She turned like a startled jay, threw up her arms and prepared to take flight. Already her feet were skimming the leaves when, alarmed by the intruder and the retreat of their mistress, the little tots raised a frightful wail. Their shrill cries caused her to think twice about abandoning her charges. She turned indecisively. No use; she was fain to go back. Like a reluctant sprite drawn by an enchanter's charm, she retraced her steps. Crouching down, she pressed the shrillest of the tots to her bosom, caressed another, and calmed them all with soothing words. As chicks seek shelter under the brood-hen's wing, so the little waifs wrapped their arms about her knees and huddled around her.

"Come," she chided them, "is it nice to be crying so? Is it polite? Why, you will frighten the gentleman. He had no wish to startle you. He is no nasty old tramp, but a visiting guest – a nice gentleman. See how handsome he is." And she looked for herself.

The Count, clearly delighting in these flatteries, smiled at her sweetly. But the girl, suddenly remembering herself, fell silent and, mantling deeply like a rose, lowered her eyes.

He was indeed a comely young gentleman: tall of stature, with an oval-shaped face, gentle eyes of cornflower blue, cheeks pale yet fresh-complexioned, locks long and fair. Tufts of grass and leaves, gleaned from his passage across the beds, clung to his temples like an unravelling wreath of bays.

"You!" he burst forth. "By what name shall I pay you homage? Deity! Nymph! Shadow! Apparition! Speak! Do you walk this vale of your own accord? By another's will compelled? Ah, I think I know. A spurned lover, some great lord or jealous guardian, keeps you prisoner in this castle park. For such as you, knights errant fought in the lists. From such as you sprang heroines of melancholy romances! Unfold, my beauty, the secret of your cruel misfortune. Your deliverer stands before you. Even now he hangs upon your beck. As you reign in my bosom, so do you reign over this arm!"

And he stretched forth his arm.

Blushing girlishly, yet beaming with joy, she listened to him speak. As a child rejoices in a book of gaudy pictures or takes pleasure in a handful of glittering game counters even before knowing their value, so she, without grasping the substance, delighted in the sonorities of his speech.

"Sir, where have you come from?" said she at last. "What do you seek here among the flowerbeds?"

The Count's eyes rounded with bewilderment and surprise. For a moment he stood speechless; then, shifting his tone, he replied: "Please excuse me, miss, I seem to have spoiled your fun. Forgive me. I was hurrying to the house for breakfast. It is running late, and I hoped to arrive there on time. As you know, the road takes a roundabout route. If I am not mistaken, the way across the garden is shorter?"

"There is your way, sir," said she. "Only do mind the beds. You will find a path in the grass yonder."

"Right or left?"

The girl raised her eyes and seemed to study him narrowly. The house stood in plain view not a thousand paces from where they stood, yet here was he asking the way.

"Do you live here, miss?" pursued the Count, eager to draw her into a conversation. "Close to the garden? In the village then? How comes it that I have never seen you in the house? Have you been here long? Visiting perhaps?"

The little gardener shook her head.

"Forgive me, but is that not your room by the window yonder?"

Meanwhile, his thoughts ran this way: *True, not your heroine of melancholy lays. But she is undeniably young and pretty. How oft it chances that a noble mind or soul blooms unseen like a rose in the woods. Yet bring such a flower into the world, expose her to the full light of day, and she blazes forth with dazzling splendor.*

Without a word, the little gardener rose to her feet, scooped up the tot clinging to her arm, seized another by the hand and, driving the rest like a flock of geese before her, went forth into the orchard.

"If you please, sir," said she with a backward glance, "be so kind as to drive my scattered birds into the grain patch."

"What! I?" cried the astonished Count. "Drive your birds?"

But by now she had fled into the shadow of the next aisle of trees. For an instant, he fancied he saw a pair of eyes flash through the intervening skein of sprays.

The Count lingered alone in the garden. As the earth grows cool after sunset, so his soul began to shed her ardor and take on darker tones. He lapsed into a reverie; but he drew small comfort from his dreams. On coming to himself, he felt vexed – why, he couldn't say. Alas, how little had come of it! His hopes had run too high. With a burning brow and leaping heart had he crept across the beds toward this shepherdess. All those graces he'd ascribed to the mysterious nymph! All those qualities imputed! All those conjectures made – and, in the event, so wide of the mark. True, her face was pretty, her figure, svelte. Yet how lacking in poise! And those ample cheeks! The ruddy hue painted a picture of simple, superabundant bliss, a sign, surely, that her mind and heart lay as yet dormant, inactive! And then her replies. How coarse! How rustic!

"Why delude myself?" he cried out. "My nymph's a common gooseherd."

With the girl's departure, the entire bewitching transparency suddenly lost its allure. The ribbonry, the charming trellis of silver and gold – alas! So was it all merely straw? In anguish, he stared at the little bent-grass broom in her hand. So much for the ostrich plumes! And the golden vessel – Amalthea's horn? A raw carrot! Even now was one of the village waifs bolting down the last of it. So, it was farewell to the charm! The spell! The wonder! Just so, spying a puffball, a boy feels drawn to the soft, delicate head. Drawing closer to touch it, he blows on the downy globe, and the flower vanishes away, leaving behind in the hand of the fastidious observer a bare stalk of grayish-green hue.

The Count rammed his hat over his eyes, spun on his heel and returned whence he came, though he shortened the way by striding across the flowers and vegetables and over the gooseberry beds. Finally, after vaulting the fence, he breathed freely again. But then he recalled that he'd spoken to the girl of breakfast. Perhaps word of their meeting so close to the house had already got out? What if they'd dispatched servants to fetch him, only to learn he had run off? No telling what they would think. Yes, it behooved him to go back.

Keeping low along the fences, he skirted the baulks and islands of weed. At last, to his great relief, after taking a thousand detours, he emerged on the road that made straight for the manor courtyard. He followed the fence without glancing at the garden. So the grain pilferer, betraying no sign of his deed or

intent, averts his gaze from the granary. Such was the Count's
chariness, though there was no one about to observe his movements. On he walked, his head turned away from the garden,
eyes to the right.

  Yonder stood a grove of birches – clean of undergrowth
and richly swarded. There he saw, gliding over the green broadloom, flitting among the white trunks under an awning of low-
hung leafy sprays, a host of shadowy figures. Bizarrely clad, executing strange dance-like motions, they floated like wraiths in
the moonlight. Some stood sheathed in black, others wore long
flowing robes as pale as the snow. One had on a broad-brimmed
hat as wide as a cooper's hoop, another went bareheaded. Still
others walked as if wrapped in vapors, headgear trailing like a
comet's tress in the breeze. Each figure struck a different pose.
One stood rooted to the forest floor. Only its lowered eyeballs
moved. Another stared straight ahead, moving like a somnam-
bulist, swerving neither to the right nor left, as if walking a line.
The shapes kept bending down in diverse directions, as if making profound bows. Upon nearing one another or crossing paths,
they exchanged neither word nor nod, so absorbed were they in
their task, so deep their distraction. The vague figures put the
Count in mind of the Elysian shades, which, bereft of pain and
cares, roam the blessed fields in quiet, yet mournful, tranquility.

  Who would have recognized in these silent folk so frugal
of movement, our friends – the Judge's companions! Having concluded their stormy breakfast, they had gone outdoors to observe
the solemn rite of mushroom gathering. Being sensible folk, they
knew the art of moderation and how to deport themselves according to the place and season. And so, before following the
Judge out into the woods, they had assumed a new demeanor
and change of garb: loose linen sarafans tossed over their robes
and straw hats for their heads – hence their pale aspect redolent
of purgatorial souls. The youth had also changed. Only Telimena
and a few others still wore their French attire.

  The unrusticated Count could make nothing of it. Intrigued to no end, he struck out with all speed for the birch grove.

  The forest teemed with wild mushrooms. The lads picked
the rosy-cheeked *chanterelle*, an object of high praise in Lithuanian lore. The song calls it an emblem of maidenhood. Worms do
not gnaw at it, nor, strange to say, do insects alight on its cap.
The girls sought after the handsome *bolete*, which the ditty calls

the "colonel of mushrooms." All hunted for the smaller *saffron milkcap*. Though less exalted in song, these were tastiest of all, for you could eat them fresh or salted, in autumn or winter. Predictably, the Steward sought out the *fly agaric*.

Other common varieties of fungi were shunned for their inferior taste or injurious effects. Yet even these were not without their use. They provided the fauna with nourishment, the insect with a nesting place, and the glade with garniture. Like a table service they stood ranged on the meadow's linen: the round-edged *brittle gills*, silvery, yellowish, or ruby-red, like goblets brimming with a variety of vintages; the *yellow boletes*, their caps dimpled like the bottoms of upturned cups; the funnel-like *clitocybes*, slender as champagne flutes; the *fleecy milkcap*, round and white, broad and smooth, like cream-filled teacups of Dresden porcelain; and the spherical *puffballs*, squat as pepper-pots, replete with their black powdery spore mass.

The rest had names found only in the tongues of the hare and the wolf. Human-folk hadn't yet christened them, though they grew in profusion. No one touched these brute varieties. And should a gatherer mistakenly stoop to pick such a one, he would angrily snap off the cap or trample it underfoot, though in so sullying the sward he behaved quite unwisely.

Telimena picked neither the brute nor human varieties. Bored and distracted, her head thrown back, she cast her gaze about her. The Notary testily observed she was hunting for mushrooms in the trees. More spitefully, the Assessor likened her to a broody bird spying out a place to build her nest.

But Telimena seemed to be seeking a place of quiet and solitude. Slowly, she drew away from her companions. Straying deeper into the forest, she ascended a gentle slope where the trees grew thicker and shadier. A grayish rock crowned the knoll. From beneath it sprang a little stream. Out it gushed and fled away, as if seeking shade, to water the tall grasses that grew rank thereabout. Here, swaddled in the herbage, couched in a bed of leaves, unseen, untroubled, and motionless, purled the little rogue. So a querulous child lies tucked in its cradle, while its mother, bestrewing the pillow with poppy leaves, laces up the green drapes. Truly a lovely purlieu – Telimena often sought refuge here. She called it her *Temple of Musings*.

Stopping by the rill, she cast off her scarlet shawl and allowed it to float to the ground. As a bather bends down, bracing herself for the plunge, so, dropping to her knees, she sank slowly to one side. Then, as if swept up by a coral tide, she flounced down and sprawled at full length on the grass. There she lay with her elbow on the turf, temple resting on her palm, her head canted to one side, eyes poring over the gleaming vellum of a French novel. And as she read, her black ringlets and rose-hued ribbons danced over the alabaster leaves.

A quaint picture she presented. Her crimson shawl spread over the emerald-green sward; she disposed at ease upon it, her frame sheathed in a coral-red frock, the blackness of her hair and slipper setting off the gown at either end, and the white line of her arm, handkerchief and hose shimmering along the length. A distant onlooker might easily have mistaken the whole for a gaudy caterpillar sprawled on a maple leaf.

To no avail did the merits of this charming scene await the connoisseur's eye. None of the gatherers paid it any heed, so absorbed were they in their pursuit of mushrooms. But Tadeusz paid heed. Casting sideward glances at Telimena, yet loath to approach her directly, he edged his way cautiously up the slope. As when, hidden behind his wheel-mounted blind, the shooter of wild fowl advances on the bustard, or when, keeping to the far side of his mount, gun held steady on the saddle or leveled under the horse's neck, the plover stalker, making like the harrower that drags his harrow along the edge of the baulk, draws ever closer to his quarry's cover; such was Tadeusz's stealthy ascent.

But then the Judge went and upset his ambuscade! Cutting in before his nephew, he strode briskly up toward the stream. The fitful breeze played with the white tails of his sarafan and the ample handkerchief knotted around his belt. His wide-brimmed hat, held fast by a string against sudden gusts, undulated like a burdock leaf, beating now over his shoulders, now over his eyes. So, stout walking stick in hand, the Judge guided his steps toward the rill. After squatting down to wash his hands, he seated himself on a large rock opposite Telimena; and, leaning forward on the ivory ball of his prodigious cane, he opened his conversation thus:

"You must know, my dear, that ever since young Tadeusz has been our guest, I have been sorely worried. I am getting on in years, and childless. The dear lad is my one solace in the world, the future heir to my fortune. God willing, I shall leave him a handsome inheritance befitting a gentleman. But he, too, must think of his prospects and learn to stand on his own two feet. Now, consider, my dear, the difficulty I find myself in. You know what a strange fellow my brother Jacek, Tadeusz's father, is. His intentions are hard to fathom. He insists on staying away. God knows where he is hiding now. He even forbids us to tell his son that he is alive, yet still he must run his affairs. First, he wants to send Tadeusz to the legions. That caused me no little distress. Then he agrees he should stay home and take a wife. That could be easily arranged. I have my eye on a certain party. None among our fellow citizens boasts a better name or set of relations than the Chamberlain. His elder daughter, Anna, is eligible. She is fair and suitably dowered. I thought I might start the process."

Upon hearing these words, Telimena turned pale. She closed her book, endeavored to rise, then sat down again.

"So help me, my brother," said she. "Can there be any sense in this? Have you no fear of God? Tadeusz's benefactor making of him a sower of groats? Why, you will dash his prospects! Depend upon it, he will end up cursing you one day. To think of burying such talent in the woods and kitchen gardens! Why, even from what I know of him, I can see he is a clever lad – not that he couldn't stand a little refining in high society. You'd do better, my brother, to send him to the capital, to Warsaw for instance, or – I'll tell you what I'm thinking – why not Petersburg? I expect to be traveling up there this winter on business. Together, you and I shall shape plans for his future. I know a good many people there and enjoy some influence. That's the surest way of getting ahead in the world. With my help, he will gain admittance into the finest houses. And once he comes to know people of note, he will find a berth, earn a ribbon. Then, if he so chooses, he can resign his post and come home. But then he will be somebody and know the ways of the world. What say you to this, dear brother?"

"True enough," said the Judge, "a change of air and scene, a chance to see the world and rub shoulders with society can profit a young man. In my own youth, I saw a good bit of the world. I went to Piotrkow and Dubno, now following the Royal Tribunal as a barrister, now defending my own causes. I even went to Warsaw. Yes, there's much to be gained by it. I, too, should like my nephew to see the world, though preferably as a traveler or an apprentice rounding off his term, that he may

learn the affairs of men – not for grades or ribbons! You'll pardon
me, my dear, but what kind of distinction are Moscow's grades
and ribbons? Since when did our notables of old, or even now for
that matter, since when, I say, did the more well-to-do squires
of our district care for such trifles? Here we esteem them for
their gentle birth, their good name or office – by which I mean
one gained by an honest vote of the local citizenry, not through
somebody's good influences!"

"If that is your view," said Telimena, "then so much the
better. By all means, send your nephew into the world as a traveler."

"You see, my dear sister," said the Judge, scratching his
head ruefully, "I should like nothing better. But what can I do?
A fresh complication! Jacek will not yield oversight of his son.
And now he's burdened me with his companion from across the
Vistula, Friar Robak, who is privy to his plans. They have already decided the lad's future: they wish Tadeusz to wed, to take
Sophie, your ward, as wife. In addition to my fortune, the couple
shall receive a portion in ready money from my brother. As you
know, my dear, Jacek has the means. It is only by his favor that
I own the bulk of the estate, so he is fully entitled to make such
dispositions. And so, my dear, think how best to smooth the way.
They must become acquainted. True, they're very young, especially little Sophie. But that shouldn't be an obstacle. Anyhow,
it's high time she came out of confinement, for by all accounts
she's growing out of childhood."

Telimena was aghast, almost in a panic. She rose and
knelt down on her shawl. Disposed to listening at first, she was
now signing disagreement with her hand, waving it about her
ear, as if to drive the swarm of unwelcome words back into the
speaker's mouth.

"What is this? What is this I hear?" she retorted hotly. "Sir, whether it be good or ill for Tadeusz, you may decide
for yourself. He means nothing to me. Lay whatever plans you
please. Make of him a bailiff, consign him to a tavern, let him
serve out drinks, fetch game from the forest. Do as you like with
him! But Sophie, what concern is she of yours? Whom she mar-
ries is for me to decide. Me alone! Just because Jacek pays for
her rearing, affords her a modest yearly allowance, and promises to give more, that does not mean he can dispose of her like
chattels. Besides, it is still widely known that your generosity

toward her is not without a reason. You Soplicas know full well that you bear the Horeszko family a heavy debt."

The Judge listened to this part of her speech with incomprehensible dismay, sorrow, and visible revulsion. As though dreading to hear the rest, he hung his head and waved assent, blushing deeply the while.

"I have stood her in the stead of mother," pursued Telimena, closing her argument. "I am Sophie's kin, her only guardian. No one but I shall provide for her happiness."

"And if she should find happiness in this match?" ventured the Judge, raising his eyes. "If she took a fancy to Tadeusz?"

"Fancy? Fig on a thistle! Fancies, what do I care for fancies? True, Sophie may not be suitably dowered, but neither is she a village wench or some smallholder's lass. By lineage, she is daughter to a noble sire – a governor, and a Horeszko by her mother's side. She *shall* find a husband. Why else did we take such pains to rear her? But here? Why, she'd run wild in this place!"

The Judge listened attentively to Telimena without lowering his eyes. He seemed to soften, for his reply was cheerful enough.

"Well, my dear," said he, "nothing more to be said. Lord knows I did my best to bring the matter forward. Only do not be angry, my dear. If you do not agree, you are quite within your rights. Sad it is, but there's no use in being angry. I urged the suit for my brother's sake only. No one's forcing the match. Since you see fit to refuse Tadeusz's suit, I shall inform Jacek in writing that notwithstanding my best efforts, a betrothal between Tadeusz and Sophie cannot come to pass. Now I can take my own counsel. I think I shall launch the process with the Chamberlain. We'll have the matter settled in no time."

But Telimena's anger had begun to cool. "Not so fast, my brother," she broke in. "I refuse nothing. You said yourself it was too soon, that they were young. Let us bide our time and consider the matter. No harm in that. We shall allow the young people to become acquainted and keep an eye on them, for the felicity of others cannot be left to chance. Only I must warn you, my brother, to refrain from putting ideas into Tadeusz's head. No forcing of his attentions upon Sophie! The heart is no slave. Love brooks no master. No chains shall constrain it."

With that, the Judge, deep in thought, rose and walked away. Meanwhile, drawn by an imaginary trail of mushrooms, Tadeusz was approaching from the other side; and bearing slowly up in the same direction came the Count as well.

All this time, the Count had been observing the Judge and Telimena from his point of espial among the trees. Deeply stirred by the scene, he produced foolscap and pencil from his pocket, (he never went anywhere without his drawing materials), spread the paper over a leaning trunk, and busied himself with sketching studies.

"Arranged as by design," he muttered to himself. "He upon the rock, she on the sward. A picturesque ensemble. Distinctive heads, contrasting lines."

He moved closer, halting from time to time to wipe his lorgnette and daub his eyes with a handkerchief, yet never dropping his gaze.

"Must this lovely, enchanting tableau vanish or be transformed upon nicer inspection?" he mused. "Shall that velvet sward resolve itself into a patch of poppies and beet-tops? Shall I, in yonder nymph, discover a bailiff's mistress?"

Although the Count had often seen Telimena at the Judge's house, as he was a frequent caller there, he never paid her much attention. What was his amazement now when he recognized the model of his sketches! The beauty of the natural setting, the grace of his subject's posture and the elegance of her attire had transformed her almost beyond recognition. Anger still smoldered in her eyes. Enlivened by the breeze, by the recent quarrel with the Judge, and now by the sudden approach of the two youths, her face flushed with tones all the more vivid and intense.

"Please forgive the bold intrusion, ma'am," said the Count. "But I come bearing both apologies and words of gratitude: apologies for stealing upon your footsteps, gratitude for the honor of witnessing your musings. A grave offense committed, a heavy debt incurred, for I intrude upon a moment of your meditations and stand obliged for several more of inspiration. Felicitous moments! Now censure the man, but the artist awaits your grace. Having risked a great deal, I will risk still more. Be my judge!"

And kneeling beside her, he handed her his landscapes.

Telimena appraised his studies courteously, yet as one knowledgeable in matters of art. Though slow to praise, she was quick to encourage. "Bravo," she exclaimed. "I congratulate you. There is talent here. Only see you do not neglect it. Seek out lovely natural settings. Italy's sunlit skies. Rome's imperial rose-gardens. Tiber's classic cataracts. Posilipo's awesome caverns. There, my dear Count, is your land for painters. Here? Lord have mercy! A child of the Muses suckled at Soplica Manor would starve to death. Dear Count, I shall have your sketches framed, or place them in my album together with several other drawings I have picked up along the way. By now I have no mean store in my escritoire."

They began to talk of azure skies, murmuring seas, redolent breezes, and craggy peaks. Here and there, in the manner of many a traveler, they dropped scornful remarks and poked fun at their native land.

Yet all around them, in all its imposing splendor, stretched Lithuania's ancient woodland! All around them stood the bird cherry with her festoonery of wild hop; the rowan, fresh and mantling like a shepherdess's cheek; the maenad hazel with her verdant thyrsi wreathed in a grape-like garniture of pearly nuts. Beneath them grew the forest children, the guelder rose in the clasp of an alder, the black-lipped bramble entwined around a raspberry bush. Leafy-fingered trees and shrubs stood by, hands joined, like village maids and their swains poised to tread a measure around the wedded pair. And there, in their midst, surpassing the forest party in comeliness and charm of hue, stood the happy pair: a silver birch, the beloved, and her groom, a hornbeam. Farther back, like elders contemplating the junior generations, stood the hoary beeches, the matronly poplars – and a moss-bearded oak. Bowed under the weight of five long centuries, he leans on the petrified trunks his grandsires' that rear from the forest floor like broken burial stones.

Tadeusz fidgeted and squirmed, bored to no end by this long discourse in which he had no share. When the Count and Telimena began to sing the praises of exotic groves and rhyme off each species of tree – the orange, cypress, olive, almond, cactus, aloe, mahogany, sandal, lemon, ivy, walnut, even the fig – and then enlarge upon their shape, blossoms, and texture of bark, he could only pout and bridle. At last, he could stand it no longer. Though a simple youth, he knew how to delight in natural beauty. His imagination set ablaze by the sight of his native forest, he began to speak his mind:

"I have been to the botanical gardens in the city of Vilna, seen those celebrated trees which grow in the Orient or down south in that fair Italy of yours. But pray tell me which of them compares with our own native trees? The aloe? Surely not. Her twigs stick up like lightning conductors. The lemon? That dwarf of a tree with her gilded knobs and lacquered leaves? Lemon-trees are short and squat, like little old ladies – rich but ugly. Your vaunted cypress? Why, that meager tree expresses boredom rather than sorrow. People say the tall cypress looks so mournful leaning over a grave. I say the thing is like a German flunkey in court mourning, who stirs neither head nor limb, lest he should offend against funeral etiquette."

"Is not our honest-hearted birch comelier? Picture her as a village woman, a mother grieving her son, or a widow her husband. She wrings her hands, her hair fetched out over her shoulders, cascading to the ground. Mute with grief she stands, and yet in her posture how expressively she weeps! If painting's your passion, sir, why not paint the trees whose shade you now enjoy? You shall be the laughingstock of the district if, biding in Lithuania's fertile plains, you paint only craggy peaks and desert wastes."

"My friend," replied the Count, "natural beauty is but the form, the backdrop, the raw material, so to speak; the soul of art is inspiration. Art ranges on the pinions of invention. Taste must polish it, sound principles ground it. Nature is not enough, neither is fervor, for the artist must lift himself into the realm of the Ideal! Not every species of beauty lends itself to the painter's brush. All this you shall learn in good time in the course of your reading. As for painting, know that a picture requires a point of vantage, grouping, arrangement, and a sky, an Italian sky! So it is with the art of landscape. That is why Italy has always been the birthplace of painters; which in turn explains why, apart from Breughel – not Van der Helle, mind, but the landscapist (there are two Breughels!) – why, apart from Breughel, I say, and Ruysdael too, we in the northern latitudes boast of so few genre painters of the highest order. Skies! Skies are what we need!"

"Take our painter Orlowski," broke in Telimena. "There was a man with Soplica taste. You should know this is a disease

among the Soplicas. They have but one abiding passion – their
native land. I refer to Orlowski, the famous artist that spent
his years in Petersburg. I keep one or two of his sketches in my
escritoire. He lived next door to the Emperor's court. A painter's paradise! Yet, my dear Count, you would not believe how he
pined for his land. He loved nothing better than to reminisce on
his youth and sing the praises of all things Polish – the fields,
the skies, the forests."

"And rightly so!" rejoined Tadeusz hotly. "From what I
hear, those clear blue Italian skies of yours are like water frozen over. Are not gales and inclement weather a hundred times
lovelier? Here, you have only to look up: no end to the sights!
How many pictures and scenes unfold from the play of the clouds
alone. Each takes a different shape. Take the lazy autumn cloud:
tortoise-wise, she creeps along, great with showers, dropping
long streamers like unbraided tresses to the earth. That's the
rain cascading down! And the hail cloud: dark-blue and round,
with a glint of yellow in her core, she flies flaw-blown, like a ball,
and all around you hear the thunderous clatter. Take even your
regular white clouds like those over yonder. See how changeable
they are! Like a flock of swans or wild geese they drive along.
The falcon-wind swoops down from behind, bunches them up.
They mass together, swell, thicken, and lo! Sprouting curved
necks, manes, and legs, they course Heaven's steppeland like
a herd of silvery-white ponies. Yet another shifting: the ponies'
necks shoot forth spars, the manes billow into broad sails, and
the herd reshapes itself into a proud schooner. Serene and leisurely, she navigates the blue plain of the sea."

Telimena and the Count sat gazing up at the cloud. Tadeusz was pointing to it with one hand while gently squeezing Telimena's with his other. Several minutes of quiet contemplation
elapsed. The Count spread a sheet of foolscap over his hat and
reached for a pencil. Just then, the mournful sound of the manor
bell burst upon their ears. Instantly, the quiet forest broke out
into a tumult of shouts and halloos.

"So, with the tolling of the bell," lamented the Count,
shaking his head, "does Destiny put a period to the things of this
world. The reckonings of great minds, the inventions of ranging
fancy, the tender diversions, the delights of friendship, the out-
pourings of gentle hearts. When the bronze roars from afar, all
falls into confusion, chaos and turmoil, and vanishes away."

And gazing tenderly at Telimena, he said, "What remains?"

"Memories," came her reply.

And to sweeten his sadness, she tendered him a freshly culled forget-me-not. The Count raised the flower to his lips, then fastened it to his bosom. Meanwhile, on the side opposite, Tadeusz was engaged in parting the leaves of a shrub. A white object, a lily-white hand, had thrust its way through the leafage. He seized it up and kissed it. His mouth sank into the palm of the hand like a bee in a lily cup. A cold object touched his lips. It was a key and a screw of white paper bearing a note. He took up these objects and dispatched them into his pocket. What the key signified, he had no idea. Doubtless the note would shed light on it.

The bell continued to clank. A thousand shouts and cries answered like echoes from deep within the silent wood. It was the sound of men and women seeking one another out, hailing and hallooing, a signal that the day's mushrooming had come to a close. Yet these echoes were anything but sad or mournful, as it seemed to the Count. Indeed, they had a prandial sound. Every day at noon, the bell rang out from under the manor gable, summoning the guests and servants to luncheon. Many of the older domains observed this custom. Soplica Manor held fast to it.

And so the party of mushroomers issued forth from the grove. All were carrying chip or wicker baskets tied down at each corner with a handkerchief. The baskets brimmed with wild mushrooms. Each young lady held a splendid bolete like a folded fan in one hand and a bundle of *honey mushrooms* and *brittle gills* of various hue, all tied together like a nosegay of wildflowers, in the other. The Steward followed with his *fly agaric*, Telimena walked empty-handed behind him, and the two youths brought up the rear.

Entering the castle in orderly fashion, the guests drew up in a circle around the table. To the Chamberlain – it being the privilege of his office and senior years – belonged the post of honor. Bowing to the ladies, elders and youth, he approached the table. The Franciscan took his station beside him, and the Judge, his, next to the Franciscan. The Friar recited a brief benison in the Latin tongue; the men took vodka, whereupon they all sat down and tucked quietly into the beet-leaf soup – chilled

Lithuanian-style.

The noonday meal proceeded more quietly than usual. Despite the entreaties of the host, no one was in the mood for conversation. The two factions embroiled in the great dispute over the two greyhounds had tomorrow's contest and wager on their mind. Great thoughts have a way of constraining lips to silence! Telimena, while talking incessantly to Tadeusz, was fain now and then to turn to the Count and vouchsafe even the Assessor an occasional glance. So the fowler keeps an eye on several gin traps at once, one for catching the goldfinch, another for the sparrow.

Both Tadeusz and the Count felt pleased with themselves. Both were happy and hopeful, and so neither felt an inclination to talk. The Count eyed his forget-me-not proudly. Tadeusz aimed furtive glances into his pocket, making sure the key hadn't slipped away. He even reached in his hand and fingered the note. As of yet he hadn't had time to read it. Meanwhile, the Judge waited attentively on the Chamberlain, serving him champagne or Hungarian wine and squeezing his knee. Yet even he lacked zest for talk; clearly, he was burdened by private cares of his own.

The plates and dishes came and went in silence. Suddenly, an unexpected guest broke the tedious flow of the meal. It was the forest ranger. Heedless of his intrusion on the lunch hour, he walked hurriedly up to the Judge. From his mien and bearing, it was clear that he bore tidings of great and unusual import. All eyes turned on him.

"A bear, your lordship!" he gasped out, after catching his breath.

The rest, they could surmise for themselves. They understood that a bear had forsaken his lair in the old forest; that the beast was striking out for the woods across the Niemen; that they must stalk it without a moment's delay. All knew this, neither counsel nor reflection was needed. General agreement was plainly to be inferred from the ensuing welter of clipped words, the lively gestures and accompanying commands, which, while flowing tumultuously from so many pairs of lips at once, all tended toward the same end.

"To the village!" cried the Judge. "Ho there! To horse! Summon the foreman! Have a troop of beaters ready at daybreak! Volunteers, mind. Those that show up with a spear get off two days' roadwork and five days' field-service."

"Bustle about!" barked the Chamberlain. "Saddle my gray, ride post-haste to the house and fetch my two bulldogs. Aye, the pair the whole neighborhood talks about. The male answers to the name Constable, and the bitch *Procureuse*. Muzzle their snouts, throw 'em in a sack, and bring 'em here on the double – on horseback, so as not to waste time."

"Vanka!" cried the Assessor to his servant boy in Ruthenian. "Run my Sanguszko hunting knife over the whetting stone – you know, the one I received as a gift from the Prince. Then fill my cartridge belt. And see that every round is armed."

"Guns!" they cried one and all. "Get the guns ready!"

"Lead, bring me lead!" the Assessor kept yelling. "I keep a bullet mold in my bag."

"Inform the priest," said the Judge, "that holy mass shall be said in the forest chapel at daybreak tomorrow, for the success of the hunt. Aye, Saint Hubert's Mass, the one with the short office."

Their orders issued, the guests relapsed into thoughtful silence. They began to look around them, as though they were seeking someone out. Slowly, the grave countenance of the Steward drew upon itself and fixed the collective stare. Clearly, they were looking for someone to lead tomorrow's hunt, and the huntmaster's baton was being conferred upon him. Accepting the investiture, the Steward rose to his feet and struck the table a solemn blow; then, plunging his hand deep into his bosom, he drew out by its gold fob a pocket-watch the size of a large pear.

"Tomorrow," he pronounced in a grave tone, "at half past four in the morning, our hunters and beaters shall meet in front of the forest chapel."

With that, he hurried away from the table. The ranger followed fast on his heels. Together, they must lay plans and prepare for the hunt. Even so commanders inform their troops that the field will be fought at first light. In the camp, the soldiers clean their arms, chew on their rations or, setting their cares aside, doze on their saddles and greatcoats. Meanwhile, the officers plot strategy in the stillness of the tent.

No more thought of lunch. The rest of the day was spent in shoeing horses, feeding the hounds, collecting and cleaning guns. Scarcely anyone bothered to attend the evening meal. Even Scut and Peregrine's backers ceased to occupy themselves with the great contest. The Notary and the Assessor were now arm in crook, busy hunting for lead.

Worn out by the day's events, the rest of the company retired early so as to be up at the peep of dawn the following day.

BOOK FOUR: DIPLOMACY & THE HUNT

Argument: An apparition in curl papers wakes Tadeusz. A mi-atake discovered too late. The tavern. The emissary. The deft use of a snuffbox steers a discussion back on the right course. The Lairs. The bear. Tadeusz and the Count in peril. Three gunshots. Sagalas vs. Sanguszko. The dispute decided in favor of a Horeszko single barrel. Hunter's stew. The Steward's tale of the duel between Doveiko and Domeiko interrupted by a hare course. Doveiko and Domeiko concluded.

Coevals of Lithuania's Grand Dukes! You trees of Bialowieza, Switez, Ponary, and Kuszelewo! Your shade once fell upon the crowned heads of dread Witenes, mighty Mendog, and Giedymin, when, sprawled upon a bearskin by a hunters' fire, he listened to his bard Lizdeiko croon. There, looking down from the Ponary Hills, lulled to sleep by the sight of the Neris and the brawl of the Vilnele, he dreamed of an iron wolf; then, roused to the task at the clear behest of the gods, he founded Vilna, the city that broods in the forest like the wolf among the bison, bear, and wild boar. As the Romans sprang from the she-wolf, so from Vilna sprang Kiejstut, Olgierd, and the entire Olgierd line – intrepid knights and hunters all, equally unswerving in the charge and the chase. And so, our future stands revealed in a hunter's dream. Always shall Lithuania rely upon her timber and iron.

You ancient forests! The last of *them* came hunting your game! The last of our princes to wear Witold's kalpak. Last of Jagiello's line of blithe warriors – Lithuania's last monarch of the chase!

O trees of my native land! If Heaven allows me to see you again, shall I still find you there? Do you still live, dear friends? You at whose feet I used to crawl as a babe! Does mighty Baublis live? His hollow chamber, reamed out by the ages, could comfortably seat a dozen dinner guests around a table! Does Mendog's grove still blossom by the parish church? And, yonder, in the Ukrainian borderlands, does the ancient lime still stand before the Holowinski house on the banks of the Ros? A hundred youths, a hundred maids found ample room to dance beneath her spreading shade!

O you, our monuments! How many toppled each year by the timber merchant! How many devoured by Muscovy's axe! Scarce a haunt remains to charm the woodland songster or the poet, who, like the birds, holds your bowers dear. Did not Jan's linden hang upon his every word, prompt him with rhymes by the score? And that prattling oak! No end to the marvels he croons in our Cossack poet's ear!

And I! Do I not also stand in your debt, my native trees? What thoughts did I not pursue in your quiet solitudes, when I, a trifling sportsman, I fled my comrades' taunts over a quarry missed; when, deep in the old forest, the hunt far behind me, I sat me down on a small knoll. Around me gleam patches of silver-bearded moss drenched in the grenadine of trampled bilberries. Before me heave swells of purple heath. Mountain cranberry festoons the slopes as with chaplets of coral. Darkness embosoms me! A roof of interlacing branches overhangs my head like a heavy overcast of dense green clouds; and, somewhere high above that stirless vault, the wind soughs and moans, whistles, wails, and booms. A strange, heady din! You fancy a boisterous sea hangs suspended there.

Below me – a ruinous city. An overthrown oak looms up like a derelict pile. Shaggy timbers and half-rotted logs lean against it like broken pillars and remains of a wall. Grasses hedge it round. None dare peer into that stronghold! There dwell the lords of the waste – the wild boar, the bear, the wolf. Halfgnawed bones – remains of unwary guests – bestrew the entranceway. Now and anon, a pair of antlers rises fount-like out of the grass. Away streaks the stag. A tawny smudge glimpsed among the trees like a fugitive sunbeam flitting through the forest!

Silence reigns again. A woodpecker taps lightly at a spruce then flies off to renew his tapping from a new hiding place. Like a child at play he beckons to be found. Fast by, a squirrel sits gnawing at a nut. His brush overhangs his eyes like a hussar's panache; yet nothing escapes those darting eyes. A guest intrudes. Away flies our dancer of the groves! Quick as the levin-flash, he leaps from tree to tree, to slip at last into a privy cleft, like a wood sprite returning to his native tree.

Silence again. A rowan tree stirs. The clustering branches part. A face mantling redder than the rowanberry pokes through the opening – a village maiden foraging for fruit and nuts! From a plain birchbark basket she offers you fresh-culled cranberries as red as her lips. A youth walks at her side. He reaches for a hazel spray; she grasps at the flashing cobs. Horn blasts! Hound music! A hunt draws near. The pair fly into the leafy thicket, melting from sight like woodland deities.

Soplica Manor was all astir. Yet neither the babbling of the hounds, nor the neighing of the horses, nor the creaking of the carts, nor yet the shrilling of the horns stirred Tadeusz from his slumbers. Sound as a marmot he slept, still in the clothes he had worn upon dropping into bed that night. None of the youths thought to look for him in the house. All were about their affairs, anxious to be at their posts. Their slumbering companion passed entirely unnoticed.

On he snored. A fiery shaft of sunlight shone through a heart-shaped opening in the window shutter and fell full on the sleeping lad's face. He would have dozed on, but, even as he turned from the glare, an urgent tapping sound awoke him. Happy awakening! His breast heaved softly. Blithe as a morning bird he felt. He smiled – and in full memory of last night's assignation, he blushed. And he sighed, and his heart began to race.

He looked up. Ye gods! There, framed within the sunlit heart above him, danced a pair of beaming orbs – fully open, as one would expect of eyes peering into the darkness from the broad daylight. A small hand, raised slantwise like a fan, screened them from the glare. The sunlight made transparencies of the delicate fingers, suffusing them with a roseate hue. He saw a pair of curious lips, slightly parted, a set of tiny white teeth gleaming like pearls in the coral, and cheeks, which, shaded by the glowing hand, flushed red as a rose.

Tadeusz was sleeping by the window. Lying supine, invisible in the gloom, he gazed in wonder at the apparition that hovered directly above him, almost touching his face. Was he awake – he wondered – or simply imagining one of those radiant little faces that haunt the dreams of our innocent youth?

The face peered down at him. Trembling with awe and delight, he gazed hard upon it and only then – to his indescribable chagrin! – recognized the short, pale-gold tresses wrapped in snow-white curl papers, the same silvery pod-like objects he had seen flaming in the sun like a saintly glory.

He sat up with a jerk. Startled by the movement, the living vision fled. He waited in vain for it to reappear. Then, he heard three more taps and an urgent voice, saying, "Sir, it is time to get up for the hunt. You have overslept yourself!"

Springing from his couch, Tadeusz dashed back both shutters with such violence that the hinges rattled and the leaves, flying open, crashed against the wall on either hand. Upon landing on the ground outside, he looked around in surprise and bewilderment. Not a soul in sight! Hard by the window ran the garden fence hung with flowers and leafy bine. The leafage still trembled as though a light hand or breath of wind had brushed over it. Long he stared at the leaves. But he was loath to venture into the garden; instead, he leaned against the fence, raised his eyes, and, with finger pressed to his lips, enjoined himself to silence, lest by a hasty utterance he should break his train of thought. Several times, he tapped his forehead, as if stirring memories that had long lain dormant there. At last, gnawing at his fingers, he drew blood.

"Serve a man right! Serve him right!" he cried at the top of his compass.

Alive with shouts and cries just moments before, the courtyard stood hushed and deserted like a cemetery. The entire hunting party had ridden out. Tadeusz raised his hands like trumpets to his ears and listened hard. Presently, bugle notes and hunters' halloos came floating toward him from the forest. Finding his horse saddled and bridled in the stable, he seized his flintlock, vaulted astride, and sped off like a madman toward the two taverns by the chapel, where the hunt had agreed to meet at dawn.

The two inns leaned inward from either side of the highway, their windows glaring at one another like sworn enemies. The older hostelry belonged by right of deed to the castle holder. The new one belonged to the Judge, who had built it to spite the castle. Gervase held sway over the one, Protase lorded it over the other.

While the new inn looked perfectly ordinary, the old one hewed to the ancient design of Tyrian carpenters, which the Jews later spread far and wide. The architectural style is foreign to builders abroad; we inherit it from the Jews. From the front, it resembled a boat, from the rear, a temple. Shaped like an oblong chest, the boat was a veritable Noah's ark. Nowadays, we'd give it the more prosaic name of stable. Livestock of every description, horses, cows, oxen, and bearded goats stood stalled within. Birds and reptiles (at least a pair of each) and swarms of insects thronged the rafters. The rear of the building resembled a marvelous temple recalling that great edifice of Solomon's, which Hiram's builders, skilled in the joiner's craft, first erected on Sion Hill. The Jews imitate it even now in their synagogues; the same plan can be seen in their stables and inns. The roof, made of thatching and roughly cut boards, tapered upward into a peak like a tattered Jewish hat. A covered gallery projected from the gable wall. Wooden pillars supported it – architectural wonders in their bearing strength, for they were rotted half through and, like Pisa's tower, out of the perpendicular. (Unlike Grecian columns, they had neither capital nor plinth.) Spanning these pillars were Gothic-style arches, also of wood, with ingenious motifs adorning their façades – all askew and bent like the branches of a Sabbath menorah. No chisel or sculpting tool but a deftly wielded carpenter's adze had shaped these motifs. From the points of the arches swung small button-like knobs reminiscent of those which the Hebrew wears over his brow and calls *tzitziot* in his language. Seen from afar, the whole tottering, lopsided hostelry brought to mind a Jew nodding his head in prayer. The roof suggested his hat; the ragged thatch, his beard; the grimy smoke-smeared walls, his black coat; and the sculpted arches, his tasseled prayer shawl.

The interior of the tavern was partitioned in two like a Jewish schoolhouse. One half consisted of a number of narrow rectangular rooms reserved for gentlemen travelers and their ladies. The other half housed an ample hall. A narrow wooden table with many legs ran the length of each of the walls; and, alongside each table ran short-legged benches resembling their sires, the tables, in every respect, only smaller.

Ranged together on these encircling benches were men and women of the village and members of the minor nobility. Shoulder to shoulder they sat; only the Bailiff sat alone. After morning mass at the chapel – the day being Sunday – they had dropped in at Yankel's for a drink and a spot of good cheer. Before each patron foamed a tumbler of home-brew spirits. The hostess, bottle in hand, hovered busily over her guests. Behind her stood the Jewish proprietor. He wore a black, silver-clasped

coat that swept down to his heels. With one hand tucked under his satin sash and the other running solemnly down his silver beard, he cast his gaze around the hall, issuing orders here,
greeting new arrivals there, striking up conversations with the
seated, settling quarrels – yet serving no one.

Yankel was an old Jew respected everywhere for his pro-
bity. In all the years he'd kept the inn, no rustic or nobleman
ever lodged a complaint at the Manor. Nor was there cause, for
his drinks were neat and choice. He kept a strict account and
cheated no one. Boisterous spirits, he put up with, but he drew
the line at drunken behavior. He was fond of parties, threw open
his house for every wedding and christening, and, on Sundays,
invited over the village band with their array of musical instruments, including a bull fiddle and a doodle sack.

Yankel knew music. Indeed, he was famous for his mu-
sicianship. He used to make the rounds of the country houses
with the cymbalon, the instrument of his people, and astounded
all with his playing and songs, which he delivered in a voice
that was trained and true. A Jew, he spoke Polish with a clean
accent. He had a special fondness for Polish folksongs. Of these,
after each trip across the Niemen, he brought back a good many:
mazurkas from Warsaw, *kolomyjkas* from Galicia. Rumor had
it – of uncertain reliability to be sure – that he was the first to
bring home and make popular the song now famous around the
world, the one our legions' bugles first pealed forth to the Lombard on the Ausonian fields. The art of singing pays handsomely
in Lithuania. Music wins people's favor, fame and wealth accrue
from it – Yankel made a fortune. In time, having had his fill
of fame and profit, he hung up his dulcimer and, settling into
the inn with his children, turned to ply his trade as a spirits
vendor. He also served as under-rabbi in the neighboring town.
Everywhere, he was received as a welcome guest and trusted
consultant, for he knew the trading wherries and the grain business – indispensable items of knowledge in the country. In short,
people esteemed Yankel as an honorable Pole.

It was Yankel who put an end to the frequent bloody
shindies that raged between the two taverns. He leased the pair
of them. Respected alike by the old Horeszko partisans and the
Judge's serving-men, he alone knew how to hold the grim Warden and fractious Court Usher in check. In Yankel's presence,
both men bridled their grudges. Grim Gervase curbed his sword-

arm, Protase, his tongue.

Today, Gervase was absent, having left with the hunting party. He wouldn't dream of allowing the raw Count to venture alone on so perilous an expedition; and so, he accompanied him as his aide and escort.

The Friar sat in Gervase's place between two benches in the corner farthest from the door where those of the Orthodox faith hang their holy icons. Yankel had seated him there himself. Clearly, the Jew held him in the highest regard, for whenever he saw Robak's mead-pot run low, he would promptly replenish it himself. By all accounts, they had befriended each other while traveling abroad in their youth. Robak often visited the tavern under the cover of night to confer with the Jew on various important matters. Word went around that the Friar trafficked in contraband, but this malicious rumor warranted no credence.

Robak sat hunched over the table, holding forth in a low voice. The nobility crowded attentively around him, their noses bent over his snuffbox. All helped themselves to a pinch, whereupon our squirearchy sneezed like a battery of mortars.

"*Reverendissime!*" snorted Skoluba. "Now there's snuff that goes straight to your head. Never in my born days has this nose of mine sniffed the like." He stroked his long appendage and sneezed again. "Genuine Franciscan! From Kowno no doubt, a city famous for her snuff and mead. I was there once. When was it now?"

"Good health!" broke in Robak. "Good health to you, gentlemen. As to the snuff, well, it hails from a deal farther than Mr. Skoluba supposes. Jasna Gora! Aye, the Pauline Fathers grind this snuff in Czestochowa, home of the wonder-working image of the Blessed Virgin, Queen of the Polish Realm. Even now she goes by her other name of Grand Duchess of Lithuania. Even now she holds the royal office. And yet schism reigns over the Duchy!"

"Czestochowa, you say?" struck up Wilbik. "I used to go there thirty years ago on pilgrimages to make my confession. Is it true the French bide there now? Do they really mean, as *The Lithuanian Courier* reports, to destroy the Basilica and seize the treasury?"

"Not true!" countered the Friar. "His Imperial Highness Napoleon is an exemplary son of the Church. The Pope himself anointed him. They see eye to eye and together they revive the faith of France. Admittedly, the faith has seen better days. Aye, Czestochowa pours ample silver into the national coffers – for the good of the Fatherland! For Poland, I say. God himself enjoins it! His altar tables have always fed the nation's coffers. A hundred thousand patriots – and perhaps soon even more – stand under arms in the Duchy of Warsaw. Who's to pay for it? Is it not up to you, Lithuanian Poles? Why, it's coppers you drop into Moscow's chest."

"Devil take it!" cried Wilbik. "They seize it by force."

"Reverend Father," piped up a meek little rustic, bobbing and scratching his head. "The nobility suffer, aye, but not half as bad as us. Why, they fleece us to the bone."

"Bumpkin!" yelled Skoluba. "Fool! It is easier for you. The peasantry are used to being skinned like eels. But we born-and-bred gentlefolk have grown attached to our golden liberty. Aye, my brothers, in the old days *'the gentleman on his grange—'*"

"Yes, yes, we know," they cried out one and all, *"The gentleman on his grange stands equal to the governor!"*

"Aye," Skoluba resumed, "but now they question our pedigree and send us rummaging through our papers to prove our gentle birth."

"Oh, spare me!" yelled Juracha. "Your sires were but ennobled peasants, whereas I spring from princes. To ask *me* for my letters patent! Why, God only knows when I got my title. Let the Muscovite inquire of the forest oak who entitled him to lord it over the shrubs."

"Beguile others with your tales, O Prince," said Zagiel. "You will find more than one house here with a coronet."

"Your arms depict a cross," cried Podhajski. "An allusion to a converted Jew gracing your line."

"Lies!" broke in Birbasz. "I spring from Crimean counts, yet there are crosses over the galley charging my shield."

"A Rose Argent, with a coronet, done on a ground of gold," shouted Mickiewicz. "Now there's a princely escutcheon! You've only to consult Stryjkowski. His armorial makes frequent mention of it."

A great murmur broke out in the inn. Robak fled to his snuffbox and proffered them each a pinch. At once, the noise subsided, as out of courtesy they inhaled a few grains and fired off a salvo. Profiting from the pause, the Franciscan resumed:

"Great men have sneezed on taking this snuff. Would you
believe it if I told you Dombrowski took four snorts from this
box?

"Not *the* Dombrowski?" they said.

"The very one, the General. I was in his camp the day he
took Gdansk from the Germans. He had a letter to write. Afraid
of nodding off, he took a pinch, sneezed, and clapped me twice on
the shoulder. 'Father Robak,' said he, 'if all goes well, we shall
meet in Lithuania before the year is out. Be sure her sons greet
me there with snuff. This Czestochowa snuff, mind! I'll take no
other.'"

Robak's words aroused so much wonder, such transports
of joy in the boisterous throng, that for a moment they fell silent.
Soon, half-audible whispers made themselves heard: "Snuff?
From Poland? Czestochowa? General Dombrowski? From Italy?" – until, at last, thought fused with thought, word with word,
and the entire assembly cried out in unison, "Dombrowski!" And
joined in that single roar, they fell into a common clasp. Peasant
embraced Crimean Count. Coronet, the Cross. Roses Argent –
Galley and Griffin. All cares went by the board. Even the Friar
sat forgotten. They sang out the Dombrowski mazurka, all the
while shouting, "Vodka! Mead! Wine!"

Father Robak suffered them to sing on, but at last it was
time to intervene. Seizing the snuffbox in both hands, he broke
up their singing with a sneeze. Before they could start up again,
he hastened to speak.

"You find my snuff praiseworthy. Is it not so, esteemed
gentlemen? But take a closer look at the box and see what's depicted there."

And wiping the dust from the lid with his handkerchief,
he revealed to their gaze a miniature depicting a tiny swarm-
like army. A mounted rider stood out like a large beetle in its
midst – clearly, the commander of the host. With one hand on
the rein and the other raised to his nose, he reared his horse, as
if urging it into the heavens.

"Now," said Robak, "look well on this awesome figure.
Guess who?"

Intrigued to no end, they examined it closely.

"He is a great man," added Robak. "An emperor, but not
Russia's emperor. Tsars never snort snuff."

"A great man wearing a gray capote?" said Cydzik. "I thought great men went about in gold. Even the lowest-ranking general among the Muscovites drips with gold like a saffron-dusted pike."

"Nay," chimed in Rymsza. "As a lad, once, I saw Kosciuszko, our Commander-in-Chief. Now there was a man for you! He went about in a peasant's caftan, a *czamara*, that is."

"*Czamara* my eye, sir!" snorted Wilbik. "You mean a *taratatka*."

"A *czamara* has braids," countered Mickiewicz. "A *taratatka's* smooth all over."

Contention broke out over the various cuts of frock and coat. Seeing the talk go astray, the artful Robak steered it back to the campfire, his snuffbox. Again, he proffered it. They sneezed and drank each other's health. The Friar resumed.

"When Emperor Napoleon takes his snuff, pinch after pinch, it is sure sign the battle is going well. Take Austerlitz, for example. The French stand beside their guns like so. The Muscovites bear down on them in a dark swarm, while the Emperor watches in silence. Every French salvo cuts a broad swath through the enemy ranks. Squadron after squadron come charging up and tumble from their saddles, and each time the Emperor takes a snort. At last, one after the other, Tsar Alexander, his brother Constantine, and the German Prince Franz decamp. And Bonaparte, seeing the battle won, breaks out into a laugh and dusts the snuff from his fingers. So, keep this in mind, should any of you gentlemen here have the good fortune of serving in the Emperor's army."

"Ah, dear Father," cried Skoluba, "when will that be? The year drags on from feast day to feast day and every time they announce the arrival of the French. We strain our eyes, we stare and stare until we blink, and still the Muscovite has us gripped by the neck. Why, by the time it dawns, the dewfall will have dimmed our eyes!"

"Come, sir," said the Priest, "grousing's for grannies. It is the Jewish thing to stand idle until a traveler comes knocking at the tavern door. With Napoleon on our side, it is no trick to beat the Muscovite. Three times, he has tanned the Swabian's hide. Hasn't he drubbed the dreaded Prussian? Flung the English back across the sea? The Muscovite will get his due, never you mind. But what will come of it, sir, if our nobility take to

horse and sword when there's no one left to fight? Having done it
all himself, Napoleon's sure to say, 'I shall manage without you,
sirs. Who are you?' It is not enough to stand waiting for a guest,
or even to invite him in. A good host summons his servants and
sets the tables. Before the feast, he must clean the house of dirt.
Clean the house, I say. I repeat, clean the house, my sons!"

There fell a moment of silence; then voices in the crowd
piped up.

"Clean house? But how?" What means Father by that?
We will do all you say. We stand ready for anything. Only pray,
Father, do make your meaning clear."

But the Priest waved silence. Something outside had
caught his attention. He leaned out the window then rose to his
feet.

"No time now," said he. "We shall have occasion to discuss this at greater length later. Tomorrow, I have errands to
run in the district town. On my way back, I shall be looking in
on you, sirs, for alms."

"Then be sure to spend the night with us in Niehrymow!"
called out the Bailiff. "The Ensign will be glad to see you. Why,
it is an old maxim in Lithuania, 'Happy as an alms quester in
Niehrymow!'"

"And look in on us, if you would," said Zubkowski. "Father can rely on us for a roll of linen, a tub of butter, a fatted calf
or sheep. Remember these words, 'In Zubkowo the alms quester
lacks for nothing!'"

"And do not forget us!" cried Skoluba.

"Nor us!" yelled Terajewicz. 'No quester left Pucewicze
feeling peckish.'"

Such were the entreaties and pledges with which the nobility plied the Priest; but by now he was well out the tavern
door.

It was a pale, sullen-faced Tadeusz he had just seen
burning up the highroad past the window. The sight of the lad
hunched low in the saddle, bareheaded, belaboring his horse
with crop and spur, caused him great consternation. Striking a
brisk pace, the Friar set out after the youth. The road took him
in the direction of the great forest, which brooded low on the
horizon as far as the eye could see.

Who has searched the depths of Lithuania's wilds, probed their innermost recesses, their deepest vitals? The fisherman on the shore scarcely sounds the deep. The hunter stalks but the fringes of Lithuania's forests, knows but their outward form and features. Their heart, their penetralia, these lie beyond his ken! The stuff of fable what passes there. Strike but deep enough into those ancient pinewoods and shaggy forests, and you run up against a vast barrier of stumps, logs and roots fortified by quaking bogs, myriad streams, masses of weed, ant-heaps, wasps' and hornets' nests, and writhing snakes. Those that by superhuman effort brave these obstacles and strike deeper, run into still greater perils. Small lakes, half overgrown with grass and deep beyond imagining, lie in wait at every turn like wolves' lairs; in all probability, demons inhabit them. Their waters give off a sheen flecked with flakes of blood-hued rust. From deep below, there wafts a foul-smelling fume, a pestilence that strips the environing trees of leaf and bark. Drooping limbs – bare, stunted, worm-eaten, sickly, and matted with moss – and bearded stumps, humped by grotesquely misshapen fungi, press up to these meres even as a coven of witches huddles for warmth around a cauldron cooking a corpse.

Beyond these plumbless pools, man's eye and foot probe in vain. All lies covered by a thick cloud of vapors which rises eternally from the quaking bogs. Yet, beyond these mists, if common report be true, there lies a fertile region of unparalleled beauty – the first city of the animal and vegetable kingdom. Yonder lie in store all the seeds of every tree and herb whence spring all the generations of plants that populate the world. Like Noah's ark the place is sanctuary to at least one pair of every race of beast. In the very heart of this city, so the people say, the monarchs of the forest hold court – the ancient Auroch, the Bison, the Bear. Sprawled in the trees around them lie their watchful ministers-of-state, the keen-eyed Lynx, the glutton Wolverine. Farther out dwell their feudatories, the Wild Boar, the Gray Wolf, the Beamed Elk; and, high overhead, like talebearers living off the board of their liege lords, the Falcon and Wild Eagle soar. Hidden away in the very heart of the wilderness, unseen by man, these archetypal pairs send their offspring forth to tenant the world, while they themselves live out their lives in peace and quiet. Neither gunshot nor dart-thrust shortens their life. The old among them die a natural death. They even have their own graveyard, where, nearing death, the fowl retires to lay down his plumage and the four-legged beast, his pelt. When the bear finds his teeth too worn to chew his food; when the grizzled roebuck grows too stiff to stir his legs, and the hoar hare feels his blood thicken in his veins; when the raven's quill turns silvery-gray, the falcon's eye grows dim, and the eagle's ancient beak grows so bent as to close for good and prevent him from eating his prey, then all these beasts repair to the graveyard. Even smaller creatures, maimed or ailing, hasten there to rest their bones in the ancestral ground; and so, no trace of animal bones is ever found in the places known to and frequented by man.

The beasts of this metropolis are said to enjoy self-government. Thence spring their gentle manners, for they live unspoiled by human civilization, innocent of the laws of property which embroil the world of men. The very notion of duels and martial arts is foreign to their nature. As their grandsires lived in Paradise, so, too, their descendants, at once wild and tame and given neither to butting nor biting, thrive today in a spirit of love and harmony. Should an unarmed man fall in upon them, he would pass serenely through their midst. The beasts would only stare at him in awe, as when their forbears in the Garden gazed upon Adam on creation's sixth and final day, before sin set them at strife. Happily, man does not enter these repairs. Toil and care and death bar his way.

Yet rash scenthounds, swift on their quarry's traces, have been known to blunder into those sloughy, mossy, gully-riven regions. Horrified by the sights that greet them there, they fly with wild looks and appalling whines; and, long afterwards, they stand trembling at their master's feet, uncomforted by his soothing hand. In the hunter's jargon, these hidden precincts unknown to man are called *The Lairs*.

Foolish bear! Had you but kept to your haunts, the Steward would never have found you out. The scent of hives? A hankering after ripe oats? Whatever the enticement, you ventured away to where the trees grew thinner; and the ranger lighted upon your tracks. At once, he dispatches his beaters, clever spies, to reconnoiter your lying and grazing grounds; and now, extending their lines between you and the Lairs, the Steward and his beaters have blocked your retreat!

By the time Tadeusz arrived on the scene, the hounds were already probing the deepest repairs of the forest.

A profound silence! To no avail the hunters strain their ears. For an age, they stand waiting, riveted to the spot, listening to a silence that speaks in the most eloquent of tongues. Only the distant rumors of the wilderness reach them. Meanwhile, the hounds breast the undergrowth like divers in the deep. Doubles trained on the forest, the shooters have their eyes intent upon the Steward. He kneels down, bends a probing ear to the ground. Even as an ailing man's friends strive to read the verdict of life or death on the physician's face, so, trusting in the Steward's skill, the hunters transfix him with a stare of anxious hope. "Yes! . . . yes!" he whispers. He springs to his feet. He'd heard it! They listen harder. Then, all at once, they hear it too. A hound speaks, then two, then twenty! The entire scattered pack noses the scent and gives mouth. Howling, baying, they seize the trail. No longer the leisurely babble of hounds tracking a fox, hare, or hind, but the full, fierce, staggered cry of a pack hunting by sight! Abruptly, the clamor breaks off. They hold him! Fresh howls and roars. The bear fights back, inflicting wounds. Increasingly, the whines and yelps of mortally clawed hounds rise above the din.

 Guns primed, bodies taut and bent like bows, the shooters face the forest and wait until they can stand it no longer. One by one, craving the quarry for themselves, they break rank and make for the woods. Bootless the Steward's warnings! In vain he circles their positions on horseback! In vain he threatens to lay his crop on the back of the next yokel or nobleman to quit his post. The gunners dash heedless into the forest. Three flintlocks discharge at once, then a whole cannonade! At last, over the detonations of the guns, the bawl of the quarry breaks forth and echoes through the forest. An appalling roar of pain, fury and despair! A moment later, the forest erupts in a thunderous din of crying hounds, shouts, and horn blasts. Some gunners strike deeper into the forest, others cock their pieces – all wrought to the highest pitch of elation.

 "They shoot abroad!" the Steward groans. Intent on heading their prey away from its den, shooters and beaters run one way. Meanwhile, the bear, frightened off by the huntsmen and their hounds, doubles back to terrain less narrowly guarded – to the forest's fringes, which the gunners have all but deserted, and where, of the once strong ring, only the Steward, Tadeusz, the

Count, and a handful of beaters remain.

Here the forest stands thinner. A roar from within! The crack of tree limbs! Suddenly, the bear bursts out of the thicket like a bolt from a cloud. The hounds encircle him, worry him, snap at his heels. He rears on his hind legs and looks about him, fending off the foe with his roars. Wrenching roots, charred stumps, and sunken rocks out of the earth, he shies them at the hunters and hounds. Then, felling a tree and swinging it right and left like a club, he makes a charge straight at the ring of beaters and their two remaining guards – Tadeusz and the Count. Fearlessly, the two youths stand their ground, guns leveled at the quarry like a pair of lightning rods thrust into the heart of a thundercloud. In the same instant – oh, the inexperience of youth! – they pull their triggers. Both guns discharge – and miss! The beast rears up. Four hands scramble for the hunting spear planted in the ground. Grappling for the weapon, the two youths look up to see, towering above them, a vast pair of red jaws flashing two tiers of fangs. Even now, a clawed paw comes sweeping down on their heads. Paling with terror, they recoil and bolt for the sparse bush. The bear, in swift pursuit, rears and slashes. Misses again! Once more, he charges, rears, and lunges at the Count's flaxen head. That swarthy paw would have dashed off his scalp like a hat, if not for the Notary and the Assessor who come leaping from either side. Gervase lags a hundred paces behind. With him – bearing no firearm – runs Father Robak. Three guns discharge as if on command. Like a hare beset by hounds the bear vaults into the air, comes crashing headlong down, rolls sideways sheer in front of the Count, and, with all the momentum gathered by his bloody carcass, bowls him clean off his feet. Still roaring, the prostrate beast struggles to rise, but, at that moment, the Chamberlain's bulldogs, the enraged Constable and ferocious *Procureuse*, pounce and hold it down.

The Steward reaches for the horn strapped across his shoulder – a buffalo horn, long and speckled and snaked like a boa's coils. Pressing it to his lips with both hands, he inflates his cheeks like balloons. Blood starts to his eyes. Half-closing his lids, he draws in his belly to the utmost degree and transfers to his lungs all the reserves of air stored therein – and he winds the horn. Like a mighty whirlwind the bugle sends its music irresistibly into the wilds, then repeats it with its echoes. The gunners fall silent, the whippers-in halt in their tracks. All marvel at the strength, the purity and strange harmony of the notes. Once more, the old master regales the ears of the hunt with all the artistry that made him famous in the forests of yesteryear. Instantly, he fills the groves, breathes life into the stands of oak and beech. You fancy it were he that set the chase in motion, that bagged in the music were the hunt itself: a brisk flourish of vibrating notes, the morning reveille; a series of whining moans, the cry of the hounds; now and anon, a harsher tone like thunder – the crack of a hunting piece.

He breaks off, but the horn remains at his lips. You imagine he is still blowing, but it is only the echoes answering. Again, he winds. The horn seems to reshape itself at his lips, expanding and contracting even as it mimics the calls of the wild. Now it stretches like a wolf's neck, howling, now it swells like the bear's throat and roars; anon, it rends the air with a bison's bawl.

He breaks off, but the horn remains at his lips. You imagine he is still blowing, but it is only the echoes answering. The trees pick up the horn-piece and pass it on – oak to oak repeats it, beech to beech!

Again, he blows. Now the horn contains a hundred horns! The full gamut of hunting sounds bursts confusedly upon the ear – the cries of alarm and rage, the gunshots, the hounds, the quarry. Then, the Steward raises the horn, and the triumphant paean smites the clouds.

He breaks off, but the horn remains at his lips. You imagine he is still blowing, but it is only the echoes answering. A sounding horn for every tree in the forest! From bole to bole, the music rebounds; from one choir to another it carries. Ever farther, ever wider it travels, ever softer, ever purer and more sublime it grows, until, reaching the gates of Heaven, it vanishes clean away.

He withdrew both hands, spread wide his arms. The horn fell free and swung loose by its baldric. Like a man inspired, his face flown and radiant with high emotion, the Steward stood staring upward, listening to the last fading notes of the horn. A thunderous ovation rang out. A thousand cheers and good wishes issuing from as many pairs of lips.

Gradually, the noise subsided. The eyes of the hunt turned to the great carcass of the freshly felled bear. Face down he lay, pierced with shot, drenched in blood, forelegs flung wide in the tangled web of grass. He still breathed; blood jetted from his nostrils, and, though his eyes were open, his head lay motionless. Meanwhile, the Chamberlain's bulldogs clung to his throat, *Procureuse* on one side, Constable on the other, gorging himself on the gore that flowed from the severed jugular.

At the Steward's command, they prized open the jaws with iron bars and rolled the carcass with their musket stocks. Three more rousing cheers smote the clouds.

"So," said the Assessor, twirling his gun by the barrel. "So, my shooting iron, it is bully for us. Aye, little iron! A simple fowling gun, but some account she gave of herself! No surprise to her, mind. She's never been known to muff a shot. See? The gift of Prince Sanguszko himself."

He showed off his gun, an exquisitely crafted piece to be sure, albeit on the small side. He was starting to list its virtues when the Notary, wiping the sweat from his brow, broke in:

"I was right on the bear's heels when the Steward calls out, 'Stay where you are!' But how could I stand there? The bear was hightailing it toward the open field. Every second he was forging ahead. Meantime, I was running out of puff and falling behind, no hope of catching up. Then, I look to my right and see him loping through the thinning brush. I put a bead on him, 'Freeze, Bear!' I say to myself, and *basta*! Dead as a doorknob he lies. Noble firearm! A genuine Sagalas! Here, have a look at the inscription, *Sagalas London à Balabanowka*. A famous Polish gunsmith set up shop there. He crafted Polish guns but adorned them in the English style."

"A hundred thousand bears!" snorted the Assessor. "What! *You* killed him? Enough of your ravings."

"Listen, you!" retorted the Notary. "This isn't a police inquiry. It's a hunt, and I take everybody here for a witness."

A fierce contest arose among the hunters, as one side took the Notary's part and the other, the Assessor's. Meanwhile, Gervase stood entirely forgotten. With men still running up from every side, no one took notice of what was unfolding before them.

"Now here at last we have grounds," said the Steward. "For, this is no jackrabbit. A bear – now there's something to fight over! Saber, pistol and ball – take your pleasure! Your quarrel is hard to settle, so, according to our ancient custom, we shall allow you to fight a duel. I recall two neighbors in my day, upstanding men of respectable families. They lived on opposite sides of the Vilnele. One was named Domeiko, the other, Doveiko. Both fired on a sow on the same instant. Who killed her was hard to determine, and what a commotion followed! They swore to shoot at each other across the length of the bearskin. That's nobility for you! All but muzzle to muzzle! I tell you, that duel set the whole neighborhood astir. Songs were sung about it in my day. I was their second. How it happened, I shall tell you from beginning to end."

But before the Steward could begin his tale, Gervase settled the matter. After cautiously circling the bear, he drew out his hunting knife and cut the head in two. Slicing open the lobes at the back of the skull, he found and extracted the ball, wiped it on his frock coat, measured the gauge, and fitted the ball to his flintlock.

"Gentlemen," said he, holding out the lead on the flat of his hand. "Neither one of you fired this ball. It sped from this Horeszko single." He raised his antique piece, all wrapped in cord. "But it was not I that fired it. Oh, no, that took nerve! I shudder to recall it. Terror dimmed my eyes, for both young gents were running straight toward me with the bear hard on their heels, a whisker above the head of the Count – aye, last of the Horeszkos, albeit on the spindle side. *'Jesu Maria!'* I cried out. And the angels sent the Friar to my aid. He has put us all to the blush. Brave priest! As I stood trembling there, my finger frozen on the trigger, he seized the gun from my hand, aimed, and fired. To shoot between two men's heads at the distance of fivescore paces and not to miss. Into the very center of those jaws – aye, that's how to knock out a tooth! Gentlemen, in all my born years, I have seen but one man capable of such marksmanship, a man once famous among us for the many duels he fought, one who could shoot out the heel from under a lady's buskin. That knave of knaves, renowned in memorable times – Jacek *vulgo* Whiskers, whose surname I will not utter! But he has no time for hunting now. I'll warrant the ruffian sits roasting in hell now, right up to his moustaches. Glory to the priest! Two men's lives he saved, perhaps three. Gentlemen, I will not boast, but had the last child of Horeszko blood fallen to those jaws, your Gervase would be breathing no more. Even now would the bear be gnaw-

ing on his brittle bones. Come, Father Friar, let us drink your
health!"

But Robak was nowhere to be found. All they could determine from witnesses was that he had remained on the scene for
a moment after the shooting, and that, upon running up to the
youths and finding them both safe and sound, he had raised his
eyes to heaven, muttered a quick prayer, and made off across the
open field like a hunted hind.

Meanwhile, bracken, dry twigs, and tree stumps were
thrown down in a heap at the Steward's behest. A blaze sprang
up. A grayish pine of smoke wreathed upward, spreading out
like a canopy overhead. In no time, a trestlework of pikestaffs
bestrode the fire, broad-bellied copper kettles hung from the
shafts, and the wagons disgorged their store of flour, bread,
roasts, and joints.

The Judge, opening a cavernous coffer replete with rows
of upright white-capped bottles, picked the largest crystal flask
– the gift of Robak himself - containing Gdansk vodka, the cher-
ished spirits of the Poles. "Long live Gdansk!" he cried, raising
the bottle. "The city was once ours. Soon may she be ours again."
And he poured the silver decoction by turns until the gold leaf
dripped out and sparkled in the sun.

The stew was on the boil. It is hard to express in words
the extraordinary taste, hue, and delectable aroma of our hunter's goulash known as *bigos*. The urban dweller hears but the
sound of the words, the iteration of the rhymes, but never shall
he divine their substance. To savor Lithuania's songs and fare,
one needs good health, rustic living, and to be homeward bound
from a hunt. Even without these seasonings, our *bigos* is no ordinary dish, for it consists in the artful blending of the finest vegetables, cabbage being the chief ingredient – finely cut and cured
and so tasty that, as the saying goes, it finds its own way into
your mouth. Cooked in a boiler, embosoming the best portions of
the choicest meats, the kraut simmers for hours until every drop
of goodness is drawn out, and the steam, hissing from the rim of
the vessel, gives off its exquisite odors.

The stew was ready! Armed with spoons, the hunters
raised three cheers and attacked the kettles with lunges and
prods. The clank of the copper! Clouds of steam! The stew fled
away, evaporating like camphor, leaving only the steam to billow from the jaws of the kettles like volcanic vapors.

At last, having eaten and drunk their fill, the hunters hoisted their bag on a cart, and mounted up. All were in glad, voluble spirits – all, that is, except for the Notary and the Assessor, who were now more incensed than ever. They argued over the merits of their guns, the one vaunting his Sanguszko, the other his Sagalas à *Balabanowka*. Equally disgruntled were Tadeusz and the Count. They burned with shame over muffing their shots and shying from the bear. Lithuania sets an enduring black mark against hunters who allow their quarry to escape the ring. Not easy to blot it out. The Count insisted that he had been the first to reach the spear; that Tadeusz had thwarted his attempt to close with the bear. Tadeusz said he'd meant to help him, he being the stronger of the two and the more adept at wielding the heavy weapon. And so, amid the boisterous noise of their comrades, Tadeusz and the Count continued to trade taunts.

The Steward, jubilant and more talkative than ever, rode between them. Wishing to divert and reconcile them, he resumed his anecdote of Domeiko and Doveiko.

"Mr. Assessor, if I urged you to a duel with the Notary here, do not suppose I am set on seeing spilt blood. God forbid! Diversion was my purpose. I had in mind a species of comedy, to revive a conceit of mine of forty years ago – a truly remarkable one. You, being young, would scarce remember it, but in my day, it caused quite a stir, from here clear to the forests of Polesia!

"Doveiko and Domeiko's strife arose, strangely enough, from the rather awkward similarity of their names. When canvassing for Domeiko during the regional diets, his backers whispered, 'Vote for Doveiko!' A nobleman, not hearing aright, would cast his ballot for Domeiko. When Marshal Rupeiko raised his banquet toast, "Long live Doveiko!' some would chorus, 'Domeiko!' while those in the middle could never quite make it out; the more so, as dinner talk is always less than articulate.

"It got still worse. In Vilna once, a drunken nobleman received two cuts in a brawl with Domeiko. Quite by chance, while being ferried home on the river raft from Vilna, this nobleman ran into Doveiko. So, there they were, riding the same craft downstream. 'Who's that?' he asks a traveling companion. 'Doveiko,' says he. And without further ado, the nobleman whips his rapier out from under his mantle. Slash! Slash! A pair of whiskers drop to the deck. Whose? Why, Domeiko's! By deputy.

"To crown all, a similar muddle took place on the hunt. Standing close to each other, our two namesakes fired simultaneously on a bear. True, the sow dropped dead on the spot, but her belly had already been riddled with a dozen rounds, and, seeing as several others carried guns of the same gauge, well, you try and sort it out!

"'Enough!' they cried. 'Time to settle the matter once and for all. God or Satan joined us, so let us put us asunder. Two suns, one planet – a sun too many.'

"They draw their sabers, take their positions. Worthy knights they were! The harder we tried to reconcile them, the more fiercely they flew at each other. They switch to pistol and ball and resume their places. 'Much too close!' we yell. To spite us all, they vow to shoot with only the thickness of the bearskin separating them. Certain death! Point-blank! And both were first-rate shots!

"'Steward, be our second!' they yell. 'Very well,' say I. 'Tell the sacristan to dig a grave, for an encounter of this sort can have but one outcome. But have it out like noblemen, I say, not butchers. No coming closer! That you are brave lads, I can see, but surely you will not shoot with your muzzles pressed against each other's belly? No, I'll not allow it! I agree to pistols, but you shall observe a distance neither greater than nor less than the full length of the bearskin. As your referee, I shall spread the hide on the field of honor with my own hands and station you myself. You, sir, shall take your ground at one end, at the point of the snout, and you, sir, at the tip of the tail.'

"'Agreed!' they yell. Time? Tomorrow. Place? Usza Tavern. They ride off. Meanwhile, I turn to my Virgil—"

Just then, a "See-ho!" interrupted the Steward. A hare broke cover right under the hunters' mounts. Peregrine and Scut tore off in pursuit. It was not uncommon for a returning hunt to rouse a hare. The Notary and the Assessor had prepared for just such an event. When the hare sprang out, their hounds had been walking free among the horses. Before the rest of the dogs could start from their slips, off they went after it. Their masters would have followed, but the Steward halted them.

"Hold hard!" he cried. "Stand and watch! No one's to move. We can see it all from here. See? He's making for the field."

Indeed, alive to the hunters and dogs behind it, the hare was pelting into the field, ears bolt upright like a young buck's horns. Across the furrows, in a long gray blur, it streaked. You would have sworn its legs were four straight rods. They seemed scarcely to move, barely to graze the ground – even so the swallow skims the pond with his beak. Behind the hare trailed a cloud of dust; behind the cloud coursed the hounds. Seen from afar, hare, dust and hounds seemed to merge into a single body and slither across the field like a snake. The hare was its head, the bluish cloud of dust, its sinuous neck, and the two hounds, its forked tail.

The rival masters watched open-mouthed, scarcely daring to breath. The Notary turned suddenly white as a ghost. The Assessor went ghastly pale. The course was going horribly wrong. The farther the snake slithered, the longer it stretched. Now, it had broken in two, and the neck of dust was melting away. The head stood within yards of the forest, the tail lagged far behind. Next moment, the head vanished into the thicket. A white tassel-like object flashed for an instant behind it, before vanishing too, and the snake's tail sheered away.

Poor hounds! Baffled and bewildered, they cast up and down the fringe of the woods. For a moment, they seemed to confer with each other and trade accusations; then, ears adroop, tails cleaving to their bellies, they turned back. Back across the furrows they limped, too ashamed to raise their eyes; and, loath to rejoin their masters, they halted well away to the side.

The Notary's head sank to his breast. The Assessor cast gloomy glances around. They began to plead their cause: the hounds were unused to going without a leash; the hare had sprung without warning; a plowed field made for a poor course; booties would have been in order with all those rocks and jagged stones about.

The two huntsmen presented a strong case. Their audience might have picked up a number of useful pointers, but no one paid much heed. Some started to whistle, others laughed out loud. The rest, the hunt still fresh on their minds, talked of little else.

The Steward gave the hare barely a glance. Seeing it make its escape, he turned his head as if nothing had happened and closed his tale.

"Now, where was I? Right! I'd secured both men's word they'd shoot across the length of the bearskin. Our nobility were up in arms. 'Certain death!' they cry. 'All but nozzle to nozzle.'

But I only laughed, for I'd learned from my old friend Maro that an animal's hide is no ordinary yardstick. Gentlemen, you all must know the story of Queen Dido, how she arrived on the Libyan coast, and how, after a deal of haggling, she took possession of all the land an ox's hide could compass. Upon that patch of ground arose the great city of Carthage. So, that night I roll the matter over in my mind.

"In the early gray of the morning, Doveiko rides up in a dogcart from one direction, Domeiko, on horseback, from the other. What do they see spanning the river? A shaggy bridge fashioned out of cut-up strips of bear-hide. I place Doveiko at the tip of the tail on one bank and Domeiko opposite him on the other. 'Now pop away to your hearts' content!' I yell. 'But until you come to terms, you stay put right there.'

"Oh, they fumed all right. Our nobility hooted with laughter. The parish priest and I held forth aloud, drawing object lessons from the Gospels and book of statutes. There was no help for it, so the two burst out laughing and make their peace.

"The quarrel eventually led to a life-long friendship. Doveiko wedded Domeiko's sister. Domeiko married his brother-in-law's sister, Mistress Doveiko. They divvied up their estate into two equal parts. And, on the spot where this unlikely incident occurred, they built a tavern under the signboard of 'The Bear Cub.'"

BOOK FIVE: THE QUARREL

Argument: Telimena's hunting plans. The little gardener pre-pares to enter fashionable society and listens to her guardian's precepts. The return of the hunters. Tadeusz experiences a great shock. A second encounter at the Shrine of Musings. A reconciliation mediated by a col-ony of ants. The case of the hunt is argued at table. The Steward's tale of Reytan and the Prince de Nassau interrupted. A shadowy figure with a key. The ensuing brawl. Gervase and the Count hold a council of war.

His hunt crowned with success, the Steward was even now re-turning home from the forest; meanwhile, deep in the solitude of the house, Telimena was only beginning her hunt. True, she was sitting motionless with her arms folded over her bosom, but her thoughts ran upon two beasts of her own. She was seeking ways of bringing to bay and bagging the two at once, Tadeusz and the Count. The Count was a well-situated youth, comely of appear-ance, heir to a noble house. Indeed, he was half smitten with her already. But what of it? His feelings might change. And how true was his love? Would he consider marriage? With a woman several years his senior? And less well to do! Would his kinsmen allow it? What would society say?

Absorbed in these thoughts, Telimena rose from the sofa and stood on the tips of her toes. Yes, she stood taller now. Bar-ing her bust to greater advantage, she leaned over sideways, surveyed herself keenly, then again sought the advice of the mir-ror. A moment later, she dropped her gaze, sighed, and resumed her seat on the sofa.

The Count was a titled gentleman. The rich had fickle tastes. The Count was a blond. Blonds lacked passion! As for Tadeusz, here was a simple heart! – an honest lad, scarcely more than a child and only beginning to discover the delights of love. Suitably watched, he would not readily break off his first roman-tic attachment. Besides, was he not now bound to her by certain favors? Young men might be given to abrupt changes of mind, but unlike their grandfathers, having tenderer consciences, they held fast to their affections. Long does a youth's simple, virginal heart savor the sweets of first love! It takes them and leaves them with equal delight, like the humble refections we share with a friend. Only gray-bearded drunkards with seared livers recoil from the liquor they drink to excess. All this, Telimena understood perfectly well, for she was wise and fully conversant with the ways of the world.

But what would society say? True, they could always seclude themselves from sight by removing to another part of the district and living out of the way. Better still, they could leave the district altogether. Make a little trip to the city, for instance. There, she could acquaint the lad with high society, shape his path, aid him, advise him, instruct his heart, have in him a companion – a brother! – in short, enjoy the world while the years allowed.

Buoyed up by these thoughts, Telimena began to pace jauntily up and down the room. But once again she dropped her gaze. Still, it would be well give thought to the Count! Could she not contrive to interest him in Sophie? The girl might not be well-to-do, but in social standing she was every bit his equal. Was hers not a senatorial family? Was she not a dignitary's daughter? If a marriage between them were to come to pass, Telimena would be assured of a harborage in their home. As Sophie's kin and the party to secure her for the Count, she would be like a mother to them both. And so, after this final consultation with herself, Telimena went to the window and called to her niece who was amusing herself outside.

Bareheaded, still in her morning chemise, Sophie was standing in the garden with a sieve in her upraised hand. Birds flew to her feet from every quarter. Here, like rolling balls of yarn, ran a flock of ruffled hens. There, wings thrusting like oars, purple helms wobbling, cockerels with long spurs came leaping over furrow and shrub. Behind them strode a turkey tom, puffed up and clucking at his giddy helpmate's strident yelps. From the meadow yonder, peafowl, steering themselves by their long tails, glided up like a fleet of river rafts. Here and yon, silver-plumed doves floated down like snowflakes. All converged on the circular grass-plat where Sophie was standing – a raucous, roiling crush of domestic fowl compassed by a narrow white band of doves. The inner circle comprised a motley of stars, streaks, and stripes. Amber beaks here, coral crests there, all rose from that mass of plumage like fish in the sea. A grove of necks thrust up, swaying gently to and fro like water lilies. A galaxy of eyes stared up at Sophie.

High above them in their very midst she stood – all white in her long chemise. Like a fountain playing in a flowerbed she whirled round, scooping up the pearled barley in her pearly white hand, scattering the provender generously over the welter of wings and heads. Fit for lordly tables, this grain! The staple of Lithuania's broths. Sophie pilfered it from the housekeeper's cupboard. To feed her birds, she inflicted material loss on the homestead.

"Sophie!" she heard someone call. That was Auntie's voice! Tossing the rest of the dainties to the birds, then twirling and beating the sieve in time, the playful girl skipped her way like a timbrel dancer through the press of hens, peacocks, and doves. The startled fowl fluttered up in a throng. Sophie seemed to soar the highest. Her feet scarcely grazed the ground. Like Venus in her dove-drawn car she flew, a flush of silver pigeons leading the way.

Bursting in through the bedroom window, she gave out a gleeful shout and dropped breathless into her auntie's lap. Telimena kissed her cheeks and stroked her chin. With joy in her heart, she studied the pretty child's lively features, as, truly, she loved her little ward. Then, resuming her grave expression, she rose to her feet and began pacing the room.

"Really, Sophie dear," said she, holding her finger to her lips, "you forget both your station and your age. Why, just today, you turned fourteen. Time you dropped your turkeys and hens. Fie on you! Are they fitting amusements for a dignitary's daughter? As for those grimy peasant children, you have cosseted them quite long enough. Ah, Sophie! The very sight of you makes me weep. How dreadfully swarthy you are! What a gypsy you have become! You move and gesture like a parish wench. All this, I shall have to address. Indeed, I shall begin this very day. I have decided to bring you out. Yes, you shall accompany me into the drawing room to meet the guests of whom we have a large number today. See that you do not put me to shame."

Sophie clapped her hands and, leaping to her feet, flung her arms around her aunt.

"Oh, Auntie," said she, at once laughing and crying with joy. "It has been ages since I last saw a guest. In all the time I have been here among the turkeys and hens, I have had but one caller, and that was a mourning dove. I find it so dull being cooped up here in this room. Even the Judge says it is bad for my health."

"The Judge!" snorted her aunt. "He never stops pestering
me to bring you out. 'She has come of age,' he keeps on muttering
to me. Of course, never having rubbed elbows with high society,
the old man has no idea what he's talking about. I know better
how long it takes to train a young lady and how best to present
her. Understand, Sophie, that, be a girl ever so pretty or clever,
if she grows up under society's constant gaze, she creates no impression, for people will have grown used to seeing her. But let a
mature and refined demoiselle suddenly appear out of nowhere,
and the whole world flocks curiously around her. People seize on
her every glance and gesture, hang on her every word, repeat
her every thought. When once a young lady comes into fashion,
then willy-nilly everyone is bound to admire her. I expect you
shall give a good account of yourself. You grew up in the capital.
Though you have lived in these parts for two years, you cannot
have completely forgotten Petersburg. So, Sophie, attend to your
toilet. You shall find everything arranged on my dressing table.
Come, do get along! The hunt will be back any minute."

She summoned the chambermaid and the serving girl.
They emptied a water-ewer into a silver basin. Sophie splashed
in the water like a sparrow in the sand. With the maid's help,
she washed her hands, face and neck; meanwhile, Telimena
broached her Petersburg stores and drew out bottles of perfume
and jars of pomade. She sprinkled Sophie with a choice perfume
that filled the room, then applied the gum to her hair. Sophie put
on white openwork stockings and a matching pair of satin shoes
from Warsaw. After lacing the bodice, the maid spread a dust-
wrap over her bosom and set about removing the curl papers.
Since Sophie's hair was short, they braided it into two plaits,
leaving a smooth fringe over the brow and temples. The maid
bound a garland of fresh-culled cornflowers and passed it to Telimena, who pinned it deftly to Sophie's head from right to left. As
in the grainfield, the blue flowers set off the pale-gold tresses to
advantage. Then, the wrap came off and her toilet was complete.
Sophie tossed a white frock over her head, folded a white batiste
handkerchief in her hand, and presented herself for inspection
– the very picture of a white lily. A few more nice adjustments
to her hair and dress, and she was made to march up and down
the room. Telimena followed her niece's movements with a drill
sergeant's eye. She frowned and grew increasingly cross. At last,

brought to despair by Sophie's curtsy, she could contain herself no longer.

"Alas the day, Sophie! See what happens from passing time with gooseherds and ganders. Why, you stride like a boy! Your eye roves from right to left just like a divorcée's. Now drop me a curtsy. Mercy me, how awkward you are!"

"Oh, Auntie!" pleaded poor Sophia. "It isn't my fault. You have kept me locked up, and I have no one to dance with. I tend the poultry and nanny the children out of boredom. But just wait, Auntie. Give me a little time to mingle with people and see how I improve."

"Of the two evils, poultry's decidedly the lesser," stated her aunt. "I should sooner have you consorting with the barn fowl than the riffraff that have graced us with their presence until now. You have only to recall our recent visitors. The parish priest mumbling his orisons or poring over the checkerboard. The barristers puffing at their tobacco pipes. The very pink of gentility; fine manners you would learn from them! Now, at least, you have someone to whom to show yourself, for we have company of consequence visiting. Mark well, my dear, the Count is here, a true gentleman, young and well-bred, a kinsman of the Governor. Be sure to mind your manners with him."

The sound of men and horses fell upon their ears. Why, here was the hunt at the gate! Hooking her arm through Sophie's, Telimena hastened to the drawing room. None of the sportsmen had yet entered. Loath to join the ladies in their shooting jackets, they had retired to their rooms to change. The young people, being the quicker dressers, were the first to appear – the Count and Tadeusz among them. Telimena discharged the duties of hostess. She greeted and seated the guests as they entered, diverted them with small talk and presented her niece to each in turn. Tadeusz, as the girl's near of kin, enjoyed the first honor. Sophie bobbed him a polite curtsy. Tadeusz answered with a low bow. He was about to speak, when, staring into her eyes, he was so seized by a state of panic that he lost his tongue. Dumbstruck, he stood before her, blushing and blanching by turns. What lay on his heart, he had no idea, but he knew he was unhappy, for he recognized Sophie – recognized her by her stature, her fair hair, her voice! This head, this body, he had seen on the fence. Only this morning, this charming voice had roused him for the hunt.

Fortunately, the Steward relieved Tadeusz of his embarrassment. Seeing the lad pale and grow unsteady on his feet, he urged him to retire to his room and seek rest. Tadeusz withdrew to the corner and leaned against the mantelpiece. From there, never saying a word, he cast wild, wide-eyed glances now at the aunt, now at her niece. The strong impression wrought on him by Sophie's glance did not escape Telimena's notice; but she could not know everything, as she was busy diverting the guests. Still, her eyes never left the youth. At last, seizing a favorable moment, she ran to him. Was he not well? she asked. Why so downcast? She pressed her questions, made references to Sophie, and even tried to joke with him. But Tadeusz, leaning on his elbow, silent and immobile, merely frowned and grimaced. This only further confused and astonished Telimena. Instantly, her face and tone of voice hardened. Rising in anger, she let loose a stream of harsh words, taunts, and reproaches. Tadeusz, stung to the quick, started up, frowned, and spat on the floor; then, kicking aside the chair, he stormed wordlessly out of the room, slamming the door behind him. Fortunately, the scene went unnoticed by the rest of the guests.

He fled out of the gate and made straight for the fields. As when the jackfish, feeling the leister's tine lodged in its breast, thrashes about in the water, then plunges deep in an attempt to break loose, yet always drags the dart and cord behind it, so Tadeusz carried within him the hurt that refused to let go. Crossing ditches and leaping fences, he wandered without aim or direction. At last, upon entering the woods, he arrived, by chance or by design, at the knoll, which only yesterday had been the scene of his joy: the place where he had received the little note in earnest of love – the spot already known to us as the Shrine of Musings.

Whom should he spy there alone and lost in her thoughts, but *her* – Telimena! Nothing about her garb and posture recalled the nymph of the previous day. There she was – all in white, seated upon a rock, as if carved from stone herself. Her face lay buried in her hands, and, though you could not hear the sobs, you knew the tears were falling fast.

Tadeusz fought a losing battle with his heart. He felt an anguish of pity and remorse. Long he watched in silence from his point of espial behind a tree. At last, heaving a sigh, he began to reproach himself. "What a fool I am!" he thought. "What right had I to lay my mistake to her account?" Cautiously he peered out, but, at that very instant, Telimena started up from the rock and began to thrash about to the left and the right. Fording the stream at a jump, she threw out her arms, and, with her hair streaming wildly behind her, pelted, pale as a ghost, through the forest. She leapt in the air, fell to her knees, then cast herself to the ground. Unable to rise, she lay writhing on the turf, clearly in the throes of terrible torments. She tore at her breast, her neck, her ankles, her knees. Convinced that an unclean spirit had taken possession of her, Tadeusz ran to her rescue. But this was not the cause of her convulsions.

The nearby birchwood was home to a mighty colony of black ants. These canny, lively little creatures were given to roaming over the grass thereabout. Be it out of need or mere fancy, they were particularly drawn to the Shrine of Musings. From their citadel on the hill to the shores of the stream, they had beaten a path along which to parade their van and file. Alas, Telimena blocked the way! Lured by the luster of her white stockings, the insects swarmed under her dress and set busily to work, tickling and biting. Telimena was forced to flee and shake them off. Finally, seating herself on the sward, she began to pluck them one by one with her fingers.

Tadeusz could scarcely refuse to come to her aid. He brushed off her frock, worked his way down to her feet. At some point, his lips strayed close to her temple; and so, in this friendly attitude, without uttering a word, the two put their morning quarrel behind them. Who knows how long their silent discourse might have lasted if the tolling of the manor bell hadn't roused them?

The summons to dinner! Time for home, the more so, as they could hear the cracking of tree limbs close by. Could there be people out looking for them? It being improper to be seen returning from the forest together, the pair took their separate ways. Telimena followed the path to the right, toward the orchard, Tadeusz, the one to the left, toward the high road. But in so retiring, neither party was spared cause for alarm. Telimena could have sworn she caught a glimpse of Robak's gaunt hooded face in the bushes; and, more than once, Tadeusz spied a tall, white shadow to his left. Who it was, he could not unerringly say, but he had a strong suspicion it was the Count in his long English riding coat.

Dinner was served at the castle. Despite the Judge's pro-
hibition, the obstinate Protase had once again, in the absence of
the company, laid siege to the castle with an *intromissio*, as he
called it, of the tableware. The guests filed into the great hall
and formed a circle around the table. The Chamberlain – it being the privilege of his office and senior years – took the post of
honor. He bowed to the ladies, elders and youth, and approached
the table. This time, the Chamberlain's wife took her station
at his right elbow, as the Franciscan was absent tonight. The
Judge, after some rearrangement of the seats, blessed the table
in the Latin tongue; the men took vodka, then they all sat down
and tucked quietly into the beet-leaf soup – creamed Lithuanian-style.

After the soup came crayfish, chicken, and asparagus,
washed down with Hungarian and Malaga wines. The guests ate
and drank in stony silence. Never did these castle walls, which
had so lavishly fêted so many sons of the nobility and resounded
with so many hearty hurrahs – never, since the day they were
built, did these walls recall such a feast of gloom! But for the
popping of corks and the rattle of plates you would have sworn
the great hall was deserted or that some evil spirit had sealed up
the diners' lips.

The reasons for this silence were many. True, the men
had returned from the hunt in a boisterous frame of mind. But
when their exuberance abated and they began to think over the
hunt, they realized they had not come out of it with any great
glory. Had it required a friar's hood 'popping up like Philip out
of the hemp' to show up the shooters of the district? O shame!
What would they make of this in the Oszmiana and Lida districts, their long-time rivals for supremacy in the hunting-craft?
Such were the thoughts that ran through their minds.

As for the Notary and the Assessor, they had, in addition
to their old animosities, the disgrace of their hounds still fresh
on their minds. An arch hare sped before their eyes. Legs outthrust, it ran, taunting them from the edge of the thicket with
an impudent flick of its scut. Like a lash that tail cut across
their hearts! So they sat, staring down at their plates. And now,
the Assessor had more pressing cause for chagrin – namely, the
sight of his two rivals seated around Telimena.

Telimena sat half-turned away from Tadeusz. She was
confused and hardly dared to look the youth in the eye. She

sought to distract the sullen Count, to draw him into a conversation and restore his humor, for he'd returned from his walk – or ambush, as Tadeusz was inclined to think – in a strangely sour frame of mind. But the Count, listening to her, only raised his brow haughtily, frowned, and stared at her in a manner just short of scorn. Then, shifting away from her in his seat, he turned his attentions to Sophie. Bowing and smiling, he poured her wine, helped her to the viands, and plied her with a thousand gallantries. Now and again, he rolled his eyes and sighed deeply. Despite the clever deception, it was clear that his flirtations had no other object than to spite Telimena. From time to time, he would turn to her with a look of feigned indifference and plant upon her an ominous stare.

Telimena could make no sense of it. In the end, she shrugged her shoulders and put it down to his eccentric ways. And so, not entirely displeased with the addresses the Count was paying to Sophie, she turned to her other partner at table.

Tadeusz sat equally sullen. Eating nothing, scarcely drinking, eyes never straying from his plate, he pretended to listen to the talk around him. Telimena topped up his glass. Her importunity made him angry. Asked about his health, he merely yawned. He no longer took kindly to her precipitate advances – so much had he changed over the course of one evening. The immodestly low cut of her dress scandalized him. But what was his surprise when he lifted his gaze! The shock almost threw him into a panic. His eyesight had grown suddenly keener. No sooner did he glance at Telimena's glowing cheeks than he discovered a terrible secret. Ye gods! She was rouged!

Was the blush of inferior quality? Had Telimena inadvertently smudged it with her hand? Whatever the reason, the rouge lay unevenly spread, revealing patches of coarse-complexioned skin. Possibly, it was Tadeusz who, on drawing too close to her at the Shrine of Musings, had smeared the carmine that overlay the whiting like the fine dust on a butterfly's wing. At all events, Telimena hadn't had time to touch up her face after her hasty return from the forest – and now, there were freckles showing through, especially around the mouth. Suddenly, like a pair of crafty spies, having found one treason out, Tadeusz's eyes began to examine the rest of her charms only to unmask a host of additional little perfidies: two missing teeth, wrinkles along the brow, crow's feet around the eyes, and a thousand more creases concealed under the chin.

Alas, all too keenly did Tadeusz regret observing a thing
of beauty with an overnice regard. The shame of playing the spy
on one's beloved! O fickle taste! O fickle heart! But who is master of his heart? In vain he charged his conscience to square his
deficit of love, to warm his heart anew with the rays of her eyes.
But now her gaze, like the moon's, bright yet throwing no heat,
glanced off the carapace of his soul – a soul grown chill to the
core! And with such regrets and self-reproaches, Tadeusz bent
silently over his plate and gnawed on his lip.

Meanwhile, an evil spirit lured him with a fresh temp-
tation, to eavesdrop on Sophie and the Count. Charmed by the
latter's gallantries, the girl had blushed at first and dropped her
gaze, but the two were soon laughing together. Their talk turned
to a certain encounter in the garden, to a certain sally into the
burdock and flowerbeds. Straining his utmost to listen, Tadeusz
swallowed the bitter words, digesting them in his heart. A terrible feast! As the fork-tongued adder sucks on a poisonous herb
then coils up on the garden path, imperiling the unwary foot,
so Tadeusz, bloated with jealousy's venom, feigned indifference
while bursting with malice.

Let but a few sit sullen at the merriest of gatherings
and their gloom quickly spreads to the rest of the company. The
hunters had long since fallen silent; and now, infected by Tadeusz's spleen, the other end of the table fell silent too. Even the
Chamberlain seemed out of sorts. Seeing his comely, well-dow-
ered daughters in the prime of life – the finest matches in the
district in everyone's estimation! – sitting mute and ignored by
the silent youth, he too showed little zest for talk. The hospita-
ble Judge was also upset; and the Steward, noticing the general
silence, called it a feast of wolves, unfit for Polish folk.

Now the Steward's ears were peculiarly averse to silence.
Garrulous by nature, he was inordinately fond of chatterers.
Small wonder! He'd spent his entire life in the company of the
nobility, attending dinner banquets, hunts, assemblies, and the
regional diets. He was used to the presence of noise around him
even when he himself was silent or prowling the rooms with his
fly swatter or merely dozing in his chair with his eyes shut. By
day, he constantly sought out conversation. At night, he insisted on having someone close by to say the beads with, or to spin
him a yarn. For this reason, he considered the tobacco pipe his

mortal foe, thought up by the German to depolonize the Pole. "A germanized Poland is a Poland bereft of her tongue," went his saying. Having prattled all through his life, the old master now thrived on prattle for his repose. Silence awoke him from his sleep. So does the din of the wheels put the flour miller to sleep. But let the wheels grind to a halt, and he starts to his feet and cries out, *The Word was made flesh.*

Bowing to the Chamberlain, then signaling to the Judge with a light touch of his hand to his lips, the Steward made known his wish to address the guests. Both men replied to his mute gesture with a nod of the head, as if to say, "By all means."

The Steward struck up: "I make bold to prevail on our youth to make merry at the banquet table as we did in olden times – and not to chew in silence! Are we Capuchin monks? The gentleman idling his tongue is like the hunter that lets his shot rust in his gun. That is why I applaud the volubility of our sires. After a hunt, they gathered round the table not only to partake of the victuals, but also to share their thoughts. Whatever lay on their hearts, be it reproach or praise for the hunter, the beater, the hounds, the shots – all was brought out into the open, producing a noise as sweet to the sportsman's ear as a second hunt. I know. I know what ails you. This cloud of somber cares wafts from Friar Robak's hood! You feel ashamed that your shots went abroad. But do not burn with shame. I knew hunters who were better marksmen than you and missed. To hit, to miss, to learn from one's mistakes – that is the life of a hunter! I, too, have shot wide on occasion, though I have hunted with a gun since I was a boy.

"The great sportsman Tuloszczyk was known to miss. Even Reytan, rest his soul, did not always hit the mark. More on him anon. As for letting the bear escape the ring and our two young gentlemen shying away, though they had a spear in the hand, well, no one shall praise or condemn it. To beat a retreat with a loaded gun has always been regarded as the height of cowardice. And shooting blindly, as many do, not closing with the quarry or taking proper aim, that is a shameful thing. But he who aims well, who allows the quarry to approach, and misses, he may fall back without disgrace. Then again, he may resort to the spear, but only as he sees fit, for he is under no obligation. The hunting spear is there strictly for self-defense. So it has always been. So, take my words to heart, dear Tadeusz and my dear Count. Let not your retreat upset you unduly. Henceforth, as often as you recall today's incident, remember this word of caution from your old Steward. Never stand in another's way. And never should a pair of hunters fire at the same time on the same game."

No sooner had the Steward uttered the word *game* than the Assessor fired back with a half-audible *dame*.

"Bravo!" cried the youth.

Murmurs and laughter began to ripple through the hall as the Steward's word of counsel made the round of the guests – some insisting on *game*, others laughingly repeating, *dame*.

"*Fillette!*" said Bolesta under his breath, to which the Assessor, glaring daggers at Telimena, riposted, "*Coquette!*"

The Steward had not meant to poke fun at anyone, nor was he aware of what was being whispered around him. Delighted to have brought mirth to the youth and womenfolk, he now sought to bring cheer to the hunters; and so, recharging his cup, he struck up again.

"I look in vain for our Franciscan. I should like to relate to him a curious incident not unlike the one that occurred during today's hunt. The Warden said he knew of but one man capable of shooting as true and at so great a range as Robak. I knew another! He saved two men with an equally well-aimed shot. I saw it myself, when the Deputy Reytan and the Prince de Nassau came up to Naliboka Forest. They did not begrudge that nobleman his glory. Indeed, they were the first to pledge his health. Past telling the gifts they heaped upon him – in addition to the slain boar's pelt! As one who was there and saw it, I shall tell you of that boar and that shot, since the event was very much like the one that took place this morning; and it happened to the finest marksmen of my day, the Deputy Reytan and the Prince de Nassau—"

But here, having replenished the Steward's cup, the Judge broke in:

"I pledge Father Robak's health! Steward, raise your beaker! If we cannot enrich our quester with a gift, then we shall at least make recompense for the spent powder. We hereby declare that the bear slain in the forest today shall guarantee his abbey's kitchen with two years supply of meat. But the hide, I will not give to our quester. Either I shall take it by force or he must yield it to me as an exercise in humility. Then again, I may purchase it, even if it costs me a dozen sable pelts. At any rate, we will dispose of it as we think meet. The first crown and glory has already been taken by our servant of God. His Excellency the Chamberlain shall now award the hide to him that earned the second prize."

Upon this, the Chamberlain rubbed his brow and frowned. Meanwhile, the hunters began murmuring among themselves. Each laid his own claim to the prize, one for rousing the bear, another for wounding it, another for setting on the hounds, still another for drawing the beast away from the river. The Notary and the Assessor seized the occasion to renew their quarrel. The former began extolling the virtues of his Sanguszko fowling piece, the latter, his Sagalas musket *à Balabanowka*.

"My dear Judge and neighbor," the Chamberlain replied at last, "The first prize rightfully belongs to our servant of God. As to the second prize, that is not easy to decide. All seem to have acquitted themselves with distinction, all showed equal address, skill, and courage. But fate placed two among us in special peril. Two came closest to the bear's claws – the Count and Tadeusz. Both have claim to the hide. But Tadeusz, being the younger and kinsman to our host, shall gladly, I am sure of it, forgo the prize. Therefore, dear Count, the *spolia opima* fall to you. May the bear hide adorn your trophy room. May it remind you of today's sport and serve you as a talisman of hunting success and a goad to future glory."

He fell silent, blithely thinking he'd cheered the Count. He could not have known how painful a thrust he'd dealt him. At the mention of 'trophy room,' the Count instinctively looked up at the stag frontlets and spreading antlers, which, like a grove of bay laurels sown by the fathers to bind the brows of their sons, stood mounted on the walls. He glanced at the pillars, the portraits adorning them, and the ancient Half Goat emblazoning the vault. All these relics harkened to him with voices from the past.

The Count roused himself, recalling where and whose guest he was, a scion of the House of Horeszko, a guest under his own roof feasting with his ancestral foes, the Soplicas; and, now, the jealousy he felt for Tadeusz only further provoked him against the Soplica clan.

"My house is too small," he replied with a bitter smile. "It has no room worthy of so superb a trophy. Better had the bear remain here among these antlered frontlets until the Judge consent to restore it to me along with the castle."

Sensing what was in the wind, the Chamberlain tapped on his gold snuffbox.

"My dear Count and neighbor," said he. "You are to be commended for minding your interests even at the dinner table, unlike so many fashionable young gentlemen of your age who live thoughtlessly from day to day, without foresight. That my court shall bring about an agreeable settlement is my earnest hope and wish. One obstacle remains, the question of the manorial farm. What I propose is an award of land in exchange for the farm on the following terms . . ."

And he launched, as always, into an orderly exposition of his plan. He was halfway through his speech when an unexpected commotion arose at the far end of the table. A number of the guests suddenly pointed at something that had caught their attention. Others looked in the direction indicated, and, now, like ears of grain bowed by a contrary gust of wind, every head stood turned away from the speaker and faced the corner of the hall.

A shadowy figure had emerged from a tiny doorway concealed among the pillars where hung a portrait of the last of the Horeszko Pantlers. It was Gervase – instantly recognizable by his demeanor, his stature, and the silver half-goats embroidered on his faded coat. Straight as a ramrod, mute and grim, he entered without doffing his cap or bobbing his head. A dagger-like key gleamed in his hand. He opened a cabinet door and proceeded to execute a number of manual rotations.

By a pillar at each of two corners of the hall, there stood a musical clock enclosed in a wooden cabinet. Quaint old fellows these! Long at odds with the sun, they often struck the noon hour at dusk. Gervase never undertook to repair the works, but he wouldn't dream of allowing the timepieces to go unwound. Each night, he tormented them punctually with his key; and now was the hour for winding the clocks.

As the Chamberlain held the attention of those who cared to listen, the Warden pulled on the weights. The rusty sprockets began to grate and grind. The Chamberlain shuddered and stopped in mid-phrase.

"I say, good fellow," said he, "attend to that urgent task of yours some other time!"

And he resumed the exposition of his plan. But the arch Warden yanked the other weight with even greater violence, whereupon the bullfinch perched atop the clock began to flap its wings and chirp out the chimes of the hour. The bird was well crafted. Pity it was out of repair. It whizzed and it quavered, and the longer it chirped, the worse it got. The guests gave out a roar of laughter. Once more, the Chamberlain was forced to interrupt his speech.

"Warden," he cried, "or should I say, screech owl? If you value your beak, you will put a stop to that racket."

Undaunted, Gervase leaned his right arm gravely against the clock, placed his left hand on his hip, and, thus buttressed, rejoined:

"My dear little Chamberlain, a great lord is free to jest. A sparrow is smaller than an owl. And yet domiciled in his own nest of shavings, he is braver than the owl that squats under another's roof. A Warden's no screech owl. Who steals into another's garret by night, he is the owl, and I mean to flush him out!"

"Show him the door!" roared the Chamberlain.

"Your lordship!" cried the Warden to the Count. "Do you not see what goes on? Is not your honor slighted enough that you should eat and drink with these Soplicas? Must now I, Gervase Rembaïlo, keeper of the Horeszko keys, be reviled under the roof of my lords? And in your presence?"

At this, Protase called out, "Come to order!" three times. "Clear the hall, I say. I, Brzechalski, bearer of two Christian names, Protase Balthazar, formerly Sergeant-at-Arms, *vulgo* Court Usher, render my examination of the case and call as witnesses every born gentleman present here, while charging the Assessor in attendance to launch a formal inquiry on behalf of the Honorable Judge Soplica concerning an *incursio*, which is to say, unwarrantable intrusion upon another party's premises, *viz.*, the castle, which the Judge holds by right of law; to which I adduce the plain fact that he is dining here tonight—"

"Why, you squawking magpie!" bellowed Gervase. "I'll show you!"

And yanking his iron keys from his belt, he whirled them over his head and shied them with all his might at Protase. Like a stone from a sling hurtled that mass of iron! It would have smashed the Usher's skull into little bits had he not ducked in the nick of time.

The guests started from their seats. For a moment, there was a dead silence. Then the Judge cried out:

"Confine that mischief raiser in the stocks! Ho there, boys!"

The servants ran briskly through the narrow corridor between the wall and bench; but the Count barred their way with a chair.

"Stand back!" he cried, placing his foot on the frail barricade. "Judge, no one shall lay a hand on my servant in my house. Whoever has a complaint against the old man, let him lodge it with me."

The Chamberlain regarded the Count out of the corner of his eye.

"Sir," said he, "I need no help from you to chide this insolent rascal of a squire. Besides, you anticipate the court's decision. You are not the lord here, nor, sir, are you the host. Sit you still as before, and if you honor not my gray hair, then defer at least to the district's highest office."

"What is that to me?" hurled back the Count. "Enough of this prattle. Weary others with your office and favors! I have been fool enough to join in your drinking bouts, which degenerate into coarse brawls. You shall answer for this slight to my honor. Until we meet again, sober of mind! Gervase, pray follow me."

Not in his wildest imaginings did the Chamberlain expect such a reply. He had been filling his goblet, and the Count's insolent outburst hit him like a thunderbolt. There he sat, bottle sloped over his glass, his head canted to one side, ears pricked up, eyes rounded, lips partly open. No sound came out. But he squeezed the glass so hard that it burst with a ping and sent the wine spraying into his eyes. You would have sworn fire poured into his soul with the wine, so flushed was his face, so inflamed, his eye.

He sprang up to speak. The first word, he ground out indistinctly through clenched teeth, until it shot forth from his lips:

"Buffoon! Why, you cub of a count, I'll . . . Thomas, my saber! I'll teach you *mores*. Mountebank! Damn him! So my office and favors weary that delicate little ear, eh? Why, I'll slice off his lobe, earring and all. Outside with you, sir, and draw your steel.

Thomas, my saber!"

The Chamberlain's friends leapt to his aid.

"Hold, sir!" cried the Judge, seizing him by the arm. "This is our affair. I was challenged first. Protase, my saber! I shall teach him to dance to it like a bear to a stick."

But Tadeusz held him back.

"Uncle! Excellency! It is beneath either of you to deal with this dandy. Are there no young men about? Turn him over to me. I shall see he is duly chastised. And you, Hotspur, who call out our elders, we shall see what a grim knight you are. Tomorrow we decide on the place and arms and settle the matter. Now go, while you have breath to draw!"

It was timely advice, for Gervase and the Count were in serious straits. While the upper end of the table hurled forth cries of indignation, the lower end was shying bottles at the Count's head. The terrified women pleaded and wept. "Alas the day!" wailed Telimena and, raising her eyeballs, went off in a dead faint. She slumped over the Count's shoulder, pressing her swan-like bosom against his chest. Mastering his fury, the Count fell to chafing color back into her cheeks.

Meanwhile, Gervase was reeling under the barrage of bottles and stools. Even now, a throng of bare-knuckled servants was bearing down on him from both sides. Fortunately, Sophie saw the charge. Moved to pity, she leapt up and shielded the old man with her outspread arms. The servants stopped in their tracks. Gervase slunk back and vanished from sight. They were still looking for him under the table when he sprang out from the other side, hoisted a bench in his powerful arms and, swinging it round, cleared half the hall. He seized the Count by the arm; and so, with the bench serving as a shield, the two men inched their way backwards to the small doorway. On reaching the threshold, Gervase halted and eyed his foe once more. For a moment, he hesitated, unable to decide if he should beat an orderly retreat or avail himself of his new weapon and seek fresh fortunes of war. He decided upon the latter course. Lifting the bench to use as a battering ram, he swung it back, dropped his head, thrust out his chest, and, raising his foot, made ready to charge – when, catching sight of the Steward, he fell aghast.

All this time, the Chief Steward had been sitting quietly with half-shut eyes as if lost in thought. Only when the Count began to quarrel with the Chamberlain and threaten the Judge did he begin to pay attention. Twice, he took a pinch of snuff and wiped his eyes. He was only distantly related to the Judge, but, having long enjoyed the hospitality of the latter's house, he had grown quite solicitous of his companion's welfare; and so it was with growing interest that he watched the unfolding brawl. Placing his fingers lightly on the table, he cupped a knife in the hollow of his hand, helve running the length of his index finger, blade pointing elbow-ward. Then, raising his arm and drawing it back, he began to twirl the knife about in his fist, as if toying with it, yet always with an eye fixed firmly on the Count.

Now the art of knife throwing, so terrible a part of hand-to-hand combat, had long since fallen into disuse in Lithuania. Only a few old timers were acquainted with it. Gervase would sometimes resort to the art during a brawl in the tavern. But the Steward was an old hand at it. You could tell by the backward stroke of his arm that the blow would be hard; and the direction of his gaze left no doubt as to who the intended target was – none other than the Count, last male representative of the Horeszkos, albeit in the female line. The less observant youths failed to comprehend the old man's gesture, but Gervase paled at the sight. He swung the bench in front of the Count and drew back to the doorway.

"Catch 'em!" roared the throng.

Caught unawares over his kill, a wolf will turn blindly on a pack of hounds that disturbs his feast. He lunges at them, ready to tear them to pieces, when, amid the canine clamor, he hears the faint click of a gun hammer. He recognizes the sound. Glancing around, he spies the hunter at the rear of the pack. Stooped on one knee, the man stares down his barrel at him, finger on the trigger. Instantly, the wolf flattens his ears and scuttles off – tail curling around his belly. Howling in triumph, the pack goes after him, tears at his shaggy flanks. Now and again, the beast turns, confronts them, snaps his jaws. The merest rasp of his white fangs sends them into a whimpering panic. Such was Gervase's grim mien; even so did he check his assailants with his eye and the sight of the bench, until, reaching the doorway, the Count and he vanished deep into the shadowy opening.

"Catch 'em!" roared the throng again.

Their triumph was short-lived. Without warning, the Warden reappeared by the old organ in the gallery. With an appalling crash, he set to ripping out the tin-lead pipes. Great

might have been the havoc he wrought from above, but by this
time the guests were legging it helter-skelter out of the hall.
Loath to be left behind, the terrified servants seized armfuls of
dishes and decamped on the heels of their lords. What remained
of the tableware, they abandoned to the victors.

And who, braving threats and blows, was the last to quit
the scene of battle? Protase Brzechalski! Standing his ground
behind the Judge's chair, the Court Usher continued calmly to
intone his formal *obductio*. Not until he'd fully discharged his
office did he retire from the deserted field – a field now bestrewn
with the dead, the maimed, and the detritus of battle. True,
there were no human casualties, but every bench had its legs
put out; and the banquet table, unlimbed of a leg and bereft of
its cloth, lay slumped over piles of wine-spattered plates like a
slain knight upon bloodied shields. Bodies of capon and turkey
lay scattered all round on the floor, each breast transfixed by a
carving fork.

Within minutes, total calm was restored to the solitary
castle. Night closed in. The remains of the splendid lordly banquet lay spread on the floor like the nocturnal repasts of Forefathers' Eve at which the enchanted spirits of the dead are said
to gather. Thrice from the gable the lych-owls screeched like
warlocks, as if greeting the rising moon. Projected through the
casement, her pale, tremulous image danced like a purgatorial
ghost on the table. Hellish rats leapt up from holes in the cellars
below to gnaw and drink. Ever and anon, a forlorn champagne
bottle popped a toast to the presiding spirits.

On the second floor, in the mirrorless room formerly
known as the hall of mirrors, the Count stood cooling himself
in the air by the door to the gallery that overlooked the terrace
and castle gate. He wore his frock coat with one arm through
the sleeve and the tails and the other sleeve wrapped about his
throat, so that the garment draped his chest like a cloak. Gervase paced the hall with giant strides. Both men were deep in
thought, muttering to themselves:

"Pistols," said the Count. "Then again, broadswords, if
they so wish."

"The castle and the village," said the Warden, "both ours!"

"Uncle, nephew . . . I'll call out the whole tribe!" exclaimed
the Count.

"I say seize the castle, the village, *and* the land!" cried the Warden; and, turning to the Count, he resumed:

"If it is peace you want, seize it all. Why bother with law-suits, old boy? The thing is as clear as day. For four centuries, the Horeszkos have owned this castle. After Targowica, they seized a part of the land and awarded it, as you know, to Soplica. Do not settle for a part! You must take it all as recompense for your legal fees and the pillaging of the castle. Have I not always urged you to forgo the courts? Have I not always urged you to mount up and raid 'em? Aye, that's how we did it! Who seizes the land is the rightful heir. Who wins on the field wins in court. As for settling our older scores with the Soplicas, we have my Jackknife here, wieldier than any court of law. And if Matthias should lend a hand with his Switch, why, the pair of us shall cut the Soplicas into thin strips!"

"Bravo!" replied the Count. "Your plan smacks of the Sarmatian and Gothic. Your idea is more to my liking than all this legal wrangling. Do you know what? We shall mount a raid such as hasn't been seen in Lithuania for years. And a high time we'll have of it! Two years have I bided here, and all the action I've seen are boundary scuffles with the local rustics. But our expedition promises bloodshed. I took part in one such raid during my travels abroad. I was staying with a prince in Sicily, when a band of robbers abducted his son-in-law. They took him into the mountains and brazenly demanded a ransom from his kin. In no time, we raised our men and vassals and mounted an attack. Two of the brigands, I ran through myself. I was the first to storm the camp and free the captive. Ah, dear Gervase, what a splendid triumphal progress we made upon our return – in true knightly-feudal style! The populace hailed us with flowers. The prince's daughter, grateful to her preserver, fell on my neck and wept. When I returned to Palermo, it was in all the papers. Women pointed me out. The incident even became the theme of a romance, entitled, *The Count; or the Mystery of Rocca Birbante Castle* – and it mentioned me by name. Tell me, are there any dungeons in this castle?"

"We have ample wine-vaults," replied the Warden, "but they're empty now. The Soplicas drained them dry."

"My jockeys," said the Count. "We must arm my jockeys and raise our vassals in the hamlets!"

"*Lackeys?* God forbid, sir," broke in Gervase, not hearing right. "Are forays acts of villainy? Whoever heard of mounting a foray with yokels and lackeys? I can see your lordship knows nothing about forays. *Wassails?* – that's different, we could do with a few wild revelers, but you don't raise them in the hamlets. For that, we go to the noble villages – Dobrzyn, Rzezikow, Cietycze, and Rabanki! Nobility since time out of mind. The flower of knighthood – all friendly to Horeszko and sworn foes of Soplica! There shall we raise some three hundred of your noble wassailers. But that's a task for me to discharge. Meantime, you, sir, return to your hall and sleep the sleep of the just. A heavy task awaits us on the morrow. You are fond of sleep, old boy, and the hour is late. Hark! A second cock crows. I shall remain here and guard the castle until daybreak. Come sunrise, I shall be darkening the doorways of Dobrzyn."

The Count quitted the gallery, but before taking leave of the castle, he took a peep through one of the embrasures. He saw the manor house ablaze with lights.

"Blaze away," he said. "By this time tomorrow, we shall have lights in the castle, while you languish in darkness!"

Gervase sat down on the floor, leaned his back against the wall and lowered his heavy brow. The moonlight fell on the polished dome of his skull. You could see him tracing designs on it with his finger. No doubt, he was plotting strategies for future raids. His eyelids grew heavier, his head nodded uncontrollably. Feeling the onset of sleep, he said his night prayers. Somewhere between the paternoster and the ave, a host of strange shadows arose and passed before his eyes. The Warden saw his former masters, the Horeszkos. Some carried sabers, others, maces. Each man flashed a fell eye, curled a moustache, struck his pose with his saber or brandished his mace. Behind them glided a somber-faced wraith with a splash of blood on its breast. Gervase shuddered. He recognized the Pantler. He blessed himself to the four winds; and, the better to drive away these horrid apparitions, he recited the litany of the poor souls.

Once more, his eyelids began to shut tight. A noise rang in his ears. A mounted troop of the nobility, sabers scintillant, thundered before him. An armed foray! The raid on Korelicze, with Rymsza riding headmost. Among them, Gervase saw himself. Full tilt astride his gray he rode, his terrible sword upraised, tunic unbuttoned, skirts flapping in the wind, his confederate's cap sliding over his left ear. Onward he sped, striking down the standing and mounted; and now, he was setting a burning brand to Soplica's barn . . .

And weighed down by these dreams, his head sank to his chest. So drifted off to sleep the last of the Horeszko wardens.

BOOK SIX: THE NOBLE VILLAGE

Argument. First intimations of the armed foray. Protase's errand. Robak and the Judge hold counsel on the common weal. Protase's fruitless errand continued. A digression on hemp. The noble village of Dobrzyn. A description of Matthias Dobrzynski and his household.

A pallid dawn crept out of the raw murk. Upon her skirts hung the morning with no brightness in his eye. Day had long since broken, but you could scarcely tell by the light. A heavy fog overhung the earth like the thatch of a lowly Lithuanian cottage. By the spread intensity of whiteness in the sky to the east, you knew that the sun had risen and from which quarter he would descend to the earth. But, clearly, his march was joyless, and he slumbered along the way.

Taking its cue from the heavens, life on earth was running behindhand. The cattle, driven late to pasture, surprised the hare at their late breakfast. Normally, wild hare return to the woodland at daybreak. Today, in the gloom of the mist, they nibbled at the chickweed or, bunching in pairs, made scrapes in the sand, intent on making the most of their break in the open air. With the arrival of the cattle, they scuttered off into the forest.

Even the forest stood silent. A small bird awoke, but he tuned no note. Shaking the dew from his plumage, he huddled up to the tree; then, tucking his head into his shoulders and shutting his eyes, he sat waiting for the sun. Somewhere by the edge of a pool, a stork clacked his bill. Crows, bedewed with mist, roosted on the hayricks. Throats agape, they plied their raucous prattle: a sound as irksome to the farmer as the prospect of dirty weather.

The field folk had long been astir. The reaper women struck up their wonted song, dull, plaintive, and dreary as a rainy day – the more dismal as the thick fog muffled its strains. The reaphooks clinked; the meadow clinked back. A line of mowers swished through the rowen, whistling their tune. At the end of each stave they halted to whet their blades, beating their mallets in time. Concealed in the mist, they reaped. Only the viewless music of their song, scythes, and sickles told of their presence.

The Bailiff sat on a grain sheaf among the harvesters. Weary of watching their labors, he kept glancing down at the crossroads where extraordinary goings-on had drawn his attention. Since daybreak, the highway and roads had been the scene of unusual traffic. A peasant's creaking cart flew past like a post-chaise. A nobleman's caleche rattled by at a full gallop. Another passed it coming the other way, then another. From the left, an errand-bound rider sped by. A dozen more riders thundered up from the right then headed off in separate directions. What could all this mean? The Bailiff rose to his feet. He'd take a closer look and find out. Long he stood by the roadside, but all he did was shout himself hoarse. No one stopped. He recognized no one in the fog. The riders flitted by like wraiths. Now and again, the thud of iron hoofs and – stranger still – the clank of sabers fell upon his ears. All this both gladdened and frightened the Bailiff. Though Lithuania was still at peace, dull rumors of war had long been circulating – rumors about the French, Dombrowski, and Napoleon. Could these riders and their arms be bodings of war? The Bailiff hurried off to report these occurrences to the Judge, hoping thereby to learn something himself.

After last night's quarrel, the inmates and guests of the manor had risen in sad, dejected spirits. To no avail did the Steward's daughter invite the ladies to read the tarot cards. To no avail did the servants hand out decks to the men for a round of matrimony. No one was in the humor for games or amusement. All brooded quietly in their corners. The men pulled at their pipes. The women plied their knitting needles. Even the houseflies drowsed.

Oppressed by the silence, the Steward threw down his fly swatter and sought out the servants in the kitchen where the shouts of the housekeeper, the threats and buffetings of the cook and the clamor of the kitchen boys better satisfied his craving for noise. Gradually, the steady roll of the roasting spits lulled him into a pleasant state of drowsiness.

Since early morning, the Judge had remained enshrined in his study, drafting a writ of summons. Protase waited patiently under the window on the turf bench fronting the house. At last, the Judge called him into the study and read out his complaint against the Count. He detailed the outrage perpetrated upon his honor and the scurrilous words the Count had used.

Against Gervase, he laid charges of mischief and mayhem. Both men, he cited before the magistrates' court for their haughty boasts and the cost of the legal process. The summons had to be served this very day – in person, by word of mouth, before the sun went down.

Seeing the document, Protase pricked up his ears and stretched forth his hand. His mien was grave; and though he stood there solemnly, his elation was such that he could have leapt for joy. The very thought of forensic action set his blood astir. He recalled the old days when, on the promise of a generous retainer, he would brave bruises to serve a summons. So, after a lifetime of fighting wars, a legless old campaigner languishes in his hospital cot. But let him hear the sound of a bugle or distant drum-beat and, starting up, he cries out with a sleepy yell, "Thrash the Muscovites!" and peg-legs it out of the ward so fast that a youth is hard put to keep up with him.

Protase hastened to get dressed. Neither the nobleman's robe nor the white tunic would do today. Such garb was for solemn sessions of the court. Errands such as this one called for a different get-up altogether: loose riding breeches, a coat with skirts that could be buttoned up or lowered to the knees, and a cap with folding earflaps tied over the head by a string and worn up in good, and down in dirty weather. Thus appareled, he seized a cane and set out on foot. Court ushers before an action, like spies before a battle, are fain to assume various guises and costumes.

It was just as well that Protase had hurried off, as he would have taken brief comfort in serving the writ. Even now, a fresh strategy was being plotted in the manor. Robak suddenly broke in upon the Judge.

"Judge," said he with an anxious look, "this mistress aunt of ours, this giddy-brained flirt, Telimena, spells trouble. When Jacek confided our poor Sophie to her care, it was with the understanding that she was a worthy matron who knew the ways of the world. But all she does is muddy the waters and engage in intrigues. She makes eyes at Tadeusz – I've seen this, having kept a close watch on her. Perhaps she has designs on the Count as well. We must ponder how best to remove her. Her actions may give rise to gossip, bad example and strife among our youngsters, which in turn may hamper your talks."

"Talks!?" cried the Judge with unwonted passion. "I've done with talks. Finished with them, broken them off!"

"What! Where is your reason? Where is your head? What nonsense are you telling me? Not another quarrel?"

"No fault of mine, as you shall see come out in court," said the Judge. "That peacock and fool of a count started it. Aye, and that scoundrel of his, Gervase . . . but that's for the court to decide. It's a pity you didn't dine with us at the castle. You would have witnessed the gross affront he dealt me."

"But whatever made you go to those ruins!" exclaimed Robak. "You know perfectly well I cannot abide the castle. Now I swear no foot of mine shall ever cross its threshold again. Another quarrel! Merciful God! Quick, tell me what happened! The matter will have to be put right. Enough of this silliness! I have more serious worries than reconciling litigious parties. But once again I shall bring you to terms—"

"Terms? What's that supposed to mean?" broke in the Judge, stamping his foot. "Why, you and your terms can go to the devil! The nerve of the monk! Treat him nicely and he thinks he can lead you by the nose. Understand, sir, Soplicas do not take kindly to terms. They sue to win! Many a time, they sat out a lawsuit in their name so as to win it after six generations. I was foolish enough to follow your counsel and file a third appeal with the boundary court. No more talks! No more, I say. No, sir! No, sir! No, sir!" And pacing the room, he pounded the floorboards with his feet. "Besides, after last night's outrages, the Count must either beg my forgiveness or grant me satisfaction!"

"But, dear Judge! What if Jacek hears of this? Why, he'll be driven to despair! Have the Soplicas not caused enough grief at the castle? Dear brother, I've no wish to recall that terrible incident, but you know yourself how the Targowica confederates seized part of the domain from the castle holder and awarded it to the Soplicas; and how Jacek, repenting of his sin, pledged, upon constraint of absolution, to make good those lands. So he took the poor Horeszko heiress Sophie into his care and spared no expense on her upbringing. His abiding aim has been to wed her to his son, Tadeusz, and so unite the disaffected houses, restoring honorably to the heiress what had been plundered from her."

"What has all this to do with me?" said the Judge hotly. "I never knew Jacek or so much as laid eyes on him. I heard almost nothing of his riotous life, as I was still a schoolboy in the Jesuit college then. After that, I served as a page with the Governor. They awarded me the estate, and I took it. Jacek bade me receive Sophie, and I received her, cared for her, and now fret over her future. And now, as if this women's business were not tiresome enough, this Count has to poke his nose in here – and with what claim to the castle? Why, you know yourself, my friend, he has barely a drop of Horeszko blood in his veins. And he's to insult me? And I'm to talk terms with him?"

"Come now, brother," rejoined the Friar, "there are compelling reasons. Do you recall how Jacek wished the lad to go for a soldier, then kept him back in Lithuania? Why? Because he reckoned Tadeusz would better serve our country at home. You must have heard the spreading rumors of which I have been the principal instigator. Well, now's the time to make it all plain! The hour is come! Momentous things, my brother. War's upon us. The war for Poland, my brother. We shall be Poles again. War is certain. When I set out on my secret errand here, the army's advance guard had already reached the Niemen. At this very moment, Bonaparte is mustering the largest array the world has seen or history recorded. The entire Polish Army is marching with the French. Our Poniatowski, our Dombrowski, our white eagle standards. Even now, they are on the move. At the first sign from Napoleon, they will cross the Niemen, and our Fatherland, dear brother, rises out of the ashes!"

The Judge removed his glasses in silence, folded them, staring at the Friar. Tears welled in his eyes; then, heaving a sigh, he flung himself on the Friar's neck.

"My good Robak," he cried. "Can it really be true? My good Robak," he said again. "Can it really be true? All those dashed hopes! Do you not remember? 'Bonaparte's on the march!' they tell us. And we wait for him. 'He's reached the Kingdom!' they say. 'He's beaten the Prussian. He's on his way to us!' Then, what does he do? Sign the Treaty of Tilsit! So, can it really be true? Are you not imagining it?"

"As God is in heaven, it's true."

"Then blest the lips that bring these tidings!" said the Judge, raising his hands. "You shall not regret your errand, Robak. I will begrudge your convent nothing. Two hundred choice muttons, I hand over to the friary. Yesterday, you took a shine to my chestnut mare and praised my bay. This very day, they shall

stand tied to your quester's wagon. Ask your will of me. I shall
refuse nothing. Only please, touching this whole affair with the
Count, say no more. He slighted my honor. I've served him a
writ. It wouldn't do to back out now."

The astonished Friar wrung his hands and stared fixedly
at the Judge.

"So," he said, shrugging his shoulders, "while Napoleon
brings freedom to Lithuania, and the world trembles in its boots,
you still have lawsuits on your mind? After all I have told you,
you are going to sit idly by, when action is called for?"

"Action?" queried the Judge. "What action?"

"Have you not read it in my eyes? Still no promptings
in your heart? Oh, my brother, if you have a drop of Soplica
blood in your veins, consider but this. The French strike from
the front? Well, suppose we stir up a popular insurrection in
the rear. What say you to that? Let Lithuania's heraldic charger
snort again! The Bear of Samogitia roar once more! Oh, were but
a thousand men – nay, five hundred! – to strike at the Muscovite from the rear, a rising would spread through Lithuania like
wildfire. What if we seized Moscow's guns and standards and
went as victors to meet our country's deliverers? We'd march up,
and Bonaparte, seeing our lances, would ask, 'Whose troops are
these?' – 'Insurrectionists, Your Imperial Highness! Lithuania's
militia!' we'd yell back – 'Who leads you?' he'd ask. 'Judge Soplica!' we'd say. Oh, who then would breathe a word of Targowica?
Aye, so long as the Ponary heights stand overlooking Vilna and
Niemen runs his course, the people of Lithuania shall exalt the
bearer of the Soplica name. To her grandsons and great-grand-
sons, Jagiello's city shall point him out, and say, 'There goes Soplica of those noble Soplicas who fathered the Uprising!'"

"Never mind what people will say," replied the Judge. "I
have never cared much for worldly praise. God knows I'm innocent of my brother's sins. I was never one to meddle in politics. I
discharge the duties of my office and till my acre of ground. Still,
as a born gentleman, I should be glad to clear my family's name.
And, as a patriot, I should be equally glad to serve my country
– aye, lay down my life for her! Swordplay has never been my
strong point, though I've dealt a few cuts in my time. Everyone
knows how during Poland's last muster of the diets I challenged
and wounded the two Buzwik brothers, who . . . but let that pass.
So, what say you? Do we take the field? Mustering riflemen will

be no trouble. We have no shortage of powder. Our parish priest keeps a field-piece or two in the rectory. I recall Yankel saying he had lance-heads in store at the inn, and we were welcome to use them in time of need. Whole crate-loads he smuggled in from Konigsberg! We'll fetch 'em and whittle shafts at once. Of swords, we have plenty. Our nobility will mount up. And with my nephew and myself leading the van – well, we shall do our best."

"O noble Polish blood!" cried the Friar, deeply moved, throwing his arms around the Judge's shoulders. "True child of the Soplicas! God charges you with the task of wiping clean your prodigal brother's sins. Always have I held you in high esteem, but, from this moment on, I love you like a brother. We shall make every preparation, aye, but now's not the time to take arms. I shall inform you of the hour and place. This I know: the Tsar has sent emissaries to Napoleon to sue for peace. War has not yet been declared, but Prince Joseph heard from Monsieur Bignon, a member of Napoleon's Imperial Council, that nothing shall come of these talks, and that war is inevitable. And so, the Prince dispatched me here as a scout with instructions that Lithuania should stand ready, upon Napoleon's arrival, to declare her desire to be reunited with her sister the Crown, and so reinstate the old Commonwealth.

"In the meantime, my brother, we must make peace with the Count. I know he is a crank, somewhat fantastical in his views. But he is young and honest – an honorable Pole. We stand in need of such men. Cranks, as I have discovered, can be very useful in revolutionary times. Even fools can be useful so long as they are honest and led by men of prudence. The Count enjoys respect among the nobility. Were he to rise, he would stir up the entire district. Knowing how rich he is, every born gentleman would say, 'It is a sure thing, since even the magnates are taking to arms. Where do I sign up?'"

"Let him come to me first!" rejoined the Judge. "Let him come here. Let him beg my forgiveness. I am his senior in years and hold an office. As to the lawsuit, the court of arbitration—"

The Friar slammed the door behind him.

"Pleasant journey!" called out the Judge.

Robak leapt into his wagon, cracked his whip, stung the horses' haunches with the traces; the wagon jolted forward and vanished into the fog. Ever and anon, a gray cowl could be seen above the mist, like a vulture riding the clouds.

Meanwhile, the Court Usher had already reached the Count's hall. Lured by the smell of bacon fat, a wily fox will hasten toward it, yet, aware of the hunter's ruses, halt every few steps, sit up, raise his brush in the air and fan it to his nostrils, ensuring that the bait has not been tainted. Just so, having swung off the road into the adjacent hayfield, Protase described a circle around the house, twirling his cane, halting from time to time, as if spotting a cow in distress. Thus maneuvering, he fetched up at last in the garden. And there, stooping down, he made a sudden dash forward – a bystander would have sworn he was after a corncrake – cleared the fence, and plunged into the hemp.

Both man and beast find a measure of safety in this odorous patch of vegetation encircling the house. Here, sprung from the cabbage patch, the hare finds surer cover than in the brushwood. Once embowered in that pungent herbage, he has no cause to fear either gaze- or scenthound. Here, the house servant, escaping the lash or the fist, lies low until his master simmers down. So, too, the peasant, fleeing the military draft, sits secure in the hemp, while the government officials vainly comb the neighboring forest. This explains why, during battles, forays and requisition drives, each side takes such pains to occupy the hemp ground, for, oftentimes, it stretches forward to the walls of the house and backward as far as the hop fields, thus providing the rival parties with suitable cover for mounting assaults or beating a retreat.

Protase, brave soul that he was, was not wholly without trepidation. The very scent of the leafage wafted back memories of previous expeditions, when the hemp patch had borne witness to his pains. He recalled the incident with the nobleman from Telsze whom he'd summoned to court. Putting a pistol to his breast, Dzindolet – that was his name – forced him to crawl under the table and bark out a retraction of the summons like a dog. That was one time Protase had to leg it into the hemp. Then there was the incident with the proud and insolent Wolodkowicz. This scourge of the dietines and disrupter of court sessions, having seized the writ from the Usher's hand and torn it to shreds, stationed a pair of cudgel-bearing Haiduks at the door and, poising his naked rapier over Protase's head, snarled, 'Either you eat these scraps or I run you through!' Being the prudent soul that he was, Protase went through the motions of chewing, inched his way to the window and took a header into the hemp.

True, greeting a summons with a sword or a whip was no longer common practice in Lithuania; and, in truth, only rarely had the Court Usher met with such abuse for his pains. But Protase could not have known of this change of custom, for he hadn't served a writ in years. Though he was always keen to go, and constantly pressed the Judge to send him, he was always refused out of regard for his age. Today, the matter being especially urgent, the Judge had accepted his offer to serve the summons.

Protase looked around and listened. Not a sound. He thrust his hands cautiously into the hemp, parted the forest of stalks, and plunged into the vegetation like a diver breasting the deep. He raised his head. Not a sound. He crept up to the windows. Not a peep anywhere. He took a look inside the house. Not a soul in sight. Heart a-flutter, he stepped onto the veranda and pushed the door open. The house stood utterly deserted – a veritable enchanted castle! Seizing the occasion, the Usher whipped out the summons and began to read the contents aloud. A footfall fell upon his ear. His heart leapt to his mouth. He was all set to make a dash into the hemp, when, to his great relief, the familiar figure of Robak appeared in the doorway. Both men stood there greatly surprised.

Clearly, the Count and his household had left – and in a hurry, for the front door stood ajar. Evidently, they had been busy arming themselves. Double-barreled guns and sporting pieces lay strewn over the floor. In the corner were ramrods, gun-cocks, locksmiths' tools, and all the necessaries for repairing firearms, as well as powder and paper for manufacturing cartridges. Could the Count have taken his entire household on a hunt? But why the side arms? Here lay a rusty saber missing its hilt, there, a sword bereft of its knot. Clearly, they had been drawing weapons and even ransacked their store of obsolete arms. After carefully examining the harquebuses and broadswords, Robak went reconnoitering around the farm in the hope that some servant might enlighten him as to the Count's whereabouts. Eventually, he ran into two elderly women in the deserted yard. They informed him that the Count and his men had ridden out, heavily armed, to Dobrzyn.

Now the village of Dobrzyn was famed throughout all of Lithuania for the courage of its noblemen and comeliness of its womenfolk. Once, it had been a thriving, populous place. When King Jan Sobieski mustered the general militia, the ensign of the voivodeship supplied His Majesty with six hundred fully armed knights from Dobrzyn alone. But now, the clan had grown small and poor. In former days, they found an easy living in the courts of magnates, serving in the army, mounting forays, and taking part in the regional diets. Now, they were forced to shift for themselves, toiling like mere peasants – except that, instead of the peasant's caftan, they wore a long white coat with black stripes and, on Sundays, the loose-sleeved nobleman's robe. The same went for the village's gentlewomen. Even the poorest of them differed in dress from their rustic neighbors. Eschewing the peasant woman's homespun vest, they went about in drill or percale. When grazing their cattle, they wore leather rather than bast shoes; and when reaping, and even spinning, they always wore gloves.

The people of Dobrzyn differed from their Lithuanian brethren in their language, stature, and physiognomy. Pure Polish blood ran in their veins. All had jet-black hair, high foreheads, and aquiline noses. The clan originally hailed from Dobrzyn in Mazovia; and, though they had struck roots in Lithuania four centuries earlier, they still preserved their Mazovian manners and speech.

When christening their young, they invariably chose the name of one of the Crown's patron saints, Bartholomew or Matthias. Matthias baptized his son Bartholomew. Bartholomew – Matthias. The women invariably took the names Catherine or Maryna. To avoid any confusion, men and women took various bynames deriving from some personal quirk or attribute. Sometimes, as a token of his fellows' scorn or esteem, a nobleman received more than one byname. The same gentleman might go by one name in Dobrzyn and by another in the neighboring village. Other noble families of the district would take after the Dobrzynskis and resort to bynames – only they called them 'nicknames.' Nowadays, almost every family uses nicknames. Few are aware that the custom originated in Dobrzyn. But there, the usage served a purpose, while, in the rest of the country, it arose out of silly imitation. And so, Matthias Dobrzynski, the family's patriarch, had originally been styled *Cock o' the Steeple*. Later, during the rising of 1794, he became known as *Hipsmiter*. Among his own folk, he went by the appellation of *Little King*, while among the Lithuanian folk he was known as *Matthias of Matthiases*.

As Matthias presided over the people of Dobrzyn, so his cottage, standing between the tavern and the church, dominated the village. You could tell it was inhabited by impoverished gentlefolk, and rarely visited. The entranceway stood gateless, and the gardens were neither fenced nor sown. Birch trees had grown up in the vegetable beds. Yet the cottage, better constructed and larger than the others, had every appearance of being the village capital. The right wing, which housed the parlor, was built of brick. Nearby stood the lumber house, granary, barn, byre, and stable, all clustered together in the manner typical of our minor gentry's habitations. Everything about the little grange had an aspect of extreme decrepitude and decay. The cottage roof shone green, as if sheeted with tin; in fact, it was overgrown with moss and grasses as rank as prairie herbage. The straw roofs of the granaries resembled hanging gardens, which abounded with all manner of plant life – stinging nettle, red crocus, yellow mullein, and the gaudy-plumed pigweed. Birds of every kind nested there. There were dovecotes in the lofts, swallows' nests in the windows. White rabbits frisked by the front door and burrowed in the untrodden turf. In a word, the cottage resembled a rambling rabbit hutch or cage.

Yet the place had known sieges! Reminders of frequent fiercely fought battles abounded everywhere. An old cannonball the size of a child's head lay rusting in the grass by the gate. This relic of the Swedish Wars had substituted for a rock to keep the gate-leaf open. In the yard, on unhallowed ground overgrown with weeds and wormwood, moldered a dozen wooden crosses – grim tokens of a sudden violent death having visited those that lay buried there. To anyone observing the cottage, the lumber house, or the granary with a keener eye, the entire face of the walls had a dappled look, as if a swarm of black insects had alighted there. Lodged deep in each of these dapples was a musket ball – like a drowsy bumblebee in its earthy cell.

Every door had its knobs, studs, and hooks shorn off or gouged by a sword-stroke. Clearly, the temper of Sigismund steel had been tested here, steel so hard that you could smite off the head of a nail with ease or slice through a hook without nicking the blade. Above the door lintel, partially obscured by shelves of cheeses and plastered up with swallows' nests, stood the Dobrzyn bearing.

The house, the stable, and the coach-house stood filled, like ancient armories, with accoutrements of every description. From the roof of the coach-house hung four huge helms, formerly adornments of martial brows, now home to Venus' birds, the doves. Here purring pigeon fed his unfledged squab. Over the manger, in the stable, swung an enormous open hauberk and ring-mail corselet – a makeshift fodder rack from which the stable boy forked clover to the colts below. Several rapiers lay about in the kitchen, their temper spoiled in the hearth by the impious maid who used them as roasting spits. A horsetail, booty plundered from the Turk at Vienna, performed the office of a duster for the grain mill. In a word, Mars had ceded the field to frugal Ceres. Together with Pomona, Flora, and Vortumnus, she presided over Matthias' house, stable, and granary. Alas! These deities must yield sway again. Mars has returned.

In the early gray of the morning, a dispatch bearer rode into Dobrzyn. Like a bailiff recruiting feudal service he went from house to house, rousing the inhabitants. The gentry scrambled from their beds and spilled into the streets. The tavern rang with shouts, the rectory window blazed with candlelight. People ran to and fro. "What is happening?" they asked. The elders held council, the youth saddled their horses, while the women held tightly to their squirming youngsters, who rared to go and fight without the slightest notion of whom they were to fight or why. Alas, stay home they must! A lengthy meeting raged in the crowded rectory. Finally, unable to come to an agreement, they decided to refer the matter to their old patriarch, Matthias.

Matthias had seen threescore summers and twelve. He was a sprightly old master of small stature – a former Bar Confederate. Friend and foe alike knew him by his prodigious saber of damascene steel, which he facetiously styled *The Switch*. With it, he could chop a pike or bayonet like chaff. He quit the Confederates and, siding with the Crown, stood with Tyzenhaus, Lithuania's Under-Treasurer. But when the King took Targowica's part, he deserted the royal cause. These changing allegiances gave rise to the byname *Cock o' the Steeple*, for he seemed to turn his standard to the wind like a weathervane. There was no understanding his turncoat ways. Perhaps he was excessively fond of war. Defeated on one side, he sought his fortunes on the other. Or perhaps he was merely a shrewd observer of the spirit of the times, crossing to whichever side he saw as tending to the advantage of his country. Who knew? One thing was certain. He was never swayed by a desire for personal glory or paltry gain. Nor did he ever side with the Tsarist cause – the very sight of a Muscovite made him foam and froth at the mouth. After the last partition of his country, he kept indoors, out of sight, like a cave-bound bear sucking his paw.

His last action was with Oginski in Vilna, where both men served under Jasinski. There, he and his Switch performed wondrous feats of valor. Legendary was his leap from Praga's ramparts in a single-handed attempt to rescue Pociej, who had been left languishing on the battlefield with twenty-three wounds. All Lithuania gave them up for lost. But though their bodies were riddled through like sieves, the pair made it back to safety. After the war, Pociej, being an upright man, sought to re-ward Dobrzynski handsomely. He offered him a homestead with five buildings for life along with an annuity of a thousand *zlotys* in gold. But Matthias wrote back to him, saying, "Let Pociej be Matthias' debtor, not Matthias Pociej's!" He refused the home-stead, declined the gold, and went home to toil by the sweat of his brow. There, he built beehives, concocted potions for the cat-tle, snared partridge for the county fair, and hunted wild game.

Dobrzyn was home to several wise elders versed in Latin and jurisprudence. Many of these sages lived in far better cir-cumstances than Matthias. Yet, of the entire clan, it was Mat-thias – poor, simple old man that he was – who enjoyed the high-est repute; and not just as the celebrated wielder of the Switch. People respected him as a man of good sense and solid views. Conversant with the history of his nation and the traditions of his family, he was practiced in law, skilled in husbandry, and ex-pert in the hunter's and apothecary's crafts. People even ascribed to him knowledge of extraordinary and preternatural events, though this the parish priest sternly disclaimed. At the very least, he was keenly attuned to atmospheric changes and able to predict the weather better than any farmer's almanac. Small wonder, then, that when it came to matters like deciding when to sow the crops, or dispatch the wherries, or harvest the corn, or yet when to launch a court action and when to seek terms – none of these things was undertaken in Dobrzyn without first seeking

Matthias' advice. Not that he actively sought out such standing; indeed, he would dearly be rid of it. He huffed at his clients. Often, he said nothing at all and pushed them out the door. Seldom did he impart advice, and then not just to anyone. Only when it came to settling the most pressing disputes and disagreements did he offer his opinion when asked, and even then, only in the tersest fashion.

Today everyone counted on Matthias to take the matter in hand. None doubted but that he would place himself at the head of an armed foray. Ever since his youth, he had loved a good brawl. Besides, he was a sworn foe of the Muscovite race.

Matthias was strolling through his deserted yard, humming snatches of *When Early Breaks the Dawn*. He was glad it was clearing. The fog, not lifting in the usual manner and forming clouds, sank steadily earthward. The breeze unfurled her fingers and stroked the mist, smoothing and spreading it over the fields; meanwhile, the sun broke through with a thousand rays, limning the mist with tints of vermilion, silver, and gold. So a pair of weavers craft the gold-fibered belts of Slutsk. A maid sits under the web, threading silk on the loom and smoothing the surface with her hand, while the master lowers down strands of purple, silver, and gold, creating brilliant flower motifs. So did the breeze weave her web of vapors over the earth, while the sun embroidered it.

Matthias warmed himself in the sun. He had said his prayers and was addressing himself to his domestic chores. Gathering up a supply of grain and leaves, he seated himself in front of his cottage and whistled. A host of rabbits started from their burrows. Their long white ears poked up from the grass like instantly sprouting daffodils. Below winked their bright little eyes, beading the velvety sward as with blood-red rubies. Up they sat, all ears and eyes; then, lured by the cabbage leaves, the entire little flock of snowballs made for Matthias. Hopping and skipping, they scampered up to his feet and leapt onto his lap and shoulders. The old master, himself white as a rabbit, loved to have them flock around him. With one hand, he stroked their warm furry bodies, with the other, he scooped millet seed from his hat and scattered it on the grass for the sparrows. A raucous throng alighted from the cottage eaves.

Suddenly, as Matthias sat delighting in their banquet, the rabbits bolted for their holes. With a flutter of wings, the startled birds returned to the eaves. A party of new guests walked smartly into the yard. The delegation from the rectory had arrived to seek Matthias' counsel.

"Praised be the Lord Jesus Christ," they greeted him from a distance with low bows.

"Now and evermore," replied Matthias.

On learning of the party's pressing business, he ushered them into his cottage. They filed inside, seating themselves on the bench. The leading delegate stood up and began to lay the matter before him. Meanwhile, more and more of the nobility arrived. Most of them were Dobrzyn folk, but there were also a good many neighbors from the surrounding noble villages. Some were armed, some not. Some arrived in britzkas, some in dog-carts. Others came mounted, still others, on foot. They drew up their rigs, hitched them to the young birch trees and, burning with curiosity over the progress of the talks, began to swarm through the house. The parlor being now filled, they crowded into the hallway. Others, thrusting their heads through the open window, listened intently.

BOOK SEVEN: THE COUNCIL

Argument. The salutary advice of Bartholomew styled the Prussian. The martial views of Matthias styled the Baptist. The political views of Mr. Buchman. Yankel's conciliatory plea cut short by Jackknife. Gervase's speech demonstrates the power of parliamentary oratory. Old Matthias' protestations. The sudden appearance of armed reinforcements breaks up the deliberations. Harrow! Hang Soplica!

It was the turn of the delegate Bartholomew Dobrzynski, the one that regularly plied the waterways to Konigsberg, to say his piece. His kinsmen jokingly styled him *The Prussian*, because he loathed the Prussians and yet loved to talk about them. He was advanced in years and had seen much of the world in his travels. An avid reader of the newspapers and a canny politician besides, he was able to shed a good deal of light on the subject under discussion.

"So, Matthias, my brother, revered father of us all," he summed up, "their aid is not to be sneezed at. In wartime, I should rely on the French as on four aces in the hand. Valiant folk, the French! Not since Tadeusz Kosciuszko's day has the world seen a military genius of the caliber of the great Emperor Bonaparte.

"I remember when the French crossed the River Warta in the year of grace 1806. I was biding abroad then, engaged in trading ventures in Gdansk. Having many kinsmen in the province of Poznan, I had gone there for a visit. So there was I, shooting small game with Joseph Grabowski – he's colonel of a regiment now, but then he was still living on his estate near Oberau. Greater Poland was at peace, even as Lithuania is now. Then came word of a terrible battle. A courier from Mr. Todwen rushed up to us. 'Jena! Jena!' yelled Grabowski, upon reading the letter. 'They beat the Prussians! We've won.' Down I leapt from my horse, and, falling on my knees, I offered thanks to God.

"We rode into the city, as if we had business there and were none the wiser. What do we see? Every hofrath, landrath, commissar and other like varlet bowing and scraping before us, all pale and trembling like cockroaches soaked in boiling water.

We laugh and rub our hands. Then, all cap-in-hand-like, we ask for news. 'So, what's the word from – Jena?' You should have seen them start! They were astounded we already knew about it. '*Ach, Hairy Got! O vey!*' they cried; and hanging their heads in shame, they ran into their houses, then helter-skelter out again. Oh, it was bedlam, I tell you! Every highway and byway in Greater Poland thronged with fleeing Germans. Like a swarm of ants they crawled along, dragging their conveyances behind them – they call them 'vagens' and 'fornagels' there. Men and women with teapots and tobacco pipes, lugging wooden chests and featherbeds, all decamped as best they could.

"Meanwhile, we quietly take council together. Harrow! To horse! Snarl up Fritz's retreat! Now's the time to thrash the landraths, make schnitzel of the hofraths, grab the *Offiziers* by their queues. General Dombrowski enters Poznan and proclaims the Emperor's command. 'Poles, rise up!' Within a week, our people have beaten the Germans and driven them out. Not a blessed Prussian as far as the eye can see.

"Now suppose we in Lithuania went it with the same verve and panache and gave the Muscovites a similar drubbing? Eh? What say you to that, Matthias? If Moscow decides to have it out with Bonaparte, it will be no ordinary fight. Napoleon's the world's foremost hero. Commands troops past telling. Eh? What say you, Matthias, Little King?"

He had had his say. All eyes turned expectantly on Matthias. But Matthias neither moved his head nor raised his eyes. Instead, he kept slapping his hip with his hand, as if reaching for a sword. Since the partition of his country, he had sworn off wearing a sword. But the very mention of Moscow brought back his old habit of slapping his left side. No doubt he was feeling for his Switch, whence his other byname, Matthias *Hipsmiter*. At last, he raised his head. A deep hush fell over the room. But, once more, Matthias disappointed the general expectation by frowning and dropping his head to his chest.

At long last, he spoke, slowly and emphatically, punctuating each phrase with a nod of this head.

"Silence!" said he. "Whence comes this intelligence? How close are the French? Who leads them? Have they declared war on Moscow? If so, where and why? Who knows their line of march? What is their strength? What foot? What horse? Who will answer these questions? Speak!"

The nobility eyed one another in silence.

"I say we wait for Father Robak," ventured Bartholomew the Prussian. "It was he who brought us the news. Meanwhile, we should send trustworthy spies to the border and quietly arm the whole district. But now we need to proceed with all due caution and not betray our plans to the Muscovite."

"What!? Wait? Prate? Delay?" broke in another Matthias whom they styled *The Baptist* after the prodigious club he wielded and dubbed his *Sprinkling Broom*. He had brought the weapon with him and was standing behind it, his hands resting on the ball, his chin on his hands.

"Wait? Prate? Debate?" he bellowed. "Hem, haw – then scram, is it? I've never been to Prussia. Konigsberg logic may suit the Prussians, but I rely on our own nobleman's sense. This I know: you mean to fight, grab your sprinkler; you mean to croak, call a priest, and that's it! As for me, I aim to live and fight. What use is the Friar? Are we schoolboys? Eh? What's Robak to me? It's us who shall be the maggots gnawing at Moscow. Spies, reconnoitering – shillyshally! You know what that means – that you're gaffers and dodderers! Eh, brothers? The pointer's to sniff and point. The quester's to quest for alms. Mine's to soak and douse. Soak 'em! Douse 'em! – and that's it!"

And saying this, he patted his club, while the entire assembly took up after him, "Soak 'em! Douse 'em!"

Another Bartholomew took the Baptist's part, the one styled *Razor* after his razor-thin rapier, and yet another Matthias, this one called *Watering Can* after the blunderbuss he carried. It had a muzzle so wide that buckshot poured out of it like water from a watering can.

"Long live the Baptist and Sprinkling Broom!" they yelled.
The Prussian tried to speak but could scarcely make himself heard over the din and laughter. "Down with the cowardly Prussians!" they cried. "Let the poltroons among us hide under a friar's habit!"

Once again, old Matthias raised his head. The noise died down. "Do not make fun of Robak," said he. "I know him. A padre, aye, but a crafty one. The little maggot has gnawed tougher nuts than you. I met him only once and was on to his little game the moment I laid eyes on him. He turned his gaze from me. Afraid I'd ask him for his confession! But that is not my business. I could say a lot on that score. Anyhow, he will not come here. No use calling the Friar. If all this news comes from him, then who knows to what purpose? Robak's one devil of a priest. If this is all you know, then why come to me? What do you want?"

"It's war, we want!" they yelled.

"What war?" he asked.

"War on Moscow!" they roared. "A fight! Thrash the Muscovites!"

All this time, Bartholomew the Prussian had been at pains to make himself heard. At last, thanks to his repeated bowing and the stridency of his treble voice, he succeeded in winning their audience.

"I, too, want to fight," he shouted, thumping his chest with his fist. "I may not wield the Baptist's Sprinkler, but I did give a proper christening to four Prussians with a barge pole the day I had a few too many, and they tried to drown me in the Pregel."

"That's the spirit, Bartholomew!" roared the Baptist. "Douse 'em, I say!"

"But for the love of Jesus," Bartholomew went on. "First, we must know whom we are fighting, and why. The world needs to know, else how will the people follow us? Where will they go if even we have no idea when or where to go? Fellow noblemen! Brothers! All this requires serious consideration. Brothers! We need order and organization here. If it's war we want, then let us form a confederacy and think the matter through. Where to raise our banner? Under whose staff to ride? That's the way it's done in Greater Poland. We see the Prussian in full retreat, and what do we do? We hold a secret council, arm the peasants and nobility, and wait for Dombrowski's order. Then harrow! We take to horse and rise up as one man."

"I beg the floor!" spoke up the estate manager from Kleck, a comely young man attired after the German fashion. Though his name was Buchman, he was of Polish stock – born in Poland proper. No one knew if he was of gentle birth, nor did anyone care to ask. All respected him for the fact that he served a great magnate, loved his country, and had a good deal of learning. He had taught himself the science of husbandry from foreign books and ran his estate in an orderly manner. On politics, too, he had formed wise opinions. He wrote a flawless hand and expressed himself with elegance. And so, when he began to speak, everyone stopped to listen.

"I beg the floor," he repeated, twice clearing his throat; and, making a bow, he addressed the conclave in a sonorous voice.

"Our foregoing eloquent speakers have touched on all the salient, essential points. They have raised the discussion to a higher plane. All that remains is to bring into focus the pertinent thoughts and considerations thus far presented. In this way, I propose to reconcile the contrary views. Our discussion, I note, runs along two distinct lines. Since the lines have been drawn, I shall pursue them accordingly. First, why undertake an insurrection, and in what spirit? This first question is of paramount importance. The second touches the matter of revolutionary power. The lines have been aptly drawn. Only, I propose to reverse the order. Begin first with the question of authority. When once we have grasped what that constitutes, we may then proceed to deduce the essence, spirit, and aims of the insurrection. So, let us start with the question of authority.

"When we survey the history of mankind, what do we see? Primitive man, scattered throughout the forests, bands together and unites for the purpose of mutual defense. He considers the problem. That is the primordial deliberation. Next, he agrees to lay aside a part of his liberty for the common good. That is the first law wherefrom, as from a wellspring, all subsequent laws flow. We can see, then, that government is created by a consensus, not by the will of God, as some mistakenly claim. Thus, since government rests on a social contract, the division of power is but its necessary consequence—"

"So, it's contracts, is it?" broke in old Mathias. "But which? Kiev's or Minsk's? There you have it – Babin government! Mr. Buchman, whether it be God or the devil that forced the Tsar upon us, I have no wish to argue, but pray tell us how best to be quit of him."

"Aye, there's the nub of it," bellowed the Baptist. "If I could just mount his throne and anoint him with my Sprinkler here, he'd never be back – not for any shady transaction in Kiev or Minsk or any of Buchman's contracts either. And no archpriest, nor yet the great Arch-Fiend himself, could raise him back to life. Give me sprinkling any day! Mr. Buchman, silver-tongued you may be, but talking is so much hem and haw. Soaking's the thing!"

"That's it! That's it!" squeaked Bartholomew the Razor, rubbing his hands and running from the Baptist to Matthias like a shuttle thrown from one side of the loom to the other. "If you, Matthias of the Switch, and you, Matthias of the Club, were but to come to an agreement, so help me, we'd make mincemeat of the Muscovites. Razor here awaits the Switch's orders!"

"Orders are for parade drills," broke in the Baptist. "Our old Kowno brigade had but one sort of order – short, with knobs on. Strike terror and never flinch! Into the fray and never give ground! Wade in often and lay 'em on thick. Slam-bang!"

"Now you're talking!" squealed Bartholomew the Razor. "There's orders for me. What need have we of treaties? Why waste ink drawing up acts of confederation? Do we need a confederacy? Is that what the fuss is about? Let our Matthias be marshal! The Switch his staff of office!"

"Long live our Cock o' the Steeple!" roared the Baptist.

"Long live the Sprinklers!" roared the nobility.

But now murmurs, vigorously suppressed in the center of the room, could be heard from the far corners. Evidently, the deliberations were resolving into two factions.

"I deplore agreements!" cried Buchman. "That is my philosophy."

"*Veto!*" cried another, "I say 'nay.'"

Others chimed in from the corners. Suddenly, the deep voice of the newly arrived Skoluba broke upon their ears.

"Gentlemen of Dobrzyn, what is all this? Some pretty mischief in the wind? How about us? Shall we be deprived of our rights? When the invitation came to our village – it was the Old Boy, Rembaïlo, that invited us – we understood that great events were at hand, events affecting not just Dobrzyn folk but the whole district, the entire nobility. Robak hinted as much, though he never finished what he had to say, always stammering and expressing himself obscurely. Anyhow, after dispatching runners to all our neighbors, here we are at last. You're not alone, men of Dobrzyn! Ten score men, we've mustered from the other villages. So, let us all confer together. If we need a marshal, then we shall all vote together. One man, one vote! Long live equality!"

"Long live equality!" yelled both Terajewiczes, the four Stypulkowskis, and the three brothers Mickiewicz.

"Agreement shall be the ruin of us," cried Buchman who was standing behind Skoluba.

"Then we will get by without you!" bellowed the Baptist. "Long live our marshal, Matthias of Matthiases! Rally to his staff!"

"Throw in with us!" cried the Dobrzyn gentry.

"*Veto!*" yelled the others.

The conclave split into two factions. Two clusters of heads waved in opposite directions, one shouting, "We say 'nay!'" the other, "We say 'aye!'"

Old Matthias, the one mute voice, the one steady head in the room, sat between them. Across from him stood the Baptist, his arms draped over his club, head swinging this way and that like a gourd balanced on a tall stake. "Douse 'em! Douse 'em!" he roared tirelessly. The Razor was darting nimbly back and forth between the Baptist's and Matthias' benches, while Watering Can paced the room slowly between the Dobrzynskis and the nobility, as if to unite the factions. "Shave 'em!" yelled the Razor. "Soak 'em!" cried Watering Can.

Matthias remained silent, but he was clearly losing his patience. For a full quarter of an hour, the uproar raged on. Suddenly, a flashing shaft shot up over the heads of the raucous assembly. It was a rapier, a fathom in length, a handbreadth wide, double-edged – clearly, a Teutonic blade cast of Nuremberg steel. All gazed at the weapon in silent awe. Though its bearer stood hidden by the throng, they guessed at once who he was.

"That's Jackknife! *Vivat* Jackknife!" they roared. "Long live Jackknife, emblem of Rembaïlo village! Long live Rembaïlo! The Old Boy! Scarpate! Half-Goat!"

Pushing his way through the ruck into the center of the room, Gervase, for it was indeed he, flourished his gleaming Jackknife. Then, lowering the point before Matthias as a sign of greeting, he spoke:

"Jackknife salutes the Switch. Fellow noblemen from Dobrzyn! Far be it for me to impart advice. I shall only tell you why I summoned this muster. What to do and how to go about it, you will have to decide for yourselves. No doubt you are aware of the rumors going about the noble villages. Great events are at hand! Father Robak has talked about it, so you must know what I'm talking about, right?"

"We know!" they roared.

"Right, then!" he went on, eyeing them sharply. "Now a clever head needs but few words to the wise, right?"

"Right!" they answered.

"Right, then," continued the Warden. "When the French emperor moves east and the Russian tsar west, it's war, see? Tsar against emperor, king against king. They'll go at it head to head. That's what monarchs do. Meantime, shall we stand idly by? When the bigwigs go for each other's throats, how say we go for the small fry, each his own man? A brawl from above and below, great against great, small against small. We shall start such a swinging match that this entire piece of roguery will come crashing down. And so, the Commonwealth shall flourish again, and gladness return. Am I not right?"

"Right!" they roared. "He puts it to a nicety."

"You said it, brother!" roared the Baptist. "It's whack, thwack, and that's it!"

"My barber's shop is always open for business!" echoed the Razor.

"But first, dear Baptist and Matthias, you must agree on who's to lead us," said Watering Can politely.

"Agreement's for fools!" broke in Buchman. "Debate never harms matters of the common weal. Be silent, gentlemen! We are listening, and we stand to gain by it. The Warden considers the matter from a fresh point of view."

"Not at all," replied Gervase. "Nothing new in my approach. Great matters are for the great to decide. For such things, we have emperors, kings, senates, and parliaments. They decide such matters in Cracow or Warsaw, old boy, not here in the village of Dobrzyn. Acts of confederation are not writ in chalk on the mantelpiece, or aboard a trading wherry, but on parchment scrolls. Writs are not for us. For that, we have our clerks of the Crown and Lithuania. Mine's to slash with my Jackknife."

"And mine to splash with my Sprinkler!" roared the Baptist.

"And mine to pierce with my *Awl*!" added Bartholomew styled *The Bodkin*, drawing his small rapier.

"I take you all as witnesses," said Gervase, coming to the heart of the matter. "Did Robak not tell us to clean house before inviting Bonaparte in? You all heard him. But did you take his meaning? Who's the scum of our district? Who's the traitor who slew the worthiest Pole among us? Who robbed him and looted his castle and even now would seize what's left from his rightful heir? Who, I say? Need I tell you?"

"Why, Soplica! He's the rascal," cried Watering Can.

"Aye, the tyrant!" squealed the Razor.

"Then douse 'im!" bellowed the Baptist.

"If he's a traitor, to the gallows with him!" shouted Buchman.

"Harrow!" thundered the throng. "Harrow! Hang Soplica!"

But the Prussian rose in the Judge's defense. Raising his arms, he called out to his brethren.

"Gentlemen! Dear oh dear! God help us! What is it now? Warden, have you gone mad? Is this what we're talking about? So, a man has a crazy outlaw brother – what of it? Shall we punish him on account of his brother? Is that the Christian way? I say the Count must have a hand in this. The Judge hard on the nobility? Not true, by thunder! Why, you're the ones suing him in court, while he would make terms with you. He waives his rights and even covers the costs. So he takes the Count to court! What of it? They're both rich. Let lord have it out with lord. What's that to us?

"The Judge, a tyrant?" he went on. "But he was the first to forbid the peasantry to bow before him. A sin, he said it was. Numbers of times have I seen a company of rustics seated with him at table. He pays the village taxes. You won't see that in Kleck, Mr. Buchman, though you run things there after the German fashion. The Judge a traitor? Why, I've known him since we were schoolboys. He was honest then, and so he is now. Poland's dearer to him than anything in the world. He preserves the Polish ways and brooks no Muscovite inroads. Whenever I return from Prussia and need to wash myself of German contamination, I visit Soplica Manor as though it were the very heart of Poland. There, a man can breathe and imbibe his native country!

"Men of Dobrzyn, I am your brother, but, so help me, I shall see no harm done to the Judge. Nothing good will come of it. This is not the way they did it in Greater Poland, my brothers. What spirit we had! What harmony! The very thought of it warms my heart. None there would dream of troubling a council with such trifles."

"It is no trifle to gibbet a knave!" roared back the Warden.

The murmurs grew louder. Then Yankel, seeking audience, leapt on a bench and drew himself up. His waist-length beard hung over their heads like a truss of straw. After removing his fur hat with one hand and righting his skullcap with the other, he thrust his left hand under his belt, and, bowing low with a flourish of his hat, addressed the throng:

"Now, gentlemen of Dobrzyn, I am but a poor Jew. The Judge is neither kith nor kin to me. I respect the Soplicas as my good lords and squires. But I also respect you Matthiases and Bartholomews as my good neighbors and patrons. Here is what I think. If you mean to do harm to the Judge, that is not a good thing. You'll come to blows, and blood will be spilt. Men will die. And what about the assessors? The constable! The dungeons! A horde of soldiery stands billeted in the village – yagers every one! The Assessor bides at the manor. He has only to whistle, and the whole troop will come marching up as ordered. *Then* see what passes! And if you're counting on the French, they still have a fair piece to come.

"I am a Jew," he went on. "War is not in my line, but I have been to Bielica and talked to my fellow Jews on the border. They tell me the French stand massed on the banks of the Lososna, and that, if war breaks out, it won't be before the spring. So, I say wait. Soplica Manor is not a market booth you can take apart and cart off as you please. It will still be there in the spring. As for the Judge, he is not a tenant publican. He won't run away. You will still find him come spring. But now, pray disperse! No more carrying on aloud about what's past, for that is idle talk. Come, my noble sirs, who will do me the honor? My Sarah has just given birth to a little Yankel. Today, I will stand you all to a round of drinks. We shall make loud music together! I shall bring in a couple of fiddlers, a doodle sack and a bass viol. My friend Matthias here is fond of old linden mead and new mazurkas. I have new mazurkas! Aren't my brats *fein* little singers, eh? I taught them myself."

Yankel's words went straight to their hearts, so dearly did they love him. Joyous shouts and applause broke out. A murmur of assent was already spreading outside the confines of the house when Gervase pointed his Jackknife at Yankel. The Jew leapt down and melted into the crowd.

"Begone, Jew!" roared the Warden. "Keep your nose out of this. It doesn't concern you. And you, old boy," said he, turning to the Prussian, "so, now that you run a pair of paltry barges for the Judge, you think you can speak for him? Have you forgotten your father sailed *twenty* Horeszko wherries down to Prussia? That's how he and his family came into their fortune. Nor was he the only one. All of you living in Dobrzyn stand in his debt. You oldsters must remember, and you youngsters have heard that the Pantler was father and benefactor to you all. Whom did he send to Pinsk to run his estate? A Dobrzynski! Who kept his books? Dobrzynskis! Who were his stewards? Whom did he entrust with the charge of his pantry? None but Dobrzynskis! His household abounded with Dobrzynskis. It was he that pressed your cases in court and secured pensions for you from the King. It was your children he boarded in droves in the Piarist schools, paying out of his own pocket for their togs and victuals, and later securing their preferment, also at his own charges. Why did he do this? Because he was your neighbor! And now the Judge's boundaries encroach on your land. What good has *he* ever done you?"

"Not a blessed thing!" piped up Watering Can. "That's because he's nothing but a jumped-up smallholder. When he huffs, it's all pshaw! pshaw! nose in the air. Remember when I invited him to my daughter's wedding? I poured him a drink. He refused it, saying, 'I don't drink like you Dobrzyn people. You, brothers, swill like bitterns.' Now there's a nob for you! A mollycoddle kneaded from Marymont flour. Wouldn't drink with us. So, we pour one down his throat. 'Outrage!' he cried. Just you wait, I'll pour him an outrage."

"The fraud!" roared the Baptist. "I too have reason to soak him one. My son used to have his wits about him. Now he's grown so daft they call him Sack, all on account of Soplica. I ask the boy, 'Why do you keep going to the Manor? God help you if I catch you there!' Then like a shot, he's back at Sophie's again. I catch him lurking in the hemp, grab him by the ear, and anoint him one. He blubbers and bawls like a peasant's babe. 'Father, beat me if you will, but I have to go there,' he sobs. 'What's the matter with you, son?' I ask him. He's in love with Sophie, he tells me. Wants to sneak a glance at her. I feel sorry for the poor lad. So I say to Soplica, 'Judge, let Sophie wed my Sack!' 'She's too young,' says he. 'Wait another three years or so, then she can decide for herself.' The knave! He lied. Even now he's lining up another match for her, or so I hear. Now see if I don't invite myself to the wedding and anoint their nuptial bed with my Sprinkler."

"Is such a knave to lord it over us?" cried the Warden. "Is he to ruin our ancient lords? Men far worthier than he? Meantime, the Horeszko name and its memory perish! Oh, where is there gratitude in this world? Clearly none in Dobrzyn! Brothers, you wish to do battle with the Russian Tsar, yet you fear to make war on Soplica Manor? Afraid of the dungeons, is that it? Do I summon you to brigandage? Perish the thought! Fellow noblemen, I stand on my rights. The Count has won the case. Several awards of court have been made in his favor. All that's left is to have them executed. That's how we did it in the old days! The court issued its decree, the nobility carried it out. Who precisely? Why, you Dobrzynskis! That's how your name became famous throughout all of Lithuania. Aye, it was Dobrzynskis that fought the Muscovites in the foray against Mysz. Voinilovich, the Russian general, led them. Aye, he and that scoundrel friend of his – Mr. Wolk of Lugomowicze! Remember how we took Wolk captive and were about to string him up from the barn rafters for being a tyrant to the peasantry and a servant of the Muscovites? But then our stupid peasants had to take pity on him. One of these days, I'll roast him alive on my Jackknife. I'll not mention the many other great forays we took part in. Always, we came away with booty, general acclaim and glory as befitted noble knights. But why bother recall them? Today the Count, your neighbor, has to waste his time with lawsuits and winning decrees. None will come to the poor waif's aid. The heir to the same Pantler that put bread on your tables now finds himself friendless – except for me, his Warden, and my trusty Jackknife!"

"And *my* Sprinkler!" chimed in the Baptist. "Where you go, dear Gervase, there I go too. So long as I have an arm to swing, I shall make it go splish, splash. Two makes a pair, I'll warrant. You have your sword, Gervase, and I, my Sprinkler. So help me, you'll slash and I'll splash, and, between the two of us, we'll clobber 'em. Splish! Splash! Let the others prattle."

"You'll not exclude Bartholomew, eh, brothers?" squeaked Bartholomew the Razor. "You just provide the suds, and I'll do the shaving."

"I'll ride with you, too," cried Watering Can, "since we can't seem to settle on a marshal. Voting and ballots mean nothing to me. I have another sort of ballot – lead!" And drawing a fistful of shot from his pocket, he rattled it in his hand. "Here's my kind of ballot. Each one of these has the Judge's name on it!"

"We'll join with you!" cried Skoluba.

"Where you go, we go!" yelled the nobility. "Long live Horeszko! Long live Half-Goat! Long live Warden Rembaïlo! Harrow! Hang Soplica!"

Even so did the silver-tongued Gervase twist his audience around his little finger. Each had his own grievance against the Judge, as neighbors often do, some over damages done, others over timber encroachments, still others over a boundary dispute. Anger goaded some, jealousy of the Judge's wealth others, hatred united them all. And raising their sabers and clubs, they pressed up to the Warden.

At last, having sat silent and dour all the while, Matthias rose from his bench. Slowly, he stepped into the middle of the room. Clapping his hands to his hips, he stared his audience straight in the eye, shook his head and began to speak. Each word, he uttered with deliberation, between emphatic pauses.

"You stupid, stupid fools! You fools! Pay the piper, face the music. So, when the restoration of Poland and the Commonwealth is in question, you – fools! – are all at loggerheads. You cannot hold a proper debate – fools! – or bring it to order, or even – stupid fools! – settle on a man to lead you. You fools! But the moment someone raises a private grievance, you – stupid fools! – are all in agreement. Begone from my sight! As sure as my name is Matthias, I'll see you all to hell. And may a hundred million drays of hogsheads and devils go with you!"

They fell silent as if a bolt of lightning had struck them; but just then a tremendous clamor erupted outside the house.

"Long live the Count!"

The Count and ten jockeys – all heavily armed – came riding into Matthias' yard. The Count sat astride a mettled charger and was suited in black. Investing his shoulders like a sheet, with a clasp at the throat, was a great sleeveless walnut-hued cloak of Italian cut. He wore a round hat with a plume and held a sword in his hand. Wheeling about, he saluted the throng with a flourish of his blade.

"Long live the Count!" they yelled. "With him we live and die!"

The nobility ran to the cottage window, then, pressing on the Warden's heels, made for the door. Gervase dashed out. The throng tumbled out behind him, whereupon Matthias, driving the stragglers out of the house, slammed the door and shot home the bolt. Then, opening the window, he stuck out his head and yelled "Stupid fools!" one last time.

Meanwhile, the nobility swarmed around the Count. They repaired to the village tavern. There, recalling the old custom, Gervase called for three noblemen's belts. With these, he had three casks hoisted from the cellar – one of vodka, another of honey mead, the third of ale. He drew the stoppers. Three streams, one silvery white, the second amber red, and the third tawny yellow, gushed out with a hiss, cascading rainbow-like into a hundred resonant goblets and cups.

The nobility milled about the yard, now drinking heartily, now pledging the Count fourscore and ten. "Harrow!" they yelled. "Hang Soplica!"

Yankel stealthily mounted an unsaddled horse and galloped off. The Prussian, ignored by the crowd despite his eloquent protestations, also tried to steal away. "Traitor!" cried the nobility, going after him. Meanwhile, Mickiewicz stood off at a distance. He had not joined in the clamor or offered his counsel. But they guessed from his demeanor that he was up to no good. They drew their swords. Up and at him! He broke away, falling back. Now he was bleeding. His back was pressed to the fence. But his friend Zan and three Czeczots arrived in the nick of time. The nobility drew back. In the skirmish, two men received cuts to their hands, another to the ear. The rest were already mounting their horses.

Marshalling their troops, the Count and Gervase distributed arms and issued orders. At last, the entire host started at a gallop down the long village street.

"Harrow!" they shouted. "Hang Soplica!"

BOOK EIGHT: THE FORAY

Argument. The Steward's astronomy. The Chamberlain's view of comets. A mysterious scene in the Judge's room. Tadeusz's skillful attempts at self-extrication land him in hot water. A new Dido. The foray. The last protest of the Court Usher. The Count takes Soplica Manor. Storm and butchery. Gervase as cellarer. The feast.

There is a moment of brooding calm before the storm when the storm cloud draws up overhead and, louring at the people below, checks the breath of the winds. With flashing eyes, she sweeps the earth in silence, marking out the places where she will shortly be hurling her bolts. Precisely such a calm brooded over the Soplica house. It was as if a foreboding of stupendous events had sealed up the lips of its inmates and borne their spirits into the realm of dreams.

After dinner, the Judge and his guests repaired outdoors to take the evening air. Seating themselves on the turf embankment in front of the house, the entire party gazed up at the heavens in an attitude of gloomy silence. The sky seemed to be sinking, contracting, pressing ever closer to the earth, until, like a pair of lovers draped in the darkness, the two substances began their intimate colloquy, confiding their feelings through stifled sighs, murmurs, whispers, and half-uttered words. All this comprised the peculiar music of the evening.

The screech owl moaning from the gable launched the concert. Bats rustled their delicate wings, flitting about by the house where the lattices and peoples' faces shone. Closer still, drawn in great numbers by the women's white dresses, whirred the bats' tiny sisters, the moths. They picked on Sophie in the worst way, beating about her face and sparkling eyes, which they took for a pair of candles. A great swarm of insects whirled round and round in the air, humming like musical glasses. Among the myriads of sounds, Sophie's ear could make out the midges' harmonies, the gnats' jarring semitones.

Meanwhile, in the field below, the evening concert had barely begun. The musicians had just finished tuning their instruments. The corncrake, first fiddle of the meadow, rasped out

three times. From the slough yonder, the bittern's booming bass
replied. Snipe rose whirling in the air, repeating their drum-like
cadences. At last, like the enchanted tarns of high Caucasia that
drowse by day and croon by night, two meres picked up the concert of the birds and insects and broke forth in a double chorus.
One of these meres had pellucid depths verged with sand; a soft
and solemn moan issued from its deep-blue breast. The other
had a miry bed and mud-choked waters; it answered back with
a cry both sad and passionate. In both reservoirs warbled frogs
without number. Each choir stood tuned to a mighty chord, one
sang *fortissimo*, the other *sotto voce*. One seemed to complain
mournfully, the other heaved sighs. So, like a pair of Aeolian
harps playing by turns, the two bodies of water conversed across
the fields.

The shades of twilight deepened. Only the eyes of prowling wolves flashed like taper-flames among the thickets and
withy beds bordering the brook. Yonder, shepherds' watchfires
could be seen glimmering on the shrinking horizon. At length,
the moon kindled her silver lamp, swung clear of the forest and
lit up both heaven and earth. Side by side, like a happy married
couple, they slept partially covered by the gloom, earth's silvery
bosom wrapped in heaven's chaste embrace. Opposite the moon,
a star winked out, then another, then a thousand, then a million! Prominent among them were Castor and his brother Pollux, whom the ancient Slavs called *Lel* and *Polel*, and whom our
common folk have now re-christened *Lithuania* and *The Crown*.

Farther out shone the two pans of the celestial *Scales*.
Upon those pans, on the morning of Creation – so the old folk
tell – God weighed the earth and all the planets in turn before
setting them in the chasms of space; then, he hung the golden
scales from the heavenly vault as a prototype for the balance
scales of men.

To the northward gleamed the circle of the starry *Sieve*.
Through this sieve, God was said to have sifted the grains of rye
when dropping them down for our forefather Adam, whom he
had banished from the garden of delights for his sin.

Somewhat higher in the heavens stood *David's Chariot*, ready for mounting, its long shaft pointed toward the North
Star. The old Lithuanians knew better. They claimed the people
erred in calling it David's, for it was the Angel's Chariot. Lucifer
rode it eons ago when, daring God to combat, he bore down on

the heavenly gates along the Milky Way, until Michael smote
him, and drove the chariot off the road. There, among the stars,
it lies ruined. No one may repair it – the Archangel Michael has
laid a ban on it.

The old Lithuanians also knew – this reportedly from the
rabbis – that the great *Dragon* of the Zodiac, which wound its
starry coils around the heavens, was not a serpent, as astronomers mistakenly claimed, but a great fish – *Leviathan* by name.
For eons, it inhabited the deeps, but after the Great Flood, it
perished for want of water. The angels then fixed its bones to
the celestial dome as both a curiosity and a remembrance for the
world. Even so the parish priest of Mir adorned the walls of his
church with the excavated ribs and femurs of giants.

With such stories, all culled from books or passed down
by oral tradition, did the old Steward entertain the guests. Although he had feeble vision by night and distinguished nothing
in the skies even with the aid of spectacles, yet he knew the
name and shape of every constellation by heart. With his finger,
he pointed them out, along with the trajectories they described.

This evening, the guests paid him scant attention. No one
took the slightest interest in the Sieve, or the Dragon, or even
the Scales. Today, all eyes and thoughts stood riveted on the new
guest that had recently risen to their ken – a comet of great size
and power. The celestial body had appeared in the west and was
bearing northward. With her bloody eye sideways intent upon
Lucifer's chariot, the comet dragged her great tress like a haul-
net behind her, sweeping a third of the heavens and gathering
up a vast multitude of stars. Meanwhile, her head bore higher to
the northward, bound straight for the Polar Star.

Every night, with a sense of nameless foreboding, the
Lithuanian folk gazed at the heavenly sign, reading dark mean-
ings into it. Nor was it the only sign. Not seldom were ill-omened
birds seen mustering in vast flocks in the bare fields. Balefully,
they cawed and sharpened their bills, as though drawn by the
prospect of carrion flesh. Not seldom were dogs seen scratching the ground, howling in terror, as though death, famine, or
war were in the air. The forest rangers claimed to have seen
the Maid of Plagues stalking the churchyard. Towering over the
tallest trees, she strode, waving a blood-soaked kerchief in her
hand.

The Bailiff drew all manner of inferences from these signs. He had come to report on the day's labors and was now standing by the fence, quietly holding forth with the accountant. But the Chamberlain, who sat on the turf bench, cut short the company's chatter. All knew he was about to speak, for his large snuffbox flashed in the moonlight – it was wrought of pure gold with a diamond inlay; a glass-covered miniature of King Stanislas adorned the lid. Drumming on it with his fingers, the Chamberlain took a pinch, and spoke:

"My dear Steward, all your talk about the stars is but an echo of what you learned at school. But when it comes to portents I should rather listen to our common folk. I also studied the stars – for two years in Vilna. Madame Puzinina, a rich and learned lady, endowed the university with a village of two hundred souls for the purchase of various lenses and telescopes. Our famous Father Poczobut, then rector of the Academy, was a watcher of the skies; eventually, he gave up his chair and telescopes and retired to his quiet cell in the abbey, where he died an exemplary death. I am also acquainted with Sniadecki, a highly learned man, though a layman. Now, as I see it, our astronomers observe planets and comets much as our townsfolk observe horses and conveyances. They are quite able to tell you if someone is driving up to the Royal Castle or departing abroad through the city turnpike. But who rides inside and why, what the ambassador discussed with the King, and whether His Majesty replied with a declaration of peace or war – this they never ask. I recall the time Branicki left for Jassy in his carriage. That vile car had a whole host of Targowica partisans in tow like a comet's tail. The common folk, who took no part in the public deliberations, guessed right away that the tail betokened treachery. I hear they called the comet a besom that would end up sweeping millions away."

"It is true, Your Excellency," replied the Steward with a bow. "I remember well what I heard as a child. Though I was not yet ten, I recall seeing the late lamented Sapieha at our house. He was still a lieutenant in the dragoons then. Later, he became Marshal of the Royal Court and died Grand Chancellor of Lithuania at the ripe old age of a hundred and ten. He served under Hetman Jablonowski's banner when Sobieski raised the siege of Vienna. The Chancellor described the moment King Jan mounted his horse for the great battle. The Papal Nuncio had just blessed him, and the Austrian ambassador, Count Wilczek, was kissing his foot and passing him the stirrup, when the King exclaimed, 'See what passes in the heavens!' Looking up, they saw a comet streaking from east to west along the path taken by Mohammed's host. Later, Father Bartochowski would compose a panegyric titled *Orientis Fulmen* for the triumphal progress through Cracow. He made much of that comet. I have also read about it in a work entitled *The Janina*, which describes the late king's entire campaign. The book includes aquatints of Moham- med's mighty standard and shows just such a comet as we see today."

"Amen to that," said the Judge. "I take your omen to sig- nal the advent of another Jan the Third. Today, we have a new champion in the West. God willing, the comet bears him hither to us."

The Steward nodded gloomily. "Aye," said he. "Sometimes they foretoken wars, sometimes just local quarrels. That this comet should appear over the Manor is not a good sign. Perhaps it por- tends some domestic misfortune. Yesterday, we had contention and disputes enough during the hunt and banquet. The Nota- ry and the Assessor argued all morning, and, in the evening, Tadeusz challenged the Count to a duel – over the bearskin, it appears. If the Judge hadn't interrupted me, I might have rec- onciled the parties at the table, for I meant to tell them about a curious hunting incident not unlike the one that occurred yes- terday. It happened to the finest pair of shooters of my day, the Honorable Deputy Tadeusz Reytan and the Prince de Nassau. And it happened like this.

"The General Starosta of Podolia, Prince Czartoryski, was traveling up from Volhynia to visit his Polish domains or, if I remember rightly, to attend Parliament in Warsaw. On the way, partly for amusement and partly to canvass for votes, he paid calls on the local nobility. He visited the late Tadeusz Rey- tan who became our deputy from Novogrodek. I had the honor of growing up in his house. To honor the Prince's visit, Reytan arranged a reception. The nobility came out in large numbers. They staged a play. The Prince loves the theatre! Kaszyc – the one who lives in Jatra – supplied the fireworks, Tyzenhaus sent down a troupe of dancers, and Oginski and Soltan – the one from Zietela – provided the orchestra. In a word, the entertainment of the house was lavish beyond compare. And, in the forest, they held a splendid hunt. Now it is well known to you gentlemen that almost all the Czartoryskis in living memory, though they trace their origins to the Jagiellos, have never much taken to hunting – not because they are lazy, of course, but because of their foreign tastes. The Prince would sooner glance at a book than a kennel, sooner peer into a lady's bower than a forest thicket.

"Accompanying him was the German Prince de Nassau who, while hunting once with Moorish kings in the Libyan desert, was said to have slain a tiger with spear in close combat. About that feat, the German Prince was given to much boasting. Now, on this occasion, we were hunting wild boar. Reytan brought down a huge sow at great risk to his life, for he'd fired his gun at close range. We were amazed and commended him warmly for his feat of marksmanship. Only de Nassau stood unimpressed. He strutted about, mumbling under his breath that a good aim proved but a bold eye, while cold steel proved a bold arm. And he began holding forth again on his Libyan hunting expedition, his Moorish kings, and the tiger he'd speared. Reytan listened to him sullenly. Always a fiery-tempered fellow, he slapped his saber and cried out, 'Your Highness, who looks boldly, fights boldly! A wild boar's as good as a tiger. A saber's a match for a spear!' There followed a heated exchange. Fortunately, Czartoryski intervened and appeased them in French. What he said, I have no idea, but it was like ashes over live coals, for Reytan had taken the matter to heart. He bided his time, swearing to play a trick on the German. That prank nearly cost him his life. And he played it the very next day. Just how, I shall tell you in a moment."

Here, the Steward paused, raised his right hand and beckoned for the Chamberlain's snuffbox. He took the snuff slowly, as if deliberately to hold his audience in the keenest suspense. At last, he resumed. But, once again, the tale that compelled such rapt attention was broken off. A servant announced a caller on a matter of urgent business. The Judge bade them all a good night. The company dispersed, some to the house, others to the barn. Soplica retired to confer with the caller.

While the rest of the household slept, Tadeusz paced like a watchman outside his uncle's door. He wished to consult with him on an important matter, and it had to be now, before going to bed. He dared not knock, for the Judge had locked the door. Evidently, a private conference was in progress. Tadeusz waited in the hall, listening intently.

He heard sobbing. Taking care not to touch the door-knob, he peered through the keyhole. A strange sight greeted his gaze. The Judge and Robak were on their knees in a tight embrace. Both wept, shedding tender tears. Robak was kissing the Judge's hand, while the Judge, wracked by sobs, clung to the Friar's neck. For a full quarter of an hour, they remained silent. At last, Robak spoke softly:

"My dear brother, God knows how I have kept these se-crets to which I bound myself in the confessional as recompense for my sins. God knows how I have lived, devoting myself entire-ly to him and my country, renouncing pride and earthly glory and intending to die a Franciscan friar, though it meant conceal-ing my name – and not just from the world, but from you and my very own son. But now, the superior general has given me leave *in articulo mortis* to disclose my identity. Who knows if I shall return alive and what will pass in Dobrzyn? Oh, my brother, what a disastrous muddle! The French are still nowhere near. We must wait until next spring. But there's no restraining our nobility. I fear I've been overzealous in stirring them and leading them on. The Warden has snarled everything up! And now, this crazy Count of ours, I hear, has gone to Dobrzyn. I daren't go after him, and this for a very good reason. Old Matthias knows who I am! Were he to give me away, I should have to forfeit my head to Jackknife. Nothing will hold the Warden back. My neck is of no account, but the discovery could doom our plans.

"Still, I must go and see what passes there, even if I should die in the attempt. Without me, the nobility are sure to run amok. Keep well, dear brother, keep well! I must hurry. If I die, you alone shall fetch a sigh for my soul. If war breaks out, the whole secret being known to you, finish what I started. Above all, remember you are a Soplica!"

Here, wiping his tears, the Friar straightened his habit, drew up his hood, and, quietly opening the shutter at the rear of the study, leapt out into the garden. The Judge remained in his chair and wept.

Tadeusz waited a moment before rattling the doorknob. The Judge admitted him. Entering quietly, he made a low bow.

"Dear Uncle," said he. "I have bided here only a few short days and barely had time to enjoy my stay with you. But I must leave this evening, tomorrow at the latest. As you know, we de-

manded satisfaction from the Count. Fighting him is my affair,
and I have issued my challenge. Since dueling is forbidden in
Lithuania, I plan to cross the border to the Duchy of Warsaw.
The Count is a braggart, I know, but he does not lack for courage. I have no doubt he will appear at the appointed place. We
shall have it out. God willing, I shall give him his due, then swim
the Lososna to join the ranks of my fellows who stand waiting on
the other side. I understand my father's last will and testament
provides for my going for a soldier. Who gainsaid it, I do not
know."

"My dear Tadeusz," replied his uncle. "Has someone
scalded you with boiling water, or are you jinking like a hunted
fox that waves his brush one way and goes another? True, we
have called out the Count and cannot back down, but to leave
now! What's got into you? It's customary to dispatch a second
before a duel, and set terms. The Count may yet offer an apology
and retract his insult. Wait a while, there's plenty of time. Or
perhaps there's some other burr under your saddle, eh? Come,
speak plainly. What is it about? I'm your uncle. I may be getting
on in years, but I know what goes on in a young man's heart."
Here, he chucked his nephew's chin. "I've been a father to you.
A little bird tells me you've been intriguing with the ladies. By
jiminy, our youth waste no time in taking to the fairer sex! Come,
Tadeusz, be honest with me. Speak plainly."

"Yes, you are right, dear Uncle," mumbled Tadeusz.
"There are other reasons, and perhaps I am at fault. A mistake!
What can I say? Misfortune! Hard to remedy. No, Uncle, I cannot stay any longer. A youthful error. Please, ask me no more
questions. I must leave the Manor without delay."

"There, I knew it!" exclaimed his uncle. "A lover's quarrel! Last night, I noticed you biting your lip and frowning at a
certain young lady. I saw the sour look on her face too. I know all
about these trifles. When a pair of children fall in love, there's no
end to these little mishaps. Happy one minute, sad and fretful
the next. Now they snap at each other over God knows what,
now they sulk silently in the corner – sometimes they even bolt
for the fields! If such a fit has taken hold of you, be patient. There
is a remedy! I shall undertake to reconcile you shortly. I know all
about these trifles, for I, too, was young once. Now tell me all, for
I've something to say as well. This way, we shall take each other
into mutual confidence."

"Uncle," said Tadeusz, kissing his hand and blushing. "I will tell you the truth. I have grown very fond of the young lady, Sophie, your ward, though I have seen her on but two occasions. They tell me you plan to wed me to the Chamberlain's daughter, a beautiful girl – a rich man's daughter. But I could never marry Mistress Rose, for I am in love with Sophie. The heart must be true to itself, and it were dishonest to marry while loving another. Perhaps time will heal the wound. I am leaving, and for a good while—"

"Tadeusz, my boy," his uncle broke in. "It strikes me as a strange way of loving. Fleeing the object of your love. I'm glad you are frank with me, but do you not see how silly it would be if you left now? What should you say if I myself arranged to wed you to Sophie? Eh? What? Not jumping for joy?"

"Your kindness astonishes me, sir," replied Tadeusz after a moment's pause. "But it is useless. Your favor would come to naught. Alas, a fool's hope! Mistress Telimena will never allow it."

"We shall ask her," said the Judge.

"She will never agree," said Tadeusz brusquely. "No, Uncle, I cannot wait. I must depart soon, at sunrise. Only please give me your blessing. I have everything in readiness. I ride for the Kingdom without delay."

The Judge curled his whiskers and glowered angrily at the boy. "You call this plain speaking?" said he. "Is this how you confide in me, first the duel, and now this romantic attachment and sudden departure of yours? Oh, some intrigue's afoot, I'll warrant. People have talked! I have had you followed. You, sir, are a philanderer and a scapegrace! You, sir, tell lies. And what were you up to the other night, sniffing about the house like a bird dog? Oh, Tadeusz! Could it be that you have seduced Sophie, and now you mean to fly the coop? Well, young cock, you shall not wriggle out of this so easily. Love or no love, you shall marry Sophie – or bear the lash! Tomorrow, you shall stand at the altar. And he talks of feelings and a constant heart! You, sir, are a lying rascal! Faugh! I shall look into this, Tadeusz. I shall make your ears smart yet. I have had trouble enough today till my head fairly aches with it. And now he would deny me a good night's rest. Off to bed with you, sir!"

With that, he flung open the door and summoned the Court Usher to help him disrobe.

Tadeusz left quietly, hanging his head, their bitter exchange heavy on his mind. Never in his life had he been scolded with such asperity. He felt the justice of his uncle's charges, and he crimsoned at his conduct. What now? What if Sophie should find out? Should he ask for her hand? But what would Telimena say? No! He could stay no longer. Engrossed in these thoughts, he had barely taken a few steps when something swept into his path. Looking up, he saw a white wraith-like figure advancing toward him. Tall, meager, and haggard, it glided along, the moonlight hanging tremulously on its garments.

"You ingrate," groaned the wraith, stopping before him. "You sought out my looks and now you shun them. You sought out my words and now you stop up your ears as though my words and glances were poison. Serves me right! Now I see what you are – a man! Not given to coquetry, I was loath to torment you. I sought to make you happy. And this is how you repay me! Conquest of my tender heart has hardened yours. Having won my heart with immoderate speed, you are as quick to scorn it. Oh, it serves me right! But depend upon it, this cruel lesson has taught me to despise myself with a scorn far greater than yours!"

"Telimena," said he. "Please believe me, it's not that I am unfeeling. Nor do I shun you out of scorn. But consider the matter yourself. People have been watching, spying on us. Can we go on like this, in the open? What will people say? Why, it isn't proper. My God, it's a sin!"

"A sin, is it?" said she with a bitter smile. "O babe in the woods! Lambkin! If I, a woman, under the power of love, care not if the whole world should discover me and blacken my name, why should you, a man, who can blithely own to having a dozen lovers? Tell me the truth. You mean to desert me."

And she burst into tears.

"But Telimena!" said the youth. "What would people say on seeing an able-bodied man of my age settling down in the country for a life of love, when so many young men, so many married men are leaving their wives and children and flying abroad to march under our nation's colors? Even if I cared to stay, does it depend on me? My father declared in his will that I should be a soldier in the Polish Army. Now my uncle has repeated the command. I leave tomorrow. I have made my decision and, by God, I'll not go back on it."

"Far be it from me to stand in the way of your fame and happiness," said Telimena. "You are a man. You shall find a lover worthier of your heart – wealthier and fairer-looking. Only before we part, grant me this one solace. Tell me that your affections sprang from the heart, that here was no idle dalliance, no wanton fling, but an instance of true love. Tell me my darling Tadeusz loves me. Let me hear once more, from his own lips, the words, 'I love you.' Let me sear them deep into my soul, engrave them in my mind, so that, knowing how you loved me once, I may the more easily forgive you."

Again she burst into sobs.

Seeing her weep and entreat him so tenderly for a trifle, Tadeusz felt an anguish of pity. Honest compassion welled up within him. Had he then searched the recesses of his heart, he would have been at pains to tell if he loved her or not.

"Telimena!" said he with feeling. "Heaven strike me if it be untrue that I was fond of – yes, even loved – you. Brief as were our moments together, they passed so sweetly and tenderly that they shall long remain in my heart. So help me God, I shall never forget you."

Telimena leapt up and flung her arms around his neck.

"There! I knew it," said she. "You do love me. So, I live again! Today, I was on the point of taking my life. But now that you love me, my darling, can you really think of leaving me? My heart and all that I own are yours. I shall follow you wherever you go. With you, every nook in this earth shall be dear to me. Depend on it, our love shall turn the barrenest of wastes into a garden of delights."

"What!" said Tadeusz, tearing himself free from her embrace. "Have you taken leave of your senses? Where? What for? Follow me!? A simple soldier? You, a camp follower!"

"Then we shall be married," said she.

"No, never!" cried Tadeusz. "I've no intention of marrying at this time. Nor will I be anyone's lover. Trifles! Enough of this! I beg you, my sweet, come to your senses. Compose yourself. I am grateful to you, but marriage is out of the question. Let us love each other, but at a distance. I cannot stay any longer. No, no, I must away. Keep well, my Telimena. I leave tomorrow."

With that, he put on his hat and turned to leave. But Telimena's medusan look froze him in his tracks. Against his will, he remained, staring in terror at the pale figure standing motionless, devoid of life and breath before him. Stretching forth her arm, she pointed a finger, sword-wise, straight at his eyes.

"Hah!" she exclaimed. "Just what I wanted to hear. Worm tongue! Lizard's heart! That by reason of you I should scorn the addresses of the Count, the Notary, and the Assessor; that you should seduce, then cast me away like an orphan – that is of no account. You are a man, and I know your knavery. That you, like others of your sex, should break faith with me is no surprise, but I had no idea you were capable of such base lying. I listened in at your uncle's door! So, it's the child, Sophie, is it? Fond of her, eh? Treacherous designs! No sooner do you beguile one hapless soul than, under her very nose, you seek out a fresh victim. Fly, if you wish, but my curse shall hound your footsteps. Remain, and the whole world shall know of your perfidy. No more shall your arts deceive others as they gulled me. Out of my sight! I scorn you, sir! You are a liar, a base scoundrel!"

Tadeusz shuddered under the force of her invective. These were mortal insults to a nobleman's ear! No Soplica had ever been so rebuked. He turned deathly pale, stamped his foot, and bit his lip. "Stupid fool!" he muttered.

He stalked off. But the word 'scoundrel' kept resonating in his heart; he cringed in anguish. Deep down, he knew he deserved the rebuke. He knew he had treated Telimena with great unfairness. Her rebuke was just, his conscience told him. And yet her reproaches made him despise her all the more! Oh, Sophie! But he dared not think of her for shame. So, his uncle had meant to wed them all along! Dear sweet Sophie! She might have been his bride. But Satan had so ensnared him in web upon web of sin and lies, and now, with a sneer, left him rebuked and despised by all. A few brief days and his prospects lay in ashes. And he felt the full justice of his requital. Suddenly, the thought of the duel flashed like an anchor of repose in the turmoil of his brain.

"Kill the Count! The scoundrel!" he cried out in anger. "Avenge myself or die!" But what exactly for, he did not know. The rage subsided as quickly as it arose. Once more was he seized by an anguish of sorrow. What if there was an understanding between the Count and Sophie? Perhaps the Count really was in love with Sophie! Perhaps Sophie requited his love and would take him for her husband! What right had he to seek to sunder their union? Who was he, hapless one, to ruin the felicity of others?

He fell into a desperate funk; saw no way out for himself except in immediate flight. Where to? His grave, no doubt! And with his fist pressed to his heavy brow, he made for the two meres at the bottom of the field. Stopping by the miry pond, he plunged his gaze into the greenish depths and drew the muddy scent lustily into his lungs. Like every wild extravagance, self-violence has its fanciful aspect. In the mad turmoil of his thoughts, Tadeusz felt an inexpressible desire to drown himself in the turbid waters.

But Telimena, guessing the youth's despair from his wild aspect and seeing him make for the meres, took fright on his account. Though still burning with righteous anger, she was at heart a caring soul. True, it pained her that Tadeusz had presumed to love another, and for this she had had a mind to punish him; but never would she wish him dead! With arms outstretched, she ran after him, crying, "Stop! No matter! Love, wed, leave as you please, but for God's sake, stop!" But he had forged on ahead at a run and was even now standing on the marges of the mere.

Now by a strange quirk of fate, the Count was at this moment riding along this very bank at the head of his troop of jockeys. Entranced by the serenity of the night and the marvelous music of the aquatic orchestra – those very same choirs that sang like Aeolian harps; no creatures sing as sweetly as our Polish frogs! – he drew rein. Forgetting all about the raid, he turned his ear to the pond and listened intently. His gaze swept the fields, the immensity of the sky – clearly, he was composing a nocturnal landscape in his mind.

It was indeed a picturesque spot. The two meres leaned inward upon each other like a pair of lovers. The waters of the pond to the right were smooth and clear like a maiden's cheek. The pond on the left had a duskier surface, like the cheeks of a youth sprouting a manly down. The first pond was verged with golden sand as with locks of shining hair. The brow of the other bristled with osiers and tufts of willows. Both meres lay draped in herbage.

From each of these reservoirs there flowed a small rill. Like two arms they met and joined as one. Farther down, the brooklet tumbled into a gloomy ravine and fled away – away, but not out of sight, for the stream bore the moon-luster along. The

water cascaded in sheets. Upon each lucent layer there sparkled
a bouquet of moonbeams. Inside the ravine, the light broke into
shivers, which the stream then snatched up and bore away even
as fresh bundles of moonbeams came showering down. You fancied the Naiad of Switez were seated there, decanting a spring
from a bottomless ewer, while dipping into her apron pocket and
bestrewing the water's surface with enchanted gold.

Once through the ravine, the brooklet flowed out upon a
level plain. There, slowing to a leisurely meander, it fell silent.
Yet still you could see it move, for the moonbeams continued to
glint along the shimmering stream. So stirs Samogitia's lovely snake, the one the Lithuanian folk call *givoytos*. Though he
seems to slumber in the heather, yet he is constantly moving, for
his enameled skin, ever changeful, turns now gold, now silver,
until it vanishes from sight among the mosses and fern. So the
meandering brook lapsed away among the alder-trees, whose
feathery forms loomed on the far horizon like phantom spirits
half seen, half wreathed in mist.

A watermill stood hidden in the ravine between the two
meres. As when, eavesdropping on a pair of lovers, a grumbling
old guardian shakes his head and, swaying, waving his arms,
belabors his charges with stern admonitions, so the mill suddenly shook its moss-crusted brow and set its bladed fist in whirling
motion. No sooner did the mill come to life and grind its mandi-
bles, than it drowned out the love talk of the meres and woke the
Count from his reverie.

Astonished to see Tadeusz standing so close to his armed
party, the Count cried out, "To arms! Seize him!" The jockeys
leapt from their horses, and even before Tadeusz had time to re-
act, they had taken him captive. Then, galloping on to the man-
or, the party quickly overran the courtyard. The house awoke.
The dogs made noise. Watchmen cried alarm. The Judge ran
out, half-dressed. At first, he took the armed troop for a band of
brigands; but then he recognized the Count

"What is the meaning of this?" he cried.

The Count flashed his sword over his head, but, seeing
the Judge unarmed, he held back.

"Soplica!" he said. "Ancestral foe of my clan! This day,
I redress your wrongs, both fresh and ancient. This day, ere I
avenge the insult to my honor, shall you render me an account
for the seizure of my domain."

"In the name of the Father and the Son!" cried the Judge, crossing himself. "Faugh, are you a brigand, sir? Heavens! Does this befit a man of your birth, your high degree, your breeding? I shall brook no harm done here."

Meanwhile, the manor servants, bearing cudgels and muskets, ran out to join their master. The Steward, eyes fixed on the Count, knife thrust up his sleeve, came hastening behind them. They would have set to on the spot, if the Judge hadn't stopped them. Plainly, resistance was futile. A new foe was even now approaching. A light flashed among the alders, followed immediately by the discharge of a harquebus. Even now, a troop of horsemen came thundering over the bridge.

"Harrow! Hang Soplica!" roared a thousand voices. The Judge recognized Gervase's battle cry and shuddered.

"This is nothing yet," the Count assured him. "Soon, there will be more of us. Judge, lay down your arms. These are my allies."

Just then, the Assessor ran up. "I arrest you in the name of His Imperial Highness!" he cried. "Surrender your sword, sir, or I shall call out the army. You know the penalty for mounting a raid at night. Ukase twelve hundred states—"

The Count struck him in the face with the flat of his blade. The Assessor fell without a sound and crawled into the nettles. All thought him dead or wounded.

"So, there *is* banditry afoot!" cried the Judge.

A collective groan went up, overtopped by Sophie's shriek. Flinging her arms around the Judge, she squealed like a child undergoing a ritual bloodletting. Meanwhile, Telimena leapt in among the horses; and, with joined hands stretched toward the Count, her head thrown back, her hair spread wildly across her shoulders, she cried out in terror:

"Upon your honor, by all that is holy, we entreat you upon our knees. Dare you refuse us, my lord Count? Harsh man! You must slay us women first."

And she went off in a dead faint.

Surprised and greatly unnerved by this scene, the Count leapt to her aid.

"Mistresses Sophie and Telimena!" he cried. "Never shall I imbrue this sword in the blood of defenseless souls. People of Soplica Manor! You are my prisoners. So did I once in Italy, at the crag the Sicilians call Birbante Rocca, when I took a robber's camp. The armed men, I slew. Those relieved of their weapons, I seized and had bound. They walked behind my horsemen – a splendid train enhancing my triumphal march! Later, we hanged them at Etna's foot."

It was a stroke of singular good luck for the Soplicas that the Count had swifter horses than the nobility. In his zeal to be the first to engage the enemy, he had outstripped the main body of horsemen by at least a mile. Well-disciplined and orderly, his jockeys comprised a regular army of sorts, unlike the rest of the nobility, who, as is often the case with insurgents, were unruly and all too quick at hanging.

Now that his ardor and rage had cooled, the Count considered how he might end the raid without bloodshed. He ordered his men to confine the Soplica family in the manor house and station guards at the doors. With a "Harrow! Hang Soplica!" the nobility rushed on in a body, encircled the yard, and took it by storm – all the more easily, as their captain had been taken and the garrison had fled the field. Still, the victors' blood was up. They sought out the enemy. Barred from the house, they ran to the farmyard, and burst into the kitchen. The sight of the pots and pans and the hearth not yet grown cold, the smell of recent cooking, and the sound of dogs crunching on the scraps of the evening meal – all this went straight to their hearts, setting their thoughts on a different course. While cooling their wrath, it inflamed their desire for food. Worn out by their march and the whole day spent in deliberations, they thrice roared in unison, "Meat! Meat!" "Drink! Drink!" went the refrain. The nobility broke into two choirs, one calling for meat, the other for drink. Their cries echoed throughout the Manor, and wherever they were heard, mouths watered, bellies growled. And so, at a signal from the kitchen, the entire host dispersed to forage for victuals.

Meanwhile, Gervase, repulsed from the Judge's rooms, was forced to defer to the Count's guards. Unable to avenge himself on his enemy, he turned his mind to his second main objective. Being practiced and skilled in the law, he was eager to establish the Count's legal title to his new inheritance. And so, he set out in search of the Court Usher. After a lengthy search, they found Protase skulking behind the stove. Gervase seized him by the collar and dragged him into the yard outside.

"Mr. Usher!" said he, prodding his breast with his Jackknife. "The Count makes bold to bid your honor proclaim before our noble brethren my lord's formal intromissio of the castle, manor, village, fields, both sowed and fallow – in a word, *cum grovesibus, forestis, et fencelinesibus, peasantibus, scultetis et omnibus rebus; et quibusdam aliis.* You know how it goes. So out with it. Let's hear you bark. And leave nothing out!"

"Now hold on a moment, Warden," said Protase, uncowed, thrusting his hands under his belt. "I am quite ready to do the bidding of either party, but I warn you, a decree proclaimed under the threat of violence and in the dark of night carries no weight."

"Threat? What threat?" said the Warden. "There's no violence here. Why, I am asking you nicely, sir. If you find it dark, old Jackknife here shall oblige and strike you a light so bright that seven churches could scarce outshine it!"

"Come now, Gervase, old fellow," Protase replied. "Why so testy? I am only the court usher. It is not for me to examine the merits of a case. Everyone knows it is the plaintiff that summons the usher. He tells him what to say, and he proclaims it. Ushers are but emissaries of the law, not subject to punishment, so I cannot imagine why you are keeping me under guard. I shall pen a writ at once. Bid someone fetch me a lamp. Meanwhile, I shall make the announcement. Brothers, come to order!"

So as to be better heard, he climbed the large pile of logs that stood seasoning by the garden fence. Directly he got to the top of it, he vanished from sight, as if swept away by a gust of wind. They heard him land with a thump in the cabbage patch below. They saw his white confederate's cap streak like a dove through the dark hemp. Watering Can took a pot-shot at it. Missed! They heard the snapping of poles. Protase had reached the hop thicket.

"I protest!" he yelled, now sure of his escape. Behind him were the withy bed and the brook's miry ground.

Protase's cry of demurral was like the last cannon shot upon the taking of a redoubt. All resistance ceased at Soplica Manor. The ravenous nobility fell to rapine and pillaging at will. The Baptist set up post in the cowshed. There, he dispatched an ox and two calves with a blow to the head. Razor slit open their throats with his thin blade. With no less expedition, Bodkin stuck the sucklings and porkers between the shoulder blades. And now, slaughter threatened the poultry. The watchful geese, ancient Rome's preservers, honked in vain for assistance. Alas!

No Manlius stood by to repel the treacherous Gaul. Matthias Watering Can broke into the pen. He wrung the necks of some, others he took alive, lashing them to his belt by the neck. In vain did the geese gurgle and writhe. In vain did the ganders hiss and nip at their assailant. Covered in sparks of goose down and borne on by the wheel-like flapping motion of the wings, Matthias made straight for the kitchen. One would have sworn he was *Chochlik* – the winged evil sprite.

But the most appalling, if quietest, butchery took place in the hen-roost. Young Sack burst inside. Using a halter, he yanked the ruffle-feathered hens and crested capons from their perches. One after another, he wrung their necks and piled them on the floor. Beautiful birds! Fattened on pearls of barley. Foolish Sack, what fit of folly took you? Now, you shall never appease Sophie's wrath!

Recalling the old days, Gervase appealed to the nobility for their ceremonial belts. They lowered them into the Soplica cellars and hoisted up casks of home-brew vodka, oak-seasoned mead, and ale. Some of the casks, they broached at once. The rest, they seized lustily and, swarming like ants, rolled them to the castle, where the entire host was gathering to spend the night. It was there that the Count had established his headquarters.

Laying a hundred bonfires, they began to boil, broil, and grill. Tables groaned with meat. Rivers of spirits flowed. The nobility intended to eat, drink, and sing the night out. Gradually, they began to drowse and yawn. Eye after eye drooped shut. The head of every man began to nod. Each dozed off where he sat, one over his bowl, another over his tankard, still another over his joint of beef. Sleep, Death's brother, had vanquished the victors.

BOOK NINE: THE BATTLE

Argument. On the perils consequent upon disorderly encampment. Unexpected succor. The sorry plight of the nobility. The alms quester's visit, a portent of rescue. Major Plut's excessive gallantry brings down a storm on his head. A pistol shot, the signal for battle. The Baptist's exploits, Matthias' exploits and perils. Watering Can's ambush saves the manor. Cavalry reinforcements, assault on the infantry. Tadeusz's feats of valor. The leaders' duel cut short by an act of treachery. The Steward tips the balance of the battle by a decisive maneuver. Gervase's bloody exploits. The Chamberlain, a magnanimous victor.

So soundly did the nobility sleep that neither the flickering glow of the lanterns nor the irruption of several dozen men roused them from their slumbers. The intruders fell upon them even as the wall spider known as the harvestman alights on a drowsy fly. Scarcely has his victim time to emit a sound when the grim assassin enfolds it in his long legs and throttles the life out of it. The nobility slept more soundly than any fly. Not a peep out of any one. All lay as dead, though strong hands seized and turned them bodily like sheaves for the binding.

Only Matthias Watering Can who held his liquor better than any reveler in the district, who was capable of draining a gallon of linden mead before growing unsteady on his legs or slurring his speech, only Matthias, though he'd feasted long and slept soundly, showed any sign of life. He opened one eye. Horrors! What a sight! Two spectral faces, each sporting a prodigious pair of moustaches, leaned directly over him. He felt their breath upon his cheeks, their whiskers trailing over his lips. Their four hands whirred like wings over his body. Terrified, he tried to bless himself, but he found his arm pinned to his side. He tried to move his left arm. Alas! The wraiths had swathed him up tighter than a new-born babe. More appalled than ever, he shut his eyes and lay motionless. His blood ran cold. You would have sworn he was dead.

But the Baptist strove to defend himself. Too late! They'd restrained him with his own belt. Undismayed, he curled himself into a ball and flipped onto his feet with such élan that he landed prone on the chests of his sleeping companions. Rolling clear of their heads, he began to toss about like a pike on a sandy shore, all the while roaring like a bear, for he had a lusty pair of lungs. "Treachery!" he cried. Instantly, the roused nobility picked up the chorus, "Treachery! Murder! Treachery!"

Their cries echoed all the way up to the hall of mirrors where the Warden and the Count and his jockeys lay sleeping. Awakened by the noise, Gervase struggled to rise, only to find himself stretched and bound on his rapier. He looked up to see a body of armed men in short black shakos and green tunics standing by the window. One of their number wore a sash and was directing his underlings with the point of his sword. "Bind them! Bind them!" he whispered. On the floor around him lay the jockeys, trussed up and docile as sheep. The Count was seated – unbound but disarmed. Two riflemen with fixed bayonets stood guarding him. Gervase recognized them at once: Muscovites!

This was not the first time he found himself in such straits. More than once in his life had he been bound hand and foot, and always he'd managed to break free. Gervase had ways of bursting his bonds, for he was uncommonly strong and full of resource. Choosing the way of stealth, he closed his eyes and feigned to sleep on. Slowly, he straightened his limbs; then, drawing a deep breath and shrinking his belly to smallest size, he began to hunch up and stretch and arch his body. As the snake, when molting, draws head and tail into its coils, so Gervase the long grew short and stout. The cords stretched, even creaked. Alas! They refused to snap. Dismayed, ashamed, livid with rage, Gervase rolled onto his belly and buried his face in the ground; then, shutting his eyes, he lay still as a stone.

Snare drums broke into a slow roll; steadily faster and louder they rolled. On hearing the signal, the Russian officer had the Count and his jockeys confined under guard in the castle and the nobility escorted to the manor house where a second company of yagers stood posted. In vain the Baptist grimaced and tossed.

Awaiting them in the courtyard were Major Plut, his staff, and a large number of armed noblemen, including the Podhajskis, Birbaszes, Hreczechas, and Biergels – all friends and kinsmen of the Judge. Informed of the raid, they had hastened to his rescue, all the more readily, as they had long had a bone to pick with the Dobrzynskis.

Who summoned the Muscovite battalion from the villages? Who so quickly mustered the nobility from the neighboring settlements? The Assessor? The innkeeper? All sorts of rumors made the rounds, but no one knew for certain, either then or later.

By now it was light. Blood red, dull-edged, and beamless, the sun glowed half visible among the inky clouds like a horseshoe embedded in the forge's coals. A keen wind sprang up from the east, driving the scud along like jagged lumps of ice. Each passing streamer sprinkled a chill drizzle. No sooner did the wind dry the rain than another moisture-laden rack came driving up; and so, by turns, the day was wet and cold.

Meanwhile, the Major ordered his men to haul down logs from the woodpile seasoning by the house. This done, he had them hew out semi-circular notches at regular intervals along the length of each log. The prisoners' legs were then thrust into the notches, another log was placed on top, and the ends were nailed together so that the two beams fastened upon the ankles like a bulldog's jaws. Even tighter were their hands tied behind them; then, to further their torment, Plut had their caps struck off and their cloaks, robes and even their *taratatkas* and tunics torn from their backs. So, ranged and confined in the stocks, they sat, teeth chattering in the growing cold and wet. In vain the Baptist grimaced and tossed.

Bootless the Judge's appeals on the nobility's behalf! Bootless Sophie's tears and Telimena's entreaties that the prisoners be more humanely treated. No doubt the Captain would have allowed himself to be swayed, for deep down Nikita Rykov was a decent man, despite his being a Muscovite. But what could *he* do? Major Plut was a man to be obeyed.

The Major, a Pole by birth, hailed from the village of Dzierowicz. Common report had it that his real name was Plutowicz and that, after converting to the Orthodox faith, he had russified it to Plut. A scoundrel, he most certainly was, as so often happens when Pole turns renegade in the service of Tsar. Even now he was standing in front of his troops with his arms akimbo, pipe in mouth, cocking his nose at the people that came bowing and begging before him. Eventually, answering them with a surly plume of smoke, he stalked off toward the house.

Meanwhile, the Judge proceeded to mollify Rykov; then taking the Assessor aside as well, he sought the two men's advice on how they might settle the matter out of court. Above all, the authorities must be kept in the dark.

"Sir!" said Rykov, approaching Major Plut. "What use to us are all these prisoners? Shall we drag them before the court? Think of the grief it will inflict on the nobility, and there's not a kopeck in it for us. Know what I think, Major? Better settle the matter amicably. Let the Judge repay us for our trouble, and we shall say we dropped in for a visit. This way, the goat will be safe and the wolf satisfied. Remember the Russian saw, 'All's possible that's prudently done.' Or this one: 'Broil your portion on the Emperor's skewer.' Or this one: 'Harmony's better than discord.' Come, sir, tie a good knot and stick the ends in the water. We'll make no report, and no one shall be the wiser. 'God made hands to be greased.' Now, there's a Russian saw!"

Upon hearing this, Plut rose to his feet and snorted indignantly: "Rykov, have you gone mad? This is the Tsar's service. Service isn't chumship, you know. Stupid old Rykov! Have you taken leave of your senses? Release these troublemakers? In times of war like these? Hah, you Polish lordlings! I'll teach you rebellion! Hah, you rascal Dobrzynski nobles! I know you! Let the scum enjoy a good soaking!" And, looking out the window, he gave out a roar of laughter. "Why, that same Dobrzynski sitting over there with his coat on. . . Hey, you there, tear his coat off! . . . that same Dobrzynski over there picked a quarrel with me at last year's masquerade ball. Who started it? Why, him of course, not me! 'Show the thief the door!' he yelled, as I was engaged in a dance. Being then under suspicion of having my hand in the regimental till, I was greatly put out. Anyhow, what business was it of his? There I was, dancing the mazurka, when he shouts 'Thief!' behind my back, and the nobility chorus 'Hear! Hear!' after him. Insulted me, see? Now, I have the rascal in my clutches. 'Hey, Dobrzynski!' I says to him. 'So the goat comes to the cart, eh? Now you'll see what's what, eh Dobrzynski? You're in for the switch.'"

And leaning over, Plut whispered into the Judge's ear:

"So, Your Honor, if you wish to get off lightly, it'll run you a cool thousand rubles per head, in cash. A thousand rubles. That's my final word."

The Judge tried to bargain with him, but the Major wouldn't hear of it. Once again, he began to strut up and down the room, trailing thick clouds of smoke like a skyrocket or lighted squib. In vain the women went begging and weeping after him!

"Major," said the Judge. "So you take the matter to court. Where's the good of it? No battle was fought, no blood spilt. So, they helped themselves to chicken and smoked goose. All right, they shall make recompense according to the law. I will not lodge a complaint against the Count. A neighborly squabble, that's all it was."

"Ever read the Yellow Book?" asked the Major.

"What yellow book?"

"Better than your Book of Statutes," said Plut. "Full of words like, 'Siberia,' 'gallows,' 'noose,' and 'knout' – aye, the book of martial law, which stands proclaimed throughout all of Lithuania. Your courts are worthless now. According to the wartime decrees, your prank shall earn you a stint of hard labor in Siberia at least."

"I shall appeal to the Governor," said the Judge.

"Appeal to the Emperor, if it pleases you," said Plut. "You know very well that when the Tsar consents to ratify a sentence, he is as likely to double the penalty. So, by all means, Judge, launch an appeal. If need be, I shall find something to pin on you too. That spy, Yankel, whose movements the authorities have long been watching, is a tenant of yours. Bides in your tavern, eh? If I cared to, I could arrest the lot of you on the spot."

"Arrest me?" exclaimed the Judge. "You'd dare? Without orders?"

Just as their exchange was turning into a fierce contest, a new caller made his entrance into the courtyard. A bizarre, tumultuous train! Gamboling ahead of the cortege like a ceremonial runner came a huge black wether, its brow bristling with two pairs of horns – one pair was hung with bells and arched around its ears, while the other protruded sideways with small brass globes dangling from the tips. After the ram came a herd of bullocks, then sheep, then goats; and after the livestock came four heavy-laden ox-wagons.

No one could mistake the arrival of the alms quester. Mindful of his duty as host, the Judge prepared to greet his guest at the door. Robak sat in the first wagon, his face half hidden by his hood. They recognized him when, driving past the prisoners, he turned and signed to them with his finger. Nor did the driver of the second wagon escape recognition. It was old Matthias Switch, dressed in rural weeds. A cheer went up from the nobility the moment he came into view. "Stupid fools!" he growled, before silencing them with a peremptory wave of his hand. The Prussian, clad in a threadbare capote, steered the third wagon, while Zan and Mickiewicz brought up the rear in the fourth.

Meanwhile, the Podhajskis, Isajewiczes, Kotwiczes, Birbaszes, Biergels and Wilbiks, observing the sorry plight of their Dobrzyn brethren, felt their old animosities cool. While it is true that the Polish nobility are prone to ructions and all too easily provoked to combat, they are not vindictive. And so, seeking direction, the entire host ran over to Matthias. He, in turn, marshalled them around the wagons and bade them wait.

Robak entered the parlor. Though habited in his usual manner, he was scarcely recognizable, so much had his expression changed. Normally solemn and preoccupied of mien, he now held his head erect, and his face beamed like a jovial friar's. Before addressing the inmates, he gave out a long hearty laugh:

"Ha! Ha! Ha! Ha! Greetings! Greetings! Ha! Ha! Ha! Splendid! Well done! Most sportsmen stalk by day, but you, my dear officers, stalk by night. Good hunting. I've seen your game. Oh, pluck 'em, pluck 'em, I say. Skin 'em. Rein 'em in, for our nobility's a restive steed. Major, I congratulate you on bagging our young Count. Lots of meat on him. Moneybags! A sire of ancient lineage. Have him cough up three hundred ducats for his release. And while you're about it, spare three groats for my convent and me, for I am always praying for your soul. We Franciscans give serious thought to the state of one's soul. Does death not snatch even staff-officers by the ear? As Baka wrote, *'Death rends the purple by the yard, / Plants heavy blows on broadcloth too, / With equal zest he linen snips, / And army serge, and cowls, and curls.'* Aye, Baka puts it well: *'Death's an onion, fetcher of tears, / Grasps all to his bosom, sparing none, / Nor sleeping tot, nor boozing sot.'* Aye, Major, now we swill, anon we rot! Ours, all that we eat and sup this day. Apropos, dear Judge, is it not time we broke fast? I take my seat at the table and bid you all join me. Major, what say you to beef stew and gravy? Lieutenant, what is your fancy? A bowl of punch?"

"Indeed, Father," agreed the two officers, "high time we ate and pledged the Judge's health."

The household gaped at the Friar. Whence came this new manner and jovial air! Meanwhile, the Judge issued orders to the cook. They brought in the punch bowl, the sugar, the bottles and the beef. Plut and Rykov fell to with a dispatch so keen that in the space of half an hour they had downed two-dozen collops and drained several quart vessels of punch.

Replete at last and in genial spirits, Plut lolled back in his chair. Taking out his pipe, he lit it with a banknote; then, wiping his lips with the tip of a napkin, he turned his mirthful eyes to the womenfolk.

"Now, pretty ladies," said he, "you shall be my dessert. By my major's epaulets, after a breakfast of stewed beef there's no better relish than a chat with pretty ladies such as yourselves. Eh, pretty ladies? A round of cards? *Elb Zvelb*? Whist? Or what say we dance a mazurka? Eh? Three hundred devils strike me dead if I ain't the finest mazurka dancer in the regiment." And saying this, he leaned over toward the women, spreading compliments and clouds of smoke.

"Yes, let's dance!" cried the Friar. "When in my cups even I, a Franciscan friar, am not averse from hiking up my habit and treading the odd measure. But look you, Major, here sit we drinking, while your yagers stand frozen to the bone outside. Now carousing's carousing! Judge, send out a keg of vodka! The Major won't mind. Let our brave yagers enjoy a tipple."

"Indeed, why not?" said the Major. "But I don't insist."

"Make it a keg of pure spirits," whispered Robak to the Judge. And so, while the officers drank merrily in the house, the men outside went on a spree of their own.

Captain Rykov downed his liquor sturdily in silence. Meanwhile, the Major caroused and paid court to the women of the house. At last, itching to dance, he threw down his pipe and seized Telimena by the hand, but she promptly tore herself free. Then, turning to Sophie, he bowed unsteadily and begged her for the pleasure of a mazurka.

"Rykov!" he cried. "Stop puffing on that pipe. Put it away! You're handy with the balalaika. See the guitar there? Strike us up a mazurka. As commanding officer, I'll take the top of the dance."

The Captain took the guitar and began tuning the strings. Again, Plut sought to entice Telimena to a dance.

"I give you my word as major, dear lady, call me no Russky if I lie. May I be a son of a bitch if I do. Ask around, if you doubt me. The officers – indeed, the whole army – will bear witness that in the Second Army, Ninth Corps, Second Infantry Division, Fiftieth Yager Regiment there is no mazurka dancer equal to Major Plut. So, come, little lady, don't be skittish or we shall have to serve you out, officer-style."

With that, he sprang to his feet, seized Telimena by the hand, and smacked her white shoulder with a loud kiss. Instantly, Tadeusz leapt up from aside and dealt him a resounding slap across the face. Kiss and slap rang out in rapid succession like a brisk repartee.

Thunderstruck, Plut rubbed his eyes. "Rebellion! Rebel!" he roared, pale with rage; and drawing his sword, he drove furiously at Tadeusz. But the Friar pulled a pistol from his sleeve.

"Shoot, boy!" he cried. "Shoot like the blazes."

Tadeusz seized the small-bore from his hand and took aim. The charge exploded. The shot went wide, though it stunned the Major and blackened him with powder. Rykov leapt up, guitar in hand. "Rebellion! Rebellion!" he cried. And he made toward Tadeusz. But at that moment, the Steward, who was sitting across from the two officers, swung back his arm and let fly. The blade sang through the air between their heads and struck home even before they saw it flash. It smote the guitar box and went clean through. Rykov dodged smartly aside, narrowly escaping with his life; but that brush with death gave him a nasty fright.

"Yagers! Rebellion! By thunder!" he cried; and, drawing his sword, he backed away toward the hall.

Just then, a large host of the nobility broke in through the windows at the far end of the room. In they swarmed, rapiers drawn, with Switch at their head. Plut and Rykov raced to the door and yelled for help. Three yagers nearest the house answered their call. Three gleaming bayonets came poking in through the door. Three stooping black shakos came gliding in behind. As a cat lies in wait for a rat, so Matthias stood by the door with his back to the wall, his Switch upraised. He struck a terrible blow. It would have trimmed all three heads from their necks, but, alas, weak eyesight, or perhaps an excess of dispatch, caused the old master to lunge prematurely. Before the necks could show themselves, he smote on the shakos and swept them off, bringing Switch down on the bayonets with a heavy clang. The Muscovites drew back. Matthias raced into the courtyard after them.

Outside, even greater confusion reigned. Soplica's men were tearing at the stocks, vying with one another to set the Dobrzynskis free. The yagers seized their muskets and flew at them. Bursting in upon the stocks, a sergeant ran Podhajski through with his bayonet, wounded two others, and fired upon a third. The nobility took to their heels.

All this happened close to where the Baptist had sat confined. His hands now free and ripe for battle, he rose up, doubled his long-fingered fist and brought it down sheer upon the Russian's back. The resulting blow was so hard that it rammed the sergeant's brow into the musket firelock. The hammer clicked, but the blood-soaked powder failed to ignite. The sergeant pitched full length on his weapon at Baptist's feet. Dobrzynski bent down, seized the weapon by the barrel and flourished it like a sprinkling broom; then, whirling it round, he smote two privates across the shoulders. A corporal caught a crashing blow on the head. The rest of the yagers took fright and backed away from the stocks. So did the Baptist raise a whirling roof over the heads of his brethren.

At last, the stocks were broken, the last cords cut. No sooner freed than the nobles made for the Friar's wagons. There, they helped themselves to rapiers, sabers, broadswords, scythes, and muskets. Finding a bag of shot and two blunderbusses, Watering Can poured powder into the muzzle of his own gun, then, priming the other, handed it to the Baptist's son, Sack.

More yagers appeared. A chaotic scuffle ensued. The nobility found themselves unable to cut and slash in the melee; nor could the yagers fire their muskets. They fought it out at close quarters. Steel clashed on steel. Blades shivered. Saber broke on bayonet. Scythe on crossguard. Fist met fist. Arm smote arm.

Captain Rykov and a handful of yagers ran to where the barn abutted on the paddock fence. From his fresh position there, Rykov called on his men to break off the disorderly combat, as, deprived of the use of their muskets, they were falling beneath the enemy's fists. His inability to open fire infuriated him, but there was no way of telling Pole and Muscovite apart. *"Стройся!"* he roared, which means "fall in!" in Russian, but in the din no one heard the command.

Meanwhile, ill-suited to close-quarters combat, old Matthias was falling back. Left and right he flailed, clearing a space for himself. Here, with the tip of his Switch, he sheared bayonet from barrel like a wick from a candle. There, lunging lustily, he cut and jabbed. Even so did wary old Matthias retire to open ground.

He found himself hardest pressed by a seasoned old *Gefreiter*, the regimental instructor and grand champion of bayonet exercise. Gathering his strength and drawing himself in, the Muscovite tightened his grip around his rifle – right hand over the lock, left midway up the barrel – and launched into a series of twists and turns, leaps and squats, now dropping his left hand and darting his stinger with his right, now drawing it back and resting the gun on his knee.

Appraising his opponent's skill, Dobrzynski rammed his spectacles over the bridge of his nose with one hand; then, holding Switch close to his chest with the other, he backed away, while carefully watching the *Gefreiter's* every movement. He feigned a drunken lurch. Emboldened by this action, the *Gefreiter* lunged forward. To reach the retreating Matthias, he was forced to rise and thrust with his weapon to the full extent of his right arm. Such was the weight and momentum of the musket that he lost his balance. And here, Matthias rammed his sword-hilt in between the bayonet and barrel, swung the musket into the air, and, bringing Switch down, took a slice at the Muscovite's arm. Then, swinging lustily again, he split open his jaw. Thus fell the finest *Fechtmeister* of all the Russias, knight of three military crosses and four-time medal winner.

Meanwhile, out by the stocks, the nobility's left flank was on the verge of victory. There, conspicuous in the distance, fought Baptist, while yonder, weaving in among the Muscovites, ran Razor, unseaming torsos even as Baptist bludgeoned skulls. As that farm machine – brainchild of German masters which we call a thresher, though, having both flails and blades, it also doubles as a chaff-cutter – even as that fell engine slices through stalks and threshes the grain, so Baptist and Razor wrought their combined havoc on the enemy, one from above, the other from below.

With victory now assured, Baptist made for the right flank where a new peril threatened Matthias. An ensign, seek-

ing to avenge the *Gefreiter's* death, was harrying the old man
with a long spontoon – something between a pike and axe, now
obsolete in the infantry though still used in the navy. The ensign, a young man, was weaving nimbly about. Every time Dobrzynski knocked aside his weapon, he stepped smartly out of
reach. Unable to shake or hurt him, Matthias could only parry his thrusts. Already, his opponent had gashed him slightly;
and now, raising his pike, the ensign stood poised for the killing
blow. Seeing he would never reach Matthias in time, Gervase
halted in mid-stride, swung his weapon and sent it hurtling with
bone-shattering force at the yager's legs. The ensign let go of his
halberd and slumped to the ground. Again, Baptist charged. A
host of noblemen followed, but scattered units of yagers from the
left flank pursued them, and so a fresh skirmish began to rage
around the Baptist.

To save Matthias, Baptist had sacrificed his weapon. The
deed almost cost him his life. Two strapping yagers leapt upon
him from behind and dug their hands into his hair. Steadying
their feet, they pulled on him even as wherrymen pull on the hal-
yards of their vessel. Baptist lashed back with random punches.
No use: he began to keel over. Then, catching sight of Gervase,
who was fighting close by, he cried out, "*Jesu Maria!* Jackknife!"

Sensing Baptist's plight by the urgency of his voice, Gervase whirled round and swung his rapier down hard between
Dobrzynski's head and the yagers' arms. With cries of terror,
they recoiled, but a severed hand hung ensnarled and ensanguined in the hair. Even so, in his frenzied struggle with a young
eagle that seizes him with one set of talons while anchoring itself to a tree with the other, the jackrabbit rips the bird in two,
so that one bloodied set of talons remains fastened to the tree in
the forest and the other is borne away into the fields by the hare.

Free again, Baptist looked about him, reached out his
hands, sought a weapon, yelled for a weapon, yet never ceasing
to rain down blows, holding his ground and keeping close to the
Warden's side. At last, his son Sack loomed up in the melee. The
lad was aiming his blunderbuss with one hand and dragging behind him a fathom-long tree, heavily knotted and bristling with
sundry knobs and pieces of flint. (No one but Baptist was capable
of lifting it off the ground.) Overjoyed at seeing his Sprinkling
Broom, Dobrzynski seized it, pressed it to his lips, then, leaping
up, whirled the club in the air and promptly imbrued it in blood.

Bootless to sing of the wondrous feats he went on to perform! Bootless to sing of the carnage he wrought on every hand! No one would believe the Muse; nor would anyone believe the old woman who, from her point of vantage atop Vilna's Ostra Gate, saw the Russian General Deyov entering the city. Even as they swung open the gate, a townsman surnamed Czarnobacki slew Deyov and put his entire Cossack regiment to rout.

Enough that everything came to pass exactly as Rykov had foreseen. The hampered yagers fell before the stronger foe. Twenty-three lay dead in the dust. Another thirty or so lay groaning from sundry wounds. Many fled into the orchard and hop field. Some made for the river, others ran to the house, seeking refuge among the womenfolk.

The triumphant nobility dashed off, shouting for joy. Some went in search of kegs of spirits, others went after plunder and booty. Robak alone refused to share in their triumph. He had not taken part in the fighting – canon law strictly forbids a priest to engage in combat; nonetheless, he had imparted expert advice and made a complete circuit of the battlefield. With a glance here, a hand signal there, he put the fighting men on their mettle and cheered them to the assault. Now, he was calling upon them to join him in a strike on Rykov and secure the victory. Meanwhile, he dispatched a runner to the Captain, informing him that if the yagers put down their arms, he would spare their lives. If they delayed, he would have them encircled and cut down to a man.

But Captain Rykov was far from begging quarter. Mustering the half-battalion around him, he cried, "Ready!" With a loud clatter, the yagers shouldered their loaded muskets. "Level!" he cried. A long line of barrels flashed upward. "Fire by volley!" he cried. One after another, they discharged their guns. One fired, another loaded, still another stood at the ready. Musket balls zipped, firelocks crashed, ramrods thudded home. The line resembled a wood louse with its myriad gleaming legs all beating at once.

But strong spirits had addled the yagers' brains. They aimed poorly and fired wide. Few inflicted wounds, and scarcely one killed his man. Even so, two Matthiases fell wounded, and one Bartholomew went down to the dust. The nobles, replying sparingly with the odd harquebus, were all for flying at the enemy with their swords, but the older men restrained them.

Meanwhile, bullets whizzed thickly around them, hitting some, driving others back. Before long, the musketry cleared the yard, and now there were balls patting around the manor windows.

All this time, Tadeusz had been biding indoors at the Judge's behest, guarding the womenfolk. But on seeing the battle take a turn for the worse, he rushed out into the yard. The Chamberlain – his valet Thomas having at last fetched him his saber – hastened after him. In no time, he joined the nobility, took his place at their head, raised his saber, and led them in a charge. The yagers held their fire, allowing them to approach, then raked the line with a hail of lead. Isajewicz was killed on the spot. Wilbik and the Razor fell wounded. Robak and Matthias, who stood at either flank, halted the charge. Unnerved, the nobility began to look about them and fall back; and now, Captain Rykov decided to mount a final strike, to sweep the courtyard clean and storm the house.

"Prepare to attack!" he cried. "Fix bayonets! Quick march!"

Lowering their heads, rifle barrels outthrust like a rack of antlers, the line advanced, gradually quickening their pace. Powerless to stem the onset head-on, the nobility fired from the flanks. By now the yagers had cleared half the courtyard.

"Soplica!" shouted the Captain, pointing his sword at the manor door. "Lay down your arms or I shall burn you out."

"Burn away!" said the Judge. "I'll fry you in the flames."

O Soplica Manor! If your whitewashed walls still stand under the limes, if the nobility still gather there to feast at the generous board of their neighbor, Judge Soplica, then surely, they must pledge the health of Matthias Watering Can, for without him, the manor would be no more.

Until now, Matthias hadn't proved much of a warrior. Though he was the first to be freed from the stocks and retrieve his beloved blunderbuss and bag of shot, he was loath to enter into the fray. He said he could never trust himself on an empty stomach; and so, having first gone over to a vat of pure spirits standing nearby, he helped himself to the liquor with generous scoops of his hand. Only when he'd adequately warmed and refreshed himself did he right his cap, seize his blunderbuss from between his knees, ram home a charge, sprinkle the pan, and take a survey of the field. He saw the wave of gleaming bayonets dashing over and scattering the nobility. Thither he swam, to meet the wave. Head down, he plunged into the dense grass in the middle of the courtyard where the nettles grew thick; and there, signaling to Sack with his hand, he lay down in ambush.

Sack was standing with his blunderbuss outside the manor house – abode of sweet Sophie, whom he still loved dearly and would gladly die for, despite her having spurned his addresses. As the yagers went marching into the nettles, Watering Can discharged his gun. A dozen chopped-up bullets poured from the flared muzzle into the Muscovite line. Sack unleashed a dozen more from the porch. The yagers fell into a panic. Surprised by the ambush, the extended line huddled up into a ball and pulled back, abandoning their wounded to the Baptist, who lost no time in dispatching them with his Sprinkler.

It being now too far to return to the barn, Rykov, fearing a drawn-out retreat, made smartly for the garden fence. Checking his company in their flight, he drew them up again, only this time he changed their formation. From a single line, he formed a triangle with its apex projecting forward like a wedge and its two sides extending back to the garden fence. He did well to do this, for, just then, a body of horsemen came bearing down upon them from the castle.

Confined in the castle until the guards panicked and fled, the Count had ordered his men to mount up. Hearing the detonations of the musketry, he urged his riders into the firing line, he at their head, steel raised aloft.

"Half-battalion, open fire!" roared Rykov.

A fiery thread ran the length of the line of leveled guns, as the pans ignited and three hundred whining musket balls sped from the blackened barrels. Three riders fell wounded. Another lay lifeless in the dust. The Count's charger took a ball and tumbled, unhorsing its rider. Seeing the yagers train their guns on the last male representative of the Horeszko line (albeit on the spindle side), Gervase gave out a yell and ran to his aid. But Robak, who was closer, flung himself in front of the Count and took the bullet intended for him. Dragging him from under the horse, he led him away, all the while shouting to the nobility to spread out, take better aim, save ammunition, and seek cover behind the fence, the well paling and the cowshed. As for the Count and his horsemen, a more favorable occasion was soon to present itself.

Tadeusz understood Robak's plan and executed it to perfection. He took cover behind the well and, being sober and skilled in the use of a double (he could hit a *zloty* piece tossed in the air), he wrought havoc on the Muscovites, picking off the officers one by one. With his first shot, he struck down the sergeant major; then, discharging one barrel after the other, he brought down two more sergeants. Time and again, he fired, here at a gold braid, there into the midst of the triangle, where the officers stood. Rykov fumed with rage, stamping his foot, gnawing on his sword knot.

"Major Plut!" he cried. "What's to become of us? At this rate, there'll be no one left to take charge."

In an access of fury, Plut called out to Tadeusz: "You, Pole! Shame on you for hiding behind a bit of board. Are you a coward? Come out in the open! Fight with honor, as befits a soldier!"

"Major," Tadeusz replied. "If you are so brave a knight, why cower inside a ring of yagers? I do not fear you. Come out from the fence! I slapped you one across the face and stand ready to do so again in close combat. What is the use of this bloodshed? The quarrel is between us. Let sword or pistol settle the matter! Choose your weapon, field-piece, poniard, it's all one to me. Refuse, and I shall pick you off like wolves in their lair!"

With that, he fired another round with such truth of aim that he felled the lieutenant standing next to Rykov.

"Major," whispered Rykov. "Go out and fight this duel! Avenge his earlier slight to your honor. Depend on it, if someone else kills this Polish lord, you will never wash away the disgrace. You must lure him into the open. Since firearms won't do the job, kill him with the sword. Old Suvorov used to say, 'Rifles are trifles. The trick is to stick 'em.' So, Major, go out into the field. Otherwise, he'll pick us all off. See? He's taking aim again."

"Rykov, old friend," said the Major. "You're the wiz with the blade. Go out yourself, my boy. Or tell you what: we shall send one of the subalterns. As the major here, I cannot desert my soldiers. I command the battalion after all."

Raising his sword, Rykov stepped boldly out into the field, waved a white handkerchief and called for a ceasefire. Tadeusz was offered his choice of arms. After some deliberation, the two men agreed upon épées. Since Tadeusz did not carry such a weapon, they were obliged to find him one; but, even as they were engaged in the search, the Count ran up, flourishing his foil.

"Mr. Soplica," said he, interrupting the talks. "With all due respect, it was the Major you called out, but I have an earlier grievance against the Captain here, for it was he who broke into my castle—"

"*Our* castle, you mean!" broke in Protase from behind.

"—at the head of a band of robbers," finished the Count. "It was Rykov who had my jockeys bound. I recognize him. Now shall I punish him, as I did those brigands on the crag the Sicilians call Birbante-Rocca."

There fell a silence. All shooting ceased, as the two armies watched their champions come together. Heads turned inwards, menacing each other with their right arm and right eye, Rykov and the Count closed for combat, but not before doffing their hats with their left hand and bowing courteously – an honorable custom this, the principals exchanging greetings before proceeding to slaughter! Then engaging their blades, they clashed. Front foot thrusting, knee flexing, the two knights lunged and parried in turn.

Meanwhile, seeing Tadeusz standing directly opposite him, Plut conferred quietly with Corporal Gont, who was reckoned the finest marksman in the company.

"Gont," he whispered. "See that gallows' bird over there? Lodge a bullet under his fifth rib, and I'll see you get four rubles in silver."

Gont drew back the hammer of his musket, put his eye to the sights, while his cronies covered him with their cloaks. He took aim, not at Tadeusz's rib, but at his head. He fired. The bullet struck home – almost! It went clean through Tadeusz's hat. The youth spun round. Baptist made toward Rykov. The nobility, cring foul, followed him. But Tadeusz threw himself in their path, and Rykov, falling back, regained the safety of his ranks in the nick of time.

Once more, Lithuania and Dobrzyn went on the attack in a spirit of amicable rivalry. Their old differences set aside, they fought like brothers, each exhorting his comrade-in-arms. The Dobrzynskis rejoiced at the sight of Podhajski prancing before the yager line and mowing it down with his scythe. "A Podhajski! A Podhajski!" they cried. "Forward, Lithuanian brothers! Hurrah! Hurrah for Lithuania!" Seeing the valiant and wounded Razor raise his sword, the Skoluba clan yelled in reply, "A Dobrzynski! A Dobrzynski! Long live Mazovia!" So, urging one another on, they sallied forth against the Muscovite. Robak and Matthias were powerless to hold them back.

Just as the nobility mounted this frontal assault on the yager company, the Steward left the battlefield and repaired to the garden. Protase padded warily beside him, listening to his instructions.

Rearing up in the garden close to the fence, which formed the base of Rykov's triangle, was an enormous old cheese house built with beams lashed crosswise like a latticework cage. Several scores of gleaming white cheeses stood piled within. All around them swung bundles of drying herbs: sage, blessed thistle, wild thyme – in short, the Steward's daughter's entire herbal pharmacopoeia. The cage measured four fathoms across, and the entire structure rested like a stork's nest on a great pillar of oak, which, being old and half-rotted, canted at a precarious angle and was in imminent danger of giving out. The Judge had often been urged to dismantle the decaying structure, but he always said he would sooner repair than take it down, or at least have it erected elsewhere. He put off the business to a more favorable time. In the meantime, he had the old pillar propped up with two supports. Thus buttressed, the unstable structure reared above the fence, overlooking Rykov's triangle.

Armed with stout spear-like poles, the Steward and the Usher advanced stealthily through the hemp toward the cheese house. Behind them came the bailiff mistress and a kitchen boy – a small lad, but strong as they come. On reaching the spot, they thrust their poles deep into the top of the rotted pillar, then, hanging from the pole-ends, began pulling down with all their might. So wherrymen thrust out from the bank with long spars, heaving their grounded vessel into deeper waters.

With a loud crack, the pile gave way. The dryer tottered and came tumbling down on the Muscovite triangle, crushing, killing, and maiming the men with its burden of beams and cheeses. Where yagers had been standing lay a wreckage of timbers, bodies, and snow-white cheeses imbrued in blood and brain matter. Rykov's triangle stood shattered into bits. In no time, Sprinkling Broom was in the thick of it, raining down blows; so, too, were Razor and Switch. Razor flashed. Switch slashed. Just then, the nobility attacked in a body from the manor house; and now, from the gate, the Count set his horsemen upon the fleeing remnant.

Only eight yagers and their platoon sergeant held on. The Warden made a rush at them. The yagers stood their ground. Nine barrels stood aimed at a point sheer between his eyes. Straight into their sights he ran, brandishing Jackknife. But Robak, seeing Gervase's blind charge, ran deliberately across his path, dropped down on all fours and struck him off his feet. Both fell to the ground the moment the platoon fired. Scarcely had the hot lead whistled past overhead when Gervase was up again, diving into the smoke. In an instant's compass, he'd hacked off two heads. The yagers fled in dismay. Gervase went after them, slapping them with the flat of his blade. Across the yard they dashed, the Warden in hot pursuit. They ran into the open barn. Thither, panting on their heels, went Gervase. He vanished into the darkness. Still, he did not desist from the fray! Groans, yells, and heavy blows echoed from within. Soon all was quiet. Gervase emerged alone from the barn, his blade dripping with blood.

By now, the nobility had taken the field and were busy pursuing, cutting down, and spiking the last of the scattered yagers. Only Rykov held out. He fought on, swearing he would never lay down his arms. At length, raising his saber, the Chamberlain stepped forward and addressed him in solemn tones:

"Captain, you shall not stain your honor by accepting quarter. Brave, hapless knight! You have proved your courage. Give up this vain struggle. Lay down your arms before we disarm you with our sabers. Your life and honor are safe. You are my prisoner."

Won over by the Chamberlain's sober manner, Rykov bowed and surrendered his saber, its blade ensanguined to the hilt.

"My brother Poles," said he. "My misfortune was in not having a single cannon. Old Suvorov put it well. 'Remember, Comrade Rykov,' he used to say. 'Never venture against the Pole without a field-piece.' What can I say? My yagers were drunk. The Major let them swill. Ah, Major Plut! He has done enough mischief for one day. He shall answer to the Tsar, for he was in charge. As for me, Chamberlain, I will be your friend. 'The better the shover, the better the lover,' goes a Russian saw. Aye, Chamberlain, you Poles spar as sturdily as you swig! But, please, no more pranks on my yagers."

  Hearing this, the Chamberlain raised his saber and ordered the Court Usher to proclaim a general pardon. The wounded were tended, the dead cleared from the field, the remaining yagers disarmed and taken captive. Long they searched for Plut. The Major had plunged deep into the nettles and was playing dead. Eventually, he came out of hiding, but only after the battle was well and truly over.

  So ended the last armed foray in Lithuania.

BOOK TEN: EMIGRATION • JACEK

The storm. Deliberations aimed at securing the fortunes of the victors.
Talking terms with Rykov. The farewell. An important revelation. Hope.

The wraiths of scud, which since morning had been driving like a flock of black birds, kept massing together, rising ever higher in the sky. Scarcely had the sun gained his meridian when the massing flock swathed half the heavens in a vast band of cloud. Driven ever more swiftly by the wind, the great cloud grew denser, sank lower, until half torn from the sky on one side, it swung earthward, spread out along the horizon and, like a great sail gathering up all the currents of air, swept the skies from south to west.

There came a moment of calm. The air fell still, as if stricken with fright. The grainfields stood stirless. A moment earlier, they had been surging like seas, bending to the ground then recovering themselves with a toss of their golden spikes. Now, they stared, stalks bristling, into the sky. So, too, the green willows and poplars ceased bowing by the wayside like women plainers over an open grave. No longer did they thrash their limbs and spread their silver tresses on the wind. Now, as if palsied with grief, they stood lifeless, like the rock of Niobe of Sipylos. Only the quaking aspen stirred her grayish leaves.

Normally loath to leave the pasturage, the cattle, huddling together, trotted briskly homeward without waiting for the herdsmen. The bull pawed the ground, plowed it with his horn, bellowing balefully at the frightened herd. The cow, mouth open wide with wonder, gazed large-eyed into the sky, sighing deeply. Meanwhile, the laggard hog fretted and gnashed his teeth; then, stealing into the grain, he made off with his plundered store of sheaves.

Birds sought refuge in the forest, under the eaves or in the depths of the long grass. Only the crows strutted in solemn flocks around the pools. Tongues protruding from their dry, gaping throats, wings adroop, they swept the jet clouds with their black eyes and waited for the coming bath. Then, sensing a storm of unwonted violence, they too rose up in a cloud, and fled to the forest. Only the fleet-winged swallow braved the skies. Like an arrow he clove the thunderhead and plunged like a spent bullet.

It was just then that the nobility had concluded their terrible battle with the Muscovites. Seeking shelter of house and stable, they trooped off, abandoning the field to the elements, which now massed for their own battle. In the west, still bathed in sunlight, the earth glowed a sullen reddish-yellow. Like a dragnet the shadow-casting cloud caught up the remnants of light and went after the sun, as if to enmesh it before it sank below the horizon. Whistling squalls sprang up, each scattering bright raindrops, large, and round, and grainy like hailstones.

Suddenly two dust whirls met. Grappling each other around the waist, they wrestled, spun round, and, whistling and twisting over the pools, stirred the waters to their very depths. Down over the meadows they swooped, shrilling through the grass and withy beds. Willow branches snapped, swathes of mown grass flew up like fistfuls of torn-out hair interwoven with curly locks of grain. The whirlwinds fell howling to the ground, rolled in the dust, plowed up and tore at the clod, making way for another twister that reared up in a column of black earth. Up it rose – a whirling, moving pyramid, its head boring into the ground, heels kicking sand into the eyes of the stars. With each stride forward, the twister thickened, funneling out at the top, until, with a triumphant blast, it blazoned the storm like a giant trumpet. And with all this chaos of water, dust, straw, leaves, branches and torn-up turf, the tempest smote the forest, roaring like a bear in the heart of the wilderness.

Drops came splashing down, thick and fast, like earth shaken through a sieve. A thunderclap rent the air. The rain coalesced into solid streams. Now, like taut cords binding earth to sky, it fell in long tresses. Now, in broad sheets, it poured, as if tossed bodily from a pail. Heaven and earth vanished under a mantle of darkness. The obscurity of the night and the inkier gloom of the storm blotted them from sight. Now and again, the horizon split open from one end clear to the other. Like a colossal sun, the storm-angel flashed his face, then, palled in darkness again, drew back into the heavens and, with a thunderous peal, slammed shut the clouds behind him. Once more, the tempest regained strength. Another thunderous cascade! The gloom deepened, thickened as to become almost palpable. Again, the torrent slackened. For a moment, the storm seemed to nod off to sleep. Then again, it awoke and rumbled. Once more, the flood came down. At last, but for the steady patter of the rain and the soughing of the trees around the house, all grew still again.

Nothing could have been more welcome this day than a torrential downpour. After shrouding the battlefield in darkness, the rainstorm flooded the roads, swept away the bridges, and turned Soplica Manor into an unapproachable fortress. Thus, news of the events at the Manor could not get out; and, for the nobility, it was precisely upon the circumstance of secrecy that the sway of the balance now hung.

Weighty deliberations were in progress in the Judge's room. The Friar lay on the bed, exhausted, pale, and blood-stained, yet in full possession of his senses. Complying diligently with his orders, the Judge called in the Chamberlain, summoned the Warden, then, bringing in Rykov as well, closed the door. The secret negotiations went on for an hour, until, tossing a hefty purse of ducats down on the table, Captain Rykov brought the talks to a stand.

"My Polish friends!" said he. "There is a common saying among you that every Muscovite is a scoundrel. Now, you can tell everyone who cares to ask that you have met a Muscovite captain – Nikita Nikitich Rykov by name. He holds eight medals and three crosses. I beg you remember it. See? This one for Ochakov, this for Izmailov, these for Novi and Preussisch-Eylau. And this one here for Korsakov's glorious retreat from Zurich. Be sure, also, to add that Rykov received a gift sword for gallantry, three commendations from the Field Marshal, and four citations along with two honorable mentions from the Tsar himself. And I have papers to prove—"

"Aye, Captain," broke in Robak, "but tell us what will happen to us if you do not accept our terms. Did you not promise to hush up the affair?"

"So I did, and I pledge it again," affirmed Rykov. "My hand and seal upon it! Why should I desire your ruin? I am an honest man. I like you Poles. Poles are a cheerful race, always good for a tipple. Brave lads too, always good for a tussle. We have a Russian saying, 'Who rides a cart often finds himself beneath it.' 'Today you ride in front, tomorrow you're in the rear.' 'Today you best 'em, tomorrow you're worsted.' So, what's to be mad about? Such is the soldier's life! Why fret and sulk over a lost battle? Ochakov was a bloody affair. At Zurich, our infantry

got soundly thrashed, On the fields of Austerlitz, I lost an entire company. Before that – I was a sergeant then – it was your
Kosciuszko at Raclawice! His scythemen cut my platoon to ribbons. But what of it? I say. Later, at Maciejowice, with my own
bayonet, I slew two of your brave noblemen. One of them was
Mokronowski. There he stood, swinging his scythe at the head
of the line. He had just sliced off the cannoneer's hand – lighted
linstock and all. Oh, you Poles! The Fatherland! Rykov knows
the meaning of the word. The Tsar gives the order – but I feel
for you. What business have we with you, anyhow? Moscow for
Muscovites, and Poland for Poles – that's what I say. But, alas,
the Tsar won't hear of it."

"Captain," said the Judge. "Those who have provided
your billets these many years know you to be an honest man.
Do not take this gift amiss, my friend. We meant no offense. We
made bold to collect these ducats only because we know you are
a poor man."

"Oh, my yagers!" cried Rykov. "The whole company cut
to ribbons. My company! And all thanks to Plut. He was the
commanding officer. He will answer to the Tsar. Keep those pen-
nies of yours, gentlemen! I have my captain's pay, such as it is.
It buys me my punch and tobacco. I like you Poles. With you, I
can eat and drink, hoot it up, and enjoy a good chat. In short, I
can live. Rest assured, I will protect you. And when the inquiry
comes around, I shall, on my word of honor, testify in your favor.
We'll say we dropped by for a visit, downed a few, hoofed the
odd measure, and got a bit pie-eyed. Then Plut accidentally gave
the order to open fire, a skirmish broke out, and somehow his
battalion got the worst of it. Meanwhile, be sure to grease the
commission's hand with gold, and all shall be well. But I must
tell you what I told this fellow with the long rapier here. Plut is
in charge. I am only second in command. Plut is alive. He may
pull a fast one and sink you yet, for he's a sly customer. You will
need to stop up his mouth with banknotes. What say you, sir?
You with the long rapier! Did you talk to Plut? Come to terms?"

Gervase looked about him, stroked his pate with one
hand and gestured vaguely with the other, as if to say he'd taken
care of the matter.

"Well?" insisted Rykov. "Will Plut keep mum? Did he
pledge his word?"

Vexed by Rykov's persistence, the Warden turned his thumb solemnly downward and waved his hand as if to close further discussion.

"I swear by my Jackknife that Plut shall not give us away," said he. "His lips are sealed!" And lowering his hand, he snapped his fingers – to dispel the mystery.

Gervase's dark gesture was understood. His listeners stared at one another in surprise. For several moments, they studied each other's faces in gloomy silence.

"So, the fox pays his skin to the furrier," muttered Rykov at last.

"*Requiescat in pace!*" said the Chamberlain.

"Clearly the hand of God," said the Judge. "But I am innocent of this bloodshed. I knew nothing of it."

The Friar rose from the pillows and sat gloomily silent. "It is a great sin to kill an unarmed captive," said he at last, eyeing the Warden sternly. "Christ forbids revenge, even on one's enemies. Oh, Warden, for this, you shall answer heavily to God! One restriction pertains: if the deed were done not from mindless vengeance but *pro publico bono*."

The Warden nodded, waved his hand, then, blinking his eyes, repeated the phrase, "*pro publico bono*."

There was no more talk of Major Plut. In vain they scoured the yard for him the next morning. A reward was posted for his body. All to no purpose. The Major had vanished without a trace as if he'd dropped into a well. Several conjectures as to his fate made the rounds, but no one knew for certain either then or later. To no avail did they pester Gervase with questions. No utterance would pass his lips except, "*pro publico bono*." The Steward was privy to the secret, but he'd pledged his word of honor, and so the old man's lips remained sealed as by a spell.

Having agreed to the terms, Rykov left the room; meanwhile, Robak had the fighting nobility called in.

"My brothers," said the Chamberlain, addressing them gravely. "This day God has smiled upon our arms, but I must be frank with you, gentlemen. Dire consequences shall follow from this untimely battle of ours. We have committed a blunder, and each one of us here is to blame. Father Robak for being overzealous in spreading the news. The Warden and the nobility for mistaking his purpose. The war with Russia will not be waged just now. Meanwhile, those that took a leading part in the battle

are no longer safe in Lithuania. So, gentlemen, you must fly to
the Duchy of Warsaw. I have in mind Matthias, whom they call
Baptist, Tadeusz, Watering Can, and Razor. These named must
fly across the Niemen where our nation's host awaits them. We
shall lay the blame squarely on Plut and on you absconders, and
thus save the rest of your kin. I bid you farewell, but not for
long, as there is every reason to hope that our liberty shall break
forth this coming spring. Lithuania, which now bids you farewell
as exiles, shall see you shortly as her conquering saviors. The
Judge shall attend to your journey. And I, insofar as I am able,
will help with the funds."

The nobility saw the wisdom of the Chamberlain's words.
Well they knew that those who ran afoul of the Tsar never found
true peace in this world. A man had either to fight or rot away
in the Siberian wastes. And so, exchanging sorrowful glances
in silence, they sighed and nodded assent. Although known the
world over for their love of their land, which they hold dearer
than life, yet Poles have always been ready to go abroad, faring
forth to the ends of the earth, suffering years of privation and
want, battling man and fate – enduring all this, so long as there
shines through it all the hope of serving their country.

They agreed to depart without delay. The sole dissenting
voice was Buchman. Being a prudent man, he had not taken
part in the battle. But on hearing of the council, he had hurried
over to cast his vote. Although favorable to the plan, he sought
to elaborate on it. He pushed for certain amendments and clar-
ifications. A formal committee had to be struck, the aims, ways,
and means of emigration duly weighed, and many other things
besides. But, alas, time was of the essence, and Buchman's advice was promptly shelved. The nobility bade a hasty adieu and
set out on their journey.

Then the Judge, bidding Tadeusz stay behind, said to
the Friar: "It is time I told you what I learned for certain only
yesterday. Our Tadeusz is truly in love with Sophie. Let him
ask for her hand before he leaves. I have spoken with Telimena.
She no longer opposes the match, and Sophia agrees to the will
of her guardians. My dear brother, if we cannot wed the young
couple today, then let us at least betroth them before the lad's
departure. You know well the various temptations to which a
young heart is subject abroad. With a ring on his finger, a youth
has merely to glance at it, recall his betrothal, and the fever

of foreign seductions cools at once. Believe me, a wedding ring possesses great power. Thirty years ago, I entertained a strong affection of my own for Mistress Martha. I had won her heart, and we were engaged to be married. But God chose not to bless our union. He left me orphaned after taking into his glory the comely daughter of my friend, the Steward. All I have left is the memory of her charms and qualities, and this gold ring. The poor lass appears before my eyes every time I glance at it. Thus, by the grace of God have I kept my plighted faith until now. I never married and remain a widower, even though the Steward has another daughter, who is very pretty and very much like my beloved Martha."

And gazing tenderly at his ring, the Judge wiped his tears with the back of his hand. "Well, dear brother," he concluded, "shall we have them betrothed? He loves her dearly, and I have the aunt's and the girl's consent."

At this, Tadeusz stepped forward and spoke with great animation. "Dear Uncle, how can I thank you enough for the constant care you take for my happiness. If Sophie were pledged to me today, if I knew she were to be my wife, I should be the happiest man in the world. But I must tell you frankly that, for various reasons, the betrothal cannot take place. Question me no further! If Sophie agrees to wait, she may soon find in me a better, worthier man. Perhaps my constancy shall earn me her affection. Perhaps a sprig of glory shall garnish my name. Perhaps I shall soon return to my home. Then, dear Uncle, shall I remind you of your promise. Then, on my knees, shall I greet my dear Sophie and – if she still be free for the asking – beg for her hand. But now I must leave Lithuania. Who knows for how long? Perhaps in the meantime someone else shall win Sophie's favor. I refuse to bind her will. To expect a return of affection – an affection I have not yet earned – would be beneath contempt."

And as the lad uttered these earnest words, two glistening teardrops, large as pearly berries, started from his large blue eyes and guttered swiftly down his ruddy cheeks.

All through their secret conversation, Sophie had been in the alcove next door, listening intently through a crack in the wall. She overheard Tadeusz's bold and forthright declaration of love, and her heart trembled. She observed the two big teardrops in his eyes. Yet she could make little sense of it! Why had he fallen in love with her? Why was he leaving her now? Where

was he bound? The thought of his leaving saddened her. Never
before had she heard so strange and novel a thing from the lips
of a youth – that she was loved! She ran to the family oratory
and took from it a holy picture and small relic box. The image
was of Saint Genevieve. The box contained a shred of garment
belonging to Saint Joseph the Bridegroom, patron of betrothed
couples. Armed with these devotional articles, she entered the
Judge's room.

"Are you leaving so soon?" said she to Tadeusz. "I have a
little gift for your journey and a word of caution too. Carry this
relic and image with you always, and remember your Sophie.
May God keep you well and happy. May he bring you home to us
soon, safe and sound."

She fell silent and stooped her head. No sooner did she
close her dark-blue eyes than tears flowed to profusion from under the lashes; and so, with her eyes closed, Sophie stood silent,
spilling tears like diamonds.

Tadeusz took the gifts and kissed her hand. "My lady Sophia," said he. "Now I must bid you farewell. Remember me.
Vouchsafe me an occasional prayer. Sophia . . .!" But he could
say no more.

Meanwhile, the Count, who had entered unbidden into
the room with Telimena, found himself moved by the young couple's exchange of tender adieus.

"Such a simple scene," he remarked, casting a glance at
Telimena, "and how much beauty contained herein! Two souls,
a shepherdess and a warrior, fain to diverge their wakes like
a frigate and its jolly boat in stormy waters. Indeed, nothing
so fires the emotions as the forced separation of two souls in
love. Time is a blast of wind. The short wick, it quenches. Great
flames, it fans to mightier conflagrations. I, too, can love more
ardently from afar. Mr. Soplica, I took you for a rival. This error
was the cause of our unhappy contention, which forced me to
take up the sword against you. Now I see where I erred. You
sighed for this shepherdess, while I'd entrusted my heart to this
fair Nymph here. Henceforth, let us drown our differences in the
blood of our enemies. We shall no longer contend with murderous steel. We shall settle our amatory quarrel by other means.
Let us see who outmatches the other in strength of affection. Let
us leave behind these dear objects of our love and hasten forth
against the lance and sword. Be it ours to strive together on the

battlefields of constancy, sorrow, and suffering – to pursue our foe with a manly arm!"

And saying this, he looked at Telimena; but she, aghast at his words, merely stared back at him.

"But, dear Count," broke in the Judge. "Why do you insist on leaving? Take my advice and remain on your estate where you are safe. The authorities may skin the minor nobility alive. But you, dear Count, are sure to come out all right. You know the regime under which we live. You are rich. You shall buy yourself out of prison with half a year's income."

"Not in my character!" stated the Count. "If I cannot be a lover, I will be a hero. Made anxious in love, I shall seek comfort in glory. If I must be a beggar of the heart, then be it mine to abound in feats of arms."

"But what prevents you from enjoying love and happiness?" asked Telimena.

"The power of my destiny!" replied the Count. "A dark prescience impels me in mysterious fashion toward foreign lands and noble feats of arms. It is true that today, in your honor, I stood ready to light the flame on Hymen's altar. But this youth has set me a more shining example, for he is ready to tear the nuptial crown from his temples and ride off to prove his heart against fortune's hurdles and the hazards of bloody war. For me, too, shall this day mark a new Epoch. Birbante-Rocca once echoed with my arms. May these arms now echo throughout the length and breadth of Poland!"

With that, he proudly smote the sword-hilt at his side.

"Indeed, it would be hard to rebuke such zeal," replied Robak. "Go then, and take your money with you. Perhaps you shall see fit to equip a company as did the young Potocki, who astounded the French by raising a million francs for the war treasury, or like Prince Dominic Radziwill, who pledged his lands and chattels to field two new horse regiments. Go, I say, and take your money with you. We have no shortage of fighting brawn in the Duchy, but we do lack funds. Go then, and God speed!"

"Alas, my knight," said Telimena, looking sorrowfully at the Count. "Nothing, I see, shall deflect you from your purpose. Therefore, I beg you, when you enter the martial lists, cast a tender glance at this love-gage."

She tore a ribbon from her frock, tied a bow and fastened it in the Count's buttonhole.

"May these, my colors, lead you forward against blazing cannon, glinting lance and raining brimstone. And when your valorous deeds spread your fame abroad, when the imperishable bay shadows your bloody casque, and victory crowns your lofty helm, then cast your eye again upon this favor and recall whose hand affixed it to your breast!"

She tendered him her hand. The Count knelt down and kissed it. And so, raising her handkerchief to one eye, while squinting down with the other, Telimena watched him bid her his soulful adieus; then, heaving a sigh, she shrugged her shoulders.

"My dear Count," said the Judge. "Make haste, it is growing late."

"Enough of this!" growled Father Robak. "Be off with you!"

The Judge and the Friar quickly parted the tender couple and showed them the door.

Meanwhile, after embracing his uncle tearfully, Tadeusz kissed Robak's hand. The Friar pressed the lad's brow to his bosom, placed his hands crosswise over his head and, gazing heavenward, said, "God go with you, my son!" And he wept.

"What!" exclaimed the Judge, as soon as Tadeusz quitted the room. "Will you tell him nothing? Not even now? Is the poor lad to know nothing at all? Even at his departure?"

"Aye, nothing," replied the Priest. For a while, he wept, his face buried in his hands. "Why should the poor boy know he has a father who hides from the world like a scoundrel . . . a common murderer! God knows how much I wish to tell him, but I forego this solace in atonement for the sins of my past."

"Then, it is time to think of yourself," said the Judge. "Considering your age and state of health, there is no question of your going abroad with the others. You say you know of a place where you can weather the storm. Tell me where it is. You must hurry, a britzka stands waiting. But wouldn't the ranger's lodge serve you better?"

Robak shook his head.

"I have until morning," said he. "Now, my brother, send for the village priest. Bid him come quickly with the *viaticum*.

Dismiss everyone but yourself and the Warden, and close the door."

The Judge, having done his behest, sat down on the bed beside him; meanwhile, Gervase remained standing, his elbow anchored on the pommel of his sword, his bent brow resting on his hand.

Before beginning to speak again, Robak turned his gaze on the Warden and eyed him strangely. As when a surgeon, before applying the knife, lays a warm hand upon the patient's body, the Friar softened the expression of his keen eyes. Long he trained his look on Gervase's face; then, as though hazarding a blind thrust, he covered his eyes and uttered forcefully:

"I am Jacek Soplica."

The Warden paled and lurched forward. Like a rock arrested in mid-fall he stood, bent at the waist, one foot raised off the floor. Wide-eyed he stared, whiskers bristling, mouth agape, white teeth bared. The rapier slipped out from under him, but he caught it up with his knees. Seizing it by the pommel with his right hand then grasping firm hold of the hilt, he drew it back. The dark blade swayed fitfully behind him. He brought to mind a wounded lynx ready to spring from a tree at a hunter's face. Puffed up into a ball, the beast stands snarling, flashing its bloodshot eyes, twitching its whiskers, vibrating its tail.

"Gervase," said the Friar. "Man's wrath no longer holds me in fear. The hand of God is upon me. I adjure you in the name of him who saved the world, who blessed his slayers from the cross and heard the robber's plea. Relent, and hear me out! I have revealed myself. To ease my conscience, I must obtain, or at least beg, your forgiveness. Hear my confession. Then, do with me as you please."

And he joined his hands, as if in prayer. The Warden, drawing back in great astonishment, smacked his brow with his hand, then shrugged his shoulders.

The Friar began to relate the story of his past friendship with Horeszko, of his love for the Pantler's daughter and the resulting enmity between the Pantler and himself. He spoke at random, often interspersing his confession with complaints and accusations. Often, he would break off his tale, as if he had fin-

ished, only to resume it again. The Warden, being privy to most
of the details, was able to make sense of the desultory tale and
supply the missing parts. But the Judge was often left in the
dark. With stooped heads, both men listened intently to Jacek's
tale. Meanwhile, Jacek's speech grew increasingly slower. Often, it broke off altogether.

"You remember, Gervase, how the Pantler used to invite
me to his banquets and drink my health. Often, he would raise
his cup and declare aloud that he had no better friend than Jacek Soplica. How he'd clasp me to his bosom! Those who saw it
would have sworn he was ready to share his soul with me. He,
my friend? He knew perfectly well what was raging in my heart!

"Meanwhile, the neighbors' tongues already wagged. 'Hi
Soplica!' – they called – 'you woo in vain. A magnate's doorbell
exceeds the reach of a cupbearer's son!' I laughed, affecting to
scoff at dignitaries and their daughters. What were aristocrats
to me! If I paid them visits, it was out of friendship alone. Never
should I match above my degree, I assured them. Even so, the
jests cut me to the quick. I was young, fearless, and enjoyed full
access to society in a land where, as you know, minor nobility and magnates could aspire to the crown on an equal footing.
Why, Tenczynski once begged the hand of a daughter of a royal house, and the King agreed without any hint of shame! Are
not the Soplicas every bit as worthy as the Tenczynskis – their
blood, their arms, and their loyal service to the Commonwealth?

"How easy, upon a single instant, to blight another's happiness so that an entire lifetime cannot set it right. One word
from the Pantler and how happy we should have been! Who
knows? We might all be living still. He might have lived out his
declining years in peace and quiet, close to his beloved daughter,
his lovely Eva, and his grateful son-in-law. He might have rocked
his grandsons' cradles. But in the event he ruined us both. He .
. . and that slaying . . . and all the consequences of that crime .
. . all my sorrows and transgressions! . . . but I have no right to
lay blame. I am his slayer. I have no right at all to accuse him. I
forgive him with all my heart. And yet he . . .

"Had he but once refused me openly (for he was well
aware of our feelings), had he forbidden me to visit, who knows?
I might have taken my leave, vented my anger, and eventually
left him in peace. But that proud fox devised another stratagem
– to behave as though it never occurred to him that I might be

seeking such a union. And yet he had need of me. The nobility valued me. I was popular among the manor holders. And so,
pretending not to notice my feelings, he continued to receive me
as before – insisting even that I should come more frequently.
But every time we were alone and he saw the tears start from
my eyes and my bosom heave, ready to burst, the old fox would
promptly turn to idle talk about lawsuits, the regional assemblies, the hunt . . .

"Oh, the times we sat in company, in our cups, and he,
moved to tears, took me into his embrace, assuring me of his
friendship – for he was always in need of my sword or my vote in
the House – and I would politely return the gesture. Each time,
fury so seized me that the spittle rushed to my lips and my hand
tightened around my sword-hilt – so much did I desire to spit on
his friendship and draw my sword. But Eva, seeing my face and
demeanor, guessed what was passing within me. How? I do not
know. She looked at me imploringly and turned pale. Ah, what a
lovely, gentle creature she was! That look of hers! So compliant!
So serene! So angelic! It was beyond my power to frighten her or
to stir her to anger. I held my peace. And so, Lithuania's notorious roisterer, who struck fear into the hearts of the mightiest
lords; who scarce let a day pass without provoking some brawl or
other; who would not permit a king much less a pantler to offend
him; who went into transports of rage at the slightest dissent
– I, drunk and incensed as I was, remained meek as a lamb, as
though I were gazing upon the Sacred Host!

"How many times I wished to bare my soul and beg on my
knees before him! But on looking into his eyes and meeting that
icy gaze, I was moved to shame by reason of my strong feelings.
And so, in the coolest manner, I would strike up again on the
subject of our court cases and regional diets. I even cracked jokes
– all this out of pride, mind, so as not to offend the dignity of the
Soplica name, or lower myself in the Pantler's eyes by suing in
vain and incurring a repulse. Imagine the canards flying if word
got out among the nobility that I, Jacek . . .

"The Horeszkos refusing Soplica the hand of their wench!
That I, Jacek, had been served up a bowl of black pottage!

"At last, at my wits' end, I decided to raise a small regiment of the nobility and abandon forever our district and homeland. I would make for regions in Muscovy or Tartary and there
wage war. I went to bid the Pantler good-bye, hoping that on

seeing me, his loyal supporter and old friend – indeed, I was practically a member of his household, having campaigned with him and been his drinking mate all those years – that, on seeing me about to leave for a distant land, the old man might be moved to show me a sliver of human sentiment. Even as a snail reveals his horns!

"Ah, who fosters at the bottom of his heart but the faintest spark of affection for a friend shall, upon the moment of parting, feel that spark rise up within him like life's expiring ember. When the gaze falls upon a dying friend's brow, even the coldest eye will shed a tear.

"My poor beloved! Hearing of my planned departure, she turned pale and slipped to the floor in a dead faint. She could not speak. A stream of tears started from her eyes, and I knew how dearly she loved me.

"For the first time in my life, I recall, I wept. Wept tears of joy and despair! I forgot myself, went raving mad. Once again, I was on the point of falling at her father's feet. Ready to coil myself like a snake around his knees, and beg, 'Dear father! Take me for your son, or slay me on the spot.' But then, sullen and cold as a pillar of salt, he raises, in that polite and distant manner of his, the subject of . . . what, you ask? Why, his daughter's wedding! At such a moment! Gervase! Friend! Judge for yourself. You have a heart of flesh.

"'Mr. Soplica,' the Pantler says to me. 'A marriage broker has just paid me a visit on behalf of the Chatelain's son. Now you are my friend. What say you to this? You know, of course, that I have a rich and beautiful daughter, and that he is but a castellan from Vitebsk and thus carries little weight in the Senate. How should you advise me, dear fellow?'

I have no recollection of what I said to him. More than likely, I said nothing, mounted my horse, and fled."

"Jacek!" exclaimed the Warden. "Full marks for all this special pleading. But what of it? Your fault stands undiminished. Why, you are not the first in the world to fall in love with the daughter of a rich lord or royal personage. Not the first to conspire to snatch her away by force, and so avenge yourself openly. But to devise such a cunning plot! To slay a Polish lord! In Poland! And in league with Muscovy!"

"There was no plot," said Jacek with sadness in his voice. "Snatch her away, you say? Of course I might have done it. Neither bar nor lock would have prevented me. Why, I should have smashed that castle of his into fine dust! Did Dobrzyn not stand behind me? And four other noble villages besides! Oh, if Eva had been like *their* women, strong and hardy, fearless of flight, pursuit and the clash of arms. But the poor child! How her parents coddled her – frail, timorous thing that she was. A delicate caterpillar! An April butterfly! To snatch her away thus, to touch her with a bloodied hand would have killed her. No, I simply couldn't.

"To avenge myself openly and storm the castle would have been contemptible, for people would have said that I was taking vengeance for the repulse. Warden! Foreign to your upright heart the hell of slighted pride!

"The demon of pride whispered better counsels in my ear. 'Take your revenge in blood, and conceal the cause. Stop visiting the castle, root out your love, put Eva out of mind, marry another, and then – only then – dream up some pretext, and take your revenge!'

"At first, I thought I'd found peace. The fiction pleased me, and . . . and I married the first poor lass I laid eyes on. I did wrong, I know – and sorely have I been punished since, for I had no love for her . . . Tadeusz's poor mother. She was a good-natured soul and utterly devoted to me. But, in my heart, I was choking back my earlier love and rage. I raved like a maniac. I tried to bury my grief in farm labor and other business, but all to no purpose. The demon of vengeance held me in thrall. Ill-humored and sullen, I found solace nowhere. And so, sinking from sin to sin, I turned to drink.

"So it was that in a short space of time my wife died of grief, leaving me with this child. And all the while despair devoured me . . .

"How must I have loved my poor Eva! All these years! Where did I not travel? Even now I cannot put her out of mind. Her dear image stands as if daubed by a brush before me. No amount of vodka would dull the edge of my memory even for an instant. All those lands I saw, and still I could not remove her from my mind. And here I lie in this bed – God's servant in a friar's habit, soaked in blood – still going on about her! To speak of such things at such a time. But God will forgive me. I want you to know the depth of my grief and despair when I committed that...

"The deed took place a short while after she was betrothed. The whole district buzzed with news of the match. People told me that on receiving the ring from the Governor's hand, Eva fainted away and grew feverish. Already, she was showing signs of consumption, and she sobbed constantly. She loved another in secret, they surmised. But the Pantler, ever serene and jovial, continued to hold balls at the castle and invite his friends. Me, he no longer invited. Of what use was I to him now? The disorder of my household, my wretched state and vile addiction had made me an object of scorn – the laughingstock of the world. I, who once had the entire district wrapped about my finger. I, whom Radziwill used to call 'dear fellow.' I, who would ride out of my village with a troop more numerous than a princely retinue . . . I had only to unsheathe my sword and several thousand blades flashed around me, striking terror into the castles of great lords. And here was I now – the butt of village urchins! So suddenly had I fallen from grace in peoples' eyes. Jacek Soplica! Let him who knows what it is to feel pride . . ."

Here, growing increasingly weaker, the Friar slumped back into the pillows.

"Great are God's judgments!" said Gervase, deeply stirred. "It is the truth! The truth! So, it has been you all along? Jacek Soplica under a beggar's hood? I knew you when you were hale and hearty, the comely squire whom lords flattered and the ladies raved about. The whiskered champion! It wasn't that long ago, after all. How grief has aged you! How did I fail to recognize the shot, when you felled the bear so expertly? Lithuania boasted no finer marksman – and, next to Matthias, no abler swordsman. It is true! Our women used to sing ditties about you.

The twitch of Jacek's whisker makes our gentry quail;
When Whisker's knot is tied, even Radziwill grows pale.

"Oh, you tied one on my lord! Hapless wretch! But is it really you? Reduced to such a state? Jacek Whisker, an alms quester? Great are God's judgments! And now, sir . . . hah! You shall not escape your deserts. I swore an oath that he that spilled a drop of Horeszko blood would . . ."

But here, Robak raised himself back to his sitting position and resumed his tale.

"I was out riding by the castle. Who could name the le-

gion of devils thronging my mind and heart? The Pantler – why,
he was killing his child! Me, he'd already slain . . . destroyed!
Satan drew me to the gate. Oh, the revels he held at the castle!
A shindy every night! Windows ablaze with candlelight. Hall-
ways ringing with music. It was a wonder the place didn't come
crashing down on his polished skull! Anyhow, give vengeance a
thought, and Satan slips you the weapon. The thought no sooner crossed my mind than he sent the Muscovites along. I was
standing there and saw it all. You know how they stormed the
castle.

"Because it is a lie that I was in league with Muscovy . . .

"Many thoughts passed through my mind as I stood
there. First, I broke out into a silly grin like a child entranced
by the flames of a fire. Then, expecting to see the castle burn to
the ground, I felt a sort of brigandish joy. At times, I felt like
charging in and rescuing her. The Pantler too . . .

"As you know, you fought them off bravely, and with
great skill. I could not believe my eyes: Muscovites dropping
like flies all around me. The cattle couldn't shoot straight if they
tried! The sight of their rout sent me into another towering rage.
Was the Pantler to taste victory? Was fortune to smile on all he
did? Was he to emerge triumphant from this terrible onslaught?
In disgust, I turned to leave. The day was just dawning. Suddenly, I saw him, recognized him. He had stepped out onto the
gallery and was facing the sun. I saw the flash of his diamond
broach. There he stood, curling his whiskers, proudly surveying
the field. He seemed to be singling me out for special abuse. He
recognized me, I thought, and was giving me the arm, like this!
Mocking and menacing me! I seized a soldier's musket, shouldered it, barely aimed, and fired. You know the rest . . .

"A curse upon firearms! Who kills with a blade must first
strike his pose, lunge, parry, break. He may disarm his foe, or
he may choose to check his mortal thrust. With a firearm, it is
enough to seize a gun, cock it . . . a split second, a spark . . .

"Gervase, did I run, when you took aim from the gallery?
No! I just stared into both barrels of your gun. Despair overtook
me. A strange sorrow rooted me to the ground. Why, oh why,
Gervase, did you miss your mark that day? You would have done
me a service. But, clearly it had to be . . . to atone for my sin . . ."
    Here again, he ran out of breath.

"God knows," replied the Warden, "I did my best to gun you down. How much bloodshed resulted from that single shot of yours! How many disasters have since befallen your family – and the rest of us! All through your fault, Jacek. And yet, today, when the yagers had their sights trained on the Count, last male representative of the Horeszko line (albeit on the spindle side), you shielded him with your own body. And when the Muscovites fired on me, you knocked me to the ground, thereby saving both of us. If consecrated friar you truly be, then your habit stands proof against Jackknife. Keep well! No longer shall I seek to darken your doorway. We are quits. The rest, we leave to God."

Jacek offered him his hand, but Gervase shrank back. "I cannot," said he, "without affront to my honor, touch a hand bloodied by an act of personal vengeance. . . and not *pro publico bono.*"

But Jacek, slumping down from the pillows, turned to the Judge. Growing paler by the minute, he asked anxiously for the village priest, then appealed to the Warden:

"I beg you, sir, stay a moment longer. I have barely strength to finish. Warden, I shall die this night."

"What is this, my brother?" cried the Judge. "But I had a look at it. It's hardly a serious wound. Why the priest? Could it be badly dressed? I'll send for the doctor. He should be at the druggist's—"

But the Friar cut him off. "No need now, dear brother. I took an earlier bullet in the same spot . . . at Jena . . . wound never healed properly . . . now it's infected . . . gangrene . . . I know about wounds. See? Blood, black as soot . . . what good is a doctor? . . . trifling matter . . . We die but once. Today, tomorrow, we must all yield up our souls. Warden, forgive me, but I must finish my tale.

"When the whole nation brands you a traitor, there is special merit in renouncing treason – especially for someone with a pride like mine . . .

"The label 'traitor' stuck to me like a plague. My fellow citizens turned their faces from me. Old friends shunned me. The timid greeted me at a distance and gave me a wide berth. Even the merest yokel or Jew, after bobbing his head, would give me a sidelong sneer. The word 'traitor' rang in my ears, echoed throughout my house and over my fields. From dawn to dusk, it danced before me like a spot on a diseased eye. But I was never a traitor to my country . . .

"Muscovy took me perforce as one of her own. The bulk of the Pantler's domain passed to the Soplicas. Later, the Targowica confederates wanted to honor me with an office. Had I then consented to turn Muscovite – Satan counseled it! I was already rich and powerful then – had I then thrown in with Moscow, the wealthiest magnates would have sought out my favor. Even our brother nobles, even the rabble so quick to discredit their own, will forgive those fortunates that serve the Muscovite! All this, I knew. And yet I couldn't . . .

"I fled the country. Where did I not travel? What did I not suffer!

"At last, God showed me the only remedy. I had to amend myself and, so far as possible, right the wrongs that . . .

"They transported the Pantler's daughter and her husband, the Governor, to Siberia. There, she died young, having here left behind her a daughter, little Sophie. I saw to it that she was properly looked after . . .

"Perhaps I slew him more from foolish pride than thwarted love, so I needed humbling. I entered a monastic order. I, once so proud of my noble birth, I, the swaggerer, bowed my head and became a mendicant friar, with Robak – Worm! – for a name. Because, like a worm in the dust . . .

"A wicked example to my country, an inducement to treason – these had to be redeemed by good example, by blood and self-sacrifice . . .

"I fought for my country. Where? How? No one need know. Not for earthly glory did I so often expose myself to bullets and steel. I'd sooner recall not my loud, valorous deeds, but the quiet, useful ones, and the sufferings that no one . . .

"Many times, I crossed the frontier, bearing orders from our leaders, gathering intelligence,   hatching plots. Nowhere did my quester's hood go unseen – not even in Galicia, not even in Greater Poland! For a year, I was chained to a wheelbarrow in a Prussian fortress. Three times, Muscovy flayed my back with the knout. Once, they had me on the road to Siberia. The Austrians buried me deep in Spielberg's vaults, as a slave-laborer – *in carcere duro*. Yet, by a miracle, the Lord delivered me. And now, he lets me die among my people, with the holy sacraments. . .

"But now, who knows? Perhaps I sinned again. Perhaps I exceeded orders in hastening the uprising? Yet the thought that Soplicas should be the first to rise up, that my kinsmen should be the first to plant our heraldic charger on Lithuanian soil . . . the thought . . . surely . . . was pure enough . . .

"You wanted vengeance, Gervase? Well, you have it! You have served as divine retribution's tool. With your sword, God has cut my scheme to ribbons. You snarled up the plot I'd been hatching these so many years. My great, all-consuming ambition, my last worldly desire, which I nursed and fondled like a beloved child – this, you have slain before its father's eyes. And yet, despite all, I forgive you. You—"

"Even so may God forgive you," broke in Gervase. "Father Jacek, if you must take the housel, then I am no Lutheran or schismatic. He sins that grieves a dying man – this, I know. Now allow me to relate something to you. Doubtless, you shall find it a consolation. When my late master fell mortally wounded and I knelt over his breast, smearing my blade with his blood, vowing vengeance, he shook his head at me. He pointed his hand toward the gate where you stood and traced a cross in the air. He was unable to speak, but it was a clear he'd forgiven his slayer. I understood what he meant, but so great was my wrath that I never breathed a word of that blessing to anyone."

The dying man's agonies broke off all further talk. A long hour of silence ensued. They waited for the village priest. At last, the clatter of hooves burst upon their ears. A rap on the door and the tavern-keeper, breathless after a hard ride, hurried in with an important dispatch addressed to Jacek Soplica. Jacek had his brother read it aloud. It was from Fiszer, then Chief-of-Staff of the Polish Army under Prince Joseph's command, with news that a state of war had been declared in the Emperor's Privy Council. Even now was the Emperor proclaiming it to the world. A General Assembly had been called in Warsaw and the federated Mazovian States were on the point of making a solemn declaration of union with Lithuania.

On hearing the news, Jacek muttered a silent prayer. Holding a blessed candle to his bosom, he raised his eyes, now ablaze with hope, and lavishly spent his last reserve of tears.

"*Now, O Lord,*" he prayed, "*let thy servant depart in peace.*" They knelt down. A bell at the door announced the parish priest with the Body of Our Lord.

Night was just departing. The first roseate sunbeams shot across the milky sky. Like diamond darts they pierced the lattice panes and, hanging on the dying man's head and pillow, wreathed his face and temples in gold, so that he shone like a saint becrowned with a fiery glory.

BOOK ELEVEN: THE YEAR 1812

*Spring omens. The arrival of the armies. The mass. Official re-
habilitation of the late Jacek Soplica. Eavesdropping on Gervase and
Protase from which a quick end to the lawsuit may be inferred. A lancer
courts his lass. The dispute over Scut and Peregrine settled at last. The
guests gather for the banquet. The betrothed couples presented to the
generals.*

Omemorable year! To have seen you in our land! Our peasantry still calls you the year of the harvest. Our soldiery styles you
the year of war. Ever the subject of old men's yarns! Ever the
theme of poets' musings! Long did a great sign in the heavens
foretoken your coming. Dull rumors began to spread abroad; and
when, at last, the spring sun dawned, a strange premonition, a
joyous, expectant longing seized the hearts of our people – as if
the world were coming to an end.

When came the time of the cattle going to grass in early
spring, they showed little eagerness to graze on the shoots that
greened the clod. Gaunt and famished, they lay lounging in the
fields, drooping their heads, bawling or chewing phlegmatically
on their winter-feed. Nor did the villagers plowing for the spring
crop rejoice as usual in the long winter's passing. They crooned
no song but toiled listlessly on, as though seed and harvest time
were out of mind. And as they harrowed the seed fields, they
checked their beasts of burden at every turn, gazing anxiously
westward – as if some great marvel were shaping there.

Uneasily they watched the birds return. Even now the
stork came whiffling down upon his ancient pine, spreading his
white pinion like spring's first battle flag. Swift upon his heels
came shrill regiments of swallows, mustering over the bodies of
water, scooping up the frozen mud to build their little habitations. Woodcock whirred in the dusky thickets. Flocks of weary geese swept over the forest, dropping clamorously into the
glades, seeking rest and refreshment; and all the while, throbbing high in the darkness overhead, the cranes gave out their
dismal moan. The watchmen wondered anxiously at this great
stir in the feathered kingdom. What storm had driven out the
birds so early?

At last, like throngs of finches, plovers, and starlings, new flocks appeared. A host of bright plumes and pennons flashed on the hilltops and streamed into the meadows. Cavalrymen! – strangely arrayed, bearing arms never before seen. Squadron after squadron came riding down. With them, like freshets in full spate, swept columns of iron-shod troops. Endless files of black shakos and glinting bayonets issued from the forest. Like swarms of ants without number, the infantrymen marched, all bearing north, as if, on the heels of the birds, man were driven by the same strange instinctive force to leave the fabled South in a mass migration to our land.

Day and night, horses, men, field guns, and eagles streamed past. Here and yon, an incandescent glow lighted the horizon. The earth shook, thunder rumbled from every quarter.

War! War! Not a nook in our land where the rumblings went unheard. Not even the rustic woodsman whose sires and grandsires departed this life without ever venturing beyond the forest's bourne; whose ear knew no sound under heaven but the rush of the wind and the wild beasts' roars; whose only visitors were woodsmen like himself – not even he, in these remotest parts, was spared the sights of war. A lurid glare flashed in the sky – a piercing shriek, and a grenade missent from the battle-field sought a path through the trees, snapping branches, up-rooting stumps. Trembling in his mossy lair, the venerable bison bristled his shaggy mane. Half rising on his forefeet, he shook his beard and gazed around, startled by the brilliant shower of sparks in the brushwood. The stray piece of ordnance spun round, spluttered and hissed, then exploded like a thunderbolt. For the first time in his life, the bison took fright; and, scrambling to his feet, he fled into the deeper repairs of the forest.

"A battle? Where? Which way?" the young men asked, seizing their arms. The womenfolk implored heaven with up-raised hands. "God's on Bonaparte's side!" cried one and all, their eyes bedewed with tears. Of victory, there could be no doubt. Napoleon stood with us!

O Spring! To have seen you in our land! Memorable spring of war! O spring of harvests! To have seen you blowing with grass and corn, glittering with valiant men, rich in events, and great with hope! Even now you stand before my eyes like a radiant apparition. Born in chains, enslaved while still in my swaddling bands, I have known but one such springtime in all my life!

Soplica Manor stood close to the high road leading up from the Niemen. Two generals, our own Prince Joseph and King Jerome of Westphalia, advanced with their armies along this very road. Having taken the part of Lithuania lying between Grodno and Slonim, the King granted the troops a three-day rest. Despite the rigors of the march, the Poles among them raised a howl of protest, so impatient were they to gain on the Muscovites.

The Prince's General Staff put up in the neighboring town. Meanwhile, an army of forty thousand together with its staff encamped around Soplica Manor. The staff included Generals Dombrowski, Kniaziewicz, Malachowski, Giedroyc, and Grabowski. The hour being late, they took up quarters anywhere they could find them, some in the castle, others in the manor house. Orders went out. Sentries were posted. The weary leaders retired to their rooms. Silence descended on the entire domain – manor, camp, and fields. Roaming patrols stirred like shades in the night. Campfires flickered. Ever and anon, a watchword rang out from a post.

All slept – master of the manor, generals and troops. Only the Steward forwent his sweet repose. Charged with preparing a grand banquet for the morrow, he was determined the meal should bring imperishable fame to the Soplica house. He'd hold such a banquet as did honor to Poland's revered guests and the double solemnity of the occasion – tomorrow being both a religious and a family feast. Three sets of betrothals were due to take place; and hadn't General Dombrowski this evening made known his wish to partake of a traditional Polish repast?

Despite the late hour, the Steward quickly assembled five cooks from the neighborhood to serve as his under-chefs. Girding his waist with a white apron, the head chef put on his hat and rolled up his sleeves to the elbow. Fly flap in one hand – any greedy fly seen alighting on a delicacy was swept away in an instant! – he donned a pair of well-wiped glasses and, reaching deep into his bosom, drew out a book and opened it. Titled *The Compleat Chef,* the tome described in detail every specialty of the Polish board. Count Tenczynski had made good use of it in Italy, where he threw such lavish banquets as to arouse the awe of Pope Urban VIII himself. Charles 'My-Dear-Fellow' Radziwill also consulted it when receiving King Stanislas at Nieswiez. So

memorable was the banquet, that its fame survives in Lithuania's local lore even today.

Whatever instruction the Steward was able to understand and convey aloud from the book, his able assistants
promptly carried out. The kitchen seethed with activity. Fifty
knives pounded on wooden slabs. Kitchen boys, black as fiends
in hell, bustled about, some lugging firewood, others carrying
pails of milk and wine. They filled kettles, pots, and pans. Vapors wafted forth. Two lads squatted by the hearth, working the
bellows. To help the fire along, the Steward had melted butter
poured over the logs – a luxury permitted only in prosperous
houses. Several more boys piled up the hearth with dry logs,
others skewered enormous roasts on broiling-spits: beef, veni-
son, haunches of wild boar and stag. Still others plucked heaps
of fowl, raising clouds of down and feathers. Heath cock, black
grouse, and chickens lay denuded of their plumage. True, there
was a general dearth of chickens. Since the night of the raid
when bloodthirsty Sack Dobrzynski assailed the hen-roosts and
made a shambles of Sophie's enterprise, the Manor had not yet
fully regained its reputation as the district's richest producer
of poultry. Still, what with the larder, the butchers' stalls, the
forests, and neighbors near and far, they amassed a great supply
of meat of every description. Indeed, there was enough and to
spare. The generous banquet host requires but two commodities,
plenty and art. Soplica Manor abounded with both.

The solemn feast day of Our Blessed Lady of the Flowers
was breaking. The weather was sublime, the hour early, the sky
cloudless. Heaven stood stretched over the earth like an ocean
becalmed, incurvate. Several stars still shone clear in the depths
like pearls on the sea-bottom. A lone white cloudlet drifted up
and plunged her wing into the azure. So vanishes the guardian
angel's pinion when, after a night of attending the prayers of
men, the ministrant spirit hastens to rejoin his fellow celestials.

The last pearls of the stars guttered and dimmed in the
depths of the sky. Heaven's brow grew pale. While the right temple reposed on a pillow of darkness, retaining its swarthy tone,
the left grew rosier by the minute. Suddenly, like a great eyelid,
the line of the horizon parted to show at its midpoint first the
white of the eye, then the iris, and then the pupil. A beam shot
forth, arced across the vault of the sky, then lodged itself like a
golden dart in the white cloud. That beam, the signal of day, un-

leashed a sheaf of flames. A thousand skyrockets traversed the heavenly vault; and the eye of the sun rose aloft. Still drowsy, it blinked, fluttering its radiant lashes, coloring sevenfold at once, sapphire blue reddening to ruby, ruby red yellowing to topaz, until shining forth, first like a crystal vessel, then like a lustrous diamond, the eye burst aflame like a throbbing star, large as the moon. Even so did the sun begin his solitary march across the bourneless sky.

Today, as if in expectation of a fresh miracle, the entire local populace had assembled early at the chapel entrance. Both curiosity and devotion had brought them here. Among those expected to attend the mass at the Manor were the army's generals, the famous captains of our legions, whose names the people knew and revered like those of their patron saints; whose every peregrination, campaign, and battle had become the gospel of our land.

Several senior officers and a host of soldiers had already arrived. Peasant folk thronged around them, staring in disbelief at their fellow countrymen – all arrayed in uniforms, all bearing arms, all free and speaking the Polish tongue.

The opening procession began. Scarcely could the small chapel contain such a throng! Kneeling on the green outside, the people bared their heads and peered in through the open doors. The white and flaxen heads of the Lithuanian folk shone like a field of ripened rye. Here and yon, crowned with fresh flowers and peacocks' plumes and trailing loose ribbons from braided tresses, a lovely maiden's head stood out among the men's heads like cornflower or cockle in the grain. The meadow teemed with the gaily-clad worshippers; and, at the sound of the bell, as under a breath of wind, all heads bowed like ears of wheat.

This was the day when village girls brought spring's first fruits, fresh bouquets of herbs, to Our Lady's altar. The entire chapel – altar, holy image, bell tower and gallery – stood garnished with posies and floral wreaths. Fresh breezes stirring up from the east blew the garlands down upon the heads of the kneeling faithful, spreading fragrances as sweet as the fumes that wafted from the swinging censer's bowl.

The mass said, the sermon concluded, the Chamberlain led the entire assembly out of the chapel. Recently elected their confederate marshal by a unanimous vote of the district estates, he wore the voivodeship's ceremonial uniform – a gold-embroidered tunic, a fringed robe of gros-de-Tours silk, and a gold, bro-caded belt. His dress sword with its shagreen-lined hilt hung at the waist. At his throat sparkled a large diamond pin. His confederate's cap was white and topped with a thick tuft of cost-ly egret crest-feathers. Only on grand occasions were such rich headdresses worn – the plumes a ducat apiece! Thus appareled, he mounted a rise in front of the chapel; and with the villagers and soldiers pressing around him, he addressed his audience.

"My brothers!" he began. "You have just now heard liber-ty proclaimed from the pulpit. His Imperial Majesty has restored it to the Crown and is even now restoring it to the Duchy of Lith-uania – to the whole of Poland. You have heard the government edict and proclamation calling for a nation-wide General Assem-bly. I have only a few brief words to say to this community. They pertain to the Soplica family, the lords of these parts."

"No one in the district will have forgotten the mischief wrought here by the late Jacek Soplica Esquire. But now that his sins are known abroad, it is time the world were apprised of the great services he has rendered. Our generals are here pres-ent among us. It is from them that I learned what I am about to relate. Jacek did not die in Rome as was reported. Instead, he reformed himself and changed his name and state in life. All his offenses against God and his country, he has blotted out by his holy life and noble deeds."

"When almost beaten at Hohenlinde, General Richepanse was on the point of sounding the retreat, unaware that Knia-ziewicz was marching to his relief, it was he, Jacek, alias Robak, who braved sword and lance to deliver Kniaziewicz's letters with news that our own lancers were taking the enemy's rear. Then again, in Spain, when our lancers took the fortified ridge at So-mosierra, Jacek was twice wounded at Kozietulski's side. Later still, as an envoy entrusted with secret orders, he traversed var-ious quarters of our land, gauging the currents of popular feel-ing, organizing and forming secret societies. Finally, at Soplica Manor, his ancestral seat, while preparing the ground for an insurrection, he was killed in an armed foray. The news of his death reached Warsaw just as Napoleon, in recognition of his earlier heroic deeds, had conferred upon him the order of Knight of the Legion of Honor.

"And, therefore, taking all these matters into account, I, representing the province, do solemnly proclaim the following:

that by his loyal service and the Emperor's grace Jacek Soplica has been cleared of the blot upon his name, and thus stands restored to honorable rank. Once again, he holds his rightful place among true Poles. Should any man, then, recall to the family of the late Jacek Soplica crimes for which he has long since atoned, that man shall, as penalty for the delict, be liable to the *gravis nota maculae* – this, in the words of our Statute, which thus reproves *miles* and *skartabella* alike should they spread calumny against a citizen of the Commonwealth. And since general equality before the law has now been proclaimed, article three is likewise binding upon burgher and peasant. This edict of the Marshal, the clerk shall duly set down in the Acts of the Confederation, and the Court Usher shall proclaim it aloud.

"As for the Legion's medal of honor, in no wise shall its late arrival derogate from its glory. If it cannot do honor to Jacek's breast, then may it serve as a lasting memorial to him. I hereby drape it over his grave. Let it hang here for three days. Then, let it be deposited in the chapel, as a votive offering to the Blessed Virgin."

And with that, he took the order from its case, tied the red ribbon in a knot, and hung the white star with its golden crown from the humble gravesite cross. The star's rays sparkled in the sun like the dying gleams of Jacek's earthly glory. Meanwhile, invoking eternal rest upon the poor sinner, the people knelt and recited the *Angelus* prayer; whereupon, the Judge went the rounds of the guests and village folk, inviting all to the manor house for the banquet.

On the turf ledge fronting the house, two old masters with a full mead-pot on their lap sat gazing out into the garden where the painted poppies grew. Standing like a sunflower among these blooms was a Polish lancer in a glittering cap adorned with gilded metal and a cock's feather. Before him, training her pansy-blue gaze on his eyes, stood a girl in a dress as green as the low-lying rue. Behind the couple, young women picked flowers, averting their heads, so as not to disturb the sweethearts.

But the old gaffers pulled on their mead, took snuff from each other's birchbark box, and ran on like a pair of millraces.

"Quite so, Protase, old boy," said the Warden, Gervase."

"Quite so, Gervase, dear fellow" said the Court Usher, Protase."

"Yes, quite right," they repeated several times in unison, beating time with their heads.

"The action has come to a strange conclusion – no denying," the Usher pursued. "But there are precedents. I recall lawsuits involving excesses far worse than ours, and yet marriage articles settled the matter. That is how Lopot patched things up with the Borzdobohaty family, as did, also, Krepsztul with Kupsc, Putrament with Pikturna, Mackiewicz with Odyniec, and Turno with Kwilecki.

"But what am I saying? The broils between the Soplicas and Horeszkos pale in comparison with those that once beset Poland and Lithuania. But then our Queen Hedwig brought reason to bear on the matter, and their contention was settled out of court. It is well for both sides to have eligible maids or widows ready at hand. This way, a compromise is always there to be made. The most protracted litigations take place among the Catholic clergy, or between close kin, where the case cannot be resolved through the expedient of marriage. That is why Poles and Russians are always at each other's throats. Lech and Rus were born brothers, after all. It also explains the number of long-drawn-out lawsuits with the Teutonic Knights in Lithuania, before Jagiello won on the field. Last, it explains why the Rymszas' famous lawsuit with the Dominicans *pendebat* so long on the court calendar – that is, until the priory's legal advocate, Father Dymsza, finally won the case. Hence the saying, 'The Lord God is greater than Lord Rymsza.' To which, I might add, 'Mead is better than a jackknife.'"

And pledging the Warden's health, he emptied his quart pot to the drains.

"True, true," replied Gervase with a show of emotion. "Strange have been the fortunes of our beloved Crown and the Grand Duchy. Why, they are like a married couple! God joins them, Satan puts them asunder. God minds his thing, the Devil, his. Ah, dear Protase, that our eyes should be seeing this! Our brothers from the Crown greeting us again. I served with them all those years ago. Brave-hearted confederates they were. Oh, if my lord Pantler had lived to see this moment. Oh, Jacek! Jacek! But what's the use of moaning? Now that Lithuania stands reunited with the Crown, all is made good and right into the bargain."

"And the marvel of it is," said Protase, "that only a year ago today we had an omen, a sign from above about our very Sophie whose hand in marriage Tadeusz is begging this moment—"

"We should be calling her Mistress Sophia now," broke in Gervase. "She is grown up. No longer a girl. Highborn too, for she is the Pantler's grandchild."

"Anyhow," Protase went on, "the sign was a clear foreshadowing of the future. With my own eyes, I saw it. Here we were on this same feast day, the servants and I, sitting and pulling on our mead, when, from the eaves above, a pair of old fighting cock sparrows come down with a plump. One was slightly younger and had a slate-gray throat. The other had a black throat. Off they go scuffling in the yard, rolling over and over in a cloud of dust. As we sit there watching, the servants say to one another, 'The black one's Horeszko, the gray, Soplica.' So, whenever the gray has the upper hand, they raise a cheer, 'Up with the Soplicas, and down with the Horeszko cowards.' And when he falls, it's, 'On your feet, Soplica! What? Yield to a magnate? A nobleman would never live it down.' And so, we sit there laughing, hanging on the contest's issue, when, suddenly, Sophie, taking pity on the little jousters, runs up and covers them with her hands. Yet still the down flew as the little scraps battled it out under her hands. Such was their fury. Meanwhile, gazing at Sophie, the old wives murmured to one another, 'The girl's destined to reunite two long-estranged families.' Now, I see they foretold rightly, though, in truth, they had the Count in mind at the time, not Tadeusz."

"Aye, the world's a strange place," said Gervase. "Who can fathom it? Now I have something to relate as well, not as marvelous as your omen, but hard to comprehend all the same. Once upon a time, as you know, I would not spit on a Soplica if he were on fire. Yet I always took a great shine to the lad Tadeusz. I noticed that whenever he got into a scrap with the other boys, he would always come out the winner. So, every time he'd visit the castle, I dared him to perform a difficult task. He was equal to anything, snatching a dove from the turret, plucking a sprig of mistletoe from an oak-tree, rifling a rook's nest in the tallest pine – there was nothing the lad couldn't accomplish handily. He must have been born under a lucky star. Too bad he's a Soplica, I thought. Who would have imagined that in him someday I should be greeting the castle heir, the husband of my lady, Mistress Sophia."

They ended their talk and drank on, deep in thought.
Now and anon, they could be heard saying, "Quite so, dear Gervase" and, "Quite so, dear Protase."

The turf bench upon which they were seated ran right
past the kitchen; its windows gaped open, belching smoke, as if
a fire raged inside. Suddenly, from out of these billows of smoke,
there shot forth like a dove a gleaming white hat, and the Chief
Steward poked out his head. For a while, he stood eavesdropping
on the two old masters; then, leaning over the sill, he passed
them down a saucer of biscuits.

"Here is something to wash down with your mead,"
said he. "Now let me tell you the curious tale of a quarrel that
might easily have ended in a bloody brawl. Once, while we were
hunting deep in Naliboka Forest, Reytan played a prank on the
Prince de Nassau. It very nearly cost him his life. I brought them
to terms. Let me tell you how it came about—"

But at that moment, the under-chefs broke in to ask who
was setting the table. The Steward withdrew his head from
the window. Meanwhile, Gervase and Protase went on drinking their mead. They gazed pensively into the garden where the
handsome lancer stood conversing with his young lady. He was
holding her hand with his left hand, for his right rested in a
sling. Plainly, he had been wounded.

"Sophie!" he addressed his lady. "Before we exchange
rings, tell me candidly, for I must be sure. It matters little that
last winter you were ready to give me your pledge. I would not
accept it then, for what good is a forced promise? My stay at the
Manor was very brief, and I would not flatter myself that a single
glance from me were enough to arouse your love. I am not a vain
man. I wished to win your favor on the strength of my merits,
no matter how long it took. But now, Sophie, you have been so
kind as to repeat your promise. How have I earned such a favor?
Could it be, dear Sophie, that you take me not out of love but at
the insistence of your aunt and uncle? Marriage is a thing of
serious moment. Consult your own heart in the matter. Yield to
no one's sway. Pay no heed to my uncle's threats or your aunt's
entreaties. If what you feel for me is mere kindness, and nothing
more, we can put off this betrothal for a time. Never would I seek
to constrain your will. So, dear Sophie, why not wait? Nothing
is pressing us, the more so, as last night I received orders to

remain behind, as an instructor in the local regiment, until my wounds have healed. What say you to this, dear Sophie?"

Sophie raised her head and gazed demurely into his eyes. "I have but a dim recollection of the past," she said. "All I know is that everyone kept telling me I should take you for my husband. I always obey the will of heaven and my elders." And, lowering her eyes, she added: "Before your departure, if you recall, when Father Robak died on that stormy night, I saw how sad you were to be leaving us. You had tears in your eyes. Those tears, I must tell you truly, went straight to my heart. Since then, I have believed that you love me. Whenever I offered up a prayer for you, you always appeared before me with those big glistening tears in your eyes. Then the Chamberlain's wife took me up to Vilna for the winter. There, I pined for the Manor and the little room where we first met by the table, and where later you bade me adieu. Somehow my memory of you was like a seedling sown in autumn. All winter long, it germinated in my heart, so that I never stopped pining for that room. Somehow, I knew I should find you there again, and so indeed I have. With such thoughts, I often held your name on my lips. It happened to be carnival time in Vilna. My companions told me I was in love. If it be so, then it must be with you."

And leaving the garden, they repaired to the lady's room, the same room that Tadeusz had occupied of old as a boy of ten. There they found the superbly attired Notary bustling to and fro, waiting on his plighted lady, fetching her signet rings, little chains, pots and jars, cosmetic powders and patches. Joyously jubilant, he watched his young mistress seated before the mirror, putting the finishes to her toilet, consulting with the Graces. Her chambermaids hovered about her. Some freshened up her ringlets with heated tongs. Others, kneeling on the floor, attended to the flounces of her frock.

While Notary Bolesta thus occupied himself with his betrothed, a kitchen boy suddenly rapped on the window. A hare, your honors! The animal had stolen out of the osier bed, skipped across the meadow and leapt in among the sprouting vegetables. There it sat even now. All they had to do was rouse it from the seedbed and release their hounds near the narrow gap by which it would be forced to make its escape.

Up dashed the Assessor, tugging on Peregrine's collar. The Notary ran after him, shouting for Scut. The Steward, hav-

ing stationed both men and their dogs by the fence, seized his
fly swatter and went stamping, whistling, and clapping into the
garden – scaring the quarry witless. Meanwhile, the hunters,
smacking their lips softly, restrained their dogs and pointed
to the gap in the fence; and the hounds, ears pricked, noses to
windward, chafed and quivered like a brace of shafts nocked to a
single bowstring.

Suddenly, the Steward cried out, "See-ho!" The hare bolted from beneath the fence and made its point to the meadow.
Like a shot Scut and Peregrine went after it. Unswervingly they
fell upon the beast from both sides at once. Like the two wings
of a hawk they descended, sinking their fangs, talon-like, into
its spine. The hare squealed once – piteously! – like a new-born
babe. By the time the hunters ran up to the quarry, it lay lifeless, and the hounds were tearing savagely at the white fur of its
underbelly.

As the two huntsmen patted their dogs, the Steward,
drawing the hunting knife that hung at his side, proceeded to
cut off the jackrabbit's feet.

"This day," said he, "your hounds receive equal dues, for
they have won equal glory. Equal was their address and equal
their labor. As the palace was worthy of Patz, and Patz of his palace, so are the hunters worthy of their hounds, and the hounds,
of the hunters. This brings your long, fierce contest to a close.
Now, I, whom you appointed your arbiter, render this final verdict – that you are both winners. I return your stakes. Let each
man stand by his word, and make peace."

And at the old master's bidding, the hunters turned upon
each other their beaming faces and wedded their long-separated
palms.

"I once staked my horse and trappings," announced the
Notary. "I also swore before the district court to deposit this ring
as an honorarium for our judge. A forfeit, once pledged, may not
be reclaimed. So, Mr. Steward, accept the ring as a keepsake.
Have your name or, if you like, the Horeszko device chased on
it. The carnelian is smooth, the gold, eleven carats. My horse,
our lancers have long since requisitioned, but the harness and
saddle are still mine. Experts praise these trappings for their
comfort, durability and pleasing looks. The saddle is narrow in
the Turco-Cossack style, the pommel set with precious stones,
and the seat padded and lined with heavy silk so that, when you

vault astride, you settle into the down between the bow and the cantle as comfortably as you would into your own bed. And when you break into a gallop . . ." – here Bolesta, who was known for his great love of gesticulation, spread wide his legs, as if bestriding a horse, and, feigning a gallop, swayed slowly back and forth – ". . . when you break into a gallop, the sunlight reflects off the housing, as though the horse dripped with gold, for the skirts are heavily sprinkled with gold and the broad silver stirrups, generously vermeiled. The bit and bridle straps are studded with mother-of-pearl, and a crescent moon – like the one our heraldry calls Leliwa – hangs from the breastplate. This singular garniture was taken, I am told, from a great Turkish nobleman at the battle of Podhajce. And so, my dear Assessor, please accept these caparisons as a token of my esteem."

To this, the Assessor, clearly delighted by the gift, replied: "And I staked the gift that I received from Prince Sanguszko: the shagreen dog collars with the gold rings and the exquisitely wrought velvet leash with its glittering precious stone of matching craft. These articles, I intended to leave to my children if I should ever marry – and children I shall have, for, as you know, this is my betrothal day. Nevertheless, my dear Notary, do me the honor of accepting these articles in exchange for your rich harness. Let them serve as a token of the longstanding quarrel that has come to such an honorable close for us both. May amity thrive evermore between us."

And homeward they went, there to proclaim at table that the dispute over Scut and Peregrine had been settled.

Now rumor had it that the Steward raised the hare at home and released it secretly into the garden as an easy quarry by which to reconcile the two rivals. So cunning was his ruse that he succeeded in beguiling the entire Manor. Some years later, the kitchen boy, wanting to set the Notary and the Assessor at odds again, breathed word of this. But the aspersions he cast on the hounds were to no purpose. The Steward denied the rumor, and no one believed the boy.

The guests, assembled in the great hall of the castle, stood by the table, talking and waiting for the banquet. At last, the Judge, dressed in the Governor's uniform, entered, escorting in Tadeusz and Sophie. Tadeusz touched his brow with his left hand and saluted his superior officers with a military bow. Sophia, stooping her gaze and blushing, greeted each guest with a curtsy – a curtsy perfectly executed in accordance with Telimena's instructions. Save for the bridal garland binding her temples, she had on the same costume she'd worn that morning in the chapel when offering her spring sheaf to the Blessed Virgin. Now, she had harvested a fresh little sheaf of herbs for the guests. Adjusting the shining sickle upon her brow with one hand, she proceeded to portion out the flowers and grasses with the other. The officers, on receiving their little bouquets, kissed her hand; and she, cheeks mantling brightly, curtsied again.

Suddenly, General Kniaziewicz seized the girl by the shoulders, planted a fatherly kiss upon her brow, and whisked her up onto the table. "Bravo!" applauded the onlookers, captivated by the girl's grace and beauty and still more by the rustic Lithuanian dress she was wearing. Upon these famous captains, who had spent so much of their nomadic lives roaming foreign lands, the national costume worked a special charm, for it recalled to mind their youth and romantic attachments of long ago. With tears in their eyes, they gathered round the table and gazed intently at the girl. Some begged her to tilt her head and show her eyes, others, to turn around. The girl swung round bashfully, veiling her eyes with her hand. Meanwhile, Tadeusz, looking on, rubbed his palms with joy.

Had someone suggested this costume to Sophie, or had instinct prompted her? For, surely it is instinct that tells a girl what best becomes her face. Enough that this morning, for the first time in her life, Sophie had braved Telimena's displeasure by stubbornly refusing to wear a fashionable dress. Moved by Sophie's tears, her aunt had given way and abandoned her to her rustic costume.

The underskirt was long and white, the skirt, short, cut from green camlet stuff, and rose-edged. The bodice, cross-laced from neck to waist with pink ribbons, and also green, enfolded Sophie's breast like leafage around a rose-bud. The billowy white sleeves of her blouse were laced in loose folds about her wrists. Bright and full, they shone upon her shoulders like the wings of a butterfly poised to take flight. The collar fit snugly round her neck; a rose-colored bow secured it. Her earrings – the proud handiwork of Sack Dobrzynski – were artfully scored cherry pits. (They were his gift to Sophie while she was still the object of his addresses. You could make out two little hearts with a dart and a flame.) About her neck, she wore a double string of

amber beads, and around her temples, a garland of green rose-
mary. The ribbons of her braids she'd tossed backwards across
her shoulders; and, over her brow, as was customary among the
field women, she'd set a curved sickle, well-polished from recent
reaping and bright as the crescent moon upon Diana's brow.

The guests cheered and applauded. One of the officers
drew a leather portfolio from his pocket. It contained a bundle
of papers. Laying out a sheet of foolscap, he sharpened a pencil,
moistened it with his tongue and, gazing at Sophie, set down
to draw. No sooner did the Judge see the drawing materials
than he recognized the artist, though the colonel's uniform, the
glittering epaulets, the seasoned lancer's mien, the blackened
moustache, and the Spanish beard had wrought a considerable
change upon him.

"Why hello, dear Count!" exclaimed the Judge. "A traveling painter's kit in your cartridge pouch, I see."

It was indeed the young Count. He had not been a soldier
long, but thanks to his immense wealth, his fielding of an entire
horse regiment at his own expense, and the splendid manner in
which he had acquitted himself in his first engagement, the Emperor had only today conferred upon him the rank of colonel. The
Judge saluted him, congratulating him on his promotion. But
the Count scarcely heeded him and went on with his sketching.

Meanwhile, the second betrothed couple made their entrance. It was the Assessor, formerly the Tsar's, now Napoleon's,
loyal servant – with a detachment of Polish gendarmes under
his command. Though he'd held that office for barely twenty
hours, he was already wearing the dark blue uniform with its
distinctive Polish facings. In he strode, spurs jangling, cavalry
saber trailing behind him. At his side, solemn and arrayed in her
full finery, walked his beloved, Thecla Hreczecha, the Steward's
lass. The Assessor had long since washed his hands of Telimena
and, so as to wring the coquette's heart the more, he'd turned
his affections to the Steward's daughter. The bride was scarcely
young; indeed, she was said to be all of fifty years old. But she
was a stout soul, an able housekeeper, and suitably dowered, as,
apart from the village she stood to inherit, a tidy monetary gift
from the Judge had increased the sum of her assets.

As to the third pair, the guests waited for them in vain.
Growing impatient, the Judge dispatched his servants to fetch

them. They returned by and by with word that the third bride-groom, the Notary, had lost his wedding ring in the hare course and was even now scouring the meadow for it. As for his lady, she was still at her dresser; and, though she was making all due haste, with her housemaids doing their best to bear a hand, yet there was not the ghost of a chance she would complete her toilet in time. Indeed, she would scarcely have it done this side of four o'clock.

BOOK TWELVE: LET US LOVE ONE ANOTHER!

The last banquet in the grand old Polish style. The centerpiece.
An explanation of its figures. Its transformations. Dombrowski receives
a gift. More of Jackknife. Kniaziewicz receives a gift. Tadeusz's first
official act upon receiving his inheritance. Gervase's observations. The
Concert of Concerts. The Polonaise. Let us love one another!

At last, the doors of the great hall unfolded with a crash, and in strode the Steward, head capped and erect. He greeted no one, nor did he take his place at the table, for today he appeared in his new role as Marshal of the Court. With staff of office in hand, he ushered each guest to his seat. The Chamberlain-Marshal, the highest authority of the voivodeship, was accorded the post of honor – a velvet chair with ivory armrests. General Dombrowski took his place next to him at his right, and Kniaziewicz, Patz, and Malachowski, at his left. The Chamberlain's wife was duly seated among them. Then came the other ladies, the lords, the officers, the manor holders, and the rest of the gentry. All took their places, men and women alternately, in the order assigned to them by the Steward.

The Judge, after bowing to his guests, withdrew from the banquet hall and repaired to the courtyard, where he was fêting a large number of his village folk. Assembling the people around a table some forty fathoms long, he seated the parish priest at one end and himself at the other. Sophie and Tadeusz, he did not seat. Theirs was to wait on the peasantry – they ate on the fly. Such was the ancient custom. The new heirs did the honors of the table at their inaugural banquet.

Meanwhile, awaiting the repast in the great hall, the guests stared in wonder at the table's grand centerpiece – an exquisite artifact wrought of a fittingly precious metal. Prince Radziwill *The Orphan* – so the story went – had had it made to order in Venice and embellished according to his taste in the Polish style. Plundered during the Swedish Wars, the object had passed, no one knew how, to the Manor; and now, retrieved from the lumber house, it rested in a mighty circle like a carriage wheel on the table.

A confection of snow-white sugars and mousses covered the vessel to the upper edges. The result was a marvelous simulation of a winter landscape. In the center was a dark forest made from fruit preserves. On the edges of the forest stood sugar-frosted cottages suggesting snowbound peasant hamlets and noble villages; and placed all round the vessel's rim were little blown-porcelain figurines in Polish costumes. Like stage players these figures seemed to be acting out some momentous event. So expressive were their gestures, so vivid their colors, that, but for the want of voices, you would have sworn they were alive.

But what did they represent, the guests wanted to know: whereupon, the Steward raised his staff and addressed his audience.

"By your leave, most highly honored guests!" he began, while the footmen served the vodka aperitif. "All these figurines you see before you are playing out the history of our regional assemblies – the voting, the upsets, the quarrels. I worked out the scenes myself, so allow me to explain them to you. On the right here, you see a large gathering of the nobility. Evidently, they have been invited to the inaugural banquet, for a table stands set. No one has yet seated them. They stand around in little knots. Each group holds council. Mark the man in the middle of each group. By his open mouth, wide-eyed stare and busy hands, you can tell he is an orator wooing his audience. Here, he underlines his point by tracing with his finger on the palm of his hand. These men are speakers vouching for their candidates, though with mixed results, as you can readily tell by their brethren's demeanors.

"True, in this second group, the nobility listen intently. Look at this fellow with his hands under his belt. See him straining to hear? And this one, hollowing his hand to his ear and twirling his moustache? No doubt he is collecting the pearls of eloquence and threading them upon his memory. The speaker looks pleased. Clearly, he has won them over. He rubs his pockets, for he knows he has their vote in his pocket.

"But what a difference in this third group here. The speaker is forced to grab his audience by their belts. See them pulling away, averting their heads? Observe this listener bridling with anger. See? He raises his arm, threatens the speaker, stops his mouth with his hand. He cannot bear to hear his rival praised. And mark this other fellow lowering his head like a bull as if to toss him. Some reach for their swords, others take to their heels.

"One man stands silent, apart from the rest. Clearly, he hasn't thrown in with either side. He is fearful. He hesitates. He hasn't a clue whom to vote for. In his struggle with himself, he leaves it all to chance. He raises his hands, puts out his thumbs, and, shutting his eyes, tries to align his nails. Clearly, he has entrusted his vote to fate. If the thumbs meet, it is, 'yea,' if not, 'nay.'

"On the left, we observe yet another scene. The nobility have converted the cloister's refectory into an electoral hall. The older men sit on benches arranged in rows. The youth stand behind them, peering forward over their heads. Here stands the marshal with the ballot urn in his hand. He counts the votes; the nobility watch with eager eyes. He has just shaken out the last one. The ushers raise their hands and announce the elected official.

"One nobleman refuses to abide by the common will. See him poking his head through the kitchen window? Observe that insolent, wide-eyed stare of his. His mouth gapes open. He'd swallow up the entire room! Easy to guess what he is vociferating, *Veto!* – I say no! And now see how this voice of discord sends the throng charging through the door. Heading for the kitchen, I'll warrant. Their blades are drawn. Oh, there will be bloodshed, I shouldn't wonder!

"But here, in the corridor, ladies and gentlemen, you will mark a priest in a chasuble – the old prior bearing a monstrance with the Blessed Sacrament. A surpliced altar boy clears his way with a bell. The nobility sheathe their sabers, bless themselves and genuflect. The priest turns to where the clash of steel persists. Soon he will have the whole lot hushed and reconciled.

"Ah, but you youngsters have no recollection of how famously our self-governing nobility, armed and unruly as they were, got along without the benefit of a police force. So long as the true faith flourished, we respected our laws. We enjoyed liberty with order, glory with prosperity. Other countries, I am told, keep bands of ruffians at hand – all manner of law officers, gendarmes, and constables. But if it takes the sword alone to guard the public security, then I refuse to believe true liberty exists in those lands."

Here the Chamberlain broke in, tapping on his snuffbox. "Come, Mr. Steward," said he, "put off these stories of yours. Granted, our regional diets are of great interest, but we are famished. Have them bring in the dinner!"

But the Steward merely lowered his staff to the floor.

"Your Excellency, grant me this pleasure," he replied. "Allow me yet a moment to explain this final scene. Here, you see the newly elected marshal leaving the refectory upon the shoulders of his supporters. See the nobility tossing their caps in the air? Their mouths are open. '*Vivat!* A long life!' they shout.' And there, opposite, broods the beaten contender. He stands at a distance from the rest, cap pulled down over his brow. Meanwhile, his wife waits in front of the house. She has guessed, poor thing! She swoons in her chambermaid's arms. Poor thing, she has been counting on the title 'Right Honorable,' and now it is another three years of plain 'Honorable.'"

With that, the Steward closed his commentary and waved his staff. Upon this signal, the footmen began filing in two by two with the dinner. *Barche royale* was the opening dish. Next came an old-Polish consommé prepared with masterly skill. To the marvelous secrets of its preparation, the Steward had added the measure of tossing in the odd pearl and coin. The broth was said to purify the blood and fortify the health. Then followed the rest of the dishes. Who could tell them all! And even if one could, who could make head or tail of specialties no longer known today – *kontuz, arkas*, and *blemas*; or dishes containing ingredients such as burbot meat, forcemeat, civet, deer musk, gum dragon, pine nut, and sloeberry. And the varieties of fish! Dried huchen from the Danube, flounder, white sturgeon, caviar – both Venetian and Turkish – large pike, medium-sized pike – eighteen inchers at least! – large carp, noble carp! And, to crown all, the chef's secret specialty: an entire fish, uncut, fried at the head, baked in the middle, and the tail marinating in a sauce.

But the guests took no interest in the names of the dishes. Nor did they take time to probe the mysteries of the fish. They dispatched the meal with military expedition, then washed it down with ample drafts of Hungarian wine.

Meanwhile, the grand centerpiece changed color. Stripped of its mantle of snow, it was turning green. The delicate layer of sugar icing had melted under the warmth of the summer to reveal below a landscape hitherto hidden from the eye. A new sea-

son emerged – spring, with its burst of greenery and many hues.
Various grains and crops sprang up as if leavened with yeast:
saffroned wheat nodding its golden ears; rye wrought from silver foil; buckwheat artfully fashioned from chocolate; flowering
orchards of apple and pear.

But the guests had little time to taste the fruits of summer. In vain they begged the Steward to stay their passing!
Like a planet governed by her ineluctable motions the centerpiece changed season again. Already, the gilded grainfields were
soaking up the ambient warmth. The grass yellowed, the leaves
reddened and fell, as under autumn's winds. The trees, gorgeous
a moment ago, now hung stark and leafless, blasted by gale and
frost. These leafless trees – cinnamon sticks! The pine-trees –
sprigs of laurel, sprinkled with caraway seeds, to simulate pine
needles!

The guests, goblet in hand, fell to breaking off these
branches, roots, and stumps, and nibbled on them as appetizers.
Meanwhile, the Steward circled the centerpiece and watched his
guests jubilantly.

"My dear Steward," said General Dombrowski, affecting
great amazement. "Is this a Chinese shadow play before me? Or
has Pinetti put his demons under your spell? Do such centerpiec-
es still exist among us in Lithuania? Do the people still feast in
this grand old fashion? Tell me, as I have spent the better part
of my life abroad."

"No, General," replied the Steward with a bow. "No god-
less arts these, but a harking back to those grand old banquets
held in the halls of our forefathers when Poland was happy and
strong. What I have done, I learned from this book. As to the custom being observed in the rest of Lithuania, alas! New fashions
are making inroads even here. Many a young gentleman baulks
at such excesses. He eats like a Jew, begrudges his guests food
and drink, and stints his Hungarian wine while draining drafts
of that infernal bogus champagne from Moscow, which is all the
rage. Then, in the evening, he loses as much gold at cards as it
takes to feed a hundred fellow noblemen. Even the Chamberlain
– and here I shall be quite candid, trusting His Excellency will
not take it amiss – even the Chamberlain scoffed upon seeing
me haul out the centerpiece from the lumber house. 'A tiresome
old contraption whose day was done,' he said. 'A child's play-
thing, not fit for such illustrious folk!' Yes, Your Honor, even you

thought our company would be unimpressed. And yet, judging by the awed looks of our noblemen here, I see it is a beautiful object eminently worthy of being displayed. Who knows if Soplica Manor shall ever again have the fortune of regaling such a distinguished body of guests? General, I see you have a discerning eye for banquets. Please accept this small tome. May it serve you well when you come to throw banquets for companies of foreign monarchs – aye, even for Bonaparte himself! But before I dedicate this book to you, allow me to relate the manner in which it came into my possession—"

A sudden disturbance broke out at the door. A chorus of voices cried out, "Long live Cock o' the Steeple!" The throng invaded the hall, pushing Matthias Dobrzynski to the forefront. The Judge seized him by the arm and, leading him to the table, seated him prominently among the generals.

"Matthias," said he. "How unneighborly of you to show up so late. Dinner is almost over."

"I dine early," replied Dobrzynski. "It is not for the victuals I came. A lively curiosity seized me to take a closer look at our army. One might say a lot on that score. Hard to make out just what it is. The nobility spotted me and fetched me in by force. And now, you have seated me, for which I thank you, good neighbor."

With this, he turned over his plate as a sign that he was not eating; and there, in moody silence, he sat.

"Dobrzynski?" said General Dombrowski, turning to him. "So, you are that celebrated hewer of men of Kosciuszko times – Matthias styled *The Switch?* I know you by reputation. Why, look at you! So hale! So spry! Yet how many years is it now? See how I have aged. Behold Kniaziewicz's grizzled locks! Yet here you are holding your own among the youth. I'll wager your Switch still puts out its buds. I hear the Muscovites got a sound thrashing at your hand recently. But where are your brethren? I'd give my right eye to see those Jackknives and Razors of yours – those last shining examples of old Lithuania!"

"General," said the Judge. "After our victorious battle, almost all the Dobrzynskis sought refuge in the Kingdom. No doubt they have joined one or other of the legions."

"Indeed, sir," spoke up a youthful squadron commander. "I have in my second company a whiskered ogre of a sergeant major by the name of Dobrzynski. He styles himself *Sprinkler*, but the Mazovians call him the Lithuanian Bear. Upon your command, sir, I could have him brought in."

"We have several other Lithuanian-born men in our ranks," added a lieutenant. "I know one, whom they call Razor, and another who rides with the flankers, bearing a blunderbuss. Two other Dobrzynski riflemen serve with the grenadiers."

"Aye," exclaimed the General. "But what of their leader? I would hear of the one they call Jackknife, of whom the Steward has told me so many wonders. A veritable giant of fabled times!"

"Jackknife did not seek refuge across the border," the Steward replied. "But, fearing the inquiry, he kept clear of the Muscovites. The poor fellow spent the whole winter roaming the forests and has only just emerged. In martial times like these, you may find him of service, for he is a valiant knight. Though, alas, the years are starting to weigh heavily on him. But look, here he comes now!"

The Steward pointed to the entrance hall where the servants and rustic folk stood crowded together. A shining bald skull rose high above them like a full moon. Thrice it rose, and thrice it vanished in a cloud of heads. It was Gervase, bowing, as he addressed his way through the throng.

"Your Excellency Hetman of the Crown . . . or is it General?" said he, having got clear of the crowd. "Whatever the title, Rembaïlo at your service! Aye, and this my Jackknife here, whose fame derives not from the hilt or the chasing but the temper of the steel, so that even Your Excellency has heard of it. Could this blade but speak, perchance it would put in a word for this ancient arm of mine. By God's grace, long and faithfully has it served our land and the family of my Horeszko lords, whose name lives on in the memory of men. Rare, old boy, the accountant that trims his goose quill as deftly as Jackknife trims a man's neck. Some reckoning that would take! As for the number of ears and noses lopped off − past telling! And yet the blade stands clean of nicks, unstained by murderous deeds. Open warfare and duels are all it has known. Alas, but once − may the Lord grant him rest − but once, I say, did it dispose of an unarmed man. But there, as God's my witness, it was *pro publico bono.*"

"Show me that Jackknife!" cried out Dombrowski with a laugh. "Oh, what a beauty! A true headsman's sword."

And running an awed eye over the prodigious rapier, he showed it to his officers.

All tried it in turn, but few were strong enough to raise it over their head. They said Dembinski of the brawny arm would have hoisted it, but he was not present. Of those who were present, only Squadron Leader Dwernicki and Platoon Commander Lieutenant Rozycki succeeded in swinging that massy bar of steel; and so the rapier went from hand to hand for trial.

It soon became apparent that General Kniaziewicz, the sturdiest one among them, also had the strongest arm. Seizing the rapier as though it were a mere fencing foil, he executed a series of lightning-fast flourishes over the heads of the guests. He recalled the maneuvers of Polish swordsmanship: the *horizontal cut*, the *circular*, the *diagonal*, the *cleaving stroke*, the *counter thrust*, the *counter-time* and *tierce* – maneuvers he had learned as a cadet in military college. While Kniaziewicz laughed and swung away, Gervase, with tears in his eyes, knelt down and clasped him by the knees.

"Splendid, sir!" he moaned at every sweep of the blade. "So, were you in the Confederacy too? Splendid! Marvelous! That's Pulaski's thrust. And there! Dzierzanowski struck his pose that way. And there! Why, that's Sava's slash! And that one! Only Matthias Dobrzynski could have trained your arm so. And this one, I'll be bound! I'll not brag, but it is my own invention – a cut known only to us Rembaïlos. They named it after me. *The Old Boy's Cut*. Who taught you that? It is my cut, mine!"

And rising to his feet, he embraced the General.

"Now may I die in peace," he went on. "Here stands one that shall take my darling child to his bosom. For years, the thought has troubled me night and day that my rapier will be hung out to rust after I am gone. Now, it shall not rust away. Your Excellency . . . Sir . . . General . . . Forgive me, but have nothing to do with those little skewers, those flimsy little German foils. A noble sire's child wouldn't stoop to grasp such twigs. Bear a sword worthy of Polish nobility! See, I lay my Jackknife, my dearest possession, at your feet. I never had a wife, I never had a child, but it has been both wife and child to me. For years, I never let it out of my embrace. From dawn to dusk, I caressed it. At night, it slept by my side. But now that I have grown old, it hangs like the Decalogue on the wall over my bed. I thought I should be buried with it clasped in my hand. But now I have found an heir. Long may Jackknife serve you!"

"Comrade!" replied Kniaziewicz, half in jest and half in earnest. "If you give away your wife and child, you will be left old and alone, childless and widowed for the remainder of your days. What can I offer you in return for such a precious gift? Tell me how I may sweeten your orphaned and widowed state?"

"Am I Cybulski," dolefully rejoined the Warden, "who, as the ditty goes, gamed away his wife in a round of matrimony with the Muscovite? It is enough to know my Jackknife shall flash before the world in a hand such as yours. Only, be sure to give it ample strap, well let out, for it's a bit on the long side. When cutting, always swing it with both hands from the left ear down. This way, you'll unseam your foe from crown to gut."

The General accepted the rapier. But since it was so long, he was unable to wear it. His servants stowed it in the baggage wagon. As to what became of the weapon, several accounts made the rounds, but the fact is that no one knew for certain, either then or later.

"Come now, comrade," said Dombrowski, turning to Matthias. "You seem unhappy with our arrival. Why so dour and silent? Does your heart not leap at the sight of our gold and silver eagles? At our buglers trumpeting Kosciuszko's reveille so close to your ear? Come, Matthias. I took you for a better fighting man. If you will not take up the sword or mount a horse, then at least join your comrades in a merry pledge to Napoleon's health and the hopes of Poland."

"Hah!" snorted Matthias. "I have heard and seen for myself what's up. Two eagles, Hetman, do not share the same nest. God's favor, sir, rides a paint horse. The Emperor, a great hero? One might say a lot on that score. I recall what my comrades, the Pulawskis, said upon seeing the great Dumouriez. Poland needs a Polish hero, they said. Not a Frenchman, nor yet an Italian. What she needs is a Piast, a Jan, a Joseph, a Matthias – basta! They call it the Polish Army, but look at these *fusiliers*, these *sappers*, these *cannoneers*, and *grenadiers*. I hear more German styles among them than native ones. Who can sort it out? No doubt there are Tartars and Turks among you, schismatics even, who care nothing for God or the faith. With my own eyes, I have seen our village lasses raped, passers-by robbed, churches looted. The Emperor makes for Moscow. Some march for an emperor that sets out without God's blessing! They tell me he's fallen under the Bishop's ban. What a farce! But then, they can all go and kiss my—"

And dipping his bread in the soup, Matthias ate, leaving the last word unuttered.

Matthias' words were scarcely to the Chamberlain's taste. The youth began to murmur among themselves, but the Judge broke in by declaring the arrival of the third betrothal party.

It was Notary Bolesta. Although he announced himself, no one recognized him. Until now, he had always dressed in the Polish manner. But in one of the clauses of their nuptial articles, his plighted lady, Telimena, had made him renounce the loose-sleeved Polish robe. *Bon gré mal gré*, he was fain to dress up like a Frenchman. Evidently, the frock coat robbed him of half his soul, for he walked like a crane, stiff and erect, as if he'd swallowed a stick – loath to look to the right or the left. Despite his composed mien, he was clearly in torments, unable to bow and at a loss what to do with his hands – he who was so very fond of gestures! He thrust his hands under his belt. But there was no belt. So, he proceeded to stroke his belly. Realizing his gaffe, he grew flustered and, blushing like a lobster, dispatched both hands into the same pocket of his frock coat. Like a man running the gauntlet he bore the murmurs and the sneers – as ashamed of the coat as of some discreditable deed. But then, catching sight of Matthias' stare, he fairly blenched.

Until this moment, the two men had enjoyed a robust friendship. Now, Matthias shot the Notary so fierce, so withering a look, that the latter paled to a parchment's hue. He began to clutch at his buttons, as if Matthias' gaze would strip him of his coat. Dobrzynski merely repeated the word "stupid!" twice. So much did the change of dress appall him that he rose at once from the table, swept out of the hall without excusing himself, and, mounting up, returned to his village.

Meanwhile, tricked out from top to toe in the very latest sartorial confection, the Notary's comely sweetheart, Telimena, was spreading her splendor all round. Bootless to set down in words the manner of gown she wore or the arrangement of her hair! No pen could portray it. It would take a painter's brush to limn those laces, tulles, muslins, cashmeres, pearls, and precious stones. And her lively glances! And her rosy cheeks!

The Count recognized her at once. Paling with astonishment, he rose from the table and felt about for his sword.

"So it is you!" he cried. "Do my eyes deceive me? You!
Clasping another's hand in my presence? Faithless creature!
Perfidious soul! And you hide not your face in the earth for
shame? Can you be so forgetful of your vow so recently made?
And I so easily gulled? Why ever did I sport this bow? Woe to my
rival who treats me with such disdain! Over my dead body shall
he mount to the altar!"

The guests rose to their feet. The Notary was horribly
put out. But the Chamberlain hastened to reconcile the rivals.
Meanwhile, Telimena took the Count aside.

"I am not yet the Notary's bride," she whispered. "If you
have anything against our marriage, then tell me this. And let
your answer be brief – and to the point! Do you love me? Does
your heart still hold the same affection? Are you ready to wed
me on the spot, now, this very day? If so, I shall renounce the
Notary."

"Unfathomable woman," replied the Count. "Your sentiments once struck me as poetic. But now they seem quite banal.
What are these marriages of yours if not chains that bind hands
and not souls? Believe me, there are ways of avowing one's love
without declarations, of being bound without plighting one's
troth! Two flaming hearts at points antipodal can converse in
the tongues of the glimmering stars. Who knows? Perhaps that
explains why Earth finds herself so drawn to the Sun, and why
she is ever the object of the Moon's desire. Perhaps that is why
they gaze eternally upon each other. Why they come together by
the shortest route, and yet never unite."

"Enough of this!" said Telimena. "I am not a planet,
thank heaven. Enough, I say. I am a woman. I see where this
is tending, so you can stop your twattle. Now heed my warning!
Breathe so much as a word against my marriage and, as sure as
God's in heaven, I shall fly at you with these nails of mine and
tear—"

"Madam!" protested the Count. "I shall not stand in the
way of your happiness."

And with his eyes filled with sadness and disdain, the
Count turned away. But to punish his faithless sweetheart, he
took the Chamberlain's daughter as the new object of his eternal
flame.

The Steward, seeking by wise examples to reconcile the
young people, resumed his story of the boar of Naliboka Forest

and Reytan's quarrel with the Prince de Nassau. But by now the guests had eaten their ices and were filing out into the courtyard, to enjoy the air.

The village folk had finished their feast. Stoups of mead were making the round. The musicians tuned their instruments and called the folk to dance. They sought out Tadeusz, who was standing to the side, whispering something of pressing moment to his future bride.

"Sophie!" said he, "I must consult with you upon an important matter. I have discussed it with my uncle, and he is not opposed. You know that most of the villages of which I am to take possession belong by right of inheritance to you. These peasants are your subjects, not mine, and I should be loath to dispose of their affairs against the will of their mistress. Now that we have our beloved land restored, shall this happy circumstance mean nothing more to our peasantry than a change of masters? True, we have always ruled them with kindness, but God knows to whom I should will them after my death. I am a soldier, and we both must die. Being an ordinary man, I fear my human caprices. I should do better to renounce my rights and entrust the fate of the peasants to the care of the law. Since we are free, what say we enfranchise our peasantry? Let us grant them title to the land on which they were born, the land they have earned by blood and toil, and thanks to which they feed us all and make us prosper. But I must caution you that by giving up these lands, we shall be earning a smaller income. We shall be forced to live on slenderer means. Now, I, from my youth, am quite used to frugal living. But you, Sophie, spring from a noble family. You spent your early years in the capital city. Can you see yourself living in the country, far from high society, like a common country girl?"

"I am a woman," replied Sophie modestly. "Governing's not in my line. You shall be the husband. I am too young to give counsel here. Whatever you decide I shall agree to with all my heart. And should we be the poorer for freeing the peasants, then you, Tadeusz, shall be all the dearer to my heart. I know little about my family and scarcely bother myself about it. This much I do know – that I was an orphan in need, and that the Soplicas took me like a daughter into their home. Under their roof, I was raised and have been given away in marriage. I do not fear country living. If I lived in the great city, it was long

ago, and I have long since put it out of mind. But I have always
loved the countryside. Believe me, my hens and roosters amuse
me far more than any Petersburg you would care to imagine. If I
felt drawn to the amusements and the people there, it was mere
childishness on my part. I know now that the city bores me. This
winter, after my brief stay in Vilna, I realized that I was born
for country living. Despite the city's amusements, I longed once
more for the Manor. Nor do I fear manual labor, for I am young
and strong. I know how to mind the household and take charge
of the keys. You shall see how I learn to keep house."

Even as Sophie uttered these last words, a stunned and
dour-faced Gervase approached the young couple.

"I know all about it," said he. "The Judge has talked to
me of this liberty. But how it concerns the peasantry, I cannot
fathom. Something un-Polish in this, I fear. Why, freedom's a
matter for the nobility! Not the peasantry! True, we are all sons
of Adam, but I was taught the peasants sprang from Ham, the
Jews from Japheth, and we, the nobility, from Shem. Therefore,
as elder brothers, we lord it over the other two. But our parish
priest preaches otherwise. Such was the case under the Old Cov-
enant, he says from the pulpit. Ever since Christ Our Lord, of
royal blood, was born of the Jews in a peasant's stable, he has
put all estates on an equal footing and made them one. So let it
be, since it cannot be otherwise. The more so, as I hear that even
my gracious lady Sophia has consented to it. Hers to command,
mine to obey. She is mistress! Only see that we do not grant
them an empty freedom, in word only, like that under the Muscovites. When the late Mr. Karp freed his serfs, the Muscovites
reduced them to starvation by burdening them with a triple tax.
So, my advice is to turn to ancient custom, enroll our peasants
upon our lineage, and let it be known that they bear our blazon.
My mistress will bestow the Half Goat upon some villages, and
my master, his Star and Crescent upon others. Even Rembaïlo
shall recognize the peasant as his equal when he sees in him an
honorable gentleman with a coat of arms. Indeed, Parliament
shall ratify it!

"And now, my lady, let not your spouse fret that he will
impoverish you sorely by giving up your lands. Heaven forbid
that I should see the hands of a noble sire's daughter calloused
by domestic toil. I have a remedy for this. I know of a treasure
chest in the castle. It contains the Horeszko family's table service

along with an array of rings, necklaces, bracelets, rich plumes, caparisons, and prodigious swords. It is my lord Pantler's buried trove, kept safe from the hands of pillagers. By rights, it belongs to the heiress, my lady Sophia. All this time, I have guarded this hoard like the apple of my eye – against the Muscovites and you, Soplica folk. What is more, I have a hefty purse of my own thalers saved up from past services rendered and sundry gifts I received from my former master. I had hoped to spend the odd penny in repairing the walls once the castle were restored to us. But now, it seems the new master and mistress will have need of it. And so, Master Soplica, I shall settle into your house, live on my lady's bounty and rock the cradle of a third generation of Horeszkos. If milady has a son, I shall train him in the use of Jackknife. And a son it will be, for wars loom ahead, and war-time always begets us sons!"

Gervase had scarcely uttered these words when Protase approached them with a solemn air. Bowing before the couple, he plunged his hand deep into his robe and withdrew a great panegyric two-and-a-half sheets long. The piece had been composed in rhyme by a young subaltern who enjoyed high repute in the capital for his odes. Later, he joined the army where he continued to cultivate the literary arts. After declaiming three hundred of these lines, the Court Usher reached the part of the poem that went as follows:

> *O thou! whose charms*
> *Rouse torments exquisite and cruel delights,*
> *Whose lovely glance, when turned on Bellon's host,*
> *Shivers the spear-shafts, breaks the serried shields,*
> *Do thou oust Mars this day, bid Hymen in,*
> *And hew the hydra heads from Strife's fell coil!*

Tadeusz and Sophie continued to applaud, as if hailing the recital, but, in truth, they had heard enough. Finally, at the Judge's behest, the parish priest mounted the table and proclaimed Tadeusz's decision to the villagers. On hearing the announcement, they rushed to their young master and fell at his lady's feet.

"Our patrons' health!" they shouted with tears in their eyes.

"And yours, fellow citizens!" replied Tadeusz. "Fellow Poles, equal and free!"

"A toast to our Common Folk!" proposed Dombrowski.

"Long live the Generals!" shouted the peasantry. "Long live the Army! The People! All the Estates!"

A thousand voices thundered out the toasts in turn. Only Buchman refused to share in the common rejoicing. He supported the idea in principle. But he suggested amendments. First, appoint a legal commission, then . . . but there was little time, and Buchman's advice was promptly relegated to the shelf.

Already, the pairs were lining up in the courtyard – officers and ladies, enlisted men and village girls. "*The Polonaise!*" they cried with one voice. The officers brought in the military band. But the Judge whispered into Dombrowski's ear:

"Pray hold off your bandsmen awhile. You know it is my nephew's betrothal day. We have an ancient family custom of betrothing and marrying to the strains of our own village music. Look there! The dulcimer player, the fiddler, and the pipers stand waiting. Honest musicians! See? The fiddler bridles, the piper bobs his head, imploring us with his eyes. If I send them away, the poor fellows will be sure to cry. Our villagers know no other music to skip to. So let our boys go first. Allow the folk to have their fun. Then, we can listen to your splendid band." And he gave the signal.

Tucking up the sleeve of his coat, the fiddler seized his instrument firmly by the neck, thrust the chin-rest under his jaw and sent the bow like a racehorse over the strings. Upon this signal, the two pipers next to him blew into the goatskins, inflating their cheeks, while flapping their arms like a pair of wings. You'd swear they would fly away like Boreas' full-cheeked babes! Only the cymbalon was missing.

Though the district abounded in players of the hammer dulcimer, no one dared play in Yankel's presence. (Where the innkeeper had spent the winter was a mystery. Now, suddenly, he had turned up in the company of the General Staff.) For sheer talent, finesse of touch, and general mastery of the dulcimer, Yankel enjoyed the first repute in the land. They brought in his instrument and begged him to play. But the Jew protested: his hands had grown stiff; he was out of practice, embarrassed to play before so a distinguished an audience. So he demurred; and, making a bow, he sought his escape. But then Sophie ran up and presented to him on her snow-white hand the two hammers he used to sound the strings. Stroking the old master's silver beard with her other hand, she bobbed a curtsy, saying: "Dear Yankel, be so good as to play. This is my betrothal day. Did you not always promise to play at my wedding?"

Now Yankel was immensely fond of Sophie. With a wag of his beard, he assented to her wish. They led him into the midst of the hall, pulled up a chair, seated him, and bringing forth the dulcimer, set it on his lap. With pride and delight, he regarded it. So, upon being recalled to active service, the old campaigner regards the sword which his grandsons have hauled down from the wall. He smiles. Many years have passed since last he gripped the steel, yet he is confident his hand will hold its own! Meanwhile, two of the Maestro's pupils knelt down to tune the dulcimer. They plucked the strings, tested the pitch. Yankel sat silent with his eyes half-closed, the hammers resting lightly in his fingers.

He brought them down. First, he beat a triumphal measure; then, he smote the strings more briskly until the hammers rained down like a torrent. The guests were astounded. But this was only a test, for he broke off abruptly, poising the hammers motionless in the air. Again, he brought them down. This time, they struck with light, tremulous movements, brushing the strings like a fly's wing and producing a scarcely audible hum. Meanwhile, the Maestro looked upward, waiting for the moment of inspiration. At last, staring proudly down on his instrument, he raised both arms and let them fall. Both hammers crashed down at once, again amazing the listeners.

A mighty sound burst forth from many strings at once. It was as if an entire orchestra of janissaries had struck up with bells, zils, and pounding drums. *The May Third Polonaise*! The lively notes breathed joy, brought joy to the ear. The girls itched to dance, the boys could scarcely stand still. Among the elders, the strains brought back memories of old. They recalled the glad days ensuing upon that momentous Third of May, when, assembled in the town hall, the Senate and the deputies had fêted the King, now formally reconciled with his nation; when they had danced and chanted, "Long live our beloved King! Parliament! The People! All the Estates!"

The Maestro kept quickening the time, swelling the sound. Suddenly, he struck a discordant note. It was like the hiss of a snake, like iron grating on glass! A collective shudder ran through the guests. A sense of dread infected their joy. Saddened and alarmed, they imagined the strings had lost their pitch. Could Maestro's hand have erred? But a Master never errs! He had a reason for sounding that perfidious string, for going off-tone. Louder and louder he harped on that sullen chord which conspired against the commonwealth of tones. Suddenly, the Warden understood the Maestro's purpose. Clapping his hand to his face, he cried out, "Why, I know that sound! It is Targowica." And with a loud twang, the ominous string snapped. Without missing a beat, the player turned to the trebles; then, breaking and blurring the measure, he dropped the trebles and crossed over to the bass.

A thousand tumultuous sounds broke forth with increasing intensity: the beat of a march, the clash of arms, a charge, the storming of a rampart, gunfire, children's cries and mothers' wails! So expertly did the artist convey the horror of the assault that the village women shuddered, recalling, with tears of anguish, the Massacre of Praga of which they had heard in stories and songs. Great was their relief when at last, after causing every string to crash like thunder, the Maestro damped the sounds, as though pressing them into the very earth.

Scarcely had the audience time to recover from their amazement when the music changed again. Once more, the first notes were light and hushed. A few thin strings whined shrilly like flies struggling in the spider's toils. But the strings grew in number, the scattered notes rallied, grouping with legions of chords until they marched in time and harmony, resolving themselves into the mournful strains of that popular song about the poor trooper who wandered aimlessly through holt and wood. Hunger and hardship often laid him low, until one day he dropped lifeless at his trusty nag's feet, and over his body the pony pawed the dust.

An old song so dear to the Polish soldier's heart! The men recognized it at once. The rank and file gathered around the Maestro to listen, recalling the harrowing time when they had crooned the song over their country's grave, then marched hence into the wide world. Their thoughts ran on those long years of wandering over land and sea, across burning sands and frozen wastes, among foreign folk, when oft in camp this song had cheered and warmed their hearts; and so, reminiscing sadly, they bowed their heads.

But they soon raised them again, for the Maestro was striking the higher notes with growing force, changing the time and introducing yet another theme. Once more, his lofty eye ranged over the strings. Then, joining his hands, he slammed both hammers down at once. The resulting blow was so strong, so deftly executed, that the strings rang out like brass trumpets. And from these horns issued forth and aloft the famous triumphal march, *Poland Is Not Yet Lost!* Onward to Poland, Dombrowski! The guests, applauding, sang out the refrain, "Onward, Dombrowski!"

As if stunned by his own playing, Yankel released the hammers and flung up his arms. His fox-skin hat slipped to his shoulders. His beard wagged solemnly. A strange ruddiness blotched his cheeks and a youthful fire blazed in his inspired eyes. Turning to Dombrowski, the old master covered his face. A torrent of tears flowed through his fingers.

"General!" said he. "Long has our Lithuania awaited you. Aye, so have we Jews waited for our Messiah. For years, the bards prophesied you to the people. Heaven heralded your coming with signs. Now, live on and wage war, o you, our . . ."

As he uttered these words, the tears streamed from his eyes. The honest Jew loved his homeland as passionately as any Pole. Dombrowski put out his hand and thanked him. Yankel, doffing his cap, kissed the General's hand.

Now it was time for the *Polonaise*. With a flick of his flowing sleeve and a twirl of his moustache, the Chamberlain stepped forward, offered Sophie his hand, and, bowing courteously, besought the top of the dance. The other couples formed a line behind them. Upon the signal, the stately promenade began.

The Chamberlain led the train. His red boots flashed on the greensward. The sun beat upon his saber. His lavishly wrought belt glittered. He walked slowly, one might say, charily; yet his every step, his every gesture, mirrored exactly what he thought and felt.

He pauses – to inquire of his lady, no doubt. He leans toward her. Clearly, he would whisper in her ear. The lady looks away. She is bashful and will not listen. He doffs his cap, bows deferentially. The lady vouchsafes him a glance, yet still she says nothing. He slackens his pace, follows her gaze with his eye. At last, delighted by the lady's response, he laughs out. He quickens his step and looks down on his rivals. Now he pulls his egret-plumed cap over his eyes, now he tosses it back on his head. Finally, cocking his cap at a rakish angle, he curls his moustache and marches forth. Jealously, the guests follow on his heels. He seems intent on stealing his lady away. Now he marks time, politely raises his hand, entreats them to pass him by; anon he steps nimbly aside and reverses his path, as if to baffle the dancers. But they pursue him doggedly with swift steps and encircle him in the evolutions of the dance. Growing angry, he claps his hand to his crossguard. "I care not," he seems to say. "A plague upon your jealous eyes!" With pride writ on his brow, defiance in his eyes, he executes an about-face and bears down upon the throng. Loath to stand in his way, the dancers step aside; then, regrouping, they set off again in swift pursuit. Meanwhile, shouts ring out on every hand: "Ah, he may be the last! Look on, you youngsters, and mark it well! He may be the last to lead the dance this way."

And so, pair after pair, boisterous and merry, they promenaded. Round and round they went – ladies, noblemen, soldiers, uncoiling and coiling anew like the thousand spires of a monstrous snake. Enhanced by the golden glow of the westering sun and the dark pillow of the sward, the smears of color of the dancers' costumes shimmered vividly like burnished scales. On and on they danced. The music played. The plaudits! The pledges!

Only Corporal Sack Dobrzynski held aloof. He neither listened to the music, nor danced, nor yet partook in the general merriment. Standing sullenly aside with his hands behind his back, he recalled the days of his courtship of Sophie. He recalled the gifts of flowers and bird's eggs he'd brought her, the baskets he'd woven for her, the earrings he'd carved for her. The little ingrate! Though he'd lavished those lovely gifts on her in vain, though she'd run from his sight, and his father forbade him to see her, yet despite all, he still loved her dearly. How many times had he sat on the fence to catch a glimpse of her in the window! How many times had he stolen into the hemp to watch her weed the garden, harvest her cucumbers, fatten her capons! Aye, the

little ingrate! – and he sank his head. But then, whistling out
a mazurka, he rammed his visored cap down over his brow and
made for the camp where the guards stood watch over the field
guns. To distract himself, he struck up a game of canasta with a
few old campaigners, sweetening his grief with a cup. Such was
the constancy of Sack Dobrzynski's feelings for Sophie.

Meanwhile, Sophie danced blithely on. Though she led
the dance, a distant viewer could scarcely make her out in the
vast, overgrown courtyard. Clad in her green skirt, garlanded
and bedecked with nosegays, she ranged unseen over the grass
and the flowers, governing the dance as an unseen angel presides
over the roll of the stars. You knew she was there by the eyes
turned her way, by the arms stretched toward her, by the bustle
of bodies thronging around her. Bootless the Chamberlain's attempts to cling to her side! Already, his rivals had dislodged him
from the first pair. Nor did the lucky Dombrowski have long to
gloat. He, too, was forced to yield her up. A third rival presented
himself, only to have Sophie snatched from him by a fourth; and
so he, too, walked forlornly away. At last, Sophie passed back to
Tadeusz; and here, weary of dancing, fearing yet another change
of partners and anxious to be with her betrothed husband, she
closed the dance. She returned to the table and began serving
out wine to the guests.

The sun was setting. The evening was warm and calm.
Puffs of cloud dotted the dome of the sky. Overhead, it was still
blue, to the westward, rosy. The clouds, foretokening fair weather, were airy and bright. Here, they floated drowsily like a flock
on the green. Yonder, somewhat smaller in size, they suggested
a flight of teal. A larger cloud loomed in the west. Like a sheer
lace curtain it hung, translucent, amply folded, pearly white on
the outside, gilded around the marges, and mauve in the center.
Still it glowed and flamed in the ebbing light. Then, at last, turning yellow, it grew pale and gray; and the sun, sinking his head,
drew down the cloud and, with one last warm and wafting sigh,
nodded off to sleep.

Meanwhile, the nobility drank on, pledging Bonaparte,
the Generals, Sophie and Tadeusz. Next, they saluted all three
betrothed couples in turn, then all the invited guests both present and absent, then all those friends remembered among the
living, and last, those of sainted memory.

And I, too, was a guest on that occasion. I drank the mead and the wine, and all that I saw and heard have I here set down in this book.

Finis

Note on the Spelling of Personal and Place Names

Polish surnames in this rendering appear without their standard diacritic marks. Thus, *Dobrzyński, Radziwiłł* become Dobrzynski, Radziwill, etc. Common given names such as *Zofia, Józef, Maciej, Bartłomiej, Dominik* have been anglicized to Sophia, Joseph, Matthias, Bartholomew, Dominic, etc. (The various diminutive forms are for the most part ignored.) The given names *Tadeusz* and *Jacek* present a special case and are discussed elsewhere (see note to Title Page). In only a few instances has the Polish spelling of a personal name been altered for easier readability in English (Yankel for *Jankiel*, Rembaïlo for *Rębajło*, Dombrowski for *Dąbrowski,* etc.). The few Russian names that occur are given as if transliterated from the Russian and not in their Polish or polonized form (e.g. Suvorov not *Suworów*, Kozodushin not *Kozodusin*). As for place names, older established English spellings have been preserved in the case of certain major cities, e.g. Vilna for Vilnius/Wilno and Cracow for Kraków; otherwise, the contemporary Polish names and spellings are used. Lithuanian and Belorussian personal and place names are given in their Polish variant form (with or without slight spelling modifications), though in the odd instance a more readable toponym is used outright in preference to the Polish one used by Mickiewicz (Neris and Vilnele for *Wilija* and *Wilijka*, Zietela for *Zdzięcioł*, etc.).

NOTES

Unless subsumed under my translator's note or integrated materially into the poetic text, Mickiewicz's notes to *Pan Tadeusz* are indicated as "*Author's note.*" They are given here in George Rapall Noyes' translation, only slightly revised by myself (cf. *Pan Tadeusz*, Dent Everyman's Library, 1930). The remaining notes are either my own or my adaptations of Noyes' translator's notes as revised and supplemented by Dr. H.B. Segel (*Pan Tadeusz or the Last Foray in Lithuania*, tr. Watson Kirkconnell, University of Toronto Press, 1962). Extensive use is also made of Stanisław Pigoń's notes to the Ossolineum 1982 "Biblioteka Narodowa" edition of *Pan Tadeusz*. [Transl.]

TITLE PAGE

Pan Tadeusz

Like *Don Quixote*, the title of the Polish masterpiece is best left untranslated. As an honorific title, Polish *pan* was traditionally reserved for hereditary noblemen and was roughly equivalent to "lord" or "sir" in English. In the nineteenth century it came to be used at all levels of society and may now be considered equivalent to the English "Mr." As in French and Spanish, when prepended to the first name, the style suggests a genteel informality that stops short of the familiarity conveyed by the use of the given name alone. As for the Christian name *Tadeusz* (pronounce *tah-DEH-oosh*), it is, like the name *Jacek* (*JAH-tsek*), very common in Poland even today. Apart from the eponymous hero, four Tadeuszes (Kościuszko, Rejtan, Korsak, and Steward Hreczecha) are introduced in the very first pages of the poem. Little is to be gained, and more lost, by englishing the name to the relatively uncommon Thaddeus – a *fortiori* in the case of *Jacek* (Hyacinth).

The Last Foray in Lithuania

In the time of the Polish-Lithuanian Commonwealth the execution of judicial decrees was no easy undertaking in a country where the executive authorities had almost no police force at their disposal, and where powerful citizens kept household regiments, some of them, e.g. the Princes Radziwiłł, even armies of several thousand. So, the plaintiff who obtained a verdict in his favor had to apply for its execution to the knightly order, that is to the nobility (*szlachta*), with whom rested also the executive power. Armed kinsmen, friends, and neighbors set out, verdict in hand, in company with the court usher (*woźny*), and took possession, often not without bloodshed, of the goods adjudged to the plaintiff, which the usher legally made over or gave into his possession. Such an armed execution of a verdict was called a foray (*zajazd*). In ancient times, while laws were respected, even the most powerful magnates did not dare resist judicial decrees, armed attacks rarely took place, and violence almost never went unpunished. The sad end of Prince [Dymitr] Sanguszko, and of Stadnicki, styled the Devil, is a matter of historical record. The corruption of public morals in the Commonwealth increased the number of forays, which continually upset the peace of Lithuania. [*Author's note*]

A Tale of the Polish Nobility

The term denoting the noble estate in Poland is *szlachta*. It has no precise counterpart in English, since the Poles made no distinction between nobility and gentry. "Every member of the *szlachta* was legally equal to any other: members addressed each other as 'brothers'; [in principle] no titles, such as lord or count, were allowed; any *szlachcic* could become a member of the Sejm [the Polish Parliament's Lower House]] or even, at least in theory, be elected king. Only members of the *szlachta* were permitted to bear arms. Membership in this class was marked by possession of a coat of arms; the same coat of arms was often shared by several families, but unrelated people of the same family name could have different coats of arms" (Zdzisław Najder, *Joseph Conrad: A Chronicle*, Rutgers University Press, New

Brunswick, New Jersey, 1984, p. 3). In the historical period por-
trayed in *Pan Tadeusz*, the *szlachta* formed about a tenth of the
population and was the only class to enjoy full political rights.
Its members fell into several categories, from the great landowners or magnates, to smallholders and even landless squires
serving as dependents in the households of the wealthy. While
representatives of the upper nobility do appear in *Pan Tadeusz*,
most notably the count, the poem deals mainly with the exploits
of the petty provincial nobility, who represent, as it were, the
collective hero of the epic. Thus, the present translation renders
the term *szlachta* variously as "nobility," "minor nobility," "gentry," "petty gentry," "gentlefolk," and "squirearchy." The term
szlachcic is rendered variously as "noble," "nobleman," "Polish
lord," "knight," "squire," "born gentleman," "country gentleman,"
or just plain "gentleman."

BOOK ONE

Lithuania – my homeland [p.4]

The opening apostrophe to Lithuania (pol. *Litwa*) expresses the Polish poet's strong sense of regional patriotism.
Mickiewicz was a posthumous child of the old Polish-Lithuanian
Commonwealth, whose final collapse and dismemberment occurred three years before his birth with the Third Partition of
Poland (1795). The Grand Duchy of Lithuania, formally joined
to the Crown of the Kingdom of Poland by the Union of Lublin in
1569, included the ethnic territory of Lithuania proper as well as
large parts of what is now Belarus, where in fact Mickiewicz was
born. The poet would frequently return to this historical notion
of the term, e.g. in Books Four and Eleven of *Pan Tadeusz* and
again in his *Books of the Polish Nation and Polish Pilgrimage*.

*Holy Virgin . . . of Czestochowa . . . Vilna's Ostra Gate. . . Novo-
grodek's castle* [p.4]

The references are to the wonder-working images of Our
Lady of Jasna Góra (Bright Hill) in Częstochowa, Poland, Our
Lady of Ostra Brama (also known as Our Lady of the Gate of

Dawn) in Vilnius, Lithuania, and Our Lady of Nowogródek (now Navahrudak) in Belarus. In his note Mickiewicz also mentions those at Żyrowiec (Zhirovichi) and Boruny.

where the rapeseed glows [p.4]

According to Stanisław Pigoń, the word *świerzop* might refer equally to the *sinapis arvensis*, commonly known as char-lock mustard, field mustard, wild mustard or charlock, and the yellow-flowered *brassica napus*, commonly known as rapeseed, rape, or oilseed rape. which was widely cultivated in the area and used, among other things, as fuel in oil lamps.

a two-horse britzka [p.5]

From *bryczka* (pol.); a long horse-drawn carriage with a folding top over the rear seat and a rear-facing front seat.

Here stood Kosciuszko in his Cracow coat [p.5]

Tadeusz Kościuszko (1746-1817), Poland's most revered national hero. In 1776 he went to America to participate in the American Revolutionary War as a colonel of engineers. He won distinction in the defense of Saratoga and saw further service with the army of the South. He returned to Poland in 1784, served as a general in the war of 1792, and led the insurrection against the Russians in 1794. After the failure of the insurrec-tion, he was imprisoned in St. Petersburg until released by Em-peror Paul who acceded to the throne of Russia after the death, in 1796, of his mother, Catherine II. Kościuszko returned to the United States in 1797 but left when news of the formation of the Polish Legions at the side of the French reached him. From 1798-1801 he was in residence in Paris. Both Napoleon and Al-exander I of Russia sought his services, but he resisted their attempts and played no direct role in the Napoleonic wars. In 1815, he appeared before the Congress of Vienna to plead Po-land's cause but his efforts to secure an honorable Polish settlement were doomed to failure.

On October 15, 1817, he died in Soleure, Switzerland, where he had taken up residence. His remains now rest in the Cathedral of the Wawel in the ancient Polish capital of Kraków amongst Poland's kings and her greatest poets. The "Cracow coat" worn by Kościuszko (referred to as a *czamara*) was actually a *sukmana*, the white caftan of the common folk of the Kraków region.

the robed Rejtan sat lamenting [p.5]

Tadeusz Rejtan (1742-1780) had taken part in the Confederacy of Bar (1768-1772) and was a delegate to the Parliament of 1773, where he distinguished himself by his vigorous protest against the first partition of Poland. Later he fell into despair over the disasters that had befallen his nation and took his life by swallowing shards of crushed glass.

Jasinski . . . Korsak [p.5]

Jakub Jasiński (1759-1794), a soldier and poet who served as a colonel of engineers in the Russo-Polish war of 1792. He organized the insurrection in Lithuania and seized the city of Vilnius. He was killed during the siege of Praga, a suburb of Warsaw. Tadeusz Korsak (1741-1794); a deputy to the so-called Four-Year Parliament and a leader in Kościuszko's insurrection. He perished with Jasiński in the siege of Warsaw.

the old Dombrowski mazurka [p.5]

Then the *de facto* national anthem of Poland; now, since the restoration of Poland's independence in 1918, her official anthem. A mazurka is a lively Polish dance originating from Poland's Mazovian province.

The Judge wouldn't dream of dispatching his guests' horses [p.7]

The Tsarist government in conquered countries never overthrows their laws and civil institutions at once, but by its edicts it slowly undermines and saps them of their vigor. For example, in Little Russia [the parts of the Commonwealth annexed by Russia in the first partition of Poland – *transl.*] the Lithuanian Statute, modified by edicts, was maintained until recent times. Lithuania was allowed to retain her ancient organization of civil and criminal courts. So, as of old, rural and town judges are elected in the districts, and superior judges in the provinces. But since there is an appeal to St. Petersburg, to many institutions of various standing, the local courts are left with but a shadow of their former dignity. [*Author's note*]

They had been waiting for the Chief Steward [p.7]

The steward or major-domo (*wojski*) was once an officer (*tribunus*) charged with the protection of the wives and children of the nobility during the time of service of the general militia. But this office without duties has long since become purely titular. In Lithuania there is a courteous custom of bestowing on respected persons some ancient title, which becomes legalized by usage. For instance, the neighbors may call one of their friends quartermaster, pantler, or cupbearer, at first only in conversation and in correspondence, but later even in official documents. The Tsarist government has forbidden such titles, and would make mock of them, introducing in their place the system of titles based on the ranks of its own hierarchy, for which the Lithuanians still have great repugnance. [*Author's note*]

to honor the year of war in which he was born [p.7]

This would mean that Tadeusz was born in 1794, the year of Kościuszko's insurrection.

The Chamberlain, his wife, and daughters [p.7-8]

Under the Tsarist government, the chamberlain (*podko-morzy*), once a noted and dignified official (*princeps nobilitatis*), has become merely a titular dignitary. Formerly, he was still judge of boundary disputes, but he finally lost even that part of his jurisdiction. Now he occasionally takes the place of the marshal (*marszałek*) and appoints the district surveyors (*komorni-cy*). [*Author's note*]

the Court Usher stood candle in hand [p.9]

The court usher (*woźny trybunalski*) or sergeant-at-arms (*jenerał – generalis ministerialis*), chosen from among the landed gentry by the decree of a tribunal or court, executed writs, proclaimed persons to legal possession of property adjudged to them, launched inquests, called cases on the court's calendar, etc. Usually this office was assigned to one of the minor nobility. [*Author's note*]

ancient seat of the Horeszkos [p.9]

The pantler's family name (pronounce: *ho-RESH-ko*.) No other name is revealed.

the time of troubles [p.9]

A reference to the period of Poland's partitions (1772-1795).

Both laid claims at the district court [p.10]

i.e. the court of the *zemstvo*, an organ of rural self-government throughout the Russian Empire; it adjudicated in local matters such as boundary disputes.

The Franciscan took his station . . . [p.10]

In Poland and Lithuania, the Franciscan Friars Observant were known as Bernardines, after Bernardino of Siena.

beet-leaf soup – chilled Lithuanian-style [p.10]

A popular Lithuanian summer dish made of young beet leaves, dilled cucumbers, eggs, meat or crayfish tails, and sour cream. Mickiewicz calls the dish by its Byelorussian name *chołodziec* (*холодец*), the standard Polish variant of which is *chłodnik*.

as an attendant of the Royal Governor [p.11]

The royal governor or voivode (*palatinus*) was the highest authority of the province or voivodeship (*województwo*), the largest administrative unit of the Polish-Lithuanian state.

Vespasian . . . cared little for the smell of his money [p.12]

An allusion to Suetonius' *Life of Vespasian*. Among other things, the Roman emperor imposed a tax on public toilets.

a carnival of license, swift on the heels of which came . . . bondage. [p.13]

The reference is to the Third Partition of Poland (1795), which effectively erased the country from the map of Europe until its restoration by the terms of the Treaty of Versailles in 1918. The liturgical penitential season of Lent, beginning with Ash Wednesday, is preceded by Fat Tuesday (*mardi gras*) or the Carnival, which was often associated with license and excess.

like swallows around a buzzard [p.13]

The buzzard (*raróg*) is a bird resembling a hawk. It is well known how a flock of small birds, especially swallows, will pursue a hawk. Hence the saying, to go swarming after a buzzard. [*Author's note*]

a plain case of the elflock [p.13]

The *plica polonica* (pol. *kołtun*), a disease of the hair, in which it becomes matted and twisted together. It seems to have been a common condition among the peasantry in the northeastern border regions of Poland.

our Suvorov gone [p.15]

Alexander Vasilyevich Suvorov (1729-1800), field marshal and later generalissimus of the Russian Empire; Tadeusz Kościuszko's nemesis. In addition to his brilliant Turkish and Italian campaigns he led two against the Poles: first, against the forces of the Bar Confederacy (1768-72); second, in 1794, to quell the Kościuszko insurrection, during which he oversaw the siege of Warsaw and the massacre of Praga. He was famous for his gnomes, which Captain Rykov evidently imitates.

Bonaparte had magic [p.15]

Among the Russian common folk there were numerous stories current about the black arts reputedly practiced by Bonaparte and Suvorov [*Author's note*]

the Notary and the Assessor [p.16]

One class of notaries (*rejenci aktowi*) have charge of certain government offices; others (*rejenci dekretowi*) record verdicts; all are appointed by the clerks of the courts. The assessors form the rural police of a district. According to the edicts, they are in part elected by the citizenry, in part appointed by the government; these last are called the crown assessors. Judges of appeal are also called assessors, but there is no reference to them here. [*Author's note*]

he was a Soplica . . . [p.17]

Soplica (pronounce: so-PLEE-tsa), the family name of the judge and his nephew Tadeusz

rorate candles [p.17]

The reference is to the early morning candle-lit masses during the liturgical season of Advent. "*Rorate*" (meaning: "Drop down like dew") is the first word of the opening verse of Isaiah 45:8 in the Vulgate Latin used during the pre-Christmas season in the divine liturgy.

a miniature of King Stanislas [p.20]

Stanisław II August Poniatowski (1732-1798), the last king and grand duke of the Polish-Lithuanian Commonwealth, ascended the throne in 1764 and ruled until the third partition in 1795.

old Niesiolowski [p.21]

Józef Count Niesiołowski (1729-1814), last voivode of Nowogródek, was president of the revolutionary government during Jasiński's insurrection. After its defeat, he retired from public life.

refused Bialopiotrowicz himself [p.21]

Jerzy Białopiotrowicz (1740-1812), the last Secretary of the Grand Duchy of Lithuania, took an active part in the Lithuanian insurrection under Jasiński. He was judge of state prisoners at Vilna. He was a man highly honored in Lithuania for his virtues and patriotism. [*Author's note*]

since the days of King Lech [p.21]

The three mythical brothers, Lech, Czech, and Rus, are said to be the progenitors of the Polish, Bohemian, and Russian nations.

crafted in Slutsk [p.22]

Located south of Minsk in what is now Belarus, Slutsk (pol. *Słuck*) was famous for its manufactories, which supplied the whole Commonwealth with gold brocade and massive belts or waist-sashes (*pasy kontuszowe*). They were owned by the fabulously wealthy Radziwiłł family.

the daily missal [p.22]

More precisely, "the golden altar" (*ołtarzyk złoty*), the generic title of devotional books commonly used in Poland in the eighteenth and nineteenth centuries.

a court calendar [p.22]

The calendar of causes (*trybunalska wokanda*) was a long, narrow little book listing the names of the parties to lawsuits in the order of the defendants. Every advocate and court usher had to own such a calendar. [*Author's note*]

yolked both gold and silver eagles [p.23]

i.e. the golden eagle of Napoleon and the silver eagle of

Poland. The Polish coat of arms depicts a white eagle on a red field.

the Pyramids, Tabor, Marengo, Ulm, and Austerlitz [p.23]

Napoleon's decisive military victories (1798-1805).

Dombrowski enlisting Poles in the Lombard plains [p.23]

Jan Henryk Dąbrowski (1755-1788), outstanding Polish military leader; creator of the Polish legions in northern Italy. He saw service in the wars of 1792 and 1794, and participated in the Napoleonic campaigns of 1806-07, 1809, and 1812. After the fall of Napoleon, he returned to Warsaw where he served as a Senator-Governor in the Congress Kingdom, the Polish state created by the Congress of Vienna in 1815.

Kniaziewicz issuing orders from the Capitol [p.23]

General Otton-Karol Kniaziewicz (1762-1842), another outstanding Polish military leader of the Napoleonic era. He participated in the wars of 1792 and 1794, and in 1798 commanded the First Legion in Italy. For a while he was commandant of Rome with his headquarters in the Capitol. In recognition of his victories he was entrusted with the commission of delivering the captured standards of the enemy to Paris.

Jablonowski faring forth . . . to exotic climes [p.23]

Prince Władysław Jabłonowski (1769-1802), commander of Napoleon's Polish Danube Legion. At the latter's orders, he led his ill-fated expeditionary force to Haiti to quell a popular revolt led by Toussaint l'Ouverture. He and almost all his legion perished there.

Pax vobiscum [p.25]

    Peace be with you (lat.)

BOOK TWO

Surge, puer! [p.27]

    On your feet, boy! (lat.)

his knotted rope girdle [p.27]

    Franciscan friars had three knots in their rope girdles, symbolizing their threefold vow of poverty, chastity and obedience.

the Count insisted his servants . . . be called jockeys [p.28]

    The quixotic count is evidently an anglophile.

Gervase was of noble stock [p.29]

    The "Tweedledum" to Protase Brzechalski's "Tweedledee". The humorous choice of given names derives from the Roman saints' names Gervasius and Protasius.

his real name, however, was Rembaïlo [p.30]

    Gervase's Lithuanian-sounding surname (written *Rębajło* in Polish), is derived from the Polish verb *rąbać*, meaning 'to hew.' His facetious nickname *Mopanek*, here rendered as "Old Boy," is a diminutive form of *Mości Pan*, a familiar address of the time.

a call to Parliament or the regional diet [p.31]

The Polish tri-cameral Parliament was made up of the King, an Upper House (Senate) formed by bishops, voivodes, chatelains and ministers, and a Lower House (or *Sejm*) made up of deputies who were elected by the regional diets or dietines (*sejmiki*). From 1573, Parliament convened regularly every two years for six weeks, except in case of emergency when more frequent sessions were held for two-week periods. Convocations of Parliament took place in Warsaw (regular sessions), Grodno (every third parliament) and Kraków (coronation parliaments).

playing airs on the organ [p.31]

An organ was ordinarily set in the gallery [or choir] of the old castles. [*Author's note*]

the Primate [p.31]

The primate of Poland, the archbishop of Gniezno, was the highest dignitary in Poland after the king. He officiated at coronations and reigned during the interregna.

the Chatelain [p.32]

The office of chatelain or castellan (*kasztelan*) was next in dignity to that of governor (*wojewoda*). Except for some very slight military duties, the post was purely titular, but it was prized because it entitled the holder to a seat in the Senate.

a bowl of black soup [p.32]

Black soup, served at table to a suitor, signified the family's refusal. [*Author's note*] *the Constitution of May Third* [p.32]

The Four-Year Parliament (also known as the Constitutional Parliament), in session from 1788 to 1792, adopted the celebrated Constitution of the Third of May 1791. By the terms of the constitution, the burghers were granted full equality before the law, the peasantry were placed under the protection of the government, and the notorious *liberum veto* was abolished. It was the first written constitution in Europe.

four stout-hearted Haiduks [p.32]

A hajduk was a Polish nobleman's servant dressed in Hungarian livery.

hetman's maces [p.34]

The mace (*bułava*) symbolized the authority of the hetman, the commander-in-chief of the Polish Army.

the trading wherries [p.37]

Wherries (*wiciny*) are large boats on the Niemen with which the Lithuanians conduct trade with the Prussians, freighting grain down the river and receiving colonial wares in return for it. [*Author's note*]

my dear darling bolonka [p.39]

A little white dog similar to the French Bolognese of today (the Polish name *bonończyk* derives from Bononia, the Latin name for Bologna). Through the connection between the Russian and French aristocracy in the eighteenth and nineteenth

centuries, the breed was brought to Tsarist Russia and became known as the *bolonka frantsuzkaya*. These lively toy dogs were favorites of the fashionable ladies of the period.
See *https://en.wikipedia.org/wiki/Bolonka*

Prince Sukin [p.39]

Not an entirely uncommon Russian surname, but the association with the expletive *sukin syn* (son of a bitch) is too strong to miss.

Kirilo Gavrilich Kozodushin [p.40]

To achieve his comical effect in Polish, Mickiewicz polonizes the Russian surname to Kozodusin, i.e. goat-strangler – from *koza* (goat) and *dusić* (choke or strangle). The Russian cognate of *dusić* is *душить* (*dushít'*). Hence the more natural Russian name would have been *Козодушин* (*Kozodushin*). But, transliterated into Polish, this would have yielded *Kozoduszyn*, and the desired association would have been obscured. Interestingly, a Russian statesman with a name of parallel etymology actually existed: namely, *Kozodavlev* – from *давить* (*davít'*), also meaning 'to choke.' Osip Petrovich Kozodavlev served as the Tsar's Minister of the Interior from 1810 to 1819. Mickiewicz would doubtless have heard of him during his period of exile in Russia.

Jaegermeister [p.40]

Master of the Hunt [*Jägermeister*] (ger.)

If Greater Poland wants to learn from the Swabians [p.40]

Greater Poland refers to the northwestern part of the old Polish kingdom, which fell under Prussian rule.

Prince Dominic . . . Marshal Sanguszko, General Mejen [p.44]

Prince Dominik Radziwiłł (1786-1813), a great lover of hunting, emigrated to the Duchy of Warsaw and at his own expense equipped a regiment of cavalry, which he commanded in person. He died in France. With him became extinct the male line of the Princes of Ołyka and Nieśwież, the most powerful lords in Poland and in all probability in Europe. General Jan Jakub Mejen distinguished himself in the national war under Kościuszko. Mejen's ramparts still exist near Vilna [*Author's note*].

Exactly which Marshal Sanguszko Mickiewicz had in mind is uncertain. The Sanguszkos were a powerful family of Lithuanian princes.

BOOK THREE

Banty née Cockalorum [p.45]

A vain attempt at rendering Mickiewicz's humorous appellation *Kokosznicka* and the run-on *Jendykowi-/Czówna*.

A radiant mist of mayflies or dames . . . [p.46]

In the eastern borderland region of Mickiewicz's birth, these dancing insects were called *babki*, probably under the influence of the Russian *babochka* meaning 'butterfly.' In standard Polish *babka* means 'dame' or 'granny.'

Tufts of grass and leaves clung to his temples [p.47]

Compare this description with that of the shipwrecked Odysseus suddenly appearing before Nausicaä's maidens "in his defilement with the sea-wrack" (*The Odyssey*, VI, 149, tr. T.E. Lawrence).

"You!" . . . *"By what name shall I pay you homage?"* [p.47]

This manner of launching an address is common to heroes of classical literature from Homer onward. The fragment bears a resemblance to the *Odyssey*, where Odysseus addresses Nausicaä: "O Queen: yet am I in doubt whether you are divine or mortal. If a goddess from high heaven..." (VI 164 inf.). Compare also Aeneas' greeting of his mother Venus in *The Aeneid*, I, 327-329:

> *o–quam te memorem, virgo? Namque haud tibi vultus*
> *mortalis, nec vox humanum sonat; o dea certe!*
> *An Phoebi soror? an Nympharum sanguinis una?*

And just as Sophie later addresses her little tots, so Homer's Nausicaä calls to her startled maidens: "Rally to me, women. Why run because you see a man? You cannot think him an enemy . . ." (218 inf.). Similar affinities have been noted with Polish neo-classical works, notably the humorous *Ode to a Bullwhip* ascribed to Adam Naruszewicz. According to Pigoń, Mickiewicz knew this ode well and evidently used it here for mock-heroic effect: "His contemporaries, knowing this verse, would have sensed the playfulness of applying it to a young girl. Though the count has a 'romantic cast of mind' and a fondness for romantic curiosities, he expresses himself in a manner typical of Polish poets of the eighteenth century. The entire phraseology of this fragment is reminiscent of Naruszewicz, Trembecki, and Koźmian, who frequently began their odes with the apostrophe, 'O ty! . . .' – 'O thou! . . .'"

Just so, spying a puffball . . . [p.49]

Mickiewicz uses the word *cykoria* (chicory) for the common dandelion – evidently a local designation, the standard Polish names for this wildflower being *brodawnik* or *mniszek*. Interestingly, *blue dandelion* is among the many English names for the common chicory flower. Both flowers belong to the *Asteraceae* family.

The forest teemed with wild mushrooms [p.50]

The popular and scientific names of the mushrooms mentioned by Mickiewicz are as follows:

chanterelle *(lisica)*. *Cantharelus cibarius*.
king bolete *(borowik szlachetny)*. *Boletus edulis*.
saffron milk cap *(rydz)*. *Lactarius deliciosus*.
fly agaric *(muchomór)*. *Agaricus muscarius*.
brittle gill *(surojadka)*. *Varieties of the russula spp*.
yellow bolete *(koźlak)*. *Boletus luteus*.
clitocybe *(lejek)*. *Varieties of the clitocybe spp*.
fleecy milkcap *(bielak)*. *Agaricus vellereus*.
puffball *(purchawka)*. *Lycoperdon bovista*.
honey mushroom *(opieńka)*. *Armillaria mellea*.

the handsome bolete, which the ditty calls the "colonel of mushrooms." [p.50]

In his notes, Mickiewicz mentions the "folksong" (*pieśń gminna*) that tells of the regiment of mushrooms marching off to war under the lead of the king bolete. The song, existing in Byelorussian and Polish versions, describes the properties of edible mushrooms.

I went to Piotrkow and Dubno [p.53]

Mickiewicz is deliberately poking fun at the judge's parochialism and limited horizons. Neither town falls outside the borders of the old Polish-Lithuanian Commonwealth. Piotrków was the seat of the Royal Tribunal, the highest court of Poland in 1578-1793; Dubno (in Volhynia) was the site of a famous annual fair.

the sudden approach of the two youths [p.56]

In the ensuing verbal contest between Tadeusz and the count, Mickiewicz once again harks back to the stock conventions of classical literature – this time to the idylls of Theocritus and Virgil in which two swains typically vie for the attentions of a nymph or shepherdess in a pastoral setting.

Breughel . . . Ruysdael [p.58]

The Breughels were a famous family of Dutch painters in the sixteenth and early seventeenth centuries. The count has in mind the brothers Pieter (1564-1638), known as "the Breughel from Hell" (van der Helle) because of his fondness for infernal scenes, and Jan (1568-1625), a master landscape painter. Jacob van Ruysdael (1628-1682) was another noted Dutch landscape painter, especially of pristine forests unspoiled by man. He was highly regarded by the Romantics.

our painter Orlowski [p.58]

Aleksander Orłowski (1777-1832), student of Norblin and Bacciarelli. In 1802 he settled in Saint Petersburg as Archduke Constantine's court painter. Residing near the Imperial court at the Marble Palace, he lovingly depicted Polish historical figures and themes (among them the Massacre of Praga). He was also fond of painting horses. As Mickiewicz observes in his notes, Orłowski was actually a genre painter. His landscapes are less well known. While staying in Petersburg in 1828 and 1829, Mickiewicz met the artist who painted his portrait. Telimena's use of the past tense is inapposite, since in 1811 Orłowski was still living and painting.

five days' field-service [p.62]

i.e. *corvée* labor (pol. *pańszczyzna*). Unpaid field labor owed by a peasant to his feudal lord.

my two bulldogs [p.62]

The breed of small strong English dogs that we call *pijawki* [literally: leeches] is used for hunting big game, especially bear. [*Author's note*]

Constable . . . Procureuse [p.62]

The Polish names of the chamberlain's bulldogs (*Sprawnik* and *Strapczyna*) derive from the Russian titles of two officials who, as Mickiewicz adds in his note, having "frequent opportunities for abusing their authority" were "held in great loathing by the people." These were the *ispravnik* (*исправник*), the chief of the Tsarist rural police, and the *strapchiy* (*стряпчий*), a sort of government procurator. *Strapczyna* (*стряпчина*) would be the feminine variant of *strapchiy* or refer to his wife or widow. Interestingly, there may be a Shakespearean connection here, namely with Malvolio's "Lady of the Strachy" of *Twelfth Night* (TN 2.5.37). According to Alexander Dyce's *Glossary to the Works of William Shakespeare*, the term *strachy* is "now only preserved in the Russian language but it was probably taken by Shakespeare from some novel or play upon which he may have founded the comic incidents of this drama. '[Corroboration can however be derived] from the list of all the Crown servants of Russia sent every year to the State Secretary of the Home Department at St Petersburg *in which for 1825 and 1826 Procureur Botwinko was reported to be imprisoned at Vilna for the above case and that the Strapchy of Oszmiana was acting in his stead as Procureur pro tem.*'" (*Glossary to the Works of William Shakespeare*, London, Bickers & Son, 1880, p. 420, emphasis mine). Other solutions for the textual cruce of Malvolio's "Lady of the Strachy" have since been proposed, including the most recent by D.E. Frydrychowski. See '*Some Old Story': A Conjecture on Malvolio's 'Lady of the Strachy*' (April 22, 2009). Available at SSRN: *http://ssrn.com/abstract=1925153* or *http://dx.doi.org/10.2139/ssrn.1925153*

Saint Hubert's Mass [p.62]

Hubert was the patron saint of hunters. According to the judge, the mass in his honor had a short office (*officium parvum*).

BOOK FOUR

trees of Białowieza, Switez, Ponary, and Kuszelewo [p.64]

The Białowieża Primeval Forest straddles the border between Poland and what is now Belarus. Świteź (*Svitez*) is a small forest-enclosed lake in the vicinity of Nowogródek (Navahrudak). Ponary (Paneriai), now a neighborhood of Vilnius, is located on a range of low wooded hills. The ancient Kuszelewo Forest is located in the southwestern part of the old Nowogródek district.

Witenes . . . Mendog . . . Giedymin . . . Lizdeiko [p.64]

Witenes (*Vytenis*) was Grand Duke of Lithuania around 1300. Mendog or Mindowe (*Mindaugas*, d. 1263) ruled as Grand Duke in the mid-thirteenth century. He was converted to Christianity by the Teutonic Knights in 1251 and crowned king in 1253 by Pope Innocent IV. His residence was in Nowogródek. Giedymin (*Gediminas*), the father of Kiejstut (*Keistutas*) and Olgierd (*Algirdas*), ruled as Grand Duke from 1316 to 1341. He founded the city of Vilnius and was chiefly responsible for the development of the powerful medieval Lithuanian state. In his notes Mickiewicz refers to the tradition according to which "Grand Duke Giedymin had a dream on the Ponary heights of an iron wolf and acting on the counsel of the bard Lizdejko founded the city of Vilna."

the sight of the Neris . . . and the brawl of the Vilnele [p.64]

Vilnius stands at the confluence of the rivers Neris and Vilnia (or Vilnele). Mickiewicz refers to these rivers by their Polish names; namely, *Wilia* (or *Wilija*) and Wilenka (or *Wilijka*) respectively. The latter is a shallow river with shoals and cataracts; hence the "brawl" (*szum*). In Mickiewicz's day it was still navigable by means of shallow-draft "ferries" (*promy*) or river rafts (*tratwy*).

last of our princes [p.64]

The reference is to King Sigismund August (1548-1572), the last lineal representative of the Jagiellonians, who ruled over the Polish-Lithuanian state from 1385 until 1572. Jagiełło (*Jogaila*), son of Olgierd (*Algirdas*) and the dynasty's progenitor, was crowned King Władysław IV after the conclusion of the Treaty of Krevo (1385). He was victor of the great medieval battle at Tannenberg (Grunwald) (1410). Mickiewicz notes that Sigismund August, an avid hunter, was "raised to the throne of the Grand Duchy of Lithuania according to the ancient rites; he girt on him the sword and crowned himself with the soft fur hat (*kołpak*)." Witold (*Vytautas*), elected Grand Duke of Lithuania in 1392, was Jagiełło's brother.

mighty Baublis [p.64]

In the district of Rosienny on the estate of Rural Secretary [Dionizy] Paszkiewicz [c. 1765-1830], there stood an oak called *Baublys*, which in pagan times was honored as a sacred tree. In the interior of this decayed giant, Paszkiewicz founded a cabinet of Lithuanian antiquities. [*Author's note*].

Mendog's grove . . . by the parish church [p.64]

The ancient limes, or lindens, that once grew near the parish church of Nowogródek. Mickiewicz notes that many of these were felled about the year 1812.

the ancient lime . . . before the Holowinski house [p.64]

The family of Herman Hołowiński resided at Steblów on the River Ros, a right-bank tributary of the Dnieper. Mickiewicz visited the estate in February of 1825 on his way to Odessa. A remnant of the old lime-tree survived until the end of the nineteenth century.

Did not Jan's linden hang upon his every word [p.65]

The reference is to Jan Kochanowski (1530-1584), Poland's greatest poet to the time of Adam Mickiewicz. In a number of poems Kochanowski describes the beauty of his hereditary estate, Czarnolas, and its limes.

the marvels he croons in our Cossack poet's ear [p.65]

Here the reference is to the romantic poet Seweryn Goszczyński (1801-1876), especially his poem *Zamek Kaniowski* (The Castle of Kaniów), published in 1828.

button-like knobs . . . tzitziot [p.68]

Mickiewicz may have confused two different things: *tefillin* and *tzitziot*. The *tefillin* are the two little black boxes or phylacteries, which the pious Jew straps to his forehead and arm for weekday morning prayer. The *tzitziot* (singular: *tzitzit* or *tzitzis* (pol. *cyces*), on the other hand, are the specially knotted 'fringes' or 'tassels,' which the observant Jew wears attached to the corners of his four-cornered garments, including the prayer shawl, the so-called *tallit gadol* (literally: "large tallit"). To liken *tefillin* to "button-like knobs" would be infelicitous. However, given Mickiewicz's characteristic economy of expression and preference for the particular over the generic term, it is also possible that he is using the word synecdochically, whereby the part (the knotted tassel) stands for the whole; the more so, as the word *tzitzis* is commonly used by Jews to refer to the "small tallit" (*tallit katan*). Confusion also arises from Mickiewicz's regional use of the word *łeb* in the neutral, non-pejorative sense of 'brow' or 'forehead' (cf. *lob* in Russian and Byelorussian). Yet here again the confusion would vanish if we saw this in light of Mickiewicz's fondness for *pars pro toto*, by which the "brow" refers to the whole (the head). Seen in this light, the "button-like knobs" (*gałki . . . na kształt guzików / Które Żydzi . . . na łbach zawieszają*) would felicitously convey the knotted fringes of the garment with which the devout Jew drapes his head.

dropped in at Yankel's [p.68]

Written *Jankiel* in Polish.

a doodle sack [p.69]

A kind of bagpipe or musette [cf. *Dudelsack* (ger.) and *dudy* (pol.)]. Mickiewicz uses the word *kozica* deriving from *koza* (goat), the bag being made of goatskin.

the cymbalon [p.69]

Also called the hammer dulcimer. A musical instrument of various shapes. Yankel's is the so-called "gypsy dulcimer" (*cymbały cygańskie*), a trapezoidal box tuned to as many as four octaves with taut metal strings. The player strikes the strings with leather-bound hammers. Jews often made a living with these instruments by going the rounds of the manors and towns.

kolomyjkas from Galicia [p.69]

The *kolomyjka* is a lively Ukrainian song and dance. Galicia took its name from Halych, the former capital of Red Ruthenia (*Czerwona Ruś*), now western Ukraine. The name referred to the southeastern portion of the old Polish-Lithuanian Commonwealth, which fell under Austrian rule.

Yankel . . . an honorable Pole [p.69]

Although the majority of the Jews in Poland lived apart from the Christian community and faithfully preserved their traditions, customs, and language, they could identify themselves with Poland's struggle for independence. History has recorded the heroism of Jews who appeared alongside their fellow countrymen on the field of battle. As a good Jew and a patriotic Pole, Yankel stands as a symbol of the mutual understanding and respect that Mickiewicz hoped one day would exist in Poland among all her citizens. [*H.B. Segel*]

the song now famous around the world [p.69]

The reference is to the Dombrowski mazurka, now the national anthem of Poland, *Jeszcze Polska nie zginęła* (Poland Is Not Yet Lost). Composed by Józef Wybicki in 1791, it was originally the song of the Polish legions in Italy under General Dąbrowski.

a city famous for her snuff and mead [p.70]

Kowno, now Kaunas, is Lithuania's second largest city.

schism reigns over the Duchy [p.70]

i.e. the Grand Duchy of Lithuania. The "schism" is a reference to the Eastern Orthodox Church and Russia's domination

over Catholic Lithuania. Częstochowa was in the Duchy of Warsaw. Father Robak envisages the reunion of Lithuania and the
old Kingdom of Poland.

The gentleman on his grange . . . [p.71]

An old jingle (*szlachcic na zagrodzie równy wojewodzie*)
expressing the equality before the law of all members of the Polish nobility.

consult Stryjkowski [p.71]

Maciej Stryjkowski (1547-1582), author of a chronicle of
Lithuania; one of the important sources for the early history of
that country. Mickiewicz enjoyed reading Stryjkowski and drew
on his chronicle for his own narrative poems about medieval
Lithuania, *Grażyna* and *Konrad Wallenrod*.

he took Gdansk from the Germans [p.72]

As the head of the newly created Polish Army of the
Duchy of Warsaw, General Dąbrowski took part in the siege and
capture of Danzig (*Gdańsk*) in 1807.

"Czamara my eye, sir!". . ."You mean a taratatka." [p.73]

Pan Tadeusz makes frequent mention of the national
Polish dress, which began to be superseded by modern Europe-
an apparel in the late eighteenth century. The *taratatka* was a
kind of long coat extending to the knees, with embroidery work
and loops for fastening. The *czamara* was a long dark-colored
frock coat, braided on the back and chest like a hussar's uniform,
with tight sleeves and a buttoned-up collar. By wearing a peasant's caftan (*sukmana*), Kościuszko demonstrated his solidarity
with the common people whose cause he made his own. Polish
noblemen traditionally wore the *kontusz*, a long vividly colored
robe with loose slit sleeves (*wyloty*) and girded by a massive bro-

caded fabric belt (*pas kontuszowy*). The *kontusz* was worn over the żupan, a light narrow-sleeved tunic with a low, open, rounded collar and ornate buttons down the front. Polish Jews traditionally wore a long black gown also called a *żupan*. Mickiewicz gives an accurate description of the garment when introducing Yankel in Book Four, though he refers to it there as a *szarafan*. The present translation renders *kontusz* and *żupan* as "robe" and "tunic" (or "coat") respectively.

the eagle's ancient beak grows so bent [p.76]

The beaks of large birds of prey become more and more curved with advancing age; eventually, the upper part grows so crooked that it closes the bill and the bird dies of hunger. This popular belief has been accepted by some ornithologists. [*Author's note*]

no trace of animal bones [p.76]

It is a fact that there is no instance of an animal's skeletal remains ever being found. [*Author's note*]

these hidden precincts . . . are called The Lairs [p.76]

The Polish term *matecznik* has no precise counterpart in English. It refers to the wildest and most inaccessible parts of the primeval forest.

a simple fowling gun [p.80]

A fowling piece (*ptaszynka*) is a gun of small caliber used with a small bullet. With such a gun a good marksman can hit a bird on the wing. [*Author's note*]

Domeiko . . . Doveiko [p.81]

Dowejko (lith. Doveikos) was a common name in Lithuania. The rhyming "Domejko" is a humorous reminiscence of the poet's friend and schoolmate, Ignacy Domejko, a professor of geology who went on to become rector of the University of Santiago in Chile. During the writing of *Pan Tadeusz*, Mickiewicz and Domejko shared the same living quarters.

vulgo [p.81]

>   commonly called (lat.)

until the gold leaf dripped out [p.82]

>   Bottles of Gdańsk vodka contain sediment of gold leaf. [*Author's note*]

our hunter's goulash known as bigos [p.82]

>   The *bigos* was not prepared on the spot. It was cooked beforehand, stored in casks, brought to the hunt and then reheated.

the forests of Polesia [p.83]

>   i.e. Polesie; one of Europe's largest marshy areas located in the southwestern part of the East-European Plain, now straddling Belarus, Ukraine, Poland, and Russia.

my old friend Maro [p.86]

>   i.e. Publius Virgilius Maro, author of *The Aeneid*.

an animal's hide is no ordinary yardstick [p.86]

>   Queen Dido had a bull's hide cut into strips, and thus enclosed within the compass of the hide a considerable piece of territory, where she later built the city of Carthage. The steward did not read the description of this event in the *Aeneid*, but in all probability in the scholiasts' commentaries. [*Author's note*]

BOOK FIVE

an intromissio, as he called it, of the tableware [p.94]

As court usher, Protase interlards his speech with macaronisms and Latin legalese. The Polish term *intromisyja* signifies the seizing of goods adjudged to the plaintiff.

like Philip out of the hemp [p.94]

Once in Parliament, a deputy called Philip from the village of Konopie [literally: hemp], having obtained the floor, strayed so far from the subject that he raised general laughter in the Chamber. Hence arose the saying, "to pop up like Philip out of the hemp" (*wyrwać się jak Filip z Konopi*)." [*Author's note*]

A germanized Poland is a Poland bereft of her tongue [p.97]

An untranslatable pun on the Polish word for German (*niemiec*), which derives from the word *niemy*, meaning 'dumb' or 'mute.'

And the Word was made flesh [p.97]

A line from the *Angelus*, a prayer to the Blessed Virgin, traditionally said at noon.

Fillette . . . Coquette [p.98]

The original terms are in Polish – *kobietka* (dim. woman) and *kokietka* (flirt) respectively.

spolia opima [p.99]

spoils of honor (lat.)

Brzechalski [p.101]

One of several of Mickiewicz's suggestive names (pronounce: *Bzhe-KHAL-skee*). It derives from the hunting expression *sroka brzecha* (the magpie squawks). In discharging his
office, a court usher was more than often required to raise his
voice.

the nocturnal repasts of Forefathers' Eve [p.105]

An ancient Byelorussian folk rite in which the spirits of
the dead are invoked. Mickiewicz made it the subject of his drama *Dziady* (Forefathers' Eve).

Lackeys? God forbid, sir . . . wassails? That's different.. [p.107]

An untranslatable word play indulged in by the poet.
Gervase, apparently hard of hearing, or simply ignorant of the
count's Anglo-Gallicisms *jockey* and *vassal*, confuses them with
the Polish words *lokiej* (lackey) and *wąsal* (whiskered one) –
large bushy moustaches being hallmarks of the Polish nobility
of the time. Given Napoleon's admiration of the Polish uhlan's
bravery in combat, whence the origin of the French saying *saoul
comme un Polonais*, my metonymical substitution of "wassailers" for Poland's whiskered nobility would not seem too egre-
gious a liberty. See *https://fr.wiktionary.org/wiki/saoul_com-
me_un_Polonais*

Rzezikow, Cietycze, and Rabanki [p.107]

Properly written: *Rzezików, Ciętycze, Rąbanki*. The fic-
tional names suggest the inhabitants' prowess with the sword in
carving (*rzezać*), cutting (*ciąć*), and hewing (*rąbać*) respectively.

Some were carrying sabers, others, maces [p.107]

A special kind of mace (*buzdygan* – from the Turkish). It was the staff of office of the higher military command in the Polish Army, just as the *buława* was that of the hetmans or generals. Each was a short rod with a knob at the top end, but the knob on the *buzdygan* was round and adorned with precious stones, while the one on the *buława* was pear-shaped and fluted.

BOOK SIX

The noble village [p.109]

The 'noble village' (*zaścianek*) was inhabited by families of the most impoverished of the minor nobility who, despite their distinctive manners, lived on the level of the peasantry. Mickiewicz notes that "the term *okolica* or *zaścianek* in Lithuania is given to a village of the minor nobility, to distinguish them from true villages, which are settlements of peasants." In point of fact, *okolica* and *zaścianek* were not the same thing. An *okolica* arose as a result of nobility of different backgrounds (and hence of different names) settling in one locality. A *zaścianek* on the other hand, arose as a result of the growth of a single family and the subdividing of the common ancestor's original domain into several farms. Thus, all the nobility inhabiting a *zaścianek* carried the same family name and were related.

A description of Matthias Dobrzynski and his household [p.109]

Pronounce the surname: *dob-ZHIN-skee*.
the Targowica confederates [p.112]

The Confederacy of Targowica formed in 1792 by Polish nobles who opposed the liberal Constitution of May Third, 1791. Their appeal for Russian assistance provided Catherine II with a pretext for invading Poland. The country was partitioned for the second time and the Constitution abolished.

barely a drop of Horeszko blood in his veins [p.113]

The literal translation of the Polish line is, "To the Horeszkos he is merely the tenth water on the *kisiel*." In explanation, Mickiewicz adds the following note: "*Kisiel* is a Lithuanian dish, a sort of jelly made of oaten yeast, which is washed with water until all the mealy parts are separated from it; hence the proverb."

Our Poniatowski [p.113]

Prince Józef Antoni Poniatowski (1763-1813), a nephew of King Stanisław August and commander-in-chief of the army of the Duchy of Warsaw. He was a brilliant soldier and a staunch supporter of Napoleon to the end of the campaigns. He was named a Marshal of France shortly before he perished in the battle of Leipzig.

the Treaty of Tilsit [p.113]

The Peace of Tilsit, concluded by Napoleon with the Prussians on July 7, 1807. By the terms of the treaty, a rump state known as the Duchy of Warsaw (*Księstwo Warszawskie*) was carved out from the territories acquired by Prussia in the second and third partitions. Gdańsk (Danzig), however, was kept as a free city and was not included. The Duchy was ruled by the House of Saxony in the person of Frederick August I under the protection of Napoleon. After the fall of Napoleon it ceased to exist in 1815 by decision of the Congress of Vienna.

Lithuania's heraldic charger . . . the Bear of Samogitia [p.114]

The coat of arms of Lithuania (*Pogoń*) depicts a knight on a white charger in full career. The Bear (*Niedźwiedź*) is the coat of arms of Żmudź (Samogitia), a Baltic region of Lithuania.

Monsieur Bignon [p.115]

Baron Louis-Pierre-Edouard Bignon (1771-1841), a French diplomat; from February 1811 to 1812 Napoleon's representative in Warsaw.

the proud and insolent Wolodkowicz [p.116]

After various brawls, this man was seized at Minsk and shot in accordance with a court decree. [*Author's note*]

King Jan Sobieski mustered the general militia [p.118]

Jan III Sobieski, the "deliverer of Vienna" (1683), reigned over Poland from 1674 to 1696. Mickiewicz notes that when the king was to assemble the general militia, "he had a pole set up in each parish with a broom or bundle of twigs tied to the top symbolizing his authority to inflict punishment. This was called 'sending out the twigs' (*rozdać wici*). Every adult man of the knightly order was obliged, under pain of the loss of the privileges of gentle birth, to rally at once to the royal governor's standard."

Dobrzyn in Mazovia [p.118]

Properly written: *Dobrzyń*. Mazovia (*Mazowsze*) is a province in central Poland; its capital is Warsaw.

Matthias baptized his son Bartholomew [p.118]

Matthias is *Matjasz* in Polish, its variant form being *Maciej* (dim. *Maciek*). The Polish form of Bartholomew is *Bartłomiej* or *Bartek* for short. The present translation eschews these variants.

bynames deriving from some quirk or attribute [p.118]

The poet inaccurately equates the *przydomek* (byname) with the sobriquet or nickname (*imionisko*). *Przezwisko* (also best translated as nickname) would be a better equivalent. The gentry took their *przydomek* from their estates, title, etc. The *przezwisko* originated in individual physical or behavioral characteristics and could not be passed from father to son, unlike the *przydomek*.

he went by the appellation of Little King [p.118]

The Polish word for "little king" (*królik*) also means "rabbit."

A horsetail . . . performed the office of a duster [p.120]

The horsetail (*buńczuk*) was a staff topped with crescent and a knot of horsehair. It served as an ensign for Turkish regiments. It was also used in the Polish Army as a symbol of the hetman's authority. After the numerous military victories over the Turks, it was a piece of booty commonly found in knightly homes and estates.

a former Bar Confederate [p.120]

The Confederacy of Bar (named after the Podolian town where it was formed), was organized on February 19, 1768 by Polish patriots who sought to free Poland from Russian political domination. Their four-year struggle ended in defeat and the first partition of Poland, 1772. The Bar Confederacy was the subject of a play in French by Mickiewicz – *Les Confédérés de Bar*.

stood with Tyzenhaus [p.120]

Antoni Tyzenhaus (1733-1785), First Grand Secretary,

later Under Court Treasurer of Lithuania, for a long time an unswerving partisan of King Stanisław August Poniatowski.

his changing allegiances gave rise to . . . Cock o' the Steeple [p.120]

During the Bar Confederacy, Matthias had opposed the king because of his subservience to Russia but rallied to his support when Stanisław August attempted to continue the process of national renewal after the first partition in 1772. Twenty years after, Matthias found himself again in opposition to the throne during the Targowica Confederacy when Stanisław August abandoned resistance to the Confederacy, submitted to it, and paved the way for the second partition. Although he is called *Cock o' the Steeple*, Matthias' behavior was consistently patriotic. He opposed whatever he considered harmful to his country's best interests.

His last action was with Oginski [p.121]

Michal Kleofas Ogiński (1765-1833), composer of the *Oginski Polonaise*; he took part in the insurrection of 1794 and was a member of the Provisional Government. Mickiewicz met him in Italy in 1830.

Let Pociej be Matthias' debtor, not Matthias Pociej's [p.121]

On his return to Lithuania after the war, Alexander Count Pociej assisted those of his fellow countrymen who were emigrating abroad and sent considerable sums to the treasury of the Legions. [*Author's note*]

When Early Breaks the Dawn [p.122]

The opening line of a popular hymn (*Kiedy ranne wstają zorze*) by Franciszek Karpiński (1741-1825).

Praised be the Lord Jesus Christ . . . Now and evermore [p.123]

A common pious greeting and reply in Catholic countries; it is used by Poles even today.

BOOK SEVEN

shooting small game with Joseph Grabowski [p.124]

Józef Grabowski (1791-1881) was in fact a second lieutenant, an adjutant to Sokolnicki, head of Marshal Murat's army. Grabowski retired from the army with the rank of lieutenant colonel and as a knight of the Legion of Honor. In 1831, he entertained Mickiewicz and his brother Franciszek on his estate of Łukowo, near Objezierze [Oberau (ger.)] in Greater Poland.

'Jena! Jena!' yelled Grabowski [p.124]

Napoleon's decisive victory over the Prussians at Jena took place in October 1806. After Jena, the emperor summoned the Poles to his standards.

like cockroaches [p.124]

One of Mickiewicz's many droll *double ententes*. Rather than *karaluch*, the standard Polish word for cockroach, Mickiewicz uses *prusak*, i.e. 'Prussian' or 'German.'

Ach, Hairy Got! O vey! [p.125]

i.e. *Ach, Herr Gott! O Wej!* (O Lord! O woe!). Bartholomew's hearing of German is obviously faulty.

maggots gnawing at Moscow [p.126]

The Polish word *robak* means 'worm' or 'maggot.'

then let us form a confederacy [p.127]

Confederacies, which date as far back as the thirteenth century, were extra-parliamentary citizens' organizations formed for the purpose of attaining specific goals, often by the use of armed force. Once the goals were realized, they ceased to exist. Some confederacies came into existence to maintain peace during *interregna*; others were used to circumvent the limitations of the *liberum veto* in Parliament (in a confederacy, unlike Parliament, majority vote ruled). The most famous confederacies in Polish history were those of Bar and Targowica.

So it's contracts, is it? . . . Do you mean Kiev's or Minsk's? [p.128]

The contracts of Kiev and Minsk were famous fairs, held annually. As these are the only contracts Matthias has heard of, the word, as used by Buchman with reference to Rousseau's *Contrat Social*, naturally puzzles him.

Babin government [p.128]

The Republic of Babin (*Rzeczpospolita babińska*) was a comic society founded in 1568 by Stanisław Pszonka (d. 1580)) on his estate, Babin, near Lublin. With sixteenth century French and Italian parodic academies and societies as its model, the Babin Republic became principally a liars' society (*omnis homo mendax* was its motto) conferring titles, offices, and rewards on notorious braggarts and liars.

"Veto!" cried another [p.129]

A reference to the notorious *liberum veto*, by which a single vote could effectively render null and void the entire body of legislation enacted to date at a session of Parliament. It was abolished by the Four-Year Parliament (1788-92).

boarded in the Piarist schools [p.134]

The Piarists, a Catholic teaching order, improved the education of the noble youth, especially, since the introduction of modernizing reforms by Father Stanisław Konarski in 1740.

a jumped-up smallholder [p.134]

The Polish term *szlachciura* refers to a rough, impoverished nobleman. The term describes the actual circumstances of the judge's brother Jacek before his being awarded the greater part of the pantler's domain after the events unfolding from the Targowica confederacy.

A mollycoddle kneaded from Marymont flour [p.134]

Marymont, a village near Warsaw, was named after Maria Kazimiera Sobieska. From the time of Augustus II, it was famous for the delicate flour produced by its mills.

they call him Sack [p.134]

The Polish word *sak* denotes a kind of duffel bag. Used figuratively, it means a "fool."

Dobrzynskis that fought the Muscovites in the foray against Mysz [p.135]

The Polish attributive *myski* makes it unclear as to whether the reference is to Mysz or Myssa. Mysz was a small Nowogródek district town belonging at the time to Józef Count Niesiołowski. An armed foray took place there, albeit in 1771, when Niesiołowski thereby seized possession of his wife's dowry. However, no skirmish with the Russian Army is recorded and the considerably younger Wojniłowicz and Wołk (noted subsequently) could not have taken part in it. Myssa, on the other hand, was a village in Oszmiana district belonging to the Bukaty family. Wołk lived in the Oszmiana area, but the details of that foray remain unknown.

General Voinilovich [p.135]

The reference seems to be to Florian Wojniłowicz (d. circa 1820), a general in the Tsar's service, owner of Mańkow estate in Nowogródek district.

Mr. Wolk of Logumowicze [p.135]

Samuel Wołk Łaniewski (d. circa 1850), owner of Logumowicze, a village situated north of Nowogródek in the western corner of Oszmiana district between the Niemen and Berezina rivers. Under Wołk's ownership, Logumowicze became the center of a vast fortune, which allegedly owed its beginnings to the provisioning of the Russian Army with grain through shady deals worked out by Wołk and the officers. The incident subsequently described in *Pan Tadeusz* is authentic, only the time was altered.

Zan and three Czeczots [p.137]

Close friends and university colleagues of Mickiewicz, whose names the author chooses to immortalize in his epic poem.

BOOK EIGHT

Lel and Polel [p.139]

Lel and Polel or *Lelum* and *Polelum*: i.e. Castor and Pollux in pagan Slavic mythology. The Polish Romantic poet and dramatist Juliusz Słowacki introduced them in his drama *Lilla Weneda*.

the circle of the starry Sieve [p.139]

The constellation is also known as the Northern Crown; it resembles a broken ring of stars.

David's Chariot [p.139]

The constellation known to astronomers as *Ursa Major*. [*Author's note*]

the excavated ribs and femurs of giants [p.140]

It was customary to adorn the walls of churches with any fossil bones that might be discovered. The people regard them as bones of giants. [*Author's note*]

a comet of great size and power [p.140]

The memorable comet of the year 1811. [*Author's note*]

the Maid of Plagues [p.140]

"When the plague is about to strike Lithuania, the eye of the seer divines its coming; for, if one may believe the bards, the Maid of Pestilence often appears in the desolate graveyards and meadows. She wears a white garment and has a fiery crown on her head. Her brow towers over the trees of Białowieża, and in her hand she waves a bloody kerchief." [Mickiewicz, *Konrad Wallenrod*.]

Our famous Father Poczobut [p.141]

Marcin Poczobut Odlanicki, an ex-Jesuit, was rector of the University of Wilno in the years 1780-1799 and founder of the Wilno Observatory. "Father Poczobut [notes Mickiewicz] published a work on the Zodiac of Denderah and by his observations aided Joseph Jérôme Lalande [1732-1807] in calculating the motions of the moon. See the biography by Jan Śniadecki."

Sniadecki, a highly learned man [p.141]

Jan Śniadecki (1756-1830), a distinguished Polish mathematician, astronomer, and philosopher. In Mickiewicz's student years he was professor (and later rector) at the University of Wilno. His hostility to romanticism in Polish literature was attacked by Mickiewicz in his poem *Romantyczność*.

Branicki left for Jassy [p.141]

At Jassy, in Romania, peace was concluded in 1792 between Russia and Turkey. Mickiewicz presents Franciszek Ksawery Branicki (d. 1819), one of the founders of the Targowica Confederacy, as the first to rush to Potemkin's camp at Jassy where negotiations with the Turks were in progress. In fact, he arrived after Szczęsny Potocki, Rzewuski, and other opponents of the Constitution of the Third of May 1791.

a panegyric titled Orientis Fulmen [p.142]

A prose panegyric in honor of King Jan III Sobieski by the Jesuit Wojciech Bartochowski (1640-1708). It was published in Kalisz in 1684. Its full title is *Fulmen Orientis Joannes II, rex Poloniarum ter maximus*.

a work entitled The Janina [p.142]

The reference is to Jakub Kazimierz Rubinkowski's *Janina zwycięskich triumfów Jana III* (The Victorious Triumphs of the Janina), published in Poznań in 1739. The *Janina* is the coat of arms of the Sobieski family.

The General Starosta of Podolia, Prince Czartoryski [p.142]

Adam Kazimierz Czartoryski (1734-1823), a cousin of King Stanisław Poniatowski, director of the Warsaw Military Academy, and one of the leading men of his time in Poland.

the German Prince de Nassau [p.143]

Properly, Prince de Nassau-Siegen (1745-1808), a famous warrior and adventurer of those times. He was a Muscovite admiral and [in 1788] defeated the Turks in the [Dnieper] bay near Ochakov; later he was himself defeated by the Swedes. He spent some time in Poland, where he was granted the *indygenat* [full rights of citizenship extended to a foreigner]. The combat of the Prince de Nassau with the tiger was noised abroad at the time by all the newspapers of Europe. [Author's note]

in articulo mortis [p.144]

at the point of death (lat.)

the Naiad of Switez [p.151]

The *świtezianka*, an undine or water sprite inhabiting Świteź, a forest-enclosed lake in the vicinity of Nowogródek. Apparently, an invention of Mickiewicz and not an authentic folk belief, as the poet suggests.

Samogitia's lovely snake . . . givoytos [p.151]

Mickiewicz refers to this half-mythical snake of ancient Lithuania in the text and notes of his narrative poem *Grażyna*. According to ethnographers Jan Łasicki and Maciej Stryjkowski, whom the poet cites, the reptile was said to enter a peasant's hut and breathe over the sleeping inmates, thereby fortifying them with the life of the earth, imparting health, strength, etc.

cum grovesibus, forestis, et fencelinesibus . . . et omnibus rebus; et quibusdam aliis [p.154]

The macaronisms reveal the limits of Gervase's command of Latin.

no Manlius stood by to repel the treacherous Gaul [p.155]

Manlius Marcus, called *Capitolinus*. Commander of the garrison during the siege of the Roman Capitol by the Gauls in 390 B.C. Awakened by the cries of the geese, he repelled a surprise night assault by the enemy and saved Rome.

Chochlik – the winged evil sprite [p.155]

According to popular belief, notes Mickiewicz, *Chochlik* was an arch sprite who led wayfarers astray by appearing as a will-of-the-wisp (*ignis fatus*). He appears as a character in Juliusz Słowacki's tragedy *Balladyna* (1834).

BOOK NINE

the village of Dzierowicz [p.158]

The fictitious name of Plut's birthplace suggests cheating, 'skinning' (from *odzierać*). Plut means 'cheat or 'swindler' in Russian.

the Yellow Book [p.160]

So called from its binding; the barbarous book of Russian martial law. Frequently in time of peace the government proclaims whole provinces as being in a state of war, and on the authority of the Yellow Book confers on the military commander complete power over the estates and lives of citizens. It is a well-known fact that from the year 1812 to the November Insurrection of 1831 all Lithuania was subject to the Yellow Book, of which the executor was the Grand Duke, the Tsarevich Constantine. [*Author's note*]

As Baka wrote [p.161]

Józef Baka (1707-80), a Jesuit, the anonymous author of the humorous *Uwagi o śmierci nieuchybnej, wszystkim pospolitej* (Reflections on Inescapable Death, Common to All), published in Wilno, 1766. The collection of doggerel verse was highly popular during Mickiewicz's student years.

A round of cards? Elb Zvelb? [p.162]

Plut's corruption of the German *Halb Zwölf* (half-twelve). The reference is to the French card game *Onze et demie*.

a seasoned old Gefreiter [p.165]

A senior private in the Tsarist Army.

Fechtmeister [p.165]

Fencing master (ger.)

No one but the Baptist was capable of lifting it [p.166]

A Lithuanian club is made in the following manner: a young oak is selected and slashed from the bottom upwards with an axe, so that the bark and bast are cut through and the wood slightly wounded. Sharp flints are thrust into these notches and in time these grow into the tree to form hard knobs. Clubs in pagan times were the chief weapon of the Lithuanian infantry. They are still occasionally used and are called *nasieki* (gnarled clubs). [*Author's note*]

Czarnobacki slew Deyov [p.167]

After Jasiński's insurrection when the Lithuanian armies retired toward Warsaw, the Muscovites arrived at the deserted city of Vilna. General Deyov at the head of the staff was entering through the Ostra Gate. The streets were empty; the townsfolk had shut themselves in their houses. One townsman, seeing a cannon abandoned in an alley, aimed it at the gate and fired, raking the thoroughfare with grapeshot. This single shot saved Vilna for a time. General Deyov and several officers perished. The rest, fearing an ambush, retired from the city. I do not know for certain the name of that townsman. [*Author's note*]

So ended the last armed foray in Lithuania [p.174]
Armed forays occurred even later still. Although not as famous, they were bloody all the same, and much talked of. About the year 1817, a man named U[złowski] in the Nowogródek province led a successful foray against the garrison of Nowogródek and took its leaders captive. [*Author's note*]

BOOK TEN

Ochakov . . . Izmailov . . . Novi and Preussisch-Eylau [p.177]

Ochakov, not far from Odessa, captured from the Turks in 1788 by Potemkin; Izmailov, a fortress in Bessarabia, captured from the Turks by Suvorov in 1790; Novi, northern Italy, memorable for the victory of the Russians and Austrians over the French in 1799; Preussisch-Eylau, a town in old Ducal Prussia, where on February 8, 1807 the French suffered heavy losses in combat with Russian and Prussian forces.

Korsakov's glorious retreat from Zurich [p.177]

General Aleksander Rimsky-Korsakov (1753-1840) was dispatched in 1799 to Zürich, Switzerland, in aid of Suvorov; he was beaten on September 25 before joining up with Suvorov and was consequently cashiered for a time.

Kosciuszko at Raclawice [p.178]

Racławice was a village northeast of Kraków. It was here that, on April 4, 1794, Kościuszko with an army of 6000, including 2000 peasants armed with scythes, defeated a numerically superior Russian force under the command of General Tormasov.

at Maciejowice [p.178]

The battle at Maciejowice on October 10, 1794, which marked the defeat of Kościuszko's insurrection. Kościuszko himself was wounded and taken prisoner by the Russians.

One of them was Mokronowski [p.178]

The name suggests a runny nose.

Requiescat in pace [p.179]

May he rest in peace (lat.)

pro publico bono [p.179]

for the common good (lat.)

equip a company, as did the young Potocki [p.183]

i.e. Włodzimierz Potocki (1789-1812), one of the sons of Targowica confederate Szczęsny Potocki. Wishing to wipe away the disgrace of his family, he joined the army of the Duchy of Warsaw. In 1808, he supplied two artillery batteries at his own expense and fought bravely at the Battle of Sandomierz (1809); he died at the young age of 23.

viaticum [p.184]

Literally, food for the journey (lat.), i.e. the Eucharist, as when given to a person near or in danger of death.

Tenczynski once asked for the hand of a daughter of a royal house [p.186]

Jan Tęczyński (d. 1562), Voivode of Bielsko, Polish ambassador to Sweden, fell in love with the daughter of the Swedish king, Gustav I. He was seized by the Danes on his way to marry her and died in prison in Copenhagen. His story has been treated in Polish literature by Jan Kochanowski in the sixteenth century, and by Julian Niemcewicz in the eighteenth.

even Radziwill grows pale [p.190]

Karol Radziwiłł (1734-1790) styled *Panie Kochanku* (My-Dear-Fellow) after the phrase he constantly repeated. He was the grand hetman of Lithuania, voivode of Vilnius, and the wealthiest magnate of his time. He led a carefree and adventurous life and was extremely popular among the Polish nobility. His estate Nieśwież was located not far from Nowogródek.

you knotted one on my lord [p.190]

Stroking or curling one's moustache coupled with the action of throwing back the loose sleeves of the *kontusz* was considered to be a signal of readiness for a fight or confrontation. The phrase "knotting one's whisker" (*zawiązać węzełek na wąsie*) has the additional suggestion of making a reminder for oneself, as when one 'knots' a handkerchief for the purpose of having something remembered.

I seized a soldier's musket, shouldered it, barely aimed . . . [p.191]

Here Mickiewicz states in his notes that the pantler Horeszko "seems" to have been slain around the year 1791, at the time of the first war. There is some confusion in the chronology of the poem. From Book One we learn that Tadeusz was born in the year of Kościuszko's insurrection, 1794. In Book One Tadeusz's age at the time of the action of the poem is given as about twenty. This would be consistent with Mickiewicz's original plan to set the action of the poem in 1814. When he shifted the action back to 1811-1812, he upset his chronology. Tadeusz then would have been born around 1791, three years earlier than the outbreak of Kościuszko's war. From Jacek's narrative (Book Ten) it appears that Tadeusz was born before the murder of the pantler. In attempting to restore consistency, Mickiewicz entered the above note. The "first war" mentioned in the note could only refer to that which followed the ratification of the Constitution of the Third of May, 1791. This war did not begin, however, until after the proclamation of the Targowica Confederacy, May 14, 1792. [H.B. Segel]

in carcere duro [p.193]

in harsh confinement (lat.)

It was from Fiszer [p.193]

Stanisław Fiszer (1769-1812), a former adjutant of Kościuszko. As Minister of War for the Duchy of Warsaw, he was Prince Józef Poniatowski's chief of staff. He died at the Battle of Borodino.

let thy servant depart in peace [p.194]

The first line of the *Canticle of Simeon* (Lk 2: 29-32).

BOOK ELEVEN

a great sign in the heavens [p.196]

A Russian historian describes in similar fashion the omens and premonitions of the Muscovite people before the war of 1812. [Exactly which historian has not been determined – *transl.*] [*Author's note*]

the fabled South [p.197]

The word used by Mickiewicz is *wyraj*. In his note he explains: "In the popular dialect the word properly means the autumn season, when the migratory birds fly away. To fly to *wyraj* means to fly to warmer lands. Hence, figuratively, the common folk apply the word *wyraj* to warm countries and especially to some fabulous, happy region lying beyond the sea."

King Jerome of Westphalia [p.198]

Jérôme Bonaparte (1784-1860), the youngest brother of Napoleon.

between Grodno and Slonim [p.198]

Two cities in the Hrodna province of what is now Belarus.

Malachowski, Giedroyc, and Grabowski [p.198]

Kazimierz Małachowski (1765-1845) returned to France in 1804 with the remnants of the Danube Legion after the ill-fated Haiti campaign of 1803. In 1812 he was still a colonel and commanded a regiment under Dąbrowski. He lived to take part in the November Insurrection of 1831. Romuald Giedrojć (1750-1824): in 1812 Napoleon named him inspector general of the cavalry of the Lithuanian Army, which was then forming. Michał Grabowski (1773-1812) commanded a brigade under General Kniaziewicz. He was killed at the siege of Smolensk.

The Compleat Chef [p.198]

A book, now very rare, published more than a hundred years ago by Stanisław Czerniecki. That embassy to Rome has been often described and painted. See the preface to *Kucharz do-skonały* (The Perfect Cook): "This embassy being a great source of amazement to every western state, redounded to the wisdom of the incomparable gentleman Ossoliński as well as to the splendor of his house and the magnificence of his table – so that one of the Roman princes said: 'Today Rome is happy in having such an ambassador.'" N.B. Czerniecki himself was Ossoliński's head cook. [*Author's note*]

Mickiewicz has his facts somewhat confused. Czerniecki's book bears the title *Compendium ferculorum albo Zebranie potraw* (Kraków, 1682) and was later published several times under the title *Stól obojętny* (The Indifferent Table). Mickiewicz confused it with W. Wieladek's *Kucharz doskonały*, published in Wilno in 1800, a book he had in his own possession. [*H.B. Segel*]

Our Blessed Lady of the Flowers [p.199]

i.e. "Lady Day" – the Feast of the Annunciation, March 25.

elected their confederate marshal by a unanimous vote of the district estates [p.200]

Upon the arrival of the French and Polish armies in Lithuania, each province formed a confederacy and elected its deputy to Parliament. [*Author's note*]

When almost beaten at Hohenlinde, General Richepanse [p.201]

General Antoine Richepanse (1770-1802) was commander of a French column, which was relieved in an emergency by
Kniaziewicz and his Danube Legion. "It is a well-known fact,"
notes Mickiewicz "that at Hohenlinden [Bavaria] General Kniaziewicz's Polish corps decided the victory." The action took place
against the Austrians on December 3, 1800.

our lancers took the fortified ridge at Somosierra [p.201]

Napoleon freely availed himself of Polish troops in his
Spanish campaign. In 1808 Polish light cavalry units under the
command of Baron Jan Leon Hipolit Kozietulski (1781-1821)
captured Somosierra, a defile in the Sierra de Guadarrama some
sixty miles north of Madrid.

militem and skartabella [p.202]

Miles (lat.) refers here to a Polish nobleman of ancient
lineage. *Skartabella* in old Polish law was applied to an individual recently elevated to the nobility. Until the third generation
he could not enjoy equal privileges with the rest of the nobility.

gravis nota maculae [p.202]

a brand of deep disgrace (lat.)

general equality before the law has now been proclaimed [p.202]

Although Napoleon decreed the freeing of the serfs in the
Duchy of Warsaw, he decided to postpone implementation of the
law in Lithuania until after the war against Russia. Later in
Pan Tadeusz, the eponymous hero enfranchises his peasants in
an independent action.

a Polish lancer in a glittering cap [p.202]

The Polish lancers or uhlans (*ułany*) serving in the Napoleonic Wars wore the distinctive *czapka rogatywka*, a high, square-topped peaked helmet derived from the four-pointed "confederate's cap" (*konfederatka*), which in turn derived from the *krakuska*, a hat traditionally worn by the peasantry of the Cracow region. The *czapka*, fronted by the regimental insignia embossed in metal, was adorned with braids, plumes, or rosettes.

Queen Hedwig brought reason to bear [p.203]

Poland and Lithuania were united in 1386 by the marriage of Queen Hedwig (Jadwiga) of Poland (1373-1399) to the pagan Prince Jagiełło of Lithuania, who thereupon embraced Christianity. The Jagiellonian dynasty endured until the last of the male line of that house, Sigismund August, died without issue in 1572, and the throne became elective.

pendebat [p.203]

remained pending or unsettled (lat.)

As the palace was worthy of Patz, and Patz of his palace [p.207]

The reference is to the magnificent palace built in Jezno (Jieznas), in Lithuania, by Antoni Michał Pac (d. 1774).

the one our heraldry calls Leliwa [p.208]

This was a Polish escutcheon characterized by a golden crescent on a red field surmounted by six-pointed star. It was borne by the Soplicas.

the battle of Podhajce [p.208]

A small town in eastern Galicia, the scene of a battle in 1665 between a combined Tartar-Turkish army and the Poles under Sobieski.

BOOK TWELVE

Kniaziewicz, Patz, Malachowski [p.212]

For Kniaziewicz and Małachowski, see notes to Books One and Eleven respectively. Michał Ludwik Patz (Pac) (1780-1835) served as Napoleon's adjutant and was elevated to the rank of general in 1812. Mickiewicz later met him in emigration.

a table some forty fathoms long [p.212]

A conservative estimate of two *stajs*. One *staj* measured anywhere between 40 to 100 paces.

Prince Radziwill The Orphan [p.212]

Mikołaj Krzysztof Radziwiłł (1549-1616) known as the Orphan, was converted from Calvinism to Catholicism largely through the efforts of the famous Polish Jesuit, Piotr Skarga. In 1582-1584 he made a pilgrimage to the Holy Land, on which he wrote his book *Peregrynacja do Ziemi Świętej* (A Journey to the Holy Land). A Latin translation appeared as early as 1610.

Plundered during the Swedish Wars [p.212]

The Polish-Swedish wars, 1655-1660. The historical novelist Henryk Sienkiewicz (1846-1916) made them the subject of his novel *Potop* (The Deluge, 1886).

Barche royale [p.215]

Barszcz królewski, a slightly tart soup made from the juice of pickled beets and fermented rye bread.

kontuz, arkas, and blemas [p.215]

Kontuz is a kind of smoked sausage or bouillon made from minced chicken or veal; *arkas*, a dessert consisting of sweet milk, saffron, lemon, and rose-scented vodka; *blemas* (blancmange), an almond jelly, laced with wine and seasoned with cloves, cinnamon or musk.

has Pinetti put his demons under your spell? [p.216]

Giovanni Giuseppe Pinetti (1750-1800), an Italian conjurer famous throughout Europe. Contemporary accounts describe his visits to Grodno in 1796 and to Wilno early in the nineteenth century.

grand old banquets held in the halls of our forefathers [p.216]

In the sixteenth century, and early in the seventeenth, at a time when the arts flourished, even banquets were directed by artists and were full of symbols and theatrical scenes. At a famous banquet given in Rome for Pope Leo X there was a centerpiece that represented the four seasons of the year in turn, and that evidently served as a model for Radziwiłł's. Table customs changed in Europe about the middle of the eighteenth century but remained unchanged longest in Poland. [*Author's note*]

rides with the flankers [p.218]

Napoleon's cavalry units made use of flankers for light skirmishes, scouting missions and the defense of their flanks. By 1812, flankers were always armed with light cavalry carbines, even if the rest of the unit did not have them. The reference to an

antique blunderbuss among them is a typical instance of Mickiewicz's droll sense of humor.

Dembinski of the brawny arm [p.219]

Henryk Dembiński (1791-1864), a Polish general who
took part in the Napoleonic campaigns, the November Insurrection and the Hungarian Revolution of 1831.

Dwernicki and . . . Lieutenant Rozycki [p.219]

Józef Dwernicki (1778-1857), a member of the Legions,
who in 1804 fielded a squadron at his own expense. In 1806,
he was promoted to general and distinguished himself in the
November Insurrection. Samuel Różycki (1784-1834) was an officer in the campaign of 1812; he held the rank of general in the
November Insurrection and commanded an expedition to Lithuania.

Pulaski's thrust . . . Dzierzanowski . . . Sava's slash [p.219]

The Pułaski family were among the organizers of the Confederacy of Bar. Józef Pułaski was the first commander-in-chief
of its armed forces. His son, Kazimierz, won fame as a leader
after his father's death. Later, in 1777, he came to America, and
distinguished himself by his services to the revolutionary cause.
He was killed in 1779 in the attack on Savannah. Michał Dz-
ierżanowski (d. 1808), a Bar confederate and adventurer famous
in the eighteenth century; he took part in almost all the wars
of this time. For a while he was king of Madagascar. Józef Sa-
wa-Caliński (d. 1771), a heroic Cossack, one of the leaders of the
Confederacy of Bar.

"Am I Cybulski," dolefully rejoined the Warden [p.220]

The mournful song of Mrs. Cybulski, whose husband
gambled her away at cards to the Muscovites, is well known in

Lithuania. [Author's note]

the great Dumouriez [p.220]

Charles François Dumouriez (1739-1823), a general sent by France to assist the Confederates of Bar in 1770.

What [Poland] needs is a Piast [p.220]

The Piasts were the first royal dynasty of Poland. In later times the name was used to denote any candidate for the Polish throne who was of native birth.

I hear more German styles among them than native ones [p.220]

All the preceding terms are of French origin, but in his simplicity old Matthias puts them all under the generic German umbrella. In common usage, the Polish word *niemiecki* (German) is often synonymous with *cudzoziemski* or *obcy*, meaning 'alien' or 'foreign.'

an emperor that sets out without God's blessing [p.221]

Matthias had probably heard something about the excommunication of Napoleon by Pope Pius VII in 1809. The following line with its implied internal rhyme is the despair of the translator.

he was fain to dress up like a Frenchman [p.221]

The fashion of adopting the French garb raged in the provinces from 1800 to 1812. A great number of the young men changed their style of dress before marriage at the request of their future wives. [Author's note].

resumed his story of the boar of Naliboka Forest [p.222]

The anecdote of the quarrel of Reytan with the Prince de Nassau, which the steward never concludes, is well known in popular tradition. We add here its conclusion for the gratification of the curious reader: – Reytan, angered by de Nassau's boasting, took up position beside him at the narrow passage through which the beasts would be forced to make their egress. At that moment, a huge boar, infuriated by the shots and the baiting, made a rush through the passage. Reytan snatched the gun from the prince's hands, cast his own on the ground, and, taking a pike and offering another to the German, said, "Now we will see who does the better work with the spear." The boar was on the point of attacking them, when Steward Hreczecha, who was standing at some distance away, felled the beast with a first-rate shot. Angry at first, the two gentlemen later came to terms and handsomely rewarded Hreczecha. [Author's note]

something un-Polish [p.224]

Here again the speaker uses the word 'German' in the sense of 'foreign' or 'non-native' (*z cudzoziemska*). More accurately, French, for since the revolution France was the chief disseminator of democratic ideas.

When the late Mr. Karp freed his serfs [p.224]

The reference is to Ignacy Karp, Ensign of Upita (Wilno province). As early as 1803, he enfranchised all the serfs belonging to his domains, around 7,000 male souls. Later, as marshal of the nobility, he oversaw, over a period of three years, the entry of 18,000 peasant families into the rolls of the nobility. As Mickiewicz explains in his note, "[T]he Tsarist government recognizes no freeman except the nobility. Peasants freed by landowners are immediately entered in the rolls of the Emperor's estates and forced to pay increased taxes in place of dues to their lords. It is a well-known fact that in the year 1818 the citizens of the Vilna province adopted in the regional diet a project for freeing all the peasants and appointed a delegation to the Emperor with that aim in view; but the Russian government ordained that the project should be quashed and no further mention made of it. There is no means of setting a man free under the Tsarist government except to take him into one's family. Accordingly, many have had the privileges of nobility conferred on them in this way as an act of grace or for money."

O thou! whose charms [p.225]

Protase's poem addressed to Sophie is considered an excellent pastiche of the neo-classical panegyric ode.

orchestra of janissaries [p.227]

The army of the Polish-Lithuanian Commonwealth had its own janissaries' division with a band that played a noisy martial music similar to that of the original Turkish janissaries.

that momentous Third of May [p.227]

The reference is to the celebrated Constitution of the Third of May, 1791.

the Massacre of Praga [p.228]

The massacre of the inhabitants of the Warsaw suburb of Praga on November 9, 1794, when the Russian forces under Suvorov took the city by storm. The event marked the end of the Kościuszko insurrection.

a game of canasta [p.231]

In the original, *drużbart* (from ger. *Drosselbart*, king of hearts); a game of Polish cards popular during the eighteenth and nineteenth centuries.

Then, at last, turning yellow, it grew pale and gray [p.231]

Although Pan Tadeusz ends on an upbeat note with the flame of Polish hope burning brightly in the year 1812, Mickiewicz's sublime image of the changing cloud contains a presentiment of the catastrophe that lies ahead. It is the crowning instance of the "theme of disenchantment," which runs like a *leitmotif* throughout the work.

And I, too, was a guest . . . I drank the mead and the wine [p.232]

These closing lines echo the standard ending of a Polish fairy tale.

About the Author

Adam Bernard Mickiewicz (24 December 1798 – 26 November 1855) is arguably Poland's greatest poet. A posthumous child of the old Polish-Lithuanian Commonwealth, whose final collapse and dismemberment occurred three years before his birth, he is regarded national bard in Poland, Lithuania and Belarus. Often compared to Byron and Goethe, he was a major figure in Polish Romanticism. In 1824, he was banished as a political subversive to central Russia. Welcomed into the leading literary circles of Saint Petersburg and Moscow, he became a favorite there for his agreeable manners and extraordinary talent for poetic improvisation. In 1829, he left the Russian Empire for a life of continued exile in Italy, France and Switzerland. For three years he lectured on Slavic literature at the Collège de France in Paris. He died in Constantinople while helping to organize Polish and Jewish forces to fight against Tsarism in the Crimean War. Among his other great works are his poetic drama *Dziady* (*Forefathers' Eve*), his historical narrative poems *Grażyna* and *Konrad Wallenrod*, and his admirable *Crimean Sonnets*. He lies buried in the crypt of the Wawel Cathedral in Kraków, Poland.

About the Translator

Christopher Adam Zakrzewski (born 1948) is a literary translator, teacher, scholar, and editor. He was raised and educated in UK and Ontario, Canada. He and his wife Wendy live in Wilno, Ontario. They have five children and nine grandchildren.

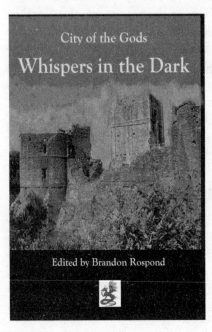
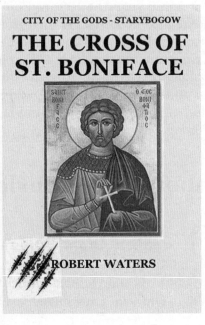

This publication has been supported by the ©POLAND Translation Program

BOOK INSTITUTE

©POLAND

ZMOK
BOOKS

"*Truly a masterpiece!* Christopher Zakrzewski has accomplished the impossible: he has rendered in prose what seemed translatable only in poetry. Poland's great epic poem can now be read as a delightful historical tale replete with Romantic irony. Zakrzewski's mastery of the English language is remarkable."
- Ewa Thompson, Rice University

"*In this extraordinarily fine prose rendering,* Christopher Zakrzewski brings his own prodigious gifts as a poet and translator to one of the great classics of world literature. The fruit of Zakrzewski's decades-long labors, this book is a treasure of immeasurable value."
- Michael D. O'Brien, novelist, painter

"*Perfectly smooth, highly expressive, subtly nuanced.* Christopher Zakrzewski's translation does full justice to this brightest jewel in the crown of Polish literature."
- Kazimierz Braun, Polish author, scholar, theater artist

"*Christopher Zakrzewski's English prose is marvelously,* not to say magically, consonant with the poetical richness of Mickiewicz's great Polish national saga."
- Olga Glagoleva, PhD, Russian historian